Also by Glenn Meade

Brandenburg

Snow Wolf

The Sands of Sakkara

Resurrection Day

Web of Deceit

About the author

Glenn Meade lives in Dublin and is a former journalist and specialist in the field of pilot training.

GLENN MEADE

The Devil's Disciple

HODDER

First published in Great Britain in 2006 by Hodder & Stoughton
This paperback edition first published in Great Britain in 2007
by Hodder & Stoughton
A division of Hodder Headline

A Hodder paperback

3

A CIP catalogue record for this title is
available from the British Library.

ISBN 9-780340-835432
ISBN 0-340-83543-5

Typeset in Plantin by Palimpsest Book Production Limited,
Grangemouth, Stirlingshire

Printed and bound by
Mackays of Chatham Ltd, Chatham, Kent

Hodder Headline's policy is to use papers that are natural,
renewable and recyclable products and made from wood
grown in sustainable forests. The logging and manufacturing
processes are expected to conform to the environmental
regulations of the country of origin.

Hodder & Stoughton Ltd
A division of Hodder Headline
338 Euston Road
London NW1 3BH

For Carolyn Mays

PART ONE

I

No night should be so cold, no winter so white, no death so chilling.

It was snowing as I pulled into the crowded parking lot outside Greensville Correctional Centre. When I stepped out, the icy January air burned like fire in my lungs. I locked my eight-year-old Bronco and walked towards the prison entrance.

A dusting of snowflakes drifted over the TV news channel crews, their trucks and satellite dishes frosted by ice crystals. My feet crunched over hardened snow, the woollen coat and scarf that I wore barely warm enough to keep out the bone-numbing cold. I was dressed in an old pair of leather calf-length boots, and my coat was pale beige, not death's black. I was here to witness an execution, but I was not mourning the imminent loss of a human life – I was celebrating death.

A killer is about to die by lethal injection and I am looking forward to his execution.

But then this was no ordinary killer. A TV reporter recognised me and called out, 'Kate, have you got anything to say to Channel Twelve viewers?'

I ignored the question and walked on.

'Miss Moran, just a few words. *Please*. Constantine Gamal is about to be put to death, for Chrissakes!'

Newspaper reporters waved to get my attention, but I ignored the media and came to a floodlit entrance. A couple of prison guards stood next to a door, and they wore scarves and uniform overcoats, their breath like smoke in the frozen air. One of them

3

opened the door and ushered me inside the warmth of the prison reception lobby. There were rows of plastic chairs for waiting visitors, and candy and soft drinks machines in a corner. At the end of the hall I saw a desk with a walk-through metal detector that led to the prison entrance. Another guard sat behind the desk and I stepped up and showed my ID and my signed letter from the warden, Lucius B. Clay. I had phoned him personally to request permission to attend as a witness tonight:

'Dear Miss Moran, You are hereby granted permission to attend the execution of Constantine Gamal at 9 p.m., January, Friday 13th.'

No postscript saying: *'Refreshments will be provided while you witness this evil bastard go screaming to hell. Enjoy the show, folks.'* Not a chance of that, but I'd figure that maybe some of the execution witnesses might have appreciated a black-humoured joke at Constantine Gamal's expense.

The guard scanned my documents, and then studied my face, as if taking nothing for granted, not even my FBI credentials or the warden's invite. 'Special Agent Katherine Moran?'

I wanted to correct the guard, to tell him that I was here as Kate Moran, *private citizen*, and not as a federal agent, but I let it pass. 'That's me.'

'The other witnesses have already been transported down to the execution chamber in Unit L in prison vans, Agent Moran.'

'I got delayed in heavy traffic outside Richmond.'

'Sure, I understand, pretty much everyone's been late tonight because of the snow. Don't worry, I'll have another van take you down. But let me call the warden and tell him you're here, ma'am.'

The guard handed back my documents, made a call and, after a brief conversation, put down his phone. 'We're all set. The warden's on his way and we've got a van coming to pick you up. Shouldn't be longer than five minutes.'

'Thank you.' *God, I'm so looking forward to this. Constantine Gamal is about to roast in hell and I've got a ringside seat.*

I glanced over my shoulder and out of the windows at the news channels crews in the frozen parking lot. They sipped hot coffee and exhaled draughts of steamy air as they stomped their feet to keep warm. The snowy winter landscape was dazzling white under the powerful lamps that flooded the lot. And that's when I realised that there was something weird about this evening. Something so out of the ordinary that my radar should have picked it up, but for some reason didn't – probably because I was late and on edge.

Forty-five minutes before the execution and there were no anti-death-penalty lobbyists gathered outside the prison. Not *one*, which was extraordinary. Usually there were legions of protesters, most of them well meaning, some holding candlelight vigils, waving placards with slogans like STOP THE KILLING and EXECUTION IS MORALLY WRONG while they prayed and sang hymns. But not so this frozen January evening.

To tell the truth, I'd have been surprised if even one among the anti-capital-punishment lobby would have seen Constantine Gamal's imminent execution as a tragedy. I was pretty convinced that some of them might have volunteered to flood his veins with poison. *But this is no ordinary execution. And the man who is about to be executed is no ordinary man.*

In fact, why don't we stick with the description of him that was coined by a Washington reporter, and with good reason – the Devil's Disciple. The day I caught him a year ago in Arizona was a milestone in my life that I can never forget. Actually, two remarkable things happened that day. The first was that I tried to blow my brains out.

2

Arizona

Two a.m. on an unusually cold, stormy morning on the edge of Sedona and I stared out at the distant rain-drenched desert with my service automatic pressed to my head. Water was beating down on the roof of my Comfort Inn motel. Every bone in my body ached with exhaustion and my eyes were smudged and swollen from lack of sleep.

The parched black landscape beyond my window was being lashed by one of those drenching Arizonian storms that made it seem as if the world was coming to an end, lightning sizzling on the horizon. My own world felt brittle, about to collapse, everything gone wrong. I brushed the barrel of my Glock pistol against my cheek and the cold steel felt soft. It reminded me of David's fingers stroking my skin. *Oh God. Why make me suffer this way? It's been such a difficult year without him and there's no end to the anguish. Please God, bring it to an end.*

My eyes felt wet as I raised the gun to my temple again. I had slept fitfully and woken ten minutes earlier in the grip of a powerful, unshakable despair that was so alien to me. Four years of agonising hard work had caused me nothing but pain and frustration. A voice inside my head told me to end it and join David and Megan, the two people I had loved most, but another voice said: *You owe it to them to catch their killer.*

My ex-husband Paul often said I was mostly tough but once in a blue moon I became fragile. At that moment I felt fragile. But this was so unlike me. A sudden pounding on my bedroom door made me jump and almost squeeze the trigger.

'Who is it?' I called out, and laid my Glock automatic on the nightstand.

'Kate, it's Lou.'

I was so relieved to hear a familiar voice and I wiped my eyes and got up off the bed and opened the door. Lou Raines stood there looking tanned but tired, his shirt and tie askew. Grumpy Lou, my boss, a guy you could always count on for a blunt word and a stinging comment. He was the Supervisory Agent in Charge of the Washington DC field office, with twenty-five years' service under his belt and a hide as tough as a jockey's ass. But he'd been like a father to me since I'd joined the Bureau and I adored him. I even figured the feeling might be mutual. 'That's some frigging rain out there, sailor. Hey, sorry for walking in on you. You look surprised.'

I let Lou in. Sailor was his pet name for me, ever since David and I had once invited him to take a ride on a Clipper sailboat that had once belonged to David's brother, Patrick. 'I thought you and Mags were on three weeks' vacation in Hawaii?'

Lou shook rain from his coat, grunted and closed the door. 'We got back yesterday morning. My wife figured another day spent alone together and one of us would wind up being charged with homicide, so I thought I'd get the hell out of her hair and see how the investigation was going. The office told me where to find you.'

'When did you get here?'

'Flew into Phoenix last night, the only last-minute flight I could get, and hired some wheels and drove up. You look beat as hell. Did I wake you?'

It wasn't like Lou to appear out of nowhere and I was on my guard. 'I was just resting. Is anything wrong, Lou?'

He looked around the room, glimpsed a coffee cup and my Glock on the table, and the rumpled bed covers not turned down. 'I'm tempted to ask when was the last time you had a good night's sleep?'

I hadn't slept for more than three hours a night all week. 'You know how it is when you've been hoping for a breakthrough.'

Lou's brow furrowed. 'We've been hoping for a breakthrough for over five years. It sounds to me like I've been missing something while I was away. Want to tell me about it?'

'Remember the theory we had about our killer?'

Lou took off his wet coat, hung it on the back of a chair and ran a hand over his balding head. 'We've had a lot of different theories, Kate. Remind me which one.'

Lou's presence had suppressed my anguish and I sat down on the bed. 'All of the twenty-eight victims that we've so far tied to the Disciple have been killed in pairs and their corpses burned. Predominantly they were father and daughter, or had an age difference that might suggest they could be so related – older man, younger woman, except in three cases the younger victims in the pair were pubescent males. Most were killed in the US but ten of the paired victims were murdered in cities abroad. Paris, London, Rome, Vienna, Istanbul. Which was why at first we figured our killer might be an airline pilot, an international businessman or company executive. Or maybe someone with a medical or vetinary background because we believe he drugged his victims with benzodiazepine beforehand.'

Lou nodded. 'That assessment made sense at the time because we found traces of the drug in some of his victims whose bodies hadn't been completely burned. Except it led us nowhere, Kate. But true to serial killer form, each murder was an effort at refinement, an attempt to carry out the perfect "kill", or as perfect as the killer's deranged mind imagined it ought to be. So what are you saying?'

'Seeing as we had no fresh leads I decided to backtrack. Rework another angle.'

'Which angle's that?' Lou asked.

'The Disciple's killings have been roughly six months apart, give or take a month. So I reckoned we were about due for another set of murders over the next month or two. Just after you left on vacation I decided to check out every international conference taking place in the country for the next six weeks. Fifty-two in total. I split the task force up into five teams and we're checking them all out. This is the eighth convention we've staked out this week alone.'

Lou raised an eye. 'That's a lot of work. What's the one in Sedona?'

'A symposium at the Sheraton for mental health professionals attended by a hundred and twenty delegates from thirty countries.'

Lou said, 'So what's the strategy?'

'To start with, the majority of the Disciple's victims were killed and butchered in remote, inaccessible underground locations, mostly caves or tunnels, disused mine shafts, underground metro stations, cellars, anywhere there's dark confinement. He'd burn his victims' bodies in a bizarre ritual, leaving a small black wooden crucifix between them. The bodies were often not found for a considerable length of time afterwards, which meant that in most cases the elements had already eradicated any tracks left by any transport he used. The two faint imprints of tyre tracks we did find were inconclusive because of heavy rainfall at the kill sites. Also, at each of the sites where we found the crucifix, it never revealed any prints.'

Lou nodded. 'We couldn't discern any real significance for the crosses, except maybe an obvious religious angle. Don't tell me, you focused on the delegates who hired cars? And maybe those with some kind of religious background? Like former priests, or serving ministers or pastors?'

I shook my head. 'We'd need more time to delve into someone's religious background, Lou. Unless it jumps out at us and the suspect's wearing a minister's collar, we'd have to deal with that issue later. But you're right about the cars. Twenty-four delegates in total hired vehicles. We discounted the third who are women because our profilers say we should be looking for a man, and we omitted another third because they're outside the age profile.'

Lou nodded. 'I'm with you. Get to the point.'

'We figured on the killer being aged between twenty-five and forty and an American citizen, because most of the killings took place in the US, which produced four people among the hirers.

I cut it down further by the car type they picked. Two hired convertibles, which usually don't have enough trunk space for transporting bodies, and besides, that kind of vehicle's too flash to carry abducted victims because it might get noticed. That left us with only two delegates worth keeping tabs on. I've already got a second team checking out the attendees at a dentists' convention tonight at the Hilton in Chicago.'

Lou's lips crinkled in a smile and he raised an eyebrow. 'It's going to be fun trying to dodge the lumps of shit that get thrown at me when the chief sees the expenses for all this manpower, but I'm impressed. You've been busy.'

'I also thought it might be worthwhile priming the park rangers in any nature reserves in the Sedona area that have caves, because that's the kind of location where our killer's likely to carry out his work. We've asked the rangers to keep a closer watch than usual on their patch over the next couple of days and contact us or the police if they notice anyone behaving suspiciously. They've promised to put every shift on notice.'

'Good work. Where's Vance Stone? Is he in on this?'

'No, he's on a couple of days' leave.'

Lou frowned. 'You didn't think to call him in? Stone's a damned good investigator, Kate.'

Vance Stone was a colleague of mine but he and I had issues. 'Sure he is, except you know the way it is between Stone and me, we fight like cat and dog. I thought it best we kept from under each other's feet.'

Lou shook his head. 'I'm not sure I agree. What about your two guys you've been watching?'

'That's where it got interesting. One hired a burgundy Toyota Camry, the other a navy blue Ford Taurus. The guy who hired the Taurus looked the most promising.'

'Why's that?'

'He's a psychiatrist named Constantine Gamal. An Armenian immigrant who came to study in this country fifteen years ago and decided to stay. His surname was originally Gamalyan but he shortened it and his citizenship application says he spent his childhood in Istanbul. Here, I had the information faxed to me.'

I handed Lou the application copy from my folder and he studied it and raised his eyes. 'Maybe the guy's got potential. Imagine. A psychiatrist who's so warped that he himself turns into a vicious killer. I'm hooked. Tell me more.'

'There's something else that's too much of a coincidence to ignore. Two of the Disciple's killings took place in Virginia, and another in Istanbul. Gamal has a connection to both territories.'

Lou's eyes sparked. 'What's his connection to Virginia?'

'Would you believe that he works at Bellevue mental health institute, near Angel Bay, ten minutes from my home? He also fits much of the profile. Highly educated professional, late thirties, unmarried, no immediate family that we can discern. I could go on. Talk about coincidence, I even met the guy.'

Lou's brow knitted. 'Are you serious?'

'Before my marriage to Paul broke up we had to visit a cop friend of his who'd suffered from a post-stress disorder and checked himself into Bellevue. Gamal was his psychiatrist and Paul and I got to meet him briefly.'

'What's he look like?'

'A nerdy, mild-mannered accountant. Slim, bespectacled, completely unremarkable. The kind of guy who blends into the background.'

Lou handed me back the copy application. 'Has the watch on him turned up anything?'

I shook my head and replaced the copy. 'That's the problem, he hasn't put a foot out of place. I figure he's probably asleep in his bed. After this afternoon's lecture on the treatment of schizophrenia and an early dinner he drew his curtains at nine p.m. and didn't leave his room. We're going to need more time watching the guy. Maybe a lot more.'

'Frig. What about the guy who hired the Toyota?'

'He hasn't panned out either. He hired in a hooker four hours ago. A woman with a big chest, big hair, long legs and high heels. She leaves after an hour and the next thing we know the guy's being wheeled through the lobby to a waiting ambulance, having suffered chest pains and a suspected heart attack. He's been in hospital ever since.'

Lou said with a tired sigh, 'Terrific. I'm beginning to think we're never going to catch this son of a bitch. He'll be another Green River killer, who'll only get apprehended when he's old and has stopped murdering.' He slumped into the chair by my bed. 'I think it's time I said something, Kate.'

I had the feeling I was about to hear the real reason for Lou's visit. 'Go ahead.'

Lightning crackled beyond the window and he looked away for a moment, as if trying to find the right words for what he wanted to say, before he looked back at me. 'The Bureau's been doing its damnedest to catch the Devil's Disciple for six and a half years now, since he first appeared on our radar after we connected two pairs of his double homicides in Chicago and DC and we set up the task force to try to catch him. You've been leading the hunt for the last four of those years, when I handed you the reins after I got promoted and I wanted someone fresh on the case. In that time no other agent I know has given more to an investigation than you. You've worked twenty-four-seven from the day you took charge. Personally, I don't know how you do it. If it was me or anyone else on your team, I bet we would have cracked up a long time ago and thrown in the towel.'

I was wary. 'Why do I get a feeling there's a "but" on the horizon?'

Lou let out a breath. 'Kate, I think it's time for you to stand down and let someone else take over the reins.'

I stared at Lou in disbelief, my black despair of a few minutes ago replaced by anger and my pride hurt. 'You're *relieving* me?'

'Kate, you've handled one of the toughest investigations the Washington field office has ever known. But you need a break for your own good. You're not just chasing a serial killer who murdered twenty-eight people. For the last six months you've been chasing the killer who murdered your fiancé and his fourteen-year-old daughter. It's deeply personal. That's why you're running yourself into the ground trying to catch this guy.'

I glanced at my Glock on the nightstand, wondering what Lou would say if he knew of my desolation of ten minutes ago. I still wore the engagement ring David had given me: a simple diamond set in a white gold band. It reminded me that I had never got over his and Megan's deaths, and sometimes I felt I never would.

I met Lou's stare. 'We both know the Disciple was the one who made it personal. He knew from the media publicity the case generated that I was narrowing the ground between us and I was determined to catch him. So he killed David and Megan because he hoped to unsettle me. But he only made me even more determined. Don't you see you're only giving him what he wants by taking me off the case? He'll have won.'

'Kate . . .' Lou shook his head. 'Kate, you've got to face the fact that despite your best efforts this investigation is going nowhere. We need someone new in the driver's seat to find this killer. The truth is, if you're not careful you're going to work yourself to death.'

A part of me knew that Lou was right: the stress was beginning to show and it frightened me. Toying with my service automatic a little while ago was so unlike me. Even the *thought* of contemplating suicide was alien to my character. 'Lou, if you'd just give me another couple of months.'

'I wish I could but my decision's final.'

'What if I take it over your head?'

'That would be a waste of time. The chief will back me up.'

'Then I'll take it higher.'

'Kate, be sensible . . .'

'Who's going to replace me?'

'I've been thinking of Vance Stone. This could give him the chance to earn the promotion he wants so badly, if he can catch our killer.'

I had no problem with Stone getting promotion, but Lou's dismissal felt like such a massive slap in the face that I was lost for words. A knock came on the door. I opened it and found an agent from the task force, his hair drenched from the rain. 'I'm sorry for disturbing you, Kate . . .'

'What is it?' I snapped.

'We just got a call from the park rangers at a nature reserve outside Sedona. They heard screams and challenged a suspicious prowler near some caves. The cops arrived and have him cornered. We think he could be our man, Kate. The bad news is he's holding a teenage girl hostage.'

3

The hunters were closing in for the kill. The Disciple ran through the limestone caves, dragging the teenage girl after him. He heard the dogs barking and he ran faster, sweat pumping from every pore in his body. Dangling from a cord around his neck was a heavy-duty electric torch and in his left hand he gripped a jagged knife, wet with blood.

Keep running.

He tried to put as much distance as he could between himself and his pursuers, but the stumbling thirteen-year-old girl was slowing him up. Her name was Melanie Colleen Jackson, he'd learned that much when he'd searched through her belongings after he'd abducted her and her father. He'd bound her hands and mouth with grey duct tape but still she emitted muffled cries of fear. He wanted to be rid of her, finish her off with the knife, but instinct told him he was going to need a hostage.

He came to a fork in the cave and saw two tunnels, left and right, and he tried desperately to remember whether he had come this way before, but the caverns all looked the same, harsh neon light from bulkheads flooding the jagged limestone walls. The Disciple had a runner's body, fit and lean, and he paused for barely a few seconds to catch his breath. He was certain he was lost, but knew that he had to keep moving, his only thought now his own survival.

He grabbed the girl's face in a vice-like grip and the teenager whimpered behind the gag as he placed the bloodied knife against her cheek. 'You keep your mouth shut and keep running or I'll butcher you the same way I did your father, have you got that, Melanie?'

She nodded, her wet eyes wide with raw fear. He took the blade away and it left a smudge of crimson on her face. 'That's a good girl. Keep those pretty legs moving.'

The Disciple started to run again, dragging the girl behind him. He heard the police dogs' frantic barking, knew he was running for his life, and he had only one question. *How did it all go wrong?*

The evening had started out flawlessly when he'd left the Sheraton Hotel at 11 p.m. He was disguised in a wig and moustache and dressed in a black Dockers windcheater, and navy chinos. He wore thin leatherette brown gloves, and a cheap pair of tennis shoes that he could dispose of far from his kill site in case he left footprints. His black doctor's bag contained the items he needed: the tan leather butcher's belt that held an assortment of knives, saws and cleavers with which to dismember his victims, surgical gloves and soap and bottled water to cleanse himself afterwards.

He had planned everything to the last detail before leaving his hotel. As usual he liked to book adjoining rooms, telling Reservations, 'I'll need connecting suites. Two of my family will be joining me later.'

No one ever joined him but the tactic allowed him to come and go from the adjoining room in disguise and without arousing suspicion, confident that no witnesses would ever identify him. He'd used his hire car to familiarise himself with the city and plan his escape routes, but before abducting his victims he would leave it in the hotel garage.

Then he had taken a cab to the east of the city, where he'd walked the streets until he'd noticed a six-year-old blue Pontiac with a big trunk parked in an alley outside a pool hall. The door was unlocked and the keys still in the ignition. He stole the Pontiac and three blocks away fitted a pair of magnetic false number plates, then he drove to the south of the city and stopped at a gas station. He'd purchased a plastic jerry can and filled it with five gallons of gas, which he placed in the trunk. Using a stolen car protected him in case someone spotted the vehicle. The stethoscope and black bag were laid on the passenger seat, along with the map and pencil torch, the hypodermic syringe and the slim iron bar, clad with thick leather, his tools of death ready for use. Then he went cruising the side streets of Sedona, seeking out his next victims, the urge to kill like a hunger in his belly.

He'd spotted at least two pairs of potential victims but the streets were either too crowded or there were witnesses in the vicinity. By midnight, storm clouds had gathered in the night sky and the streets had emptied. He'd given up hope of finding any victims that night and was about to ditch the Pontiac ten blocks from the Sheraton and retrieve the false plates when his luck changed. As he coasted past a flickering pink neon sign that said 'Dance Studio', he saw a man and a young girl step out of a doorway on to the pavement. The man locked the front door of the darkened studio and the girl was about to climb into a Toyota sedan parked out front. The Disciple noticed that most of the street lights were out and the road was deserted – no pedestrians, no passing cars. He felt his pulse quicken and his palms begin to sweat at the prospect of a kill, his body tingling with excitement.

He halted the Pontiac, rolled down the window and quickly surveyed his potential victims. The girl was no more than thirteen with mousy hair, soft lips and innocent eyes. He glimpsed a green dance leotard under her coat. *Father and daughter?* He hoped so. That kind of close victim relationship always made the kill more exciting. The Disciple picked up the stethoscope from the seat and slipped it around his neck. The instrument was a simple ploy. He knew that psychologically it made people drop their guard, thinking they were in the company of a doctor. He stuck his head out of the window. 'Hi there. Can you tell me the way to St Catherine's Hospital? I seem to be lost.'

The man finished locking up the premises as thunder cracked in the night sky. He noticed the stranger's stethoscope and approached the Pontiac, shaking his head. 'Never heard of it, sir. You're sure about the name?'

The Disciple observed the man's slender, fit-looking body. A dancer, probably, like the girl. He reckoned he could take him with little difficulty. 'Yes, it's a private hospital. I'm a doctor and need to get there urgently for an emergency. But I'm unfamiliar with the streets around here. I do have a map, if that's any help?'

The Disciple handed the man the map and a pencil torch and climbed out of the car. He was pleased to see that the girl had lingered by her passenger door, five yards away – she'd be easy to deal with, no trouble at all – and he gave the empty street one more glance up and down before he committed himself to abducting his victims. His pulse surged through his body like an electric current as he anticipated what was going to happen next.

The man studied the map as a drizzle of rain began to fall. 'I can't see no St Catherine's around here, Doc.'

Without replying the Disciple raised his arm and in an instant had stabbed the hypodermic into the man's neck.

'What the . . .' The man put a hand to his neck, staggered back in a daze, then collapsed like a sack of grain. The horrified girl clapped a hand to her mouth. *Daddy . . . !*'

The Disciple grabbed her roughly by the throat and jabbed her arm. She whimpered and slumped to the ground. *Terrific stuff, benzodiazepine.* Benzo for short, a powerful narcotic that induced immediate sleep, often used to sedate difficult psychiatric patients.

The Disciple sweated as he hefted each of his unconscious victims into the Pontiac's trunk and wrapped duct tape around their hands and mouths. He locked them in, then picked up the map and the man's car keys and stuffed them in his pockets, but he held on to the pencil torch. The rain fell more heavily now, spattering the empty street. He used his torch to check the ground in case he or his victims had dropped any evidence, but when he found nothing he climbed into the Pontiac and drove off.

By 1 a.m. he had arrived at the caves. He parked the car behind some trees and covered his shoes with thick plastic Cleaneze slip-covers and dragged the unconscious couple fifty yards inside the cavern, one after the other, the rain still sheeting down, the storm getting worse. He was drenched as he laid his drugged victims side by side on the ground. He had already checked out his kill site on three previous visits. The tourist attraction boasted native art daubed on the walls by Apache Indians, and no one used the caves after sunset except teenagers who drove there in pick-ups to swill beer on the edges of the park. But in the early hours of the morning, in a storm, the place was totally deserted.

The Disciple wiped rain from his face. It was time to begin his slaughter.

Halfway through his work he heard the girl moan and come awake. By then the man's corpse was blood-spattered, and the Disciple had placed a hand-sized black wooden cross next to the body, the gas can lying next to him on the ground, to burn the bodies with once he had finished with the girl.

The Disciple never felt so alive as in the moments after he had killed and butchered a victim, and that moment was no exception. He felt exhilarated, his body on fire with excitement. The assortment of knives and cleavers he had used to slaughter the man were laid out neatly on the rocks, the organs he had removed with surgical precision from his victim's torso were piled in a bloodied mess on the floor: heart and lungs, pancreas and spleen, liver, bowel and stomach. He moved over to the girl, ready to go to work again, when her eyelids flickered. She became conscious, looked around her dazedly.

He hadn't figured on her coming awake, or the duct tape on her mouth coming loose – he must have somehow misjudged the amount of benzo he'd used. The second the girl saw her father's eviscerated corpse lying next to her she gave a piercing scream that rang around the cavern like a siren. The Disciple fumbled in his black bag for more duct tape and struggled to cover her mouth.

It shut her up, and the girl looked petrified. Minutes later, as he selected another knife to recommence his butchery, he heard a noise like clattering stones. He frowned and cocked his ears but heard nothing more. Had the girl's scream alerted someone, or disturbed some wild cavern animal? He needed to be certain so he left her tied up and took his torch and walked back the fifty yards to the cavern mouth to investigate, the jagged knife clutched in his hand, his senses more alert with every step. He was suddenly caught in a powerful burst of torchlight as two uniformed park rangers appeared out of nowhere. 'Stop! Stay where you are!'

The caves exploded with light as someone flicked on the neon strips that were housed in metal bulkheads at intervals along the walls. The Disciple felt blind panic as he fled back to the girl and dragged her after him. He raced through the caves, but after fifteen minutes he'd ended up back where he had started, in the clearing with the girl's dead father. He was going round in circles.

The Disciple pushed the girl to the ground and slumped on to a mound of rocks. He panted as sweat dripped from the pores of his arms and lathered his face. He rarely carried a gun, preferred the knives and the hypodermic that put his victims to sleep, but he wished now that he had a gun. The rangers had disappeared but he heard voices echoing around the limestone chambers and saw the shadows of his pursuers flitting on the cave walls and heard dogs barking in the distance. They were coming closer, coming to get him. *How had they found him?*

He was trapped, but it wasn't over yet, not by a long shot. He still had an ace to play. He slipped his arm around the girl's throat and pressed the knife between her budding breasts. A little pressure and the blade would slip between her ribs and pierce her heart. *She was his hostage. His ticket out of here.* She sobbed behind the gag and he sweated as he whispered in her ear, 'You do exactly as I say, Melanie. Stay still and we both get out of here alive. Otherwise I'll cut your pretty heart out. You understand?'

The girl fell silent. He felt her young body trembling and her fear excited him. But this was no time to be distracted. He had a proposition to make to his pursuers, one they would be forced to accept or else his hostage would die. He steadied the knife against the girl's chest and waited for the enemy.

He heard noises and saw three men and a woman appear. They were armed and wore navy FBI windcheaters, and they pointed their weapons at him as they inched their way into the cave. He instantly recognised the woman, had seen her face on TV and in newspapers. *Kate Moran.* The bitch who had pursued him for years, who had proclaimed she was going to hunt him down and bring him to justice. He saw hatred in her eyes, an emotion so powerful that it consumed her. He held the knife between the girl's breasts. 'Stop right there or she dies like her father.'

He saw the agents glance at the butchered corpse on the lime-stone slab and said to Moran, 'You. Holster your gun and step forward. The others remain where you are. Put your firearms down but remove the magazines first and throw them away, or I'll kill the girl. There's no discussion.'

The agents looked uncertain until an older, tanned man who looked to be in command said, 'Kate, let me handle this . . .'

But Moran was having none of it. 'It's still my call, Lou. Everyone lay down their weapons.' She holstered her gun and waited for her colleagues to remove the magazines from their automatics and toss them away, then lay their empty weapons on the ground.

The Disciple heard the distant sound of barking dogs. 'It sounds like maybe you've got quite an army out there?'

Moran said flatly, 'Every exit out of the caves is blocked. You've got no way out, Gamal.'

The Disciple shook his head and slid the knife tip slowly across the girl's breasts. 'I think you're about to be proven wrong on that prognosis. Step ten paces towards me, Moran. The others don't move.'

Moran looked around the enclosed walls and briefly shut her eyes before taking ten paces forward. The Disciple smiled when he noticed that her face was bathed in perspiration, her hands shook, and her breathing was rapid.

'You're afraid of enclosed spaces, aren't you, Moran?'

'What . . . what makes you say that?'

'After years of dealing with patients the signs of claustrophobia are easy to recognise. Shallow breathing, trembling hands, and you look as if you're in hell. I bet you're afraid the cave walls are going to crumble in on you.'

'Maybe it's just your devilish company that makes me nervous, Dr Gamal.'

The Disciple laughed hoarsely. 'I doubt it. It seems we've come face to face at last. Except why do I get the feeling we've met before?'

'Bellevue. Five years ago.'

'Now that's interesting. You had problems with your phobia?'

'No. And it's irrelevant. Why don't you let the girl go, Doctor?'

The Disciple raised his eyes. 'Do you think I'm an idiot? It was courageous of you to enter the caves despite your fear. But maybe your decision will prove to be more stupid than brave.'

'What do you mean?'

'You'll find out soon enough. How did you locate me, Moran? No, on second thoughts, don't answer that, at least not yet. The longer we delay the more of your colleagues will arrive and the more my escape will be burdened with danger.'

Moran said, 'What escape? You're going nowhere. We've got helicopters, local cops and Feds outside. All we're short of is the National Guard.'

The Disciple shook his head and glanced at Moran's colleagues. 'You're very wrong to assume I can't escape. This is what I want you to do or else I kill Melanie. First, take your gun slowly from its holster and place it in front of you, then step well back until I tell you to stop. Do it *now*, or I'll cut her.'

The Disciple pressed the knife tip into the girl's chest and her eyes shut tight with pain. Moran hesitated, then took her weapon from its holster and slid it along the ground in front of her before she stepped back. 'That's far enough,' the Disciple ordered.

He knelt forward, still holding the girl in his arm lock, picked up Moran's Glock and stood, then grinned as he pointed it back at her. 'You know what? You can quote Freud and Maslow all you want on human motivation, but I much prefer what a certain US president had to say on the subject. When you have them by the balls, their minds and hearts will follow.'

'You disguised yourself before every kill, didn't you, Dr Gamal? That was clever. I bet you even made a habit of leaving your hire

22

car at the hotel and stealing another and fitting it with false plates, just like the one outside?'

'What does it matter?'

'Because I've got questions I've wanted answered for years. *Why?* Why kill all those victims? Why butcher them in pairs? Was it for the same reason you killed David and Megan? Some kind of revenge?'

The Disciple saw anger spark in Moran's face and he said dismissively, 'You'd never understand, Moran. Besides, I don't have the time for psychoanalytical discussion. You have ten minutes to arrange a helicopter and then I'm going to walk out of here and you're coming with me. If you don't get the chopper, the girl's dead. The same applies if anyone follows us or I notice anything amiss. *Anything*, and she's dead. Clear? Nine minutes left. You're wasting time.'

'There's one problem. I can't do as you say,' Moran answered.

The Disciple sweated as he pushed the gun barrel against the girl's temple. 'I'm holding the ace, Moran. You follow my instructions or you say goodbye to sweet little Melanie here. You want me to start cutting her here and now? Prove to you I mean business? You know I'll do it.'

Moran took a deep breath. 'Before you squeeze that trigger or use that blade you better know something too, because what I'm about to say is going to decide whether *you* live or die.'

The Disciple frowned. 'What the fuck are you talking about?'

'You're not a gun expert, are you? The safety catch, that little red button near the hammer. It's on. You can't shoot.'

The Disciple panicked and studied the weapon in his hand. He couldn't see a red button. The distraction lasted a bare two seconds but it was enough for Moran to reach behind her back and produce a small automatic. 'I like to keep this for emergencies. There's something else I forgot to mention. The Glock doesn't have a safety. Lay the weapon down. *Right now or I'll shoot.*'

'You bitch!' The Disciple pressed the Glock to the girl's head. A split second later a gunshot exploded.

23

4

Virginia

Greensville Correctional Centre is a high-security prison. Twenty-foot steel-wire walls, watchtowers with powerful searchlights and thick rolls of razor wire are everywhere. Visitors get electronically body-scanned before entering and leaving.

I have waited a year for this day.

I knew that across the snow-covered prison courtyard was Unit L, an isolated grey concrete building that houses the death chamber. This is where condemned prisoners spend their last five nights of life in a holding cell before being led to their execution – a fifteen-by-twenty-foot room where a stainless-steel gurney or electric chair awaits them. The prisoner is allowed to choose how they wish to die, but if no choice is exercised then the state carries out the execution by lethal injection. Tonight, it was Constantine Gamal's turn.

For most of my life I was never a great believer in the death penalty, but when you've spent over a decade working in law enforcement you get to realise that there *are* evil murderers in our midst who don't deserve the right to walk this earth. Gamal is one of them. Without doubt, he was the most evil, brutal murderer I have ever met in my ten years as a federal agent. He has murdered twenty-nine beloved human beings, some of his victims barely teenagers – and all of them were cherished by their families. Their deaths have left behind such deep rivers of pain.

Something else the victims had in common – none was shown a shred of mercy. Nor did their killer ever express a sliver of regret. I feel no sorrow that he is about to be executed – the truth is, I'm hoping that he dies in agony. I never thought that as a woman I would hear myself say that, but I'm damned sure that all the families of the victims he slaughtered feel the same way: *Kill him and be done with it and may he rot in hell*.

Minutes after the guard finishes his phone call, a man appears from an office at the end of the hallway to my left. I recognise the warden from newspaper photographs. Lucius Clay is a tall, elegant man in his late fifties, with watery blue eyes and the silky pale skin of a lifelong teetotaller. But today he looks as if he carries the burden of the world on his shoulders, though with the moral certainty that God is on his side.

'Miss Moran?'

Clay's handshake feels limp, as if he is reluctant to meet me. 'Are we all ready to begin, Warden?' What I really want to say is: *Are we ready to rock-and-roll and poison this bastard?* I felt chirpy this evening, would never have believed that the prospect of a human death would appeal to me so much, but it honestly did.

Then I realised something was wrong: Lucius Clay's face reddened slightly and he looked uncomfortable in my company. 'I'm afraid there's been a slight hitch, Miss Moran.'

I felt my heart quicken. I wanted to see Gamal gone from this earth just as soon as was possible and I didn't want delays. 'What kind of hitch?'

'There's a possibility that I may have to seek a temporary stay of execution from the state governor.'

I couldn't believe what I was hearing. 'For what reason?'

Lucius Clay sighed. 'I emphasise that it's a *possibility*, Miss Moran. Gamal claims that he has some startling new information to reveal.'

'*What* information?'

'Fifteen minutes ago he told the captain in charge of the death watch that he wishes to confess to another two murders.'

That completely threw me. I knew that deathbed confessions before an execution were common. And knowing Gamal as I did, I wasn't surprised that he might have killed other victims. But I wasn't expecting any last-minute admissions and I felt suddenly suspicious. 'Do you think he's being truthful?'

'I honestly don't know, Miss Moran.'

'I'm concerned about this stay of execution you're talking about. Did Gamal request it?'

Gamal had already been on death row for almost eight months and had not submitted an appeal. Legally, he couldn't offer new evidence and he was scheduled to die tonight. His only chance of survival was either a pardon from the state governor – and that seemed about as likely as a blizzard in July – or a stay of execution for up to thirty days, issued by either the courts or the governor.

'That's the strange thing,' Clay admitted. 'Gamal hasn't requested a stay. He says that he wants to put the record straight, then the execution can proceed. *I'm* the one who's suggesting a stay may be necessary until any new evidence is gathered. Then again, as I said, it's a *possibility* and may not be needed.'

'What does he mean, put the record straight?'

'I don't know. He's refused to elaborate. But those were his exact words, Miss Moran.'

I noticed the warden stare at me and I was wary. 'Why do I get the feeling that there's more to this than you're saying?'

Clay let out a sigh. 'He says he'll talk only to you, and no one else. Just the two of you alone, face to face, that's the deal if he's to tell us where he buried the bodies.'

'You're kidding me? The two of us, *alone*?' Constantine Gamal was the most cunning, wicked killer I had ever encountered and the bastard scared me. After that fateful morning in Arizona when I'd shot and wounded him before his arrest I'd had to endure his evil, disturbing presence during his interrogation and trial. The man had the ability to unsettle *anyone* he came in contact with. Could I go alone into a room with such a killer? Whose signature was to slaughter his victims the way a butcher slaughters livestock, their bodies hacked to pieces? I wanted to see him die. Now.

The warden sounded sympathetic. 'Personally, I wouldn't

consider allowing a condemned prisoner being left alone with a visitor, not ever, and especially a prisoner as dangerous as Gamal. But that's what he's insisted upon, otherwise he takes his secret with him to the grave.'

'He said that?'

Clay nodded. 'His exact words, Miss Moran.'

I considered before replying. 'If he *is* offering us a confession and new evidence, I think we're duty bound to allow him to talk, especially considering that it may give relief to the victims' families.'

Clay nodded. 'I agree, but I have to tell you I'd be most uncomfortable leaving you alone in a room with a man like him, even if I can make that room completely secure. But the decision really is yours. You can choose not to listen to him and nobody's going to call you a coward.'

'How long are you figuring on delaying the execution?' I asked.

'I'm seeking clarification on that point from the governor's office. But I do have a lawyer ready to take down any statement Gamal may wish to make. What do you think, Miss Moran? Is this something you want to do? I completely understand if you don't.'

I mulled over Clay's words. I figured that the relatives who had travelled from all over the country to witness this execution were not going to be pleased by the delay. But what if by talking to Gamal I could help any families of his undisclosed victims find closure? I figured that was important.

'You're certain the room will be secure?'

Clay nodded. 'Most certain. And Gamal will be shackled and handcuffed. But again, this is entirely your decision. I'm not enthusiastic.'

'I'll do it. Have you told the relatives about the hitch?'

'I'm just about to,' Clay admitted. 'They look to me like they're very keen to see the sentence carried out. To tell the truth, it's the largest and most eager executioner's audience I've seen in all my years as a warden. You'll forgive me, but I almost feel like I ought to be handing out soda and popcorn.'

I was tempted to say: *It's easy to understand their eagerness, Warden. They want the evil bastard gone from this earth.* But I didn't have to. I figured Clay understood.

He consulted his watch. 'And now, if you could please follow me, Miss Moran, I'll take you to the room where you can meet Gamal face to face.'

5

The warden and I made a short journey by van to a snow-covered prison yard flooded with brilliant white light. We entered Isolation Unit L through a pair of thick steel doors manned by guards.

We came to the door of a private room with grey-painted concrete walls and thick mirrored Plexiglas. A white, hard plastic table circled by eight green plastic chairs, a speakerphone on the wall and a neon light overhead. The room is an annexe with two thick steel entrance doors and just a short walk to the execution chamber.

A glass window separates the chamber and annexe, and beyond the glass I noticed two men, one of them tall and wearing a silver tie and black-framed glasses, setting up an array of video equipment, as if they were about to video the execution.

Once we enter the private room, Lucius Clay sits. I notice he has pale hands, no calluses, rough skin or bitten nails. Despite his refined appearance, his steely cobalt eyes suggest to me that in his professional capacity he has most probably witnessed every human weakness, every frailty and depravity known to man, and I'd take a guess that he's figured that the only way to muddle through life is with God as his anchor.

'Take a seat, Miss Moran,' Clay offered. 'Gamal had his last meal about half an hour ago. Last meals are mostly pizza but Gamal proved quite the gourmet. Beef heart, pan-fried in olive oil, rare, topped with a sliver of *foie gras*. Boiled potatoes smothered in garlic and rosemary butter. Crème brulée. A half-bottle of Californian Merlot. Oh, and a pack of Juicy Fruit gum.' Clay shrugged. 'It's the first time I've heard of a request for a beef heart.'

I shuddered as I joined Clay at the table. 'It sounds gross.'

'Forgive me, but I never asked if you'd like some coffee, Miss Moran.'

'No, thank you.'

Clay offered a tiny, apologetic smile. 'I never eat supper before an execution. But coffee keeps me going. I've had at least a dozen cups since I woke at six a.m. I could surely do with another.'

'Nerves?'

Clay raised a neatly trimmed grey eyebrow. 'Good Lord, no. Caffeine's my addiction, I'm afraid.'

For a coffee addict, the warden didn't seem all that jittery – until I noticed that he was tapping his slender fingers on the table. 'Is there anything else on your mind, Warden?'

Clay glanced away with an uncomfortable look towards some distant point on the blank white wall, and a few moments passed before he turned back to face me. 'I guess like me you're surprised by Gamal's last-minute offer of a confessional. You're thinking why would he wait until now? He's had every opportunity to make a statement long before his execution.'

'I thought last-minute confessions aren't all that uncommon on death row?'

'They happen. However, I never expected one from such a brutal killer.'

Nor did I. Which made me think: *Has Gamal got something up his sleeve?* Before I could answer, Clay looked me in the eyes. 'Is it too much to expect,' he suggested quietly, 'that he's had some kind of reconciliation with God? That this is all part of a seeking for forgiveness?'

I wasn't in the least bit convinced. The man who was about to be executed was probably one of the most evil serial killers since John Gacy or Ted Bundy. This much my team had learned in the last twelve months: fifteen years ago, aged twenty-three, Constantine Gamal had immigrated to the United States and begun an international killing spree that was to claim twenty-nine lives.

Gamal's modus operandi went back over twenty years to when

he'd carried out his first killings in Istanbul, of his father and his younger sister. He had managed to escape blame for the crimes – no one had been charged by the Turkish police – and his motive had always remained sketchy. I knew that his father had been an Armenian immigrant to Turkey and ran a butcher's shop. He kept a slaughterhouse in the basement and as a child Gamal would sneak down to watch his father at work. Something about the dark, underground slaughterhouse and the sight of brutal, animal death had encouraged a depraved seed to flourish in Gamal's warped mind. In every one of his subsequent killings he chose to emulate those dark moments in the basement slaughterhouse when he had murdered his father and sister. After their murder he had panicked and set fire to the basement to mask the crime. It was a desperate, juvenile attempt to destroy the bodies and the evidence, but the fire was extinguished by neighbours who stopped the blaze spreading. Those first murders gave Gamal a lust for killing that endured.

'People like Gamal are an aberrant human strain, Mr Clay. They're the dark and malignant side of human nature and they're closer to evil than they can ever be to God. Especially given the brutal way he killed his victims. I can't see such a man suddenly finding religion, can you? Or maybe your prison experience has taught you that leopards *do* change their spots at the last minute?'

Clay didn't fail to detect the bitter tone in my voice and must have seen that he had struck a raw nerve, because he put his hand across to touch mine. His milky skin didn't feel soft, but surprisingly tough. 'It isn't that uncommon for killers to seek last-minute absolution for their crimes or confess that they've committed others. Though I must admit I've often wondered about Gamal since he's been imprisoned here. Despite what you say, I feel there's a certain tragedy about his case.'

'What do you mean?'

'It's a supreme irony that a man with such a gifted intellect, a man who understands the psychiatry of warped minds, should himself turn into a vicious killer. But I'm truly sorry if my remark has caused you pain or offence. I didn't mean it to. I know you've

31

suffered personally, Miss Moran. However, even if it's not much consolation, I'm sure that some of that pain will be avenged tonight.'

Clay sounded genuine, but as I slid my hand away he didn't look all that certain of the truth of his remark. Suddenly the door opened behind him and a uniformed guard appeared. Clay acknowledged the guard's nod, then stood, raised the blinds in the room and said to me, 'We're ready to bring in Gamal. One more thing that ought to reassure you, Miss Moran. You'll both be watched through the two-way mirrored glass and we'll record your conversation. Half a dozen armed guards are on hand, so just in case you're worrying, he can't do you any more personal harm. He really can't.'

6

The warden left. Four guards entered, Constantine Gamal between them, wearing orange prison overalls. His wrists and ankles were shackled and with a rattle of steel chains he sat and faced me. Our eyes met and I felt nausea in the pit of my stomach. His eyes were dangerous, black pools, as cold as ice. One of the guards must have noticed my discomfort because he said quietly, 'Are you OK, Miss Moran?'

'Yes.'

Gamal removed the pair of wire-rimmed glasses he wore and stared across at me. Just stared, without a word, without a gesture. I knew it was a power thing with him – see who'd blink first, who'd talk first, who'd lose the game.

What struck you most about Gamal at first glance was that he looked such a *regular* guy. Thin, cleanly shaven and extremely fit – I'd heard he ran and meditated even in prison. A high, intelligent forehead and bland features. We'd found evidence in his apartment in Alexandria that he'd exploited his plain features to great effect by his trademark use of simple disguises while carrying out his heinous crimes, which helped him remain at large. Stashed in his bedroom and his Ford SUV were a big selection of wigs and false moustaches and hair dye, a postal worker's uniform, an army uniform, a priest's garb, an array of glasses and tinted contacts, racks of clothes and pots of stage make-up.

A practised psychiatrist, Gamal didn't look like a killer until you noticed his eyes – dark, murderous, deep-set eyes that reminded me of Charles Manson. I knew that on each of his forearms was a small tattoo of a black serpent's head with red-inked

Satan horns. But today his arms were covered by the sleeves of his orange overalls.

The guards withdrew, and the door clanged shut. Gamal said nothing, just continued to stare, looked at me all over: my face, my hands, my body, until about a minute later his razor lips moved and he spoke in an accent that was just faintly eastern European. 'How have you been, Kate? Is life agreeable for you?'

The familiarity of him using my first name got to me, no doubt as he intended, but I didn't reply. I'd learned from interrogating Gamal that he always had a habit of opening a conversation with a couple of probing questions, and sure enough a moment later came another one, his voice sedate and controlled. 'Have you ever been to an execution before?'

I remained silent and he said quietly, 'I imagine that the experience ought to be enjoyable for you? Something you're looking forward to? No?'

I ignored his taunts. 'Whatever it is you have to say to me, get it over with.'

'You forgot something, Kate.'

'What?'

Gamal was calmly defiant. 'That bit you wanted to say at the end. It should have been: "Whatever it is you have to say to me, get it over with, *you piece of shit*." Isn't that what you wanted to say, Kate?'

I was losing my patience. I wasn't here to be toyed with and already I'd had enough. I stood up to leave. 'Have a wonderful time in hell, Gamal.'

The defiance never left his face. 'Unlike so many who have gone before me, I'm truly looking forward to the experience. But before I enter Satan's bosom I want you to know something, Kate.'

I didn't answer. I was certain that Gamal was playing with me, and I didn't know why – he was a sicko and maybe that was reason enough – but I wasn't going to allow him to derive pleasure from taunting me. I had almost reached the door when he caught me off guard.

'Hey, I see you're still wearing an engagement ring. Was that the one David gave you? *Nice* ring. Are they real diamonds? I bet they are.' Gamal's tone changed to a mock bedside manner. 'Do you miss David, and Megan? I'm sure you do. It hurts thinking about how much you miss them, doesn't it? Day after day, night after night. Deep inside, and not the way this hurts.'

He raised his right shoulder as if wanting to show me the gunshot wound I'd inflicted beneath his prison overalls. 'A clean shot, Kate. Punched a hole in my shoulder blade, enough to knock me off my feet. Neat trick, the safety-catch thing. And our little friend Melanie lived to tell the tale.'

'If you can call it living after the hell you put her through. I doubt the child will ever be the same,' I answered.

The Disciple smiled. 'We've all got crosses to bear. But we've digressed. My point is that so many of my colleagues in psychiatry tend to think of Freud as passé, but I always thought that he perfectly encapsulated the reason for sadness when he said that the cause of all human depression is the loss of someone's love. Wouldn't you agree?'

I looked back and saw Gamal stare at me, unblinking. 'You evil, sick, unfeeling bastard,' I said.

'Call me what you want but I didn't kill them, Kate.'

I stared reluctantly at him. 'Kill *who*?'

'David and Megan. I didn't butcher either of them.'

'*What* . . . ?'

'You're killing the wrong man for their murders.'

7

Gamal's words stopped me in my tracks. I felt my mouth go dry. Seven months earlier a five-week trial had found him guilty on four counts of premeditated murder, including David and Megan's. Gamal had dismissed his lawyer mid-trial and never admitted his part in any of the murders, and that was despite being caught having just slaughtered one of his victims. In fact, he'd pretty much said nothing in court, just sat there, expressionless. He'd already gone through a battery of psychological tests and been diagnosed as sane enough to stand trial.

Gamal sat back in his chair with a self-controlled look and his chains rattled again. 'You heard me. I didn't kill them. I killed all the others I was found guilty of, even all the ones you've got on record that I wasn't charged with, but those were two crimes I didn't commit.'

I stared back at him in profound disbelief and thought: *There's some of kind strategy being played out here except I can't figure out what it is.* But I *knew* Gamal was up to something, something cruel and desperate, some last-ditch effort to wield power and inflict pain, because that was his way, that was how he got his kicks. But I couldn't fathom his motive. I stared at the mirrored glass. *I wonder what the warden and guards and the lawyer sitting behind than make of Gamal's words? Are they as astounded as me?* 'If this is some kind of ploy . . .' I began.

Gamal's deep-set eyes stared calmly back at me. 'It's not a ploy, Kate. I just wanted you to finally know the truth. I thought it was time you heard it from the horse's mouth. When you and your friends interrogated me, you asked me about a couple of inconsistencies at the Bryce crime scene. Like the fact that the

36

crucifix was left in a different position to where I usually placed it between my victims, and the other fact that your fiancé was shot in the head, unlike any of the others I killed. Doesn't that make you think I might be telling the truth? You know that I was pretty much consistent in my methods when I killed. Maybe I didn't always burn the bodies, that was always down to how much time I had. But I never used a gun on any of them. I preferred using my knives.'

I took a deep breath, reviled and perturbed by Gamal's words. 'Why is it that I still don't believe a single word you say?'

'Ask me how I can prove that I didn't kill them.'

I didn't reply. Gamal was eerily composed. 'Go on, ask me, Kate.'

'How?'

'Because when I was supposed to be killing your loved ones, I was killing someplace else.'

Gamal said it so matter-of-factly, so callously, that I felt my legs go weak. I knew why he was the most evil man I had ever encountered – he hadn't even a shred of human emotion.

He fixed me with a stare. 'You still don't believe me, do you? It's the truth. It was the same Thanksgiving Day, about the same time, but in the District that I killed my victims.'

'You're lying,' I said.

'You really think so?'

I stared back at him, unconvinced. 'Why didn't you tell your lawyer?'

Gamal waved a hand dismissively. 'He was useless. I didn't owe him a thing.'

'Why are you telling *me* this, *now*?' I asked.

He looked away, then back at me. 'Truth? Because I despise you. Because it pissed me off that you captured me. And I want you to pay for that.'

I knew there had to be an angle, had figured part of it out, but not all. 'So that's what this meeting is really all about? Revenge.'

Gamal said nothing, his face expressionless.

37

'So how am I going to pay?' I pressed him.

Gamal looked me calmly in the eyes. 'You can't see it, can you? You're going to pay because you're going to have to go through all that agony all over again. Hunting down the real killer and catching them if you can, going to trial and looking for a conviction. Should be a hoot, don't you think? All those sleepless nights, all those fucked-up weekends while you're working the case. The frayed nerves, the headaches, the constant wondering: will I catch the guilty? Still, look on the plus side, I guess there's all that overtime to look forward to, all those air miles to clock up.'

I felt a knot of anger in my stomach and found it difficult to control myself. But I still didn't believe him. *What's he really up to?* 'I don't buy your confession, Gamal. For one, you're a liar. And two, the killings of David and Megan had your hallmarks written all over them. They linked you to the crime.'

He shrugged again, as if my accusations were a mere irritation. 'Hallmarks prove nothing, don't mean a thing. How many times do I have to say it, or are you stupid? I'm telling the truth. It wasn't me. I was killing elsewhere.'

Gamal's callous admission made me feel like throwing up. 'Who were your victims?'

He shrugged. 'The kind no one misses, least of all the cops. Worthless street people – a homeless black guy and his kid. She was about eleven, twelve maybe. I killed them in my usual manner.'

I swallowed with disgust. 'Where?'

'I did them both in a tunnel near the Chinatown metro station and buried them there. I didn't have time to burn them, just like some of the others.'

'Why not?'

'A couple of maintenance personnel appeared and I vanished before they spotted me.'

'That's a big help. Tell me where *exactly* in the metro.'

'You'll have to find that out, Moran. Or else you'll have to wait until we meet in another life.'

38

This cold-blooded admission of two more murders didn't shock me. But I still had no way of knowing whether his claim was true or not. 'Why did you pick those two victims?'

Gamal relaxed farther back in his chair. 'They were in the wrong place at the wrong time. Simple as that, Kate. And I killed them for the same reason I started picking my victims again eight years ago. It was an opportunity to see if I could get away with it one more time and get the same thrill I got when I settled scores and did my sister and my old man. Does that answer it, Kate?'

He was doing it again, using my first name, but it would have been a waste of time getting angry with him. His statement sounded so damned cruel. I said, 'For killers like you I'm not so sure there is another life.'

Gamal said hoarsely, 'Now that's where you're wrong. So very wrong, Kate. See, the Devil's real. I *know* my next life exists.'

'So long as it's in hell I'm happy.'

'Don't mock hell. And the trip's well worth the admission price. Like the writer said, "Compared to evil's immortality, what is death but a truly small and painful thing?"'

'Edgar Allan Poe.'

Gamal studied his fingertips a moment before he stared at me. 'He's one of my favourite writers. Did you ever visit his house in Richmond? Worth a trip some time. Wonder if they'll ever have a memorial to me someplace?'

'I wouldn't count on it.'

The guy was Looney Tunes. He may have been declared legally sane, but he was as close to the border as anyone could come. And I still wasn't sure whether he was telling the truth or playing with me. 'I'm not in the mood for your games.'

Gamal said quietly, 'You think this is a game? You think I'm here for the fun of it? Just locate the bodies and you'll find out.'

Gamal's attitude was driving me up the wall and I'd had enough of his smugness. My patience snapped. 'You make me sick. You haven't an ounce of human decency. You know what else I think? Your little satanic worship rituals were just a sham. At the bottom of it all you're just a cowardly, brutal, scummy serial killer.'

I saw purple veins rise on Gamal's neck. 'People like you under-estimate the power of the occult. There are things you can *never* understand, Kate.'

I stood up. '*Bullshit.* There are things *you'll* never understand. Like basic human decency, and love and respect. Because you've never been even close to human. You know one of the lessons I've learned after years of hunting down vermin like you? It's that there are some people who really don't deserve to live, and you're one of them. This world will be a better place after you've gone. And I'm glad that I played a part in that.'

Gamal said, 'You see, that's what gets me off. I could have had a long and pleasurable career if you hadn't become involved. That's why you're going to pay, and pay dearly.'

This time I mustered the courage to stare him in the eyes. 'The only one who's going to pay is you, Gamal. You're history.'

'I wouldn't count on that, Kate.'

'I would,' I answered. 'Your killing spree was partly just a game to you, wasn't it? A game to see who had the brains and the cunning to win the race. Well, you lost, Gamal, and do you know why? Because behind your arrogance, your conceited intellect, you've always been a loser. I thought you were a psychiatrist, *Doctor* Gamal. But you couldn't even recognise your own fail-ings and try to rectify them. And don't even think about a memo-rial. Six months from now you'll be forgotten. Just bones in an unmarked grave.'

It happened so quickly that I barely had time to react. In an instant Gamal was up on his feet and with a rattle of chains he grabbed the table and slid the rim under the door handle to prevent the door from opening. In my panic I tried to jump away but Gamal lunged at me and I felt the full force of his weight slam into my body. I was winded, knocked off my feet, and Gamal landed on top of me as we both crashed to the floor, a tangle of arms and legs and chains.

'*Bitch!*' He spat the word like venom and fixed me with a manic stare. '*Fucking bitch!* I'll fucking kill you!'

I tried to scream but the weight of his body was crushing my chest and I could smell his sour breath. The guards were already forcing in the steel door – their voices frantic, the warden shouting, 'Push it in, for *God sakes!*'

And then I felt Gamal's teeth sink into my shoulder, a bite so deep that it might have struck bone. A stab of pain rippled through my body and felt like a jolt of high voltage, the agony excruciating. My eyes misted as Gamal squirmed like a rabid animal trying to bite off a chunk of my flesh, the agony so unbearable that I felt I was going to pass out. *God, what's keeping the guards? Why can't they help me?*

I saw that the table was still wedged against the door. I was blinded by pain but I summoned all my strength and kicked out repeatedly at the table with my heel. It dislodged a fraction and the next thing I knew the door had burst in and then came the noise of chains rattling as hands grabbed Gamal. There was a hard slapping sound as a baton struck his skull, again and again. Finally his teeth released their grip and I felt a surge of relief in my shoulder, and then a wave of intense pain. Gamal was still conscious, his lips stained with my blood as he fixed me with a cold stare.

He was calm again as he said hoarsely, 'Enjoy the show. Because you'll pay for this. You don't believe me? Just wait and see. I will defeat death and come back and take you to hell with me, Kate. That I promise you.'

The last thing I saw before I almost passed out were the guards dragging Gamal from the room.

8

For the next few minutes it seemed as if all hell had broken loose. Three guards propelled me to a room down the hall and nursed me into a chair. One of them snapped open a first-aid kit and another helped open my bloodstained blouse, the pain excruciating as he examined my wound. 'That's a pretty nasty bite you've got there, ma'am.'

He studied the livid bite mark and as he probed the flesh I felt a stab of pain and dug my nails into his arm. '*Jesus . . .*'

'Sorry, ma'am. We've sent someone to fetch a doctor.'

Finally the door opened and I was surprised to see Warden Clay escort an elegant woman into the room. She was dressed smartly in a charcoal two-piece suit and she smelled of lemon-scented soap. Brogan Lacy was David's ex-wife and she was a tall, good-looking brunette in her late forties, who worked for the Richmond Medical Examiner's office as the Assistant Chief Medical Examiner. She gave me a curt nod before she studied my wound. 'Warden Clay tells me you had an accident and he asked me to help.'

Clay said, 'I hope you don't mind, Miss Moran? Dr Lacy was the nearest medical practitioner I could find. She came as an execution witness.'

I had never really got to know Brogan Lacy – David and she had been divorced for a year when we met – but she and I had seen each other in court pretty much every day for the time that Gamal's trial had lasted. Our relationship was cool; no matter how hard I had tried to get to know her she had maintained her distance. But I understood that her grief had been intense – she had lost her only daughter. 'Why should I mind?

But it was hardly an accident, it was an attack,' I corrected Lacy.

Clay said quietly, 'Yes, I explained. But if you ladies could excuse me a moment, I have some matters to attend to. I'm sure you're in excellent hands with Dr Lacy.'

Clay left us with one of the guards for company, and Lacy slipped on a pair of latex gloves from the first-aid kit and scrutinised my shoulder, her touch almost rough. I wondered whether it had more to do with the fact that she was used to dealing with dead bodies instead of live ones than any dislike for me. I flinched. '*Ouch.*'

Lacy said coolly, 'It's not as bad as it looks, just a deep and ugly flesh wound.'

'Will I need to be stitched?'

'No, it isn't wise to stitch human bites or they won't heal properly. This may hurt some more. Try to bear up.'

Lacy went to work, dabbing on some antiseptic, as I tried to ignore the agony. She finished by applying the gauze and sticking plaster and gave me a shot. 'It's Diclofenac, to ease the pain. You still better go see your own doctor and get some antibiotic as a precaution. A human bite is often more dangerous than a dog bite.'

I put my hand gently to my shoulder and felt a painful ache. 'You're kidding?'

Lacy removed the latex gloves and tossed them in a garbage bin. 'No, I'm not kidding, Miss Moran. The human mouth is full of very harmful bacteria. But the news is you're going to live, unlike the man who attacked you.'

The door opened and Warden Clay came back, his forehead beaded with sweat. 'How is she, Doc?'

'The bite was close to the bone, but I'm pretty certain she'll suffer no long-term physical effects.'

I said to Lacy, 'Thanks. I think I owe you a coffee some time.'

She raised an eyebrow. 'That really won't be necessary, Miss Moran.'

Lacy left. Clay had the look of a man who was scared I'd institute a legal case against him and the prison. I eased myself up off the chair. 'It was my decision to enter the room, so don't worry, I won't be suing, Warden. But I thought you said I'd be safe.'

Clay dabbed his forehead with a paper tissue and said apologetically, 'Miss Moran, I am truly sorry. I had absolutely no idea that something like this might happen. Gamal was shackled, I didn't anticipate that he'd harm you, and everything happened so quickly . . .'

I felt angry. 'That's no excuse. I could have been killed.'

'That wouldn't have happened. We were inside the cell within seconds. Though I'm sure it didn't seem like seconds to you at the time. And an attack such as you experienced is one of the reasons I told you we usually *never* allow prisoners to be alone with visitors unless guards are present. That's why I was reluctant.'

Clay sounded genuinely apologetic and I let it pass. 'What's happened to Gamal?' I asked.

'He's been restrained in his holding cell.'

'Did you hear everything he said?'

'Yes, and it was recorded.' Clay sighed and dabbed his forehead again. 'Of course, it's disturbing. He obviously meant to hurt you by these claims. I can understand his motives for doing so because you apprehended him. But is he telling the truth?'

I struggled to my feet and almost cringed as a jolt of pain shot through my shoulder. 'I don't know. He may be having a last laugh at my expense by sending me on a wild-goose chase, but anything is possible where Gamal's concerned. What happens now?'

'I spoke with the governor. He insists that even if Gamal didn't kill David and Megan as he claims, he was convicted on three other counts of murder. He also confessed to them on the tape we just made, though he's never admitted it up until now. But if Gamal's past silence is anything to go by, the governor doubts we'd get more information about these other murders from him.'

'What exactly are you saying, Warden?'

'The execution goes ahead.'

9

Imagine a small theatre. Four rows of tiered seats facing a stage. Imagine the audience taking their seats and waiting for the curtains to part and the show to begin. Except that it's not a play or school pantomime they're about to witness, but the execution of a human being.

In Greensville, there are two separate viewing rooms facing the execution 'stage'. One is for the state's twelve chosen witnesses, but the room I was ushered into was packed with victims' relatives, most of whom I had become familiar with during Gamal's trial. Three seats away was Gaby Stenson, an Oregon mother of three children, and now a widow. I knew she was thirty-six, but grief had etched another decade into her face. Painfully thin, her mousy brown hair tied back, her eyes soulless: Gamal had killed her husband Mack and his teenage niece, Marie, a pretty girl aged seventeen.

Seated near by was Rob Mercier, a Chicago banker whose wife and daughter had been savagely murdered by Gamal four years earlier, dressed immaculately in a pinstripe business suit and a navy silk tie and cream silk shirt. Pain was carved into Mercier's being: his mouth tightly set, his eyes dark and intensely lonely.

Melanie Jackson sat with her mother in the third row. I was so glad to see her here, the one victim I had saved, and her widowed mother had never stopped thanking the Bureau for rescuing her daughter. Melanie noticed me and waved. She appeared much more adult in the space of a year, but thinner, and I knew that the trauma of witnessing her father's murder had matured her early. But something else about Melanie sent a shiver down my spine. I had only really noticed it when I questioned her in the days after her cave ordeal: she so much resembled Megan that it was uncanny. The same almond-brown eyes, raven hair, pale oatmeal skin, and braces on her teeth. And a warm, spirited manner that made her such a pleasure to be with. Seeing her again, and thinking of Megan, I felt that same shiver down my back.

I noticed Brogan Lacy sitting in the last row, her expression blank, her face taut. I guess all of us who had suffered because of Gamal looked lost. Grief might fade, but its mark is indelible, its blemish impossible to erase from the human heart. I was greeted by some of the witnesses, and heard their voices whisper, 'Hello, Kate.'

I waved and nodded back. We had almost become like a family. We had survived the horror of losing loved ones because of a killer's brutality, and had lived through the crushing stress of his trial. And I guess like me they wanted to move on with their lives and get some kind of closure.

But now that Gamal's execution was imminent, I found myself having mixed feelings. I was absolutely certain that I wanted him to die and that his execution was righteous. But as evil as Gamal was, and as much as I hated him and could never forgive him his crimes, it somehow made me feel tainted that I was a willing witness to his execution.

A prison official addressed the audience. 'Ladies and gentlemen, my apologies for the delay but we're now ready to begin. Please remember that if anyone wishes to leave the viewing room during the execution, they may do so. Thank you.'

I had read pretty much all I could about death by lethal injection. I'd been trying to psyche myself up for the actual event, but I figured nothing really prepared you. Behind the thick viewing glass, heavy blue plastic curtains were already open to reveal a sterile-looking chamber that could have passed for a hospital operating theatre.

It contained a stainless-steel trolley or 'gurney', in the shape of a crucifix, the 'arms' set at a downward angle. Six plastic drip lines fed through a patch of the thick blue curtain, which was

46

fitted with a clear plastic viewing hole. Behind this curtain waited the prisoner's executioners, ready with their lethal chemicals and electronic cardiac monitoring equipment. I knew that killing the condemned prisoner involved the intravenous injection of a deadly quantity of three different drugs.

First, the prisoner would be strapped down on the gurney, and his legs, arms and wrists secured with leather restraints. He would be prepped with IVs, then cardiac monitor electrodes would be attached to his body, along with two sets of three drip lines inserted into his veins, one set in each arm. Once the saline drips started, the inmate would be covered up to his chest with a sheet. Then the saline lines would be turned off and sodium thiopental injected, causing the condemned prisoner to fall into a deep sleep. The second chemical, pancuronium bromide, relaxed the prisoner's muscles and paralysed his lungs, causing his breathing to stop. Finally, a shot of potassium chloride stopped his heart.

Usually the whole process would take anything from three to ten minutes. The execution over, the dead prisoner would be body-bagged, toe-tagged and in Gamal's case his corpse would be immediately transported by van to the Medical Examiner's office in Richmond, and stored overnight before being autopsied the next morning and then buried.

Lethal injection might be considered the most humane form of execution, but some doctors claimed it could be difficult to administer because so many condemned prisoners have scarred veins due to drug abuse, or diabetes. And I'd read of the horror stories when it all went wrong, as in the case of a retarded Arkansas murderer. It took the medical orderlies almost an hour to find a vein and insert the IV tube in his arm, and in the end the prisoner himself had to help his own executioners insert the IV.

During another execution in Texas, the syringe popped out of the prisoner's vein and sprayed deadly chemical on prison officials, and the curtain had to be drawn for fifteen minutes so witnesses couldn't see the chaos. I knew that condemned prisoners had experienced violent reactions to the lethal drugs they were administered, and that some didn't go to meet their deaths quietly.

But I tried to put aside those disturbing thoughts and hoped that tonight nothing would upset the execution. Those of us in the room had endured enough trauma already – this wasn't the theatre, and none of us wanted drama.

But as always Constantine Gamal was about to surprise us all.

IO

As I waited for the curtain to part, I thought of something my mom used to say – that every sin has its own avenging angel. In Constantine Gamal's case, he'd soon have twenty-nine avenging angels descending upon him.

But as the minutes passed and nothing happened, the witnesses began to cough and shuffle their feet. Everyone was uneasy and wanted it over and done with. Then suddenly the steel door on the right clanged open and Gamal was frog-marched into the execution chamber by six tall, burly guards. A gasp went through the audience, and I wasn't sure whether it was one of satisfaction or revulsion now that they were finally about to witness the execution. What happened next was quick.

Gamal was strapped down on the gurney, his hands, arms and legs tightly bound. Then the blue plastic curtain closed for several minutes, and when it opened again the IV catheters had already been inserted into his veins, three tubes attached to each arm.

I'd heard of prisoners going quietly to their death, but Gamal was not going to be one of them. In a supreme effort of defiance he violently arched his back and reared up against the leather straps, his face purple and his dark eyes bulging as they flicked around the room. I thought: *For a man who said he isn't worried about going to his death, he sure doesn't behave like one*. Until I realised that it wasn't fear I saw in his face, but livid anger as his eyes settled on *me*.

Gamal fixed me with a burning, hateful stare that made me remember his exact words. '*Enjoy the show. Because you'll pay for this. You don't believe me? Just wait and see. I will defeat death and come back and take you to hell with me, Kate. That I promise you.*'

I was tempted to wonder what he had meant by those seemingly insane words, but suddenly the cocktail of lethal drugs began to work. Gamal's eyes flickered like dying electric light bulbs and his head suddenly slumped back against the gurney. It seemed as if he had slipped into a rapid coma, and he began to utter a rasping snore. I figured the sodium thiopental had been injected, sending him into a deep sleep.

Minutes later, he went into a fit of coughing and his chest reared up against the restraints. I guessed the second deadly chemical, pancuronium bromide, was already flowing through his veins to paralyse his lungs. He gasped as he fought for breath, his body jolting so violently that he would have broken his back had he not been belted down to the gurney. Then his lips quivered, his body shook fiercely one last time and he gave a final gasp of air and lay still. The final shot of potassium chloride had stopped his heart.

A hushed silence descended in the viewing room as one of the guards stepped behind the curtain, then reappeared and crossed the room to whisper something to Warden Clay, who had stood with the red wall-telephone in his hand from the moment Gamal had been marched into the room. Clay listened, then dismissed the guard with a nod, studied his wristwatch and spoke into the receiver to the director of the Department of Corrections.

'Mr Director, inmate Constantine Gamal is pronounced dead at twenty-one hundred hours and nineteen minutes.'

I would always remember those words that affirmed Gamal's death. *Always*. Because so much that was to happen afterwards would make me question their truth.

But at that moment all that mattered was that I sensed something strange: it felt as if all the air had gone out of the room and a sense of *evil* had departed with it. That's the only way to describe it. I heard what sounded like a collective sigh of relief as witnesses stood up and in a daze began to file out of the viewing area. Melanie Jackson left her mom's side and came over and placed a hand on my arm. I saw her mom wave to me and I waved back.

'How are you doing, Kate?' Melanie asked.

'I'm OK, or getting there, I guess,' I answered, and saw concern in her face.

'You're sure?' she asked softly.

Again I saw Megan in her face, the same caring almond eyes, and I touched her hand gratefully and felt close to tears but somehow held them back. 'I'm fine, truly I am, Melanie. Just a little shaken. How do you feel?'

She shrugged her thin shoulders. 'I guess after waiting a year for this I thought it might somehow lessen my grief pretty much instantly. It hasn't, but killing him was the right thing, I earnestly believe that. The moment he died it felt as if an evil spirit had left the room. You know what I mean?'

Melanie sounded so adult, and I knew exactly what she meant. She handed me a slip of paper. 'You look after yourself, Kate. If ever you're in Arizona, promise you'll come see me? I'd like us to meet again.'

I felt touched. 'Thank you, Melanie. I'd like that too.'

We embraced, and Melanie moved back to her mom. Other relatives were hugging each other and crying, as if it was all too much. I suddenly felt that the atmosphere was so brittle with subdued pain that I needed to get away. Besides, I had a feeling that the warden would want to talk to me again and I really didn't feel up to it.

I had wanted to see Brogan Lacy one last time, to thank her again for dressing my wound and just to be there for her at such an intense moment, but when I looked around she was nowhere to be seen. Maybe she had already left?

I stepped outside, determined that once I exited the prison I'd dodge the waiting media crews – I didn't want to talk to them, for there was no point in raking over Gamal's death. The Virginian night sky was obscured by tiny flakes of snow that brushed my face like ghostly fingertips. A few witnesses came out behind me, their conversation whispered, their faces grim, and there was a strange air of unease. And then I realised why: we were all still devastated by what we had witnessed.

The warden was right: it is so starkly brutal seeing another human being die, even if the victim is someone as wickedly evil as Constantine Gamal. A line I had read somewhere sprang to mind. *Look long enough at evil and it looks back at you.* I was relieved that our ordeal was over and that Gamal was finally dead. But the irony wasn't lost on me, that by our executing him he had forced us to become a willing party to his wickedness, and that made me feel a twinge of anger.

But above all I was glad.

So very glad it was all over.

II

Outside the prison I ignored the media crews and climbed into my Bronco. I drove north on Interstate 95, past Richmond and Fredericksburg, then just near Quantico turned east towards Widewater Beach. The night was freezing cold but the farther north I drove the more the roads were bare of snow.

In summer sunshine, Widewater is a beautiful expanse of sandy beach overlooking the Potomac river, as it wends its way down to Chesapeake Bay, its pretty coves dotted with marinas and attractive bay properties. But on this cold winter's night, as I drove along the beach road, it was a haunting, wind-lashed place. It was just before midnight when I pulled up outside the stone entrance gates to a grey-bricked cottage that overlooked a small harbour with a wooden jetty. This was what I'd called home for the last two and a half years since I'd moved in with David and Megan.

I remembered the first time I had driven down here from DC with David. I'd known him barely four months and most of the time we'd met at the artist's gallery he kept in Georgetown, where he had an overhead apartment, but he wanted to show me where he'd grown up. A hundred yards from the cottage was Manor Brook, a magnificent, big neo-Gothic Victorian house on a dozen acres. It had been built by David's great-grandfather, a local doctor, in the Vanderbilt style so common in the late 1800s, with thick granite walls, stone gargoyles, a watchtower and a heavy church door entrance.

The house had long ago fallen into disrepair, but there was a modest two-bed cottage where David lived with his daughter Megan, and it had wonderful views of the harbour. That day with

David I looked admiringly at the view and a couple of neighbours' kids enjoying themselves, fishing off a boardwalk.

I remembered David stepping out of the Bronco and studying the sea views, his hair falling in a fringe across his forehead. From the first time I'd met him I thought he looked striking, with his athletic figure, elegant hands and blue eyes. He was an artist, and had done well for himself with a number of big commissions. Dozens of his paintings hung in major corporate offices all over the country – he'd even been exhibited in London – and by most artists' standards he was a roaring success. But what I loved about David – the three qualities that had first attracted me to him – was his kindness, his quiet, unassuming confidence and the fact that he was always ready with a smile. He was also one of the sexiest men I'd ever met, but that part was hidden until I got to know him. 'Don't you think it's pretty, Kate?'

A flock of geese flew overhead, and their shrill calls harmonised to sound like a single bleat carrying across the salt marshes that stretched along the bay. David said, 'The geese hibernate here from Canada. You'll see them a lot in winter, *and* you'll hear them. When I was a kid I used to love that sound – I'd leave my bedroom window open in the evening and hear the geese passing. It felt . . . I don't know, I guess kind of comforting.'

'It looks like a great place. You mind telling me where we are?'

David shielded his eyes from the sun as he skimmed a stone out over the harbour waters. 'It's called Angel Bay. It's where I learned to paint when I was a kid, starting with harbour sketches and charcoals. We used to live in the manor until my parents died and then I moved down to the cottage – I've got an office studio out the back that I use when I'm here. I had terrific plans for refurbishing the manor house but somehow time and money always got in the way. And then Brogan and I divorced so the cottage seemed more than big enough for Megan and me. Let me show you around.'

I was sharing a rented two-bed apartment in Falls Church at the time with another female agent and by comparison Manor Brook looked like a palace, even in disrepair. We walked around the grounds, the gardens that had once been well tended overgrown, and the gurgling streams that wended around the property made me see that it had obviously once been a wonderful old house.

'It's terrific,' I said, and I meant it.

'Some tender care and hard work and it could be an interesting house once again. And I know it's a little secluded but it's probably still a lot safer than that apartment of yours in the District. Most people around here never bother to lock their front door.'

'Hey, don't tell me you're worried about me?' I said.

'Might be. I'll admit to sometimes fretting about your safety.'

I smiled with unconcealed pleasure when I heard the concern in David's voice. It was good to know he *cared*. 'Come on, my neighbourhood isn't that bad. Anyway, I'm able to look after myself. Even if I don't wear a cop's uniform any more, I've still got a gun and a badge.'

David slipped his arm around my waist and said with a glint in his eyes, 'You're right, you're a big girl now, and I'm pretty sure all you Feds are able to shoot the eyes out of a fly at fifty yards.'

'Forty, max. But it's got to be a big fly.'

His smile broadened. 'You know what I was thinking?'

'What?'

'It's a pity I never knew you when you wore your cop's uniform. Might have been interesting.'

I planted a kiss on his lips. God, I loved his lips. They were to die for. 'You never told me you like women in uniform.'

He smiled as he softly returned the kiss. 'A guy's got to keep some secrets.'

I bit his lower lip. 'Remind me to hire a uniform out for you some night. No flats, high heels and maybe stockings. That appeal to you?'

David beamed. 'Anyone ever tell you that you're a tease?'

Actually, no one ever had. But with David, flirting seemed to come naturally. I drew away, holding his hand. 'You never know, I could be tempted to use my handcuffs.'

'Don't entice me or I'll take you to bed. OK, the flirting's over for now, let me finish showing you around.'

David led me up a gravel path to the cottage. I felt so close to him, as if we had already become a couple, and for the first time in years, after a failed marriage, I was hoping this time round I had found the right man.

The cottage was protected from the Potomac winds by a cluster of fir trees and right behind it was a separate work studio, linked by a covered walkway. A hundred yards away, the shore sloped down to a long stretch of sandy beach. David unlocked the front door and stepped through a short hallway into a cosy front room. Hanging on the walls were a handful of charcoal drawings of schooners and frigates, marine bric-a-brac garnished the walls, and a big old brass telescope on a tripod pointed over a view of the bay that was stunning. 'Well, what do you think?'

I took in the room's decor. It was spotlessly clean but a little dated and definitely needed a woman's touch. I punched David's arm playfully. 'I think with all this marine stuff you'll probably qualify for honorary membership of the seamen's union.'

He smiled as he guided me out to the work studio at the back, which doubled as an office, with desk and phone. The studio was crammed with paint pots and canvases, and works-in-progress. 'Hey, stop trying to be funny. This is really such a wonderful old place, Kate.'

'Tell me.'

'My brother Patrick and I would spend our summers swimming down on the beach, or clam-fishing, or we'd all go berry-picking on the headland with Mom. Manor Brook was a special place. I often miss those times.'

'What about your dad, were you close to him?' I asked.

David's face suddenly took on a pained look. 'Not really. He could be a difficult man, stern and disciplined and prone to dark moods. Too stern to cope with two lively kids. He'd spent twenty years as a naval doctor before he finally decided to settle down.'

'You two didn't get on?'

'Let's just say we barely tolerated each other. Mom made up

for Dad's deficiencies, and she and I were closer. I guess I also felt sorry for her. The older she got, the more unhappy she became in her marriage, and she used to try to drown her discontent with a vodka bottle. But I still enjoyed my childhood.'

'Maybe you were just a happy kid?'

David smiled. 'Maybe you're right. I don't often talk about my dad. See the effect you're having on me?'

He led me around the studio and showed me a couple of his favourite paintings, one of them a colourful oil of Angel Bay harbour. 'So what about you, do I get to hear about Kate's past?'

I remembered his hand reaching out, his fingers intertwining with mine. His disclosures made it feel like a special moment of intimacy. 'I guess I would have loved the feeling of belonging to a stable, happy family but that wasn't exactly my experience,' I admitted.

'Tell me.'

I told David about my past. Dad was a gambling ex-detective who had walked out on us when I was eleven. My mom had held the family together with strict authority and vague affection, but she had died twelve years ago from ovarian cancer and I guess afterwards the family had splintered. My two younger sisters had moved west to California when they finished high school and we had drifted in and out of each other's lives ever since, mostly with phone calls at Christmas and Thanksgiving. My older brother Frank and I were closer and kept in touch, but he had a basket of his own troubles to keep him busy. 'There's no such thing as the perfect family, and every single one of them is dysfunctional, even if some are more dysfunctional than others, but in the end they're all we've really got.'

David said honestly, 'I know what you mean.' He looked at me. 'You're right about family. Maybe some day we can have our own.'

I stared back in shock. David had spoken the words with such apparent conviction that I knew he meant them, and I flushed. 'Careful, or a girl might think you were serious.'

David sounded earnest. 'I am. You want kids?'

'Sure I want kids.'

'I'd like more, too. But not only because I think Megan needs to feel part of a family.' He thought for a moment before continuing. 'I know we've only been together under four months but it's long enough for me to know the kind of woman you are. I think it would be great if things worked out between us, don't you? I feel good about us, Kate. Really good. Marry me?'

I thought: *You're kidding me? This is exactly what I want.* And I knew he wasn't kidding. I also knew that for the first time in years I'd met a man I truly wanted to have a serious relationship with. But I didn't want to sound like I was rushing headlong into marriage, just because I was thirty-five and a borderline case of bio-clock. 'Can . . . can I think about it for a day or two?'

'Sure. But don't think too long, or else I'll get worried.'

'I promise I won't.' But even as I squeezed David's hand and said the words I knew my mind was already made up, and I figured he knew it too.

'How about dinner tonight? There's a good seafood place three miles down the coast. Let me go book it.' He crossed the studio, picked up the office phone and called the restaurant.

We ate there at seven, a wonderful meal of shrimp and steak, followed by lemon cheesecake and brandy coffee, and when we returned to the cottage David poured us both some wine and then I let him take me upstairs and we undressed each other, our love-making full of tenderness and energy, his tongue finding mine. He planted tiny kisses over my neck and breasts and then he finally entered me and I cried out with pleasure. And then afterwards we'd lain together on his big old brass bed, listening to Norah Jones and the beating wings of a flock of winter geese crossing the Potomac. But tonight I felt devastated as I looked out towards the darkened river. The cottage had become my home when three weeks after David's burial his lawyer called me and invited me to his Georgetown office. What he had to say stunned me: the entire property at Manor Brook was David's bequest to me in his will. It was still in disrepair and far too big for me to live in alone so I'd chosen to remain in the cottage. The lawyer also told me that

David had left me a dozen of his favourite paintings and half a million dollars in cash. It was a lot of money to me, but I still hadn't touched a cent. It lay in the bank gathering interest while I figured what to do with it. I *couldn't* touch it. It sort of meant nothing to me, except for a vague idea that I might one day set up some kind of charitable trust in David's name.

But that's another day's work.

Tonight I was on edge. I made some hot chocolate and as I stood looking out at the cold lake and sipping from the cup I let my mind go back to the terrible day I'd learned that David and Megan had been killed . . .

12

I'd spent a week in Philadelphia chasing down a lead on the Disciple which ultimately proved worthless. I'd called David from my motel to tell him I'd be home early the next afternoon, which was Thanksgiving, and that I didn't want to miss the holiday for anything. I'd been working eighteen-hour days, the case had exhausted me, and I was so looking forward to having some time with David and Megan.

But as I drove home from Philly the next day I was so racked by tiredness that I started to fall asleep at the wheel. The next thing I knew I heard a horn blaring like crazy and I snapped open my eyes to see a silver Mack truck hurtling towards me like a rocket. I thought: *I'm going to die.* I swung the steering wheel to the right and slammed on the brakes, skidding to a halt. My hands shook – I knew I'd escaped death by inches. I'd wandered over to the wrong side of the road and I didn't want to run a further risk of getting killed so I pulled over to the side of the road and levered back the seat. The instant I closed my eyes again I fell asleep. When I woke, three hours had passed.

When I finally arrived home I saw that David's car wasn't in the driveway. When I stepped into the cottage Megan was nowhere to be seen. The Thanksgiving dinner they had prepared languished on the kitchen table. I checked the studio but it was empty. I picked up the desk phone and called David's cell but got his messaging service, as I did all that afternoon. By six that evening he and Megan still hadn't showed and I started to worry. It wasn't like David to disappear and not contact me. The only explanation I could think of was that he had decided to visit one of his buddies and his cell phone was dead or out of coverage.

An hour later I got a call from Lou. 'Where are you, Kate?'

'At the cottage waiting for David and Megan so we can start dinner, except I don't know where the heck they are. Hey, happy Thanksgiving, by the way. Is that why you called?'

Lou sounded tentative. 'Kate, can I come over? I'm not far away. I can be there in ten minutes. Would that be OK?'

I suddenly picked up a bad vibe. 'What's it about? Is there something wrong?'

'I'll tell you when I see you, Kate. I'll be there soon,' Lou said mysteriously, and hung up.

By the time he knocked on the cottage door I was already fearing that something bad had happened to David and Megan, and the moment I saw Lou's ashen face I knew I was right.

He put a hand gently on my arm. 'Kate, I don't know how to say this, except to tell you what I know. About three hours ago the bodies of an adult male and a teenage female were discovered in a cavern at a disused quarry mine four miles from here by a couple of teenagers out hiking. David was ID'd by his driving licence, found in his wallet. It also contained a photograph that resembled the female victim. I've just seen the bodies. It's definitely Megan and David, they've both been murdered, and I've just heard that David's burned-out car was found near by. From the scene evidence and the way they were killed, it pretty much looks like the Disciple's work. I'm so sorry, Kate.'

I remember my legs felt weak and I put a hand to my mouth and screamed hoarsely, 'No!'

Lou held me as I collapsed into his arms. Everything else that day was a blur. A blur of tears and depression and grief and anger until finally I felt numb.

The next morning I had to identify David and Megan, and the ordeal almost killed me. Their faces were recognisable but their bodies had been butchered and scorched. The signature and MO of the crime scene all pointed to the Disciple. The method of killing – the partly burned and eviscerated bodies – and the black wooden cross. But this time there were two inexplicable inconsistencies. Instead of being placed midway between the bodies, the crucifix had been laid at Megan's feet, and David had been shot twice in the head. Gamal had admitted to nothing during his interrogation and the inconsistencies had never been explained.

I'd left the police morgue in a trance and driven out to Angel Bay. A fog had rolled in and I parked the car in the driveway and followed a worn track until I came to the beach, the one that Megan, David and I sometimes used to walk along together. Tortured by precious memories, I had pushed on for mile after mile along the sand, driven by sorrow, so completely lost in my heartache that it seemed as if I could still hear Megan out there in the fog, giggling as she and I shared a joke, and imagine David's laughter as he joined in.

Finally I could take it no more and knelt in the sand and screamed out their names until my throat was raw. God, how I hated their killer. Even if it had cost my own life to capture the Disciple I'd gladly have given it, because at that moment my life felt worthless. I was haunted by the absolute certainty that David and Megan had died because of me, and no matter how hard I tried I couldn't find a release from my guilt.

The cause of my certainty was a bold decision I'd made. There had been dozens of media reports about the Disciple's killings in the previous six months, and because I led the investigation my name had featured large. I remembered in particular a report in the *Washington Post* three weeks earlier: FBI SPECIAL AGENT KATHERINE MORAN CLAIMS THAT WITH NEW LEADS FROM EXHUMATION THE NET IS CLOSING IN ON THE DEVIL'S DISCIPLE, THE NATIONS MOST WANTED SERIAL KILLER.

But in truth our investigation was going nowhere, and in an attempt to unsettle the Disciple I'd come up with the idea of trying to psych him out, and introduce what we liked to call the 'ass-pucker' factor.

I deliberately gave an interview to the *Post* and several TV stations claiming that the investigating team was convinced that new evidence would help us track down the Disciple. I disclosed that we were applying to the court to exhume two of the Disciple's victims from a Virginia cemetery in the coming days, and that if the bodies were in good shape and turned up the evidence we expected, then we would be close to solving the case.

We figured that all this would be a tremendous stressor on the Disciple. He would be concerned and inquisitive. He'd be in suspense about what state the bodies were in and worried that he might have left minute trace evidence behind that would help apprehend him. Above all, we were hoping he'd drive by or visit the cemetery to take a look at the exhumation for himself. It was common for killers to visit the grave sites of their victims, and the reports of an exhumation in the newspapers might prove too much for his curiosity. So we intended to videotape and photograph everyone who showed up at or near the cemetery grounds.

I had the neighbourhood near the grave site staked out with over three dozen undercover agents as we carried out the exhumation. The entire watch lasted four days but the videotape and the photographs eventually turned up nothing. The Disciple had avoided our trap.

But the next time he struck he murdered David and Megan. I felt certain that my plan had backfired and cost the lives of the two people closest to me. It was clear that the Disciple had made it his business to find out where I lived and spent time observing me before he deliberately selected David and Megan as his next victims. I felt violated, unsettled. He was making a statement. It was his way of telling me: *You think you're smart but I'm more clever than you are.* Right then, I was convinced he was. While I had been hunting him, he had been hunting me.

Why hadn't I spotted him? Why hadn't I sensed I was being stalked? He had been around my home, he had most likely followed me, just as he must have followed David and Megan before he'd struck.

After that I even bought a spare pistol and kept it with me at all times. At night, I hid it under my pillow, secured in its holster that was tied to the metal bed frame with bale twine. It was a 'lady' Glock, a smaller 9mm version of my larger Glock service pistol, and I could release it by a simple flick of the metal clasp holding the weapon in its holster.

I *wanted* the Disciple to come to my home again. Longed for him to try it some dark night so that I could shoot the bastard dead in self-defence. My heart felt seared by loss. It still did. Nothing had really changed: I still missed David and Megan, ached for them to come back, longed to hear their voices.

Since their deaths I'd often been troubled by a disturbing belief: if I hadn't been so tired driving back from Philly and hadn't pulled over to sleep, maybe I could have saved them? But now another disturbing notion began to seep into my thoughts: what if Gamal *was* telling the truth and someone else had killed them? What if I'd been racking myself with misplaced guilt on that count? I crushed the irony of the thought as being impossible. I was still certain Gamal was the killer.

It was after 2 a.m. when I stepped into the office studio. It was the first time in six months I had come in here, and my home-help lady, who cleaned the cottage twice a week, usually kept it dusted. But the studio was still much as it was after David and Megan had been killed: an unfinished canvas on the easel, a painting of the ruins of Manor Lodge. The room felt so cold and lifeless. I looked around at the finished and unfinished canvases, at the paints and dried-up brushes, at the splashes of bright colours on the floor where David had spilled paint while working, and one crimson spot in particular that almost looked like blood and always disturbed me.

For the first time in a year I touched his unfinished canvas of Manor Lodge, ran my hand over the image and felt the coarse edges of the paint and the smoothness of the canvas cloth. I turned towards the studio desk, still scattered with David's paper-work. I ran my fingers over the untidy stacks of papers, and then the desk phone, remembering how David would sometimes call me internally in the cottage and tell me he'd finished another new painting and did I want to come and see? The excitement in his voice made him sound like a young boy.

The room brought back such vivid memories, and when I could take them no more I pulled up my coat collar, closed up the studio and crossed the gravel back to the cottage. I went up to my bedroom to undress, wiped my eyes and flicked out the light. It was over now, I tried telling myself as I lay in the darkness. *The butcher who killed David and Megan has paid with his life.* Only Melanie was right: it didn't make me feel much better and it didn't bring them back.

But I knew for certain I wanted to put the past behind me and try to move on with my life. I wanted relief from my agony. I wanted a normal life again. I wanted peace. *Am I hoping for too much?*

I lay there on the bed trying not to cry, hoping my grief would go away, but it wouldn't. And then something wonderful happened: I closed my eyes and drifted into the deepest sleep I'd had in months.

13

Buck Ryan loved his prison guard job and he especially loved the execution detail. Transporting the bodies of executed prisoners to the Richmond Medical Examiner's Office was usually a piece of cake and it got him out of the prison for a few hours, but tonight was a different matter entirely. For one, it was snowing and Interstate 95 to Richmond was a ribbon of white, lit up by occasional blazing road lights. Two, his companion guard that night was Jackie 'The Whine' Dole, a pain-in-the-ass complainer.

Ryan gripped the steering wheel of the Ford box van as he drove along Interstate 95, barely touching twenty, and Dole didn't look happy as he peered out at the falling snow. 'At this rate we're going to be lucky to make Richmond for fucking breakfast,' he complained.

Ryan grunted. 'Can't help it. In these conditions I've got to take it slow. But at least we'll get there alive, not like our friend in the back.'

Ryan studied the freezing landscape of thick pine forest either side of 95 as the wipers brushed away white flakes. The road was completely deserted and only the powerful cones of light from the Ford's headlamps lit up the snowy road, giving it an eerie luminescence. 'Feels like we're the only guys alive on the planet. Kind of creepy out there, don't you think?'

Jackie Dole didn't seem to care. He had the interior light on and was flicking through the sports pages of *USA Today*. 'See the Reds lost. *Assholes*. I had ten bucks on that game.'

'Any other good news?'

Dole threw his newspaper down in disgust. 'Yeah, my dog's

66

got testicular lumps and the vet says he's going to have to cut off his coconuts. Operation's gonna set me back three hundred bucks. *Hey*, what the fuck was that?'

They both heard the thump that came from the rear of the van and Ryan braked slowly. 'Sounded like something hit us.'

'You think it's kids throwing snowballs?'

'At this hour? In the middle of nowhere? Get real, Dole.'

'That's what it sounded like. Hey, there it is again,' Dole said.

They heard another thump strike the van and Ryan said, 'What the fuck's going on?' He removed his pistol from his holster.

Dole said, 'Hey, what's with the gun? We've got a fucking corpse in the back. Who's afraid of a dead man?'

But Ryan wasn't really listening as he pushed open his door and a flurry of snow billowed against his face. 'Jeez, what a fucking night.'

He climbed out and Dole followed. Both men moved cautiously round to the back of the van. Ryan studied the deserted landscape all around them, and took a moment to marvel at the mammoth pine trees either side of the road which were dusted with thick snow. It really *did* feel as if they were the only two guys on the planet. He checked the rear door. And that's when he got a shock. It was *open*. 'What the fuck . . . ?'

'What's up?'

'That's what's up.' Ryan gestured to the open door. 'It must have been slapping in the wind. But I'm damned sure I locked it down.'

'Seems to me like you didn't.' Dole gripped the frozen door handle – it felt like ice – and pulled open the door. Inside was the white body bag, containing the human form of the executed prisoner. 'The Devil's Disciple, huh? He sure don't look so frightening now, does he?'

'Naw.'

'Let's lock this thing up.'

Ryan scratched his head. 'How the hell did the door open?'

'The cold weather. I've seen it happen before when we've taken bodies to Richmond in winter. Ice causes metal to contract, you know that? I've known locks to snap open in freezing weather.'

Ryan peered back along the road and said suddenly, 'Whatever you say. Hey, you see lights back there?'

'Where?'

'Back along the road. Hard to tell how far. Maybe a couple of hundred yards. I'm pretty sure I saw a pair of headlights just now.'

'So?' Dole asked.

'They disappeared. Like someone switched them off. You know, I'm pretty sure I saw headlights behind us earlier. Like as if someone's following us.'

Dole narrowed his eyes as he stared into the snowy darkness. 'I see nothing except fucking falling snow. Get real, man. Why the hell would someone follow us?'

'Maybe a reporter? You know the way those newspaper folks like to follow a story.'

'What story? The guy's dead, for fuck sake. Are we getting going again? I'm freezing my baguettes off out here.'

Ryan frowned as he stared out into the landscape where he thought he'd seen the headlights, but they were definitely gone, then he slammed the truck's rear door and the noise echoed in the white forest. As the noise died he took a final look around the frozen wastes – with the lights reflecting off the vast acres of snow it seemed a creepy place to be alone. He shivered and nodded towards the front cab. 'Come on, let's get out of here.'

14

It was after 3 a.m. and the moon flitted behind wisps of freezing fog that rolled in across Angel Bay. The man wore a navy blue boiler suit and thick roll-neck sweater as he sat in the dark blue Bronco, over a hundred yards from the cottage. He watched the house through a pair of powerful night-vision binoculars that coloured the darkness a fluorescent lime green. Only when he spotted Kate Moran close the curtains and saw the bedroom light extinguished did he put down the binocs.

He picked up a set of keys from the coin recess near the hand-brake. He tossed the keys in his hand. They were a copy set to Kate Moran's cottage, along with the alarm code on the tag. Moran had never changed the code. But Angel Bay was far enough away from the nearest big town to be at risk of burglary, one of those homely places where locals didn't always bother to lock their doors. He could enter the cottage any time he chose.

He'd already been in the cottage and walked through the rooms and smelled her perfume. He'd taken some of her personal stuff he needed, was even tempted to take a pair of her flimsy panties just for the fun of it, but he kept his sexual urge under control. He wasn't going to mess up his plan. He'd return the items when Moran left the cottage. But tonight he had other business. He had the killings planned down to the last detail.

But what happened next he hadn't planned on. His heart flipped when he saw the blue flashing lights of a cop car pull up behind him. The siren gave a single *whoop* and died. He immediately hid the binoculars under his seat and grabbed his cell phone. The cops flashed their lights at him and he decided to step out of the Bronco and give them a friendly wave.

One of the cops climbed out of the blue-and-white and came towards him flashing his torch, his other hand on his weapon, ready to draw it if necessary. '´Night, sir. You mind me asking what you're doing parked here?'

The man smiled and waved his cell phone. 'I had to pull in to make a call, Officer. I didn't want to risk driving and using my phone. I figured I might be breaking the law.'

'That's very wise, sir. And commendable.' The cop shone his torch on the man's face, then flashed it into the car, before he settled back on the man's face again. 'Have you got your driver's licence?'

'In my pocket.'

'Let me see it, sir.'

'Sure, Officer.' The man took out his false licence and handed it over. He had already made up his mind that if the cops got suspicious he'd kill them both. A pity, because it could fuck up his plans, but there might be no other way. The cop studied the picture, then flashed his torch in the man's face again and handed back the licence. 'Thank you, sir.'

'My pleasure, Officer.'

The officer hesitated, as if uncertain. 'Hey, you look familiar. Are you from around these parts?'

'I'm afraid not. I was just visiting a good friend of mine, Miss Kate Moran. She's a federal agent. Maybe you know her?'

The officer nodded. 'I don't know her personally, but I heard of her.' He swung a look over towards the cottage, then turned back to stare directly into the man's face. 'Hey, you know you really remind me of someone but I just can't figure it out. You're *sure* you're not from around here?'

'I'm from DC.'

'Then you better take it slowly if you're heading back that direction. Some of the roads along the way are pretty icy tonight.' The cop still looked confused and shook his head. 'I could have sworn I knew your face.'

The man smiled. 'Hey, we all make mistakes. And thanks for the warning, Officer.'

★   ★   ★

70

It had been a close call and he was sweating. The cop was right, he *had* seen him before, but the dumb asshole hadn't figured it out, and hopefully he never would. He started the Bronco and drove for well over an hour towards the north of DC, turning on to 270 until he came to the trailer park at Rockville. Along the route he'd stopped at a lay-by to check that he had everything he needed, then he fitted the false number plates and donned the woman's wig and the female clothes. He kept the revs down as he cruised into the park and came to a halt near an old Suncruiser motor home. He read the name on the mail box out front: O. Fleist.

There was a flickering blue-grey light on in the Suncruiser that he knew belonged to Fleist – a TV was on, he guessed – but no lights on in the nearby trailer homes. He reached behind his seat and pulled out a canvas knapsack: inside was a slim Maglite electric torch, a roll of grey plastic duct tape and a jagged butcher's knife.

He opened another of the zipper pockets and found the short plastic syringe and two vials of clear benzo liquid. He pulled back on the plunger as he loaded the syringe from one of the vials and popped it into his pocket. Before he stepped out of the Bronco he slipped a pair of thick Cleaneze dust covers over his shoes and pulled on a pair of black leatherette gloves.

Then he strolled up to the motor home's veranda and knocked softly on the front door. A few seconds passed and a curtain flicked, then a man came to the door. He was unshaven and looked groggy, as if he'd fallen asleep watching TV, and he wore a grubby vest and pyjama bottoms. He took one look at his visitor and his mouth dropped as if he'd seen a corpse. '*Jesus* . . .'

'I'm impressed that you recognise me, Otis. Even dressed like this. You're good.'

'What . . . what are you doing in those clothes? I thought you were dead.'

The visitor grinned, and thought he heard a whimper somewhere inside the motor home. 'Not any more, Otis. Is your daughter still with you? Is she in bed, asleep?'

The man named Otis was suddenly wary. 'G . . . Get out of here, you madman.' He attempted to close the door but his visitor put his foot firmly against it.

'Is that any way to treat an old acquaintance, Otis?'

Confusion and fear ignited simultaneously in Otis's face. 'I . . . I don't get it. How come you're alive?'

'You don't have to get it, you moron. It's payback time.' The visitor plunged the syringe into the man's chest. He staggered back and collapsed in a heap on the floor.

The visitor moved into the hallway and saw a German shepherd dog lying on a couch, its ears cocked, its mouth set in a snarl. The visitor clicked his fingers, trying to coax the dog, but it snarled again and stood up on all fours. The visitor didn't give the animal a chance. He thrust out with the butcher's knife and buried it in the dog's neck. The animal emitted a strangled whimper and collapsed.

The visitor kept the momentum going and moved into the daughter's bedroom, his steps muffled on the worn carpet. *Cute.* Her blonde hair was strewn about the pillow – fourteen and pretty in a pink nightdress. The syringe was still half full with benzo and he jabbed it into her arm, at the same time slapping a hand over her mouth in case she screamed.

But she didn't – all she did was murmur and then she was out cold in seconds.

It took him three minutes to carry the two unconscious bodies out to the Bronco. When he'd dumped the kid and her father into the vehicle's rear, both trussed up and their mouths bound with duct tape, he locked the doors.

He saw a light come on in one of the nearby trailers. When he noticed a curtain flicker he grinned. Perfect. You could always count on a nosy neighbour. He couldn't ask for more.

He went through his spiel, raising his voice to a female pitch, directing it towards the Suncruiser, saying the words that he had planned to say, adding a touch of anger to his performance, and then he climbed back into the Bronco.

He couldn't help but snigger to himself. It had all gone *exactly* to plan. He keyed the ignition and kept his headlights dipped as he drove slowly out of the park. He felt terrific. Killing made him feel so *alive*, as if by the act of taking a life he invigorated his own existence. All part of Satan's work. Two more would soon be added to his total, and there were lots more victims yet to come.

The Devil's Disciple was back in business.

PART TWO

15

I was woken by my cell phone ringing. I squinted at my bedside clock: 3 p.m. I'd slept for twelve hours and I felt groggy. I'd been so exhausted I'd completely zonked out. I almost knocked over the nightstand lamp as I fumbled for the phone and heard Lou Raines' voice.

'Hey, you doing OK, Kate? You see the newspapers yet?' he asked gruffly, without waiting for a reply.

Judging by the background noise, I guessed Lou was at his desk in the DC field office by Judiciary Square. I could picture him pacing the room, the phone glued to his ear, looking like a grouchy old owl with his hunched shoulders and squirrel-tail eyebrows, a pair of black-rimmed bifocals perched on his nose. I rubbed my eyes and pulled on my robe. 'I slept in, Lou. Your call woke me.'

'Hey, time to rise and shine. Kinda thought you might like to hear today's headlines. The *Richmond Times-Dispatch* leads with: "Psychiatrist turned serial killer is executed". Sorta blandsy, don't you think? The *Washington Post* wasn't any better – "Cavern Killer Dies". But the one I liked best was the editorial in the *Charlottesville Daily Progress*. God bless 'em but there's no Waltons' Mountain bullshit from the Charlottesville folk. "*Devil's Disciple sent to hell*". Kinda apt, don't you think?'

'It has a certain ring to it.' I stared out of the cottage window. A cold winter sun glinted on the ice-cold waters of the Potomac beyond Angel Bay, though in another couple of hours it would be dark again. I had heard what Lou said but I was resolute about my decision to put the past behind me. And that meant doing my damnedest to eradicate *everything* to do with Constantine Gamal from my mind. I tried to forget about headlines.

'You OK?' Lou asked.

'Mostly tired, I guess. How about you?'

'Firing on all cylinders since they executed the bastard. Where are you?'

'Angel Bay.'

'I guess last evening was difficult, huh? Maybe I should have gone with you to Greensville for support?'

Since his wife's menopause had started giving him grief, Lou was in the habit of working eighteen-hour days at a stretch. I figured he deserved a night off so I'd insisted on travelling to Greensville alone. 'It wasn't a problem, Lou. It was a good day considering I finally got some closure. All I've got to do now is try and move on. That's sort of the hard part.' I took a deep breath, let it out slowly and padded into the kitchen and filled the coffee maker with Costa Rican Gold. 'But the execution wasn't exactly a barrel of fun.'

I heard Lou blow out air. 'That's partly why I'm calling. I've been hearing a few stories about last night. You want to fill me in?'

I told him about Gamal's denial, his admission of another two murders and his frenzied attack on me. But I didn't tell him about the insane threat he had made. I figured it would have sounded too bizarre.

'*Jesus*,' Lou breathed, 'sounds like you had a fun-packed night. How're you doing?'

'Apart from the bite marks, reasonably fine.'

'I'll bet the warden's scared shitless you'll sue his ass. He should never have left you alone with Gamal.'

'It was my decision and to tell the truth Clay wasn't exactly enthusiastic. But I didn't have much choice. Gamal made it a pre-condition.'

Lou said, 'Do you think he was telling the truth about the Chinatown metro killings?'

'I can't be sure. I still believe that there's no question he murdered David and Megan. But he could have committed both sets of murders the same day.'

78

'I agree,' answered Lou. 'I've made a decision to liaise with the Metropolitan police and tell them we intend to check out this claim. Shouldn't be a problem seeing as the Bureau had primary jurisdiction in the case.'

Gamal had killed in six different states and after his second set of murders, seven and a half years ago, the hunt for him had become a federal case.

'How soon can we get going on this one?' I asked.

Lou said bitterly, 'I guess it'll have to be right away. As if we didn't have enough work. The bastard's hardly cold in his grave and he's still causing us frigging grief. He sure knew how to pull our chains.'

'Let's hope that's all he's doing.' I was off duty that day, but I suggested I could drive into the District and help with the search at the Chinatown metro. I didn't want to stick all the burden on Lou's slim shoulders.

But he was firm. 'Like hell you're coming in. Everything's ticking over pretty nicely here. I really just called to say that I'm thinking of you and so is everyone in the office, and we know that you've been through the grinder and thank God it's over. But the fact is, I want you to take some time off. I think you need it after the effort you put into the case. I really ought to give you a couple of weeks' paid leave, but as I'm such a miserable bastard, you'll have to settle for three days. I know you're off at the weekend but I want you to forget about work until next Thursday.'

'Lou, there's really no need . . .'

'I'll assign someone else to the metro search. And I don't want no for an answer. It's an order, you rest until Thursday and no negotiation. Got it?'

I was touched by Lou's concern. 'The fact you're suddenly all maternal, I may start thinking you're taking your wife's HRT pills.'

'My secret's out. Two a day. I figure once I grow breasts the guys in the office will start to pay more attention at my weekly progress meetings.'

I half smiled. 'OK, Lou, but on condition that if I get bored I can come back sooner.'

'No way, sailor.'

'What if you turn up something at the metro?'

'I'll call you. And I'll call you anyway just to see if you're OK. We'll keep this whole metro thing and Gamal's confession under our hats for now and out of the press, just in case we're being played for fools. But do me a favour. How about you take yourself away for a few days? I've got a feeling it might do you good.'

'You're a sweetheart, Lou.'

'Tell anyone and so help me you're fired. By the way, you'll have the new guy joining you when you get back.'

'*What* new guy?'

Lou said, 'Didn't I tell you about him already?'

'No, you didn't.'

'This keeps up I'm going to get myself checked out for Alzheimer's,' Lou answered.

'So we're finally getting a replacement for Galvin after he's left us almost a year. Do I need to know anything about this guy? He's not some pain in the ass they're trying to dump on us, is he?'

Lou said, 'He's a good agent, Kate. His name's Josh Cooper, just so you'll know, and he's been transferred from the New York field office, but I'll fill you in properly when you get back. Listen, I've got a call coming in, I better go. Take care, we'll talk soon.'

The line clicked, Lou was gone, and I was alone again. I prayed there would not be two more of Gamal's victims and that his last-minute 'confession' was just a heartless ruse. But it bothered me that Gamal had waited until right before his execution to make his move. It didn't make a whole lot of sense. I closed my eyes, trying to figure it out, but I couldn't.

I listened to the sound of the water lapping and the gulls screeching out on the water. When I opened my eyes again I knew what I had to do next.

16

I drove to the cemetery and walked past tombs of granite and bronze. Past the uprooted earth of freshly dug graves and a handful of mourners hunched in their own personal grief. David and Megan were laid to rest on a small hill shaded by some birch trees, and I placed a bunch of flowers on their simple marble headstone. I said the prayers and the words that I wanted to say, the same words I always said, that I missed them, that their passing had left such a terrible sorrow, that I wished for them back.

Standing there in the shadow of the birches, my eyes swept over the smooth marble and the simple gold-leaf words that inscribed my pain.

> *Here lies David Bryce*
> *And his beloved daughter, Megan.*
> *May they rest in peace.*

For a long time after their deaths I had visited the cemetery almost daily and felt haunted by their absence. I'd sit by their headstone, talking to them, but sometimes my imagination would intrude and I'd visualise their bodies being brutalised by Constantine Gamal and it would traumatise me for days. The David I had adored and the Megan whom I'd grown to love as if she were my own daughter – both their lives destroyed by an evil, satanic butcher. After that, I'd come less and less.

David had come into my life three years earlier, after my husband Paul had walked out on me one fall weekend and left behind a parting letter: 'Kate, this isn't working for me and I want a divorce. I can't explain why exactly, but I think I need to find someone else. There's nothing more to say, except that I know I'll always think of you. Take good care of yourself.'

We'd been having problems for about a year and attended counselling but it hadn't helped. I'd known Paul since high school when we were both seventeen. He was darkly handsome, great fun and a terrific quarterback. Added to the fact that he was a budding actor in the school drama group it was no wonder I fell madly in love with him. Later we'd joined the DC Metropolitan police within three months of each other. I'd moved to the Bureau but Paul had stayed with the Met and was promoted to homicide detective. I was crazy about him, even if I'd learned that he could be controlling and possessive.

Maybe he was just being honest, but that letter was the saddest thing I'd ever read. It cut my heart to shreds and I hit rock bottom. Actually, that's not strictly true – for the first time in my life I hit the tranquilliser bottle and turned into a mush-head and *then* I hit rock bottom. What made it worse was I'd learned that Paul had met a twenty-year-old civilian secretary named Suzanne who worked at his precinct.

For months I didn't think I could muster the energy to kick-start my life all over again. Then one rainy Friday after work a female work colleague took pity on me and dragged me along to an art exhibition she had been invited to in a Georgetown gallery. 'You need to get out, for Christ sakes, Kate, honey. You've got a face on you that looks like you've been given two weeks to live.'

'Art isn't always my thing, Adele.'

'Hey, it isn't always mine either. But this guy's work is hot. His name's David Bryce and the law practice where my sister works bought one of his works. She says all the critics are calling him the next big thing. Besides, there's *free* wine and nibbles. And who knows, maybe we'll see a few cute men.'

Men were the last thing on my mind. I walked through the gallery's cream-painted rooms, barely giving the striking, colourful Bryce paintings a second glance. I saw a water dispenser and headed towards it. I was feeling so down I palmed a couple of pills and filled a paper cup with water. A guy walked by. He had pastel-blue eyes, a compassionate face, his dark hair cut short, and he stopped in his tracks when he saw the pills. 'Difficult day?'

'Pretty much.'

'Headache?'

I felt the need to explain to the guy and I held up the pill bottle. 'Ciprimil. My doctor prescribed them.'

The Ciprimil was a relaxant that was supposed to help me sleep at night but more often than not I'd begun to use it to help me get through the bad days. The stranger locked eyes with me and offered his hand. 'I'm David Bryce.'

I remembered the name. 'You're the artist?'

'Guilty. I don't think we've met before . . . ?'

I shook his hand and studied him some more: with his elegant hands and athletic figure he looked striking, the kind of man with presence who stood out from the crowd, and yet at the same time he came across as just an ordinary guy. 'I'm Kate Moran.'

He gave me a studied look as if he were reading me like a book. 'Ciprimil, huh? Do you know where the best pharmacy is around here, Kate?'

I didn't follow what he was getting at. 'No, where?'

He tapped his temple with his finger. 'In your own head. That's where the problem's always got to be solved. Do yourself a favour and stay away from those pills or they'll only turn you into a zombie.'

For some reason at that moment the guy's attitude needled me. He may have been well intentioned but he sounded kind of patronising, and I thought: *It's none of your damned business what I do.* Who the hell was *he* to dispense advice? But that's me – I get irritated when someone starts telling me how to behave, and now I got sassy. 'Are you speaking as a medical professional, or just an interfering wiseass?'

Bryce struggled to hide a smile. 'Would it make a difference?'

'Probably not.'

He met my stare with a steely look. 'Hey, I really wasn't trying to meddle, you do what you want. But someone close to me hit the pills years ago and never managed to get off the treadmill. Believe me, if you can help it you're best keeping your nose out of the drug cabinet in the first place. Bet you can, you even look the type. So long, Kate. I hope to see you back here again some time.'

I looked at him as he walked away. That day I figured he was a meddlesome pain in the neck and disregarded his advice – besides, I never thought I'd see him again. I took the pills that morning, and the next. But on the third morning I started to think about David Bryce's advice. And I got to thinking that he was so damned right. Since I'd first started taking the little white pills I'd felt like a sleepwalker. And I knew they were a crutch. He was right about something else too: the best pharmacy was inside my own head, and that's where the battle had to begin.

So I stopped taking the pills and started reasoning with myself. It was so much tougher than I thought, and took a hell of a lot of effort, but a month later I was off the Ciprimil. Six months later my divorce from Paul went through. I got a big surprise when he rang me the day he got the papers. He sounded lost and unhappy, as if he were suddenly having difficulty accepting that our marriage was over. 'Kate, I've got to tell you, I've been having second thoughts about us getting divorced.'

I was stunned. 'Second thoughts? What are you talking about? We've been apart for over a year, Paul. We live separate lives.'

'I still love you, Kate.'

'I don't believe this. What's going on, Paul?'

He sighed. 'Suzanne and I have parted. The bitch even accused me of being controlling and violent, would you credit that? She made a 911 call to the police saying that I beat her up, but I swear it ain't true. She's going to ruin my career. Look, Kate, I'm going to be honest and tell you I'll eat humble pie if you take me back. How about it? We can make a go of it, start over fresh. Make it better than it ever was.'

I'd known Paul to be aggressive, and he had a ferocious temper, but he'd never actually struck me. Maybe he'd crossed the line?

But it hardly mattered. Too much water had passed under the bridge. 'Paul, it's over, and we both know it. If you don't accept that, then you've got a problem. Let's just go our different ways and be done with it. Someday maybe we can be friends.'

'I don't want to be just friends. I want us to stay married.'

'Be sensible, it's far too late for that, Paul.'

I heard a touch of anger flare in his voice. 'The way I see it, you'll always be my wife, no matter what happens. Are you still seeing that artist guy, Bryce?'

'How'd you know about David?'

'A cop always hears things. Will you please reconsider, Kate?'

I told him honestly, 'Paul, you're the one who walked out in the first place. There's nothing to reconsider, it's just that right now you're being irrational and feeling sorry for yourself. You'll get over it when the next bimbo comes along.'

I couldn't help my stinging remark, but I felt that I'd earned the right to unburden my hurt. Then Paul's temper erupted. 'You know something? You're just like all the other bitches out there. Maybe one day you're going to be sorry you said no. *Fuck you*.'

Paul slammed down the phone. I felt cynical about marriage that day. And if anyone had told me that within three more months David Bryce and I would be planning to marry, I'd have told them they were crazy. I *did* go back to the gallery, got invited by David to dinner, and that was where it started.

David, with his soft hands and his caring eyes, who helped me find a reconnection to life. And being around Megan had made me feel what it was like to be a mother, and I had cherished that feeling. Now the two people I loved had been gone for almost two years and I still felt crushed by their absence.

I touched their marble gravestone. I had come here simply to reflect on the sacred time that David, Megan and I had spent together, but as I felt the marble's glacial coldness seep into my flesh I felt sad. I knew that I had to move on, to make another life for myself. Not because I wanted to but because I had to let go of the past, if only for the sake of my own sanity. I wasn't forsaking the two people I had loved most: I was trying to do what David would have wanted me to do – kick-start my life all over again. But this time I was doing it on my own, and it felt daunting, almost scary.

I miss you, David. I miss you, Megan.

When I had finished my whispered words to the dead, when I had said my goodbyes, I touched my fingers to my lips, kissed the tips and laid my hand upon their headstone, then I walked back down the hill to the Bronco.

Across the road from the cemetery the Disciple sat watching from behind the dark-tinted windows of a wine-coloured GM van. He saw Kate Moran climb into the Bronco. She didn't have an inkling that she was being followed. His eyes moved briefly past the Bronco to the graveyard, where he knew David and Megan Bryce were buried.

He shifted his focus back to Moran again and saw that she looked downcast as she started the Bronco. Her indicator light flashed and she started to pull out into the passing traffic. He started the van, hung a U-turn and followed her, grinning to himself in the knowledge that whatever misery she felt now was absolutely *nothing* compared to what was in store for her. But best of all, she didn't have a clue that her worst nightmare was just about to begin.

17

That weekend I took almost no phone calls, and made none. I visited my doctor on Saturday and got the antibiotic prescription Brogan Lacy had suggested, and I slept a lot, the deep sleep of someone who has lived on their nerves for months. The kind of sleep the body induces to help it recover from a bout of exhaustion or ill health.

I knew I was getting fitter, I was eating well, but I wasn't gaining weight. My walks were the reason. Every morning after breakfast I borrowed Banjo, my neighbour's black Labrador, and in hail, rain or snow we'd walk for five miles along the coastal dunes to Miser's Point and then back again. Bob and Janet Landesman lived two hundred yards away and ran their accounting business from home: they always seemed relieved if I offered to take their slobbering, sixty-pound dog from under their feet. Banjo didn't seem to mind either – he spent as much time mooching around my home as he did theirs, so that at times it felt as if we were joint owners.

I enjoyed my walks out to Miser's Point with Banjo. It was a trail I knew well. I used to jog another nearby path – the locals unkindly called it the 'Psychopath' – around the cove to where the secure wing of Bellevue's psychiatric hospital dominated a hill overlooking the point. The hospital had been built of the same solid granite block as Manor Brook and in the same year, 1894. But I had come to avoid Bellevue, where Gamal had worked as a resident psychiatrist – the association only served to trigger memories of him that I wanted to avoid.

One morning it snowed and Banjo and I managed only a mile, but at least I kept to my walking regime. I was getting fit again, but my mind was still in turmoil. Gamal's 'confession' had unsettled me, but so far I'd had no word from Lou. On Tuesday I decided to call him.

'Hey, I thought I told you to forget about work, sailor.'

'I've been trying to, honest. How's it going, Lou?'

For some reason I could picture Lou smiling. 'What you're really asking is, have we found any evidence in Chinatown?'

'I guess I am. Have you?'

'Not a damned thing.'

Thank God for that. 'That's great, Lou.'

'It's all good news so far. I'll give you a call tomorrow, see how you're doing, Kate.'

The bad news was that I started having nightmares again. They were always the same: gruesome images of Gamal torturing David and Megan in the quarry mine where their bodies had been found. The crime scene photos of his prey were among the most horrific I'd ever seen, and it was hardly any wonder I suffered nightmares. The memories were so vivid that I would jolt from my sleep: I'd see the horrified reactions on their faces as they were subjected to Gamal's brutal cruelty. I could visualise the contours of the damp rock walls and hear the terrible screams of the two people I had adored most. And sometimes it wasn't even David and Megan I saw, but complete strangers – victims whose faces I'd never seen before. The nightmares perturbed me.

Then on the Wednesday morning Lou Raines phoned.

I had begun to feel stronger in myself. I had stopped feeling hyper-sensitive and it felt as if my mind had started to heal. After breakfast, I took Banjo for another walk to Miser's Point and when I got back and had showered and dressed in a fresh grey Notre Dame T-shirt and a faded pair of blue Levi's, the phone rang. It was Lou and he again sounded considerate. I was getting worried about the guy. 'Thought I'd just call and see how you're doing. You feeling any better?' he asked.

'I don't know about better, but I'm feeling stronger. I'm walking a lot, and taking care of myself. I'm getting there, Lou.'

'Glad to hear it.'

'I think I'm ready to come back to work.'

'Hey, I didn't call to rush you. The mission is to rest and get well.'

'I feel fine, really I do. And I need to get busy again, otherwise I might start rusting.'

'To tell the truth that's sorta why I rang. To see if you're really up to coming back.'

My pulse had raced the moment I'd heard Lou's voice on the line and now it got quicker. 'Why? Did you turn up anything at the Chinatown metro?'

Lou said, 'I've had a team down there all week and they've found absolutely zilch, apart from the buried remains of a dog that Forensics say have been there a long time. The metro people are pissed off with us getting in their way and the station manager's frothing at the mouth because of the disruption he says we've been causing. So if nothing turns up by next week I'm calling our people off.'

I felt a sense of relief. 'That's good news. Let's hope it stays that way.'

'But there was something I wanted to talk to you about, sailor. Something important. You *sure* you're up to coming in?'

'Sure. Why?'

'How about you get in by noon today? Think you could manage that?'

I was surprised because the request sounded kind of urgent and a warning bell started going off inside my head. 'What's up, Lou? Let's hear it.'

I heard him emit a heavy sigh. 'We may have ourselves a copycat killer. Someone who's mimicked Gamal's MO and crime signatures.'

'*What?*'

A puzzled tone crept into Lou's voice. 'It's kinda bizarre, Kate.'

'*What* is?'

'The sheriff's office in Culpeper County notified us this morning that they turned up a double homicide. They found two bodies in a disused mine twenty miles west of Fredericksburg. An adult and an adolescent. We don't have ID yet, but the victims look like they could have been subjected to a Gamal-style killing, and there are some pretty strange aspects to the crime scene.'

'Like what?'

Lou sighed again. 'Kate, I'd rather we talked face to face.'

My pulse started to hammer against my ribs. 'I'll get in by noon. How long have the victims been dead?'

'Sheriff says two days.'

18

Washington, DC

The FBI field office on 4th Street is a bland concrete struc-
ture that houses several hundred special agents, near the
mayor's office on Judiciary Square. It serves the Washington
District and is dwarfed by its more famous big brother – located
seven blocks from the White House, the J. Edgar Hoover Building
is the Bureau's headquarters and crammed with over five thousand employees.

I took the elevator up to Lou Raines' office but it was empty.
I figured he had stepped out for a couple of minutes, or was at
a meeting, so I headed for my own desk down the hall. On the
way I saw a couple of agent colleagues busy on their phones and
they waved to me as I went to check through my mail. As usual,
it was mostly in-house, so I filed what I had to and binned the
junk and headed for the percolator to pour myself a cup of black
coffee.

'You back from vacation, Moran?'

I turned and saw Vance Stone leaning against the door frame
of one of the offices. Stone was a touch over forty, a big and
burly New Yorker with thick red-haired forearms and cautious
green eyes that suggested there was a touch of Irish blood in his
veins from somewhere in his past. The friction between as went
back years. He was an excellent investigator, and I had tried my
damnedest to get on with him, but Stone was a difficult son of
a bitch, and a complex man.

I corrected him. 'It wasn't exactly a vacation. It was an order
from Lou.'

Stone grinned. 'Whatever. A week off on full salary while the rest of us are sweating our butts off in the salt mines sounds a good deal to me. I guess Lou still has his favourites.'

'I've worked flat out for almost five years on the Gamal case, so I reckon I've earned the break, Stone.'

The grin never left his face. 'You think so? I guess you reckon the rest of us must have been sitting on our butts?'

I figured that as usual Stone was looking for an argument but I didn't take the bait. I tried being pleasant in return but I didn't hold out any hope that it would work – it rarely did in Stone's case. 'You want some coffee?'

Stone didn't even bother to acknowledge my offer. Some days he had the manners of a pig. Maybe I was being kind. Pretty much most days.

He strolled towards me. 'I hear you witnessed the execution.'

'That's right.' I poured a cup of coffee, headed back to my desk and leafed through some paperwork, hoping Stone would leave me in peace, but he hovered over me.

'Guess you must have got a kick out of seeing Gamal get the needle, seeing as it sort of neatly tied up the case.'

'Do you mind, Stone? I've got work to do. Let's have this conversation some other time.'

But Stone pulled up a chair and sat down. Despite being a good investigator, over the years he'd been passed over for promotion, and when I was given the lead ahead of him in two major investigations he had taken an instant dislike to me. I was also the only woman in our bunch and I suspected that Stone's two failed marriages had left a bitter aftertaste when it came to the opposite sex. He liked to offer a pithy little gem to the guys about his second wife: 'My ex got the gold mine – and I got the shaft.'

'So what was it like seeing Gamal go to hell?'

I offered him a stare. 'I told you, Stone, let it be.'

'Hey, you know what really tickled me? I heard that Gamal claimed he didn't do the Bryce murders?'

'You heard right,' I answered.

Stone grinned again. 'Now isn't that interesting? Guess there's a chance that I may be proven right about the Bryce case after all. Leaves you wondering if justice was completely done that night, doesn't it?'

I could see where the conversation was heading – in a direction I didn't want it to go. I was beginning to feel uncomfortable and I got to my feet. 'You know where Lou is?'

Stone's hardened green eyes fixed on me before he reached for his jacket. 'Already at the scene in Culpeper County. He decided to get there early. The fact is, he asked me to join you. So it looks like you and me will be travelling together, now ain't that something?'

'That's just what I need, Stone. More of your charming company.'

'Hey, and I've a feeling we're going to be seeing a lot more of each other in the future.'

'And what's that supposed to mean?'

'You'll find out,' Stone said mysteriously. 'There's a chopper on the helipad in five minutes. Be there, Moran.'

As usual, Stone's arrogant tone got right up my nose. 'You're not my boss, Stone. You don't give me orders.'

Stone glanced around the office to make sure we were alone, then lowered his voice as he hurled a final volley. 'No, but wouldn't that be nice? Be careful if that happens, Moran. Because when it does then I'll make it my business to nail you on two counts of murder. Five minutes, don't be late.'

Stone immediately headed towards the elevator. I wasn't stunned by his words but I felt angry as I grabbed my coat to follow him. Even though Stone and I had worked the Constantine Gamal case together, he had never believed that Gamal had slaughtered David and Megan.

The fact is, he thought *I* had murdered them.

19

The Bell helicopter circled once before it came in to land. As the whir of the rotor blades died I climbed out. We had landed in the middle of a snow-covered field next to what looked like an old quarry or mine. Landing at such a similar crime scene to where David and Megan had been murdered sent a cold shiver through me. Something else troubled me – Lou had said it looked like we had a Gamal copycat. I began to think about Gamal's denial that he had killed David and Megan and even consider the unthinkable: *could he have actually told the truth?* I tried to dismiss that thought from my mind.

Stone had barely spoken on the short flight but I still remembered his words: *'I'll make it my business to nail you on two counts of murder.'* It was hard to imagine that Stone believed I was guilty of a double homicide but he did. *Why* he thought I might have killed David and Megan was another story.

I saw Lou Raines wave to us both and as I went to greet him a gust of wind from the dying rotor blades threw snow in his face. 'Ain't that just terrific,' Lou scowled before he looked up at me. 'Sorry to have to mess up your first day back, Kate, but I thought you ought to see this.' He nodded to Stone, who came up behind me. 'Vance. Good flight?'

'I've had worse. What's the picture here, Lou?'

I was thinking the same question as I pulled up the collar of my dark blue FBI windcheater against the biting chill. I saw a dozen sheriff's cars and Bureau vehicles parked near the mine, and clusters of uniforms stood around, chatting and rubbing their hands. A couple of my colleagues stood off to one side, away from the crowd.

'You're both about to find out,' Raines said as a local sheriff carrying a walkie-talkie approached us.

He was tall and robust, with a beer gut, and as he came closer he touched his hat and said politely. 'Afternoon, ma'am. Afternoon, sir.'

Raines said, 'Meet Sheriff Moby. I'll let him explain. His men found the bodies about seven a.m., after they got a call from a drifter who hangs around the mine. Sheriff, Special Agent Kate Moran. And this is Special Agent Vance Stone.'

Stone grunted at Moby and I shook the man's hand. 'Sheriff.'

'Do either of you agents know this area?' Moby asked.

'Can't say that I do,' I answered.

Stone shook his head. 'Naw.'

The sheriff tipped back his hat. 'In case you don't know it, we're about five miles west of the Culpeper county line, near a town called Acre. Used to be a pretty prosperous gem mining area, but the stones ran out a long time ago.' He waved a hand towards a shaft entrance that we approached. 'The last company to own this place moved out almost thirty years ago, left it to crumble and rot.'

The sheriff wasn't kidding. Even though the ground was mostly covered in snow, I could make out a jumble of junk: rotting timbers, scrap machinery, and a couple of cannibalised old Ford trucks that had been scavenged of parts, their hoods open like the yawning mouths of corroded metal monsters. A big rusted sign that said MINE NO. 2 had long ago been shredded by shotgun pellets, a hole the size of a fist punched through the O.

The sheriff rubbed his gloved hands. 'The place looks even worse when it ain't covered in snow. It started coming down last week, and it's been falling on and off until two days ago.'

'Tell me about the bodies,' I said.

'There's an old guy used to work here as the nightwatchman who found them. His name's Billy Adams. When the mine closed he was kept on by the company for about a year to caretake the place. After that they let him go and he just hung around here, drinking mostly.'

'You mean he *lives* in the mine?'

'No, ma'am, but close enough. He's got a hut right over there that used to be the old company office. When he's sober enough he sometimes drives his old Harley into town.'

I saw the derelict hut the sheriff pointed to. It was twenty feet away, a crooked, rusted stove pipe sticking out of its roof and a dented, ancient black Harley parked near the door. 'Go on.'

'Five thirty this morning he found them. Says he got a smell of gasoline coming from the shaft and decided to take a look. He found the bodies about a hundred feet inside the mine. They were disembowelled and burned beyond recognition.'

I shivered, but not from the cold. These were all typically Gamal's trademarks, eviscerating, butchering and burning his victims. 'Any ID yet?'

Sheriff Moby removed his hat and wiped his brow. 'Nope. Our forensics people say they were a middle-aged man and a young woman, possibly teenage, but I can't be any more specific until their work's done.'

Lou Raines nodded towards the entrance shaft, ten feet away. 'The mine's pretty level and burrows straight into the rock. The crime scene boys are in there now doing their thing.'

Inside the tunnel I saw brittle limestone walls, and stanchions of rotting wood supporting the beamed roof. 'Is it safe to enter?' Stone asked, as if reading my mind.

The sheriff nodded. 'Yep. According to Billy, the mine's drilled into solid limestone and the oak beams are still in pretty good shape.'

'You trust Billy's judgement?' I asked.

The sheriff shrugged. 'He's a bottle-of-Scotch-a-day man when he can afford it, which might cloud his judgement a tad, but in this case I think he's right. The mine's never had a cave-in, far as I know.'

I saw that the sheriff's men had run power cables from a mobile electrical generator to provide light in the tunnel. The entrance was about ten feet wide, and yellow crime scene tape had been strung across the tunnel mouth except for a narrow gap on the right-hand side which allowed just enough space to enter. Stone moved on ahead, and then Lou gave me a troubled look. 'I hope you're ready for this, sailor?'

I wasn't sure whether he meant the depravity I was about to witness, or my phobia. I *hated* enclosed spaces. I'd suffered from claustrophobia since I was seven years old, when one of my kid sisters accidentally locked me in a big old freezer in our back yard. I was stuck inside, banging frantically on the walls and barely able to breathe. When my brother Frank finally heard my cries after half an hour and pulled me free, I was gasping for breath and a physical and mental wreck.

Lou knew that I found confined spaces pretty hard to deal with. This was definitely one of those times. But Lou had a hard-assed attitude to any fear or phobia which stemmed from his time in the military. It could be summed up in six words: *Face it. Fight it. Defeat it.* When he'd put me in charge of the Gamal investigation, he'd forced me to face my phobia head on, and I remembered he'd even sugared the pill with praise and a smile: 'I know the crime scene's underground, Kate, but you're the best agent I've got for the case, so go do it.'

But every battle can't be won, and no matter how hard I tried my fear hadn't gone away. Right on cue, I felt my heart race and my palms perspire, and the veins in my neck pulsed. I stared into the mine shaft but I was reluctant to move inside. Stark fear rose up like bile in my stomach. What had Lou meant by 'I hope you're ready for this?'

As if sensing my terror, Lou took a firm grip of my arm and started to guide me into the tunnel.

20

We moved into the cavern, stepping over the electrical cables as the sheriff flicked on his torch. It was warmer inside the tunnel, but not by much, and our breath fogged. My heart quickened when the limestone walls suddenly narrowed by at least two feet. I felt a sense of panic, but I knew that when I was *with* someone my fear became manageable.

But I still didn't like the idea of having to go a *hundred feet* inside the passageway. It scared the living hell out of me and I gave a gasp and felt my breathing quicken. Stone was about ten paces ahead and Lou shot me a concerned look. 'You OK, sailor?'

'Sure, I'll manage.' But it was total bravado as my heart beat faster and my mouth felt dry.

Sheriff Moby noticed my discomfort. 'Anything the matter?'

'Enclosed spaces bother me,' I admitted. 'But it isn't so bad if I'm in company.'

'You'll have plenty of that. I've got three of my men in here, and there's at least six of your folks.' The sheriff flashed the torch past Stone, to where halogen lights saturated the damp limestone walls with a brilliant glow, lighting up the passageway like a movie set.

As we moved forward I had a sudden sense of dread. I thought: *Copycat.* Less than a week ago I had witnessed the execution of a man who had used a similar modus operandi. Now it seemed that we might have another comparable crime. It wasn't unknown for a big-name killer like Gamal to have sicko admirers who'd try to imitate his methods.

We came round a bend and were confronted by a blaze of white light. We were in a chamber about the size of a large living room, the rock walls glistening with moisture. The walls soared upwards for at least twenty feet, and the ground was scattered with limestone chips. Powerful halogen illuminated the floor area, most of it sealed off with crime scene tape, and clusters of agents and deputies moved carefully around the scene.

A pair of Crime Scene (CS) techs had just finished taking photographs, and in a corner another couple of techs in white disposable overalls brushed the ground for clues. I noted a sharp smell of petroleum. Lou raised his palm in silent greeting to a good-looking Latino with wire-rimmed glasses who had a black doctor's bag open at his feet, and a scarf wrapped around his neck. Armando Diaz was from Forensics, and his breath clouded in the cold air as he came over to join us. 'Guys. How've you been, Kate?'

'Surviving. How about you, Armando?'

He winked at me, as only a Latino can wink, full of sugges- tion. 'Cold as an Eskimo's ass. This place is like a freezer. How come I always get the best ones?'

'Must be luck,' I offered. Diaz was one of our best forensic pathologists, and had a reputation as a ladies' man. His spiky hair was bleached almost white and he wore a gold stud in his left ear. There was an office rumour that the guy had had his nipples pierced with two silver rings. Diaz was certainly a tad weird – as Lou liked to remind us, 'Anyone who skates to work wearing skin-hugging Speedo gear and a crotch cup has to be.'

Diaz didn't know about my phobia but I figured I must have *looked* scared – it felt as if my pulse was beating at way over a hundred. The company of at least ten people in the chamber helped to ease my discomfort, but it didn't make it go away.

Diaz grabbed a powerful electric torch from his black bag and nodded towards the centre of the cavern. 'Let me show you what we've got. They're both round the corner, right over here. But I better warn you, it's unpleasant.'

I noticed a cautioning look in Lou's eyes, as if he was trying to prepare me for something deeply disturbing. 'How unpleasant?'

Lou's mouth tightened with a look of disgust. 'You'll see for yourself.'

21

I followed Diaz and Stone and got my first shock when I saw a flat slab of rock about the size of a large dining table. The charred remains of two bodies lay on top.

I stiffened with rage. It looked as if their skeletons were fused together in a deadly embrace, the flesh horribly burned and their features scorched beyond recognition. I've seen a lot of corpses in the last dozen years but at every scene I always feel a shiver both of revulsion and compassion. And this time was no different. What flashed through my mind was that these were human beings: someone had loved them and cherished them. I put my hand over my mouth: the stench of burnt flesh was nauseating, and it was mixed with the sharp smell of petroleum.

I always got a feeling of restless unease at a freshly committed murder site. I could feel dark secrets in the cold air, thick with horror. The bodies were so badly burned that it was impossible to tell even their gender. A small black wooden crucifix about eight inches long lay midway between both corpses. I closed my eyes, then opened them again and had to take a deep breath as I stared at the charred human remains and the crucifix.

The sheriff said, 'I worked on the Gamal case we had outside of Culpeper six years ago. Mathew and Carol Brians. Father and daughter, found in a quarry cavern. You know the case?'

I hadn't worked with the team back then but I was familiar with all of Gamal's known cases. 'Sure. Go on.'

'I thought there was a strong similarity between both crime scenes. Which seemed pretty weird, considering Gamal was executed last week. I guess that's why we decided to notify you guys as a courtesy.'

'Bet you wish you hadn't?' I was tempted to break a smile, for I could see that despite his courtesy the sheriff wasn't exactly happy about the Bureau walking all over his case; most local officers wouldn't be, but this guy was putting a brave face on it.

'Only did what I thought was proper, ma'am.'

Stone said to Diaz, 'What can you tell us about the victims?'

'Not much until we have them in the lab. Most of the skin tissue and internal organs are burned to cinder – so we may have our work cut out. From the smell, it seems petroleum spirit was used. But we found no containers lying around.'

The crime scene was indeed eerily reminiscent of many of Gamal's that I'd witnessed: two bodies, usually a parent and their teenage offspring, the victims butchered and their remains often burned beyond identification. Sometimes they suffered mutilation before death. I studied the charred bodies and thought: *What a horrible way to die. I just hope they were drugged with benzo before they perished.* That was another Gamal MO. It was a tiny consolation to think their pain may have been at least partly diminished. If it hadn't, their agony was almost too much to contemplate. I indicated Diaz's torch. 'Mind if I borrow that?'

'Be my guest.' Diaz handed over the torch and I shone the powerful cone of light on to the larger of the corpses. The male's grotesque blackened skull stared back at me, the flesh the colour of tar and the texture of brittle charcoal, the jaws open in a final agonised scream. I felt like turning away in horror. '*Christ.*'

'Reminds me of that painting, the one by that crazy artist, Munch,' Lou remarked. 'I can't remember the name of the frigging thing . . .'

'*The Scream.*'

Lou nodded. 'That's the one. Pretty macabre.'

Diaz said suddenly, 'Take a look above your head.'

I looked up, and Lou and Stone did likewise. A dull circle of light hung over the chamber. It came from a hole in the cavern roof. I couldn't tell its distance or even whether it was a natural fissure in the rock or an old bore hole. I could see a ring of white cloud in the sky far above the hole. Lou Raines pointed up as a burst of piercing white sunlight suddenly drenched the cavern and reflected brilliantly off the limestone walls. 'The opening's about thirty feet above us, and about four feet wide. I figure that sun and moonlight shine directly on to the rock slab at certain times of day and night when there's no cloud cover.'

I knew what Lou was getting at. A ritual sacrifice aspect was yet another Gamal MO. A light shaft shining down into the cavern would have been just the kind of symbolism that would have appealed to his warped mind. *But Gamal's dead and buried*, I reminded myself.

I turned back to the bodies. The heads were a blackened mess: nose and lips, ears and cheeks, looked like tarry gunge. I shone the torch on the female's face. It was a disturbing experience: scorched, black locks of hair were burned into her forehead. The head was smaller, the teeth in better condition, the bones less developed. I reckoned she hadn't been much more than a couple of years into puberty. 'You said they've been dead about two days?' I addressed Lou.

'Can't say for certain until after the autopsy. But the sheriff's people believe so on account of their witness. The last time he was in the mine before he discovered the bodies was forty-eight hours prior, and the corpses weren't there.'

I was about to ask more about the witness but was distracted by the chamber's floor. 'Was all the ground around here checked?'

Diaz blew on his frozen hands and rubbed them. 'Sure.'

'And?'

'Nothing, apart from some charred clothes. They were stripped before they died, and the clothes burned separately.'

'Where?' Stone asked.

'Right over there.' Diaz nodded to several clear plastic evidence bags propped against the far wall, and I went over and picked one of them up. Inside the bag a bunch of clothes were fused together in a tangled blackened mess. 'They'll be labbed as soon as we're done here,' Diaz said.

I handed the evidence bag to Stone and shivered. Not from the cold, but because my body felt as if it was overheating and

I knew that this was caused by naked fear. The enclosed space was really getting to me, even with company – I was lucky to have lasted this long. My palms perspired, my mouth felt bone dry and my heart was flipping. *I have to get out of here soon.* 'Did you talk with the witness, Lou?'

He shook his head. 'Not yet. Our friend Billy Adams was so traumatised that one of the deputies had to take him to the local hospital. I'd like you to go see him, Kate. Vance has a court hearing to attend this afternoon and I've got to high-tail it back to the District for a three p.m. meeting.'

'Are you saying I'm in?'

'You feel up to the case?' Lou asked.

In truth, I didn't exactly know if I was, not after spending over four solid years on Gamal's case. 'Do I have an option?'

'After all you've been through, I'm not going to make it an order, Kate. But you did the business by finding Gamal, so I'd like you in and taking charge if you feel able. Seems to me we're dealing with a copycat. What do *you* think? Can you handle it?'

I didn't speak. Lou was acutely aware that David and Megan had died in similar surroundings and circumstances and he knew my emotions would take a battering if I accepted the case. But I also knew Lou's attitude: *Face it. Fight it. Defeat it.* I took another look around the chamber. I tried to keep my phobia under control for a few more minutes as I found my mind pondering the same old questions it always posed at a homicide scene. *Who, what, when, why?* What depravity had taken place here, committed by whom, and when and why? Would we be able to decipher a picture from the grisly jigsaw puzzle we'd found? I knew I was hooked. 'If I think I can't handle it I'll let you know.'

Then something vital suddenly struck me, something so obvious that I'd completely ignored it. 'What about footprints? The sheriff said it's been snowing around here all week and only stopped two days ago.'

Lou shot me a look. 'He figures the snow had already stopped several hours before the murders took place but he's waiting for confirmation of that from a local weather channel. So the killer should have left footprints in the snow. But that's one of the things the sheriff meant about this case being weird, Kate.'

'What do you mean?'

'Apart from Billy Adams' footprints in the snow, it seems there were no others.'

22

As we moved outside I saw that CS and the sheriff's men were still scouring the area for clues. I followed Lou over to his Ford Galaxy. I found it hard to believe what I had just heard. 'Someone had to walk in and out of the cavern, Lou. They didn't *float* in. There had to be some other marks or footprints.'

Lou sighed. 'There were none. Or maybe I should qualify that. So far we've found no trace of any, apart from Billy's. We matched his sneakers to some prints in the tunnel – it's the only pair of footwear he's got and they're the only marks we've so far discovered.'

'If there was snow on the ground whoever went in and out *had* to leave footprints,' I persisted.

Lou nodded. 'Even if our killer climbed down through the frigging hole in the cavern roof, we should have found *some* markings near the slab, but there weren't any, believe me. And there's something else.'

'What?'

'Our friend Billy sleeps in the hut, which is right near the mouth of the cave. But he claims he was awake most of the night the murders had to have occurred and he didn't hear a sound, apart from the wind. No screams from the victims and no signs of a perp.'

'Was he drunk or drugged?'

Lou pulled up his coat collar against the freezing cold. 'Claims he wasn't, but he admits he had a few drinks. I asked the sheriff to make sure the hospital checks him for other stimulant traces. You can ask when you get there.'

I studied the landscape. 'You think Billy's suspect material?'

'I'm pretty sure he isn't and you'll see why when you meet him. I'd bet my pension the old guy's not a psycho killer, Kate,' Lou answered.

'No footprints. No screams. No evidence. No sense.'

'Who are you telling,' Lou said with a shrug.

I looked towards the narrow road that snaked up to the mine. Another track led away to what I guessed was a rear exit. 'Is that a back way in?'

'Yep. We checked it too.'

'For recent tyre marks?'

Raines nodded. 'Yep, and found zilch.'

'That's *crazy*. How the hell did the killer get here? Even if he came by chopper we ought to see evidence.'

'Hey, I'm on your side. But until we figure out what the frig went on here, we're stumped.'

I stared out again at the landscape. The mine was remote. I couldn't see a single property among the distant rolling hills. 'This isn't the kind of place that everyone would know about. Unless they were local or had maybe worked for the mining company.'

'Yeah, I thought about that too,' Lou answered with a nod.

'It might do no harm to get a list of former mine employees who are still alive. Maybe somebody in town can help us with that,' I suggested.

Lou climbed into his car. 'The company went bust thirty years ago. But it's your baby, so you do whatever you see fit. The really shitty news is you'll have Stone for company.'

I felt a flush of annoyance. 'Lou, we'll need to talk about that . . .'

'Sorry, Kate, but you two are the best I've got and I want you working on this together.' Lou smiled. 'Besides, a little competition never hurts.'

I didn't feel happy about working with Stone. In fact, I *hated* the idea. But once Lou made up his mind it was difficult for anyone to change it. 'Any other lousy news I should know?'

'No, and I've kept the good news until last. The new guy, Josh

Cooper, joined us while you were on leave and he's on the team. He's a New Yorker, his old man and I knew each other way back, so don't be surprised if he calls me Uncle. I sent him on ahead to the hospital with one of the deputies. The sheriff will give you a ride. Sorry I can't be there to make the introductions.'

'What's Cooper like?'

Lou started the engine. 'Just what your doctor would have ordered. Bright, good looking and sexy, or so my wife always says. And he's divorced. What more do you want?'

'I meant to work with.'

Lou smiled and gunned his accelerator. 'With all those other credentials, I didn't think that would matter, but I'll let you be the judge. Be good, sailor. We'll talk later.'

23

The drive to Acre took barely fifteen minutes, but in the sheriff's company it was forty questions most of the way. The guy was a true cop who never stopped taking statements. 'You long with the Feds?' he asked.

'Ten years.'

'From DC?'

'Baltimore.'

'Born there?'

'No, Clarkson airbase.'

'No shit. Your dad served with the air force?'

'For a time, then he became a cop.'

The sheriff gave me a look. 'Hey, mine was in Clarkson maybe five years. So how come you joined the Feds?'

'I guess after I stopped dancing topless in Vegas, I was looking for a pensionable job.'

That got a stare. Then Sheriff Moby cracked a smile. 'Almost got me there. So where are you living? In DC?'

I had to listen politely to his questions until I suggested I had some things to mull over and he fell reluctantly silent. After witnessing the horror in the cavern my mind was in overdrive. The questions that that plagued me were the usual ones my mind threw up after I'd visited a homicide scene: *Who are the victims? Did they know each other? What happened at the crime scene?* And then the crazy, niggling question that again reared its head: *How could there be no footprints in the snow?* It didn't make sense.

I was distracted as we passed a few sporadic ranch-style wooden homes, and then we turned off the highway and I saw a sign that said WELCOME TO ACRE. The place appeared to be a few dozen stores and offices along a main street and that was it, apart from a couple of churches, one either end of the town. I guess the mine had once been the big thing around here. The sheriff pulled up outside a two-storey breeze-block building. 'We're here,' he announced. A sign on the lawn said: ACRE GENERAL HOSPITAL.

'At least you have a hospital,' I suggested.

'Yeah, and it services nearly half the county.'

I opened my door. 'Did you already question Billy?'

'Not entirely, ma'am. To tell you the truth, he was too traumatised so I only had about ten minutes with him. I told Agent Raines the gist of what he had to say, but I'm hoping Billy's calmed down by now and able to tell us the entire story.'

'You think he's a reliable witness?'

The sheriff nodded. 'I know he likes his bottle and he's got a reputation as a wild man who's broken up a few bars in his day, but he's nobody's fool.'

'Then let's go hear what wild Billy has to say.'

24

As soon as I stepped into the hospital lobby I saw my colleague, Mack Underwood, eating a bagel and sipping from a cup of machine coffee. He waved his bagel when he spotted me with the sheriff. Mack and I had partnered on cases – he was ex-military and swore like a marine. I once bet him a hundred bucks that he couldn't string a sentence for an entire day without a cuss word in it – Mack lost after five minutes and I was surprised he'd even lasted that long. He greeted me with a wink. 'Well, well, I guess my favourite girl's back in business. How the fuck are you doing, sailor?'

'Considering I've just come from the mine, not so hot. What's been happening here, Mack?'

'I've got a massive butt pain from waiting for two fucking hours to see Billy Adams, that's what's happening.' Mack wiped his mouth with a tissue, put down his unfinished bagel and licked his fingers as I introduced Sheriff Moby.

'Let me go and find out what the story is,' the sheriff offered.

'Hey, I'd appreciate that,' Mack said, tossing his paper tissue into a garbage bin as Moby disappeared in the direction of a pair of swing-doors leading into ER.

'So where's the new guy?' I asked Mack.

'Cooper?' He pointed with his cup towards a guy of about medium height with short dark hair slipping change into a coffee machine down the hall. 'That's him right there. Went to get himself a coffee.'

Cooper looked to be in his mid-thirties, with strong shoulders, and wore a button-down blue shirt and silk tie, and a stylish long black overcoat, his shoes polished like ceramic. 'What do you think?' I asked.

Mack gave me one of his grins. 'Hard to say. He's opinion-ated, but for a New Yorker he ain't too much of a wiseass, so that in itself is refreshing. You ask me, he's a guy who knows where he's going. Dresses well, too.'

That was a big compliment coming from Mack, considering that his assessment of most people he met was that they were a piece of shit. 'It sounds as if you might like him, Mack.'

'Sure, we already made a date for Tuesday. By the way, I hear he used to be a partner of Stone's when they worked together in the New York office. I thought I'd warn you.'

'That's news to me.' *Why didn't Lou mention that?* It was bad enough having to work with Stone, but now I had one of his old partners for company. I turned back as the new guy came up to us carrying his coffee. Now that he was closer, I guessed he was a year or two older than me, but his face had the telling lines of someone who had put in his time. He carried himself well and I noticed a glint in his pale blue eyes that I figured most women would find attractive. He looked confident and secure. And Lou's wife had been right, Cooper was sexy, but he looked too confi-dent for my liking.

Mack did the introductions. 'Kate, meet Josh Cooper, the new kid on the block. He's got the lowdown on the case. Coop, this is Kate Moran.'

We shook hands and Cooper oozed a practised, assured air. 'Agent Moran, it's good to meet. I've heard a lot about you from Lou Raines.'

I noted that his shake was firm but his hands were soft. I also noticed he had dark circles under his eyes as if he hadn't slept much. Lou had said he was divorced. I figured he might be the kind who had been out doing the clubs.

'Is that right? Would that be good or bad?' I countered, and got the uneasy feeling he was studying me.

'Mostly good, in fact.'

Mack said in mockery, 'They've been misleading you, kid. She's a ball-breaker. But you'll learn the hard way. And don't believe her if she says I'm twisted and bitter because I'm always being passed over for promotion. I'm just naturally twisted and bitter.'

Cooper said, 'I guess you two have been working together a while?'

Mack grinned as he finished his coffee. 'Five years too long.'

I met Cooper's eyes with an evaluating stare. 'So this is your first week. How's it going?'

He rubbed his eyes with his thumb and forefinger. 'So far so good. Sorry, but I had a late night last night. I've been trying to keep awake all morning.'

'Bet it was a woman,' Mack said. 'You know the terrible truth? Sex is really only for the under forty-fives. So enjoy it while it lasts, kid.'

'You reckon?' Cooper answered with a smile.

I was businesslike as I said to him, 'Late nights and early morning starts don't exactly go along together, not on this team.'

Mack winked. 'What she means is you better stay the fuck awake if you want to keep playing with the band, kid.'

Cooper looked back at me squarely. 'I'll try and remember that advice, Agent Moran. Don't worry, I try not to let my private life interfere with my work. By the way, I'm tempted to assume by your tone you're in charge of this investigation. I thought it was Lou?'

'As of half an hour ago, it's me. Why, do you have a problem with that?'

'Not right now,' Cooper replied, still eyeing me directly. 'But if ever I do I'll be sure to let you know.'

I got the feeling Cooper was being a smartass by throwing me a barb like that but I ignored his jibe. I could feel that the disturbing, copycat case was already making me irritable, which was probably partly why I was being unfriendly with Cooper. The rest of it had to do with the fact he was a former partner of Stone's. Mack tossed his empty coffee cup into a garbage bin and said with a grin, 'Good to see you guys getting along so sweetly.'

Over Cooper's shoulder I saw Sheriff Moby come out through

the swing-doors and cross to join us. 'Billy's calmed down enough so we can have a talk with him,' he announced.

Mack was already heading towards the swing-doors when the sheriff caught his arm. 'Hold on a minute, there's something you all better know.'

'What's that, Sheriff?' I asked.

'Billy's been talking with Dr Farley, who's been looking after him.'

'I'm listening,' I said.

'The doc says that a little while ago Billy mentioned that he saw someone in the mine. He thinks he may have seen the killer.'

25

A deputy kept guard outside as the sheriff ushered us into a private room. A female nurse was busy taking Billy Adams' blood pressure. He looked like an elderly hobo down on his luck, with scraggy silver hair and beard stubble. Faded tattoos stained his arms and his watery eyes turned towards us as we entered. The nurse finished her work, plumped up Billy's pillows and gave a nod as she left. 'Call if you need me, Sheriff. Let me know when you're through.'

'Sure will, Thelma.' The sheriff stepped over to the end of the bed. Billy Adams offered us a silent nod and I got the feeling that he was still doped with sedative.

The sheriff took off his hat. 'I need to talk with you, Billy. And so do these folks from the FBI. We'll try to keep it short.'

Billy had a weary look that said: *Can't you just leave me alone?* 'I'm pretty beat, Sheriff. I don't feel much like talking.'

Billy didn't sound to me like he was up to being interviewed – he sounded drowsy – but he was the only lead we had, so I said firmly, 'Mr Adams, we wouldn't be here if this wasn't important. Every minute that passes is vital in helping us catch whoever murdered the mine victims.'

Adams' eyes started to fill with tears and he turned his face away. 'I'd like to leave it for a while.'

'I understand you might need some privacy to recover, Billy,' I answered. 'But when things are still fresh in your mind is the best time to talk. And the longer this killer is on the loose, the greater are the chances of him murdering again. You could help us stop that, Billy. Help us save lives. You need to understand that your evidence may be vital.'

I didn't know whether my words had hit home or not, because Billy fell silent again. Sometimes with witnesses who have been traumatised the best thing is not to apply pressure but let them find their own way to telling their story, even if that takes time. I was impatient to find answers, and I tried to think of another tack, anything to get our guy talking, when without even so much as a look in my direction for approval Cooper pointed to a faded Redsocks tattoo on Adams' left arm. 'You a fan, Billy?'

'Used to follow the 'Socks a long time ago.'

At least he had spoken again, but it seemed like Cooper was pulling teeth. 'Not any more?' he asked.

'Got tired of watching.'

'So what hobbies have you got now?' Cooper continued.

'Drink when I got the cash, stay dry when I don't.'

'What about last night? Did you drink last night?'

Billy shrugged. 'Yeah, I had a few beers.'

'What's a few?' Cooper queried.

'One or two.'

'Glasses?'

'Pitchers. And maybe a couple of shots.'

'Where was that?'

This time Billy gave us all a stare. 'The Silver Lagoon bar. You can ask the bartender. I was there until about midnight.'

Billy sounded a touch defensive, as if he was scared that we might consider him a suspect. 'What happened after that?' I interrupted.

'Drove my Harley back to the mine. Parked right by the old office, just like I always do.'

Billy dried up again, so I said, 'Then what happened?'

'I tried to sleep. But my prostate acts up after I've been drinking and I can't sleep more than a few hours without needing to go to the can. I got an old bucket I use outside the door and I padded out to take a leak maybe three or four times during the night. The last time was about five-thirty. That's when I got it.'

Silence again. 'Got what?'

'The smell of petroleum. Seemed kind of weird seeing as I'd

never got that smell in the mine before, so I grabbed my torch and went in.'

'Go on,' I prompted.

'That's when I found the bodies. They were still smouldering, wisps of smoke coming offa them.'

Billy's eyes became moist. Our interview was an effort, and I put a hand on his bony shoulder. 'It's OK, Billy. You're doing fine.'

I could see that he was close to breaking down but I pressed on, not wanting to lose the momentum. 'Did you notice anything unusual when you got to the mine? Did you see anyone, or hear anything strange? Anyone moving about in the dark? Anything at all that struck you?'

'Ma'am, I didn't see or hear anything.'

I was confused. I glanced at the sheriff, who shrugged his shoulders. I turned back to Billy. 'I hear you told the doctor that you saw someone at the mine.'

'Yeah, but I didn't see them this morning. It was three evenings ago.'

'Then I misunderstood. Tell me exactly who or what you saw, Billy.'

'It was about five in the afternoon, just getting dark, and I was in the hut when I saw a guy dressed in black coming out of the shaft entrance. Sometimes you get locals up there shooting vermin – rats and possum – but this guy wasn't carrying no gun as far as I could tell, and I never saw him before.'

'What was he doing?'

'Like I say, I saw him coming out of the mine. What he was doing inside was anybody's guess. I reckon it was getting dark and I couldn't see so good but it was like he just walked out into the twilight and disappeared. The next morning I took a look in the mine but I didn't see nothing unusual.'

'Disappeared?'

'Yeah, like a phantom. That's how it seemed. But the mine's a junkyard. The guy could have stepped behind some piece of wreckage or other and I wouldn't have seen him.'

'How often do you see people at the mine?'

'Not often. A couple of times in a year.'

'What did this guy look like?'

'Hard to say, seeing as I didn't see him clearly. But I'd say medium height, dark haired. Kinda round features.'

'That's all you remember?'

'Yes, ma'am, that's all.'

'Did he see you?'

'Not so far as I could tell. He didn't look into the hut.'

'If we got a sketch artist to help, do you think you could come up with an image of this guy?'

'I guess.' Billy's voice sounded strained and uncertain. 'Ma'am, I really don't want to talk no more. Not right now.'

Billy wiped his eyes with the back of his hand. It was plain that he'd had enough. The sheriff's eyes met mine, and I said to Billy, 'Sure.'

The sheriff added, 'We'll talk again, Billy. Get some rest first, you hear?'

'I'll try.'

I prepared to leave. 'Thanks for your help, Billy. I know it's been a difficult time, but how about we have the artist come see you later today, after you rest?'

'Yes, ma'am.'

A moment later the sheriff crossed to the door and summoned the nurse and we filed out of the room.

26

'So, why did you transfer to Washington? Promo?'

I tossed the question at Cooper as he drove me back to DC in a green Ford Taurus from the car pool. Mack Underwood had remained at the hospital and would contact us if we got an E-fit from Billy Adams. We were on Interstate 95, half an hour from the District, and for the last thirty minutes we'd talked about nothing except the cavern murders, and I figured it was time to change the subject.

'The truth is I didn't want to move to DC, but that's another story,' he answered.

Before I could reply my cell phone beeped. A message symbol had popped up on screen. 'I need to check this,' I said.

'No problem. Work away.'

I hit the call button for the message service and put the phone to my ear. '*Miss Moran, this is Lucius Clay. I wonder if you could call me as soon as possible, please.*'

That took me by surprise. I wondered what the Greensville warden wanted.

'Problems?' Cooper asked.

I shook my head. 'Just a call I've got to make later. By the way, I didn't mean to stick my nose into your private life.'

Cooper answered with a smile. 'I didn't think you were. Only natural you'd like to know about someone new on the team.'

I had to admit his smile was attractive. I noticed that he had a boxer's scarred knuckles and figured he was able to handle himself. Now that I looked more closely at his face I saw that his nose had once been broken: there was a tiny ridge midway along where the shattered bone hadn't set properly. But it gave him a kind of rugged charm. 'Lou tells me he and your dad go way back.'

Cooper nodded. 'They grew up together, stayed lifelong friends. Lou spent so much time in our house I used to think I had three parents.'

'You two are that close?'

Cooper said, 'Sorta. I guess you could say we're friends. Lou's like an uncle. He's a good-hearted guy under that titanium exterior.'

I know what you mean. 'He pull any strings for you to transfer to DC?'

Cooper looked offended. 'I wouldn't have that, and it's not Lou's style either. You work on your own merits, which is how it should be.'

'So why *did* you transfer to DC? To help your promotion prospects?'

'No, that wasn't the reason,' Cooper said. He didn't offer to explain and fell silent as he stared out of the window, and we continued the ride in edgy silence.

I thought: *He's got a bee up him about something.* Somehow I didn't believe him about the promo. Minutes later we hit the District, the wedding-cake Capitol building straight ahead, and Cooper said, 'Lou told me you worked the Gamal case. I remembered your face from the media briefings and the newspaper reports at the time.'

'I'm flattered. My one shot at fame, but then I guess it was a pretty public case.'

'For a long time it was *the* case. Lou also told me that you and David Bryce were engaged.'

'We were due to get married the week after he and Megan were murdered,' I answered. 'Is that all Lou told you?'

'I guess there might have been a little more.'

I glanced at him and said, 'It's OK, Cooper, you can tell me.'

Cooper spoke reluctantly. 'He said that Gamal took it personally and murdered them because you were getting too close to catching him. He wanted both to taunt you and repay you for trying to hunt him down. I'm sorry, their deaths must have been really tough on you.'

You've no idea, I wanted to say. And I wondered whether Lou had told him about Gamal's claim to have been innocent of their deaths. 'Lou seems to have told you a lot.'

We entered Judiciary Square and Cooper eased on the brakes. The Ford screeched as we nosed down into the underground parking lot. Cooper said, 'I'm pretty sure it was well intentioned.'

I didn't know whether I felt irked or not that Lou had told Cooper so much about me, but something about it rankled. 'Just like when you butted in during Billy's interrogation.'

'What do you mean?' Cooper asked.

I said firmly, 'You did well to get Billy to open up and talk some more, but in any future interrogation or interview we're doing I'd appreciate it if you waited until I gave you the nod to jump in.'

Cooper fell silent, as if he disliked the rebuke, then nodded ahead as we cruised through the parking lot. 'Do I need your permission to find a parking space, too, Agent Moran, or can I just go ahead and find one all by myself?'

'There's no need to be smart, Cooper.'

'Is that what you call it when I use my initiative?'

I didn't get a chance to reply because just as Cooper pulled into a free space my phone buzzed. This time it was Armando Diaz. 'Kate, how's my favourite Bureau chick? Been looking for you, babe.'

Being a Latino, *every* FBI female employee was Armando's favourite Bureau chick. 'I'm just pulling into the basement pool. What's up, Armando?'

'I think I may have an ID on one of the victims.'

'That was quick.'

'It helps if you're a genius, babe.'

'What have you got?'

'Meet me in the lab in five minutes. I think maybe we just got lucky, big time.'

27

'Look closely,' Diaz said.

We were in the basement lab, Diaz, Cooper and me. A couple of techs wearing white lab coats were working away at their own counters and paying us no attention. 'I don't see anything,' I replied, staring down the barrel lens of an electron microscope.

'Here, let me show you how to adjust the focus.' Diaz adjusted a knob and suddenly I was looking at a series of faintly distinguishable numbers. The markings were on a ticket stub of some kind. The stub was scorched as hell, and it seemed impossible to tell its original colour, but under the electron microscope the dim line of inked numbers it contained had come into view.

'You see the figures now?' Diaz asked.

'Yeah, I see them.'

'Most of the ticket stub is cinder and totally unreadable. We were lucky to get this much by using a chemical treatment.'

I could just make out the letter and digits: they looked to me like M442379.

'What's the ticket for?'

Diaz said, 'I figure dry cleaning. It was pinned inside the girl's skirt. You know the way they pin those stubs inside clothes and sometimes forget to remove them? I figure we may be able to match the numbers to a dry cleaning outlet.'

I took my eye from the scope viewer to let Cooper take a peek, and offered Diaz a sceptical look. Apart from being a good-looker he was occasionally a snappy dresser, when he wasn't wearing skin-tight Speedo: today for a change he wore crisp khaki chinos, a white button-down shirt and a gold silk tie. 'How often do you get your clothes dry-cleaned, Armando?'

He grinned. 'Not that often. It's expensive. My wife does most of my cleaning.'

'You've got a *wife*? I never knew.'

Diaz grinned. 'Just kidding. You getting jealous, babe? I call her my wife. She's my live-in of the moment. But to tell the truth, it ain't working out. I figure I'm going to have to start interviewing for the post again.'

'Whatever. Have you got any idea how many dry-cleaning stores there are in the District?'

'I'd figure it must be in the hundreds.'

'*Many* hundreds. Maybe it even gets into the thousands when you include the Tri-state. We're talking about an area that's home to hundreds of thousands – no, make that millions – of military personnel, uniformed government employees, Bureau employees, dress-conscious politicians and lobbyists and lawyers, not to mention the many other millions of office workers. If DC isn't the dry-cleaning capital of America, then it's got to be up there near the top, along with New York and LA.'

Diaz shrugged. 'OK, but at least we've got *something*, Kate. If we can match this ticket number to a dry-cleaning establishment, then we may be able to get a customer name.'

'I guess I was hoping for more,' I admitted. 'And sooner. Finding a match could take us for ever.'

Diaz gave an exaggerated shrug. 'OK, so I was overly optimistic. I should have said I'm *hoping* this may give us a lead. But I've had two cases in the past three years where dry-cleaning stubs helped identify murder victims. Granted, the stubs weren't as burnt as this one, but we've got a lead, Kate, and that's what's important. And besides, I still got a list of contacts in the dry-cleaning business from the last cases that I can call on and pick their brains. You say you hoped for something sooner.' Diaz winked and offered me a smile. 'For you, I'll work on it all night if I have to. Want to join me?'

Cooper looked up from the microscope, raised an eye at me and smiled when he heard Diaz's offer.

'It's good of you to tempt me but I'm too busy, Armando,' I

answered. He was such a ladies' man I couldn't help but smile. I was also tempted to remind him that the ticket stub might have remained for years on the victim's clothes. In that case, we had very little hope of ever finding its owner. Another thing, a lot of dry cleaners used the same kind of ticket books. And we were only assuming the dry cleaners would be situated in the Tri-state area – in fact it could be anywhere in the country. *I'll need a lot more than the remains of a ticket stub to get me excited.*

I mentioned all this to Diaz. 'Did you find anything else worthwhile?'

'No prints on the crucifix, apparently, but some dark cloth fibres under the girl's nails. They may be relevant, they may not. But it's still early days. That's about it so far.'

'What about prints from the bodies?' Cooper asked.

Diaz said, 'We're working on it. I like to use a soap detergent to soften the charred skin and try and get a print, but my gut feeling is the victims' hands are too badly burned to lift prints.'

No fingerprints meant that all we could hope for was that the couple turned up on a missing-persons list and could be matched by DNA. *More hard work.*

I made a mental note to check the recent missing-persons lists for myself.

'That everything or you want to depress me some more?'

'Yeah, one more thing.' Diaz started to rifle through a bunch of papers on his desk until he found a slip of paper on which he'd written a note. 'Mack Underwood called fifteen minutes ago to say he'd finished at the mine shaft. We discussed the victims' time of death and he confirmed that according to the local weather channel it stopped snowing in the region about two days before our witness Billy Adams found the bodies. Mack said to pass you on a message.'

'What?'

'He says they still haven't found a damned single footprint apart from Billy's. He said to tell you that whoever else went into that cave, they must have floated in and out of there on thin air.'

*　　*　　*

It was almost 6 p.m. and I sat in the canteen with Cooper, sipping a weak café latte and staring at the rain-drenched glass.

'You look bothered,' Cooper said quietly, stirring his coffee.

'Wouldn't you be?' I offered. 'Not a single damned footprint found. It doesn't make sense.'

'The perp could have brushed the snow afterwards, or burned off any footprints,' Cooper suggested. 'That's not beyond the bounds of possibility.'

'True, but that would have taken a lot of time and effort. A lot of pre-planning and preparation. And brushing would probably have left bristles or bristle marks, but CS didn't find any.'

'Have you got any other suggestions that might make better sense, Agent Moran?'

I got the feeling Cooper was hitting the ball back at me. I put down my cup and stared across at him. 'Not right now. You didn't have much to say in the lab.'

'I thought you liked me to stay quiet.'

Touché. 'I hear you and Stone worked together in New York?'

Cooper nodded. 'Three years. We partnered for a year.'

'You two get on OK?'

'Pretty well. Stone's a good investigator. Resolute, determined. Kind of like a Dobermann, he never lets go.'

'It sounds like you admire him?'

'I give credit where credit is due.'

'I guess you two must have been buddies?'

Cooper glanced at the wall clock, finished his coffee and stood, leaving the question unanswered. 'I've got to go. I guess I'll see you in the morning.'

With casual ease, he draped his overcoat over his shoulder and headed for the door. 'And don't worry, Agent Moran, I'll do my best not to have a late night.'

28

It was raining hard and after seven that evening when I finally arrived home. On the drive to Angel Bay it looked like there was a storm brewing, the clouds foaming black, the sky so dark it appeared as if the world could end at any minute. When I stopped off at a gas station and bought some groceries the icy rain had already started with a rumble of thunder, and it was still pelting down when I pulled into the driveway and ran up to the cottage.

For the first time in a week I actually felt hunger pangs. I looked as if I'd lost about ten pounds, no bad thing, but my blood sugar was low and my energy levels felt zapped. I popped a Zesto Chicken Maryland dinner into the microwave and checked my phone messages.

There was another call from Lucius Clay asking me to phone his office. I still hadn't got round to calling him back yet. Clay hadn't left his home number so I phoned the Greensville Correctional Centre and explained who I was. The reception desk told me the warden had gone home for the evening.

I figured it would be a waste of time asking for his home number so I left a message. 'Tell the warden that Kate Moran returned his call and she'll call him again tomorrow.'

'Yes, ma'am. Good evening, ma'am.'

I put down the phone and pulled my dinner out of the microwave. The news about the lack of footprints still bothered me, big time. Whoever the perp was they had to have removed their foot marks *somehow*. Cooper had a point: what if they brushed away the snow, or used some method to melt the prints? But that would have taken time, and immense effort, and it was hard to believe they wouldn't have left *some* trace in their wake. I had barely got the first forkful of chicken into my mouth when the phone rang. I didn't recognise the cell phone number that appeared on the handset but I picked up. 'Miss Moran? It's Lucius Clay.'

I was surprised to hear back from Clay so soon. 'I just called the prison a couple of minutes ago and they told me you'd left your office for the day. Did they give you my message?'

'No, Miss Moran. I was simply calling again on the off-chance that I'd find you in. I tried your cell earlier.'

'Yes, I got your call. Is it that urgent, Warden?'

'Well, I wonder if we could meet and talk, Miss Moran?'

I heard the hesitation in Clay's voice. 'If it's about the Gamal incident, my shoulder's on the mend.'

'I'm relieved to hear that, but actually this is about something else.'

I couldn't imagine what else Clay might want to talk about. 'What is it?'

'I'd really rather meet, if you don't mind.'

'When?'

'Would tonight be inconvenient?'

I was surprised by the warden's sense of urgency and the fact that he sounded almost secretive. 'I'm pretty tired, Mr Clay. Won't it keep until tomorrow?'

'Tomorrow I fly to New York early for an important conference. To be honest, I'm passing near enough to your neighbourhood tonight. I have a bridge game to go to, and I thought, well, maybe you were free?'

How does the warden know where I live? And how does he know my home number? I ignored both questions for now. 'What time's your bridge game?'

'Nine. There's a diner called Jasper Johnson's about five miles from where you live.'

'I know it.'

'I could meet you there about eight. The coffee's mediocre, but I think I can promise you that the chocolate pecan pie is worth the drive.'

'I'll try to make it for eight. But can't you just tell me what it's about?'

'I prefer to talk when I see you, Miss Moran. Let me give you my cell phone number in case you're delayed.'

29

I was so preoccupied by the warden's call I couldn't finish eating my chicken dinner. What the hell did he want to talk about and why was he so secretive? And I couldn't relax – my head was in a muddle and began to thump with a blinding headache. I took two Tylenol, chipped off some ice from the freezer compartment. I wrapped the ice chips in a clear plastic bag, went up to my bedroom and lay on my bed with the freezing-cold bag placed against my forehead. As I lay there, iced water dripping on to the pillow, I noticed the cardboard box jutting out from under the bed.

After David and Megan had been buried, I couldn't bring myself to throw out all their belongings so I had kept some of their photographs and a few of their personal things stored in the cardboard box. I sat up, strapped the ice bag in a towel, pulled out the box and lifted the lid. On top of a stash of leather photographic wallets was a portable CD player and a collection of CDs that Megan had loved – David had bought the player for her on a business trip we'd taken to Montreal one summer. Her favourite Slipknot CD was still in the player. I picked it up, slid in some fresh batteries from the box and flicked it on.

It was rock, sung by a bunch of wacky guys wearing evil-looking masks, not to my liking or David's, but it was something Megan's peers were into and I'd reckoned it just a teenage rite of passage. As the music played, I felt tears slide down my face, remembering it blasting from Megan's room when she had her teenage friends sleep over. I knew I was only torturing myself so I turned off the CD.

There were still days when I was overcome by a painful urge

to look through the photographs and play Megan's music. *Why do I persist with such torment?* I recognised that the simple answer was that sometimes we just *need* to weep for the loved ones we've lost – need to keep reminding ourselves that we're human and that death touches us to our marrow. This was one of those moments.

But what made the torment worse was Stone's cruel taunt. '*I'll make it my business to nail you on two counts of murder.*'

Stone despised me, that much was obvious. But what made him dangerous was the fact that he actually *believed* I was guilty of a double homicide. I'd heard the reasons for his suspicions whispered in the office: David leaving me the property and money in his will. The fact that there were certain minor inconsistencies in the murders of David and Megan compared to the other Gamal murder scenes. The fact that I had no alibi for three hours on the day they were killed because I'd been overcome with exhaustion and pulled in off the highway to sleep. And there was another reason.

Stone had overheard me threaten to kill David.

30

David and I had pretty much planned our wedding down to the last detail: our marriage was meant to be a simple affair in the local church with a few close friends invited to dinner afterwards at the Blue Peppercorn Restaurant, one of our favourites, not glitzy by any means but the food was excellent – their steaks and fish dishes were to die for.

The hectic weeks leading up to a wedding are fraught with danger: tempers get shortened, nerves are frayed, there are a million last-minute details to arrange, and as my mother used to say: *'People can get killed pre-nup.'* What's meant to be an enjoyable time can sometimes turn into a nightmare. And that weekend it did.

After I'd had a tiring five days of finalising a whole long list of preparations and organising a mock run-through at the church, David and a bunch of his friends went on a last-minute stag night to New York. The trip didn't bother me in the least – I was happy that David and his buddies were going to have a blast together, and I *trusted* him. Some of the guys had planned a trip to a New York lap-dancing club and that was OK too – David had told me about it and it didn't niggle me either, all part of the ritual.

What didn't help was that by early Monday morning David hadn't returned on his scheduled flight – I'd even driven to the airport to meet him. But he'd had a few drinks too many the night before – not like David, but then this *was* his stag and it was excusable – then there was fog at La Guardia, and he and his pals had to reschedule their flights for later that evening.

Meanwhile, I was saddled with trying to deal alone with florists;

the pastor; a moody lady soprano who threw a hissy fit about the songs we wanted her to sing at the wedding, saying they weren't her 'style', even at five hundred bucks for the gig; the picky, gay restaurant manager who was a perfectionist and wanted to go over the menus down to the last detail, God bless him; and poor Megan, who'd got her period.

All Monday morning I was running around like I was high on crack, and when I made it to the office in the afternoon David called me to say he couldn't get a flight until late that evening and apologised that I'd had to hold the fort.

'Well, did you have a good time, sweetheart?' I teased.

'Do I have to tell?' David laughed.

'You can tell me about the lap dancers for a start.'

'The blonde or the brunette?'

That niggled a *little*. 'Both. Don't tell me, you had one on each knee?'

David ribbed me. 'Actually, it was one at a time, and I guess the brunette kind of took my fancy.'

I knew he was only kidding – I trusted David implicitly – but I replied in a serious voice, 'If you slept with her I'll kill you!'

David laughed. 'You know me better than that. It was all harmless fun. Hey, I've got to go, looks like we're on an earlier flight after all. Be good, see you soon, sweetheart.'

Before I had a chance to say goodbye David was gone, and as I put down the phone I looked up and saw Vance Stone standing in my doorway. He had a thick report in his hand. He offered me a tight smile. 'Kill who, Moran?'

I smiled tightly in return. 'A joke. I was talking to my fiancé. Is that report for me?'

'Yeah. Enjoy. It's only two hundred pages long.' He grinned. 'Maybe you can read it on your honeymoon night, if you don't kill your fiancé meantime?'

Stone turned and left my office. A week later, David and Megan were dead. I remember getting weird looks from Stone even after Gamal was caught and charged. That phone conversation he'd interrupted had obviously stuck in his mind. My stupid threat –

a throwaway remark – could have been taken out of context. On its own it didn't mean much, but given the fact of my inheritance from David's will, the inconsistencies in his murder and my missing three hours, I could grudgingly understand how a shrewd investigator like Stone might have niggling qualms about my credibility. But every one of his colleagues knew he was consumed by jealousy, and I didn't know of one who entertained his doubts.

Now, I emptied the bag of ice chips into the sink. My headache had started to ease but it hadn't gone away. I went to find a mirror and my make-up bag, then left the house and climbed into my Bronco. Twenty minutes later I pulled up outside Jasper Johnson's, a burger-and-fries diner next to an Amoco gas station. Despite recommending the pecan pie, the warden didn't strike me as the kind of guy who might be a regular. Which was just as well, because the dozen or so diners in Jasper Johnson's that evening mostly looked like they might have been one-time inmates at Greensville.

Lucius Clay was already nursing a coffee and a slice of chocolate pecan when I arrived. As I approached his booth he wiped his mouth with a napkin before he stood and politely shook my hand. 'It's good of you to see me at such short notice, Miss Moran. My apologies for dragging you out so late.'

'So tell me why I'm here.' At the counter sat a couple of truck drivers with tattooed arms, but the tables around us were all empty. The warden looked out of place in a greasy diner – he wore a polka-dot bow tie and pale blue shirt, a tweed jacket and Farah slacks.

'We'll get to that in a second,' Clay replied, as I slipped into the booth. His face looked washed out. A woollen winter coat and a black baseball hat lay on the seat beside him. 'I live near Ashland and usually drive close to this neck of the woods for my weekly bridge game, so I thought it might be convenient for us both. I'm sorry if I put you out.'

'You didn't. I guess you've got to be a fanatical bridge player to come all this way for a game?'

Clay smiled. 'It's in the blood, I'm afraid. My father was a club captain. He used to say that the nice thing about bridge is that it's the only card game that actually allows a player to seem half respectable. Coffee, some pie?'

'Coffee is fine.'

Clay raised a finger to attract a waitress, and when she had filled my cup and left his face became serious. 'Let me tell you why I called you, Miss Moran. But first, I think I should confess that I find this quite a bizarre situation.'

'Bizarre in what way?'

Clay's eyebrows knitted in a painful expression. 'I suppose because I find myself acting as a messenger for a dead person.'

I frowned. 'I don't follow.'

'On the evening Gamal was executed, something very strange happened.'

'You don't have to remind me, I was there.'

Clay shook his head, his face drawn. 'I didn't mean the incident in the interview room. It was something else, Miss Moran.'

That got my attention and I stared back at Clay. 'I'm listening.'

'Right before we escorted Gamal into the execution chamber, he whispered something to me. I thought you should know what he said.'

I shuddered as I gave the warden my full attention. 'What did he say?'

'Gamal's exact words were: "Tell her from me that I meant what I said. That I'm coming back. Make sure she knows that. It's important.'

I felt a chill go through me and I turned away, towards the traffic passing the diner's window. It seemed there was no end to Gamal in my life. Despite his death his presence still hadn't gone away. *Will it ever?* I felt the warden put a hand on mine and I turned back.

Clay said, 'It's obvious that Gamal bore a powerful hatred for you, Miss Moran. And I'm truly sorry if I've upset you by what I've disclosed, but I really thought you'd want to know.' He hesitated before he spoke again. 'I figured your nerves were frayed enough after the execution and by the other events of that night, so I thought it best to wait a little while to tell you. I did call your office a few days later but they informed me you were on leave.'

'I had some time off.'

'I'm curious, Miss Moran. There seemed to be some significance in Gamal's words when he spoke them. Do you know what he meant?'

I was tempted to tell the warden what Gamal had said to me, but I resisted. 'No, but I'm inclined to think they're just the desperate mutterings of a deranged man.'

Clay frowned, and looked as if he was about to pursue his question further, but then suddenly he changed his mind and took out his wallet to pay the bill. 'And now, I better say goodnight, Miss Moran. I don't want to miss my game or detain you any longer.'

'How did you know where I live, Warden?'

I saw Clay glance at my engagement ring before he said, 'Would it surprise you to know that I knew David Bryce's parents? I'd often play bridge with them at Manor Brook, but that was many years ago, before the building went to ruin. It was a magnificent old house back then, before David's folks died. But it had such a lot of tragedy associated with it I used to wonder if the place was blighted.'

'What do you mean?' I asked.

'There were David and Megan's deaths, of course, and the death of David's brother, Patrick.' Clay lowered his voice. 'And some years before he died Patrick faced a serious accusation of attempted sexual assault. Or did you know?'

'Yes, I knew.'

Clay said, 'My own son and Patrick were in the same year at Virginia State University. What a pity his life had such a terrible outcome.'

I had met David's older brother Patrick only once. He'd been a brilliant young student who'd suffered from serious bouts of depression all his adult life. As brothers they had been close, and

David had often visited him at Bellevue Hospital, where Patrick was a long-term patient in the psychiatric wing. But six months after David and Megan's murders Patrick had been so depressed he left Bellevue, walked down to the Potomac and drowned himself, his body dragged out to sea by the powerful river. I'd hardly known Patrick, and his suicide was another tragedy that had barely added to my anguish. And I'd been so grief stricken that I'd left it to Lou and Stone to break the news to him about the deaths of his brother and niece. 'David told me about the case of assault against his brother. But I got the feeling it was kept private. You must have been a close family friend to know about the accusation, Warden?'

Clay cleared his throat. 'Reasonably close.'

'One more question. Did Gamal say anything else?'

'Nothing.' Clay's face tightened, and for some strange reason I got the feeling he was uncomfortable. Was it my imagination, or did the warden look furtive? *Why do I get the feeling there's something he's not telling me?*

He avoided my gaze, glanced at his watch and picked up his coat and hat.

'I'm sorry, I really better be going, Miss Moran.'

'I forgot to ask how you got my home number.'

Clay appeared to have been caught off guard for a second, and then he said calmly, 'Didn't you leave it with the reception desk at Greensville?'

Did I? I could have, but I didn't recall. 'I guess I must have done.'

Clay stood and pulled on his coat. 'If you don't mind me saying so, Miss Moran, you look exhausted. You should get some sleep.'

'I've been out since six a.m., working a case.'

The warden tugged on his cap. 'Really? Anything interesting?'

I shook my head, not saying what I thought: *Warden, you've got no idea.*

31

The Disciple had been busy all morning at the shopping mall. By noon he had bought almost everything he needed for his trip, the suitcase, the clothes – lots of clothes because he was going to need plenty more disguises – and then he'd gone to a Superpharm and bought the other stuff he required: the packs of hair dye, the spectacles, five different pairs of sunglasses, the electric razor and the Vidal Sassoon personal grooming kit, and some groceries. The wigs and the make-up he'd already bought. He'd spent a small fortune. He dumped the bags in his car and drove back to the apartment in Alexandria.

He laid all his purchases out on the bed, including the most important of all: his much-needed weapons. Most people thought of guns and knives as being the ideal tools of death, but he was faced with a major problem – he intended to travel internationally by air and security these days was as tight as a frog's ass.

To counter that problem he used a slim, three-inch-long 26-gauge insulin syringe, as used by diabetics, who were allowed to carry their hypodermics and drugs on board. But the Disciple had drained the insulin vials and replaced them with benzo. He also needed another weapon – one that would not set off the airport metal detectors – and he had the perfect choice. It was ideal for killing and undetectable.

He took a long brown paper bag from his purchases and tipped out the contents. Eight slender, grey plastic knitting needles. Plastic wouldn't set off the metal detectors and he could insert the thin needles along the inside of his carry-case, replacing the wire formers that shaped his bag. That way they would be undetectable.

He would purchase the assortment of butcher's knives he needed when he reached each of his foreign destinations, but he didn't like ever being unarmed, anywhere. The needles were his back-up. He grinned as he picked up a heavy grocery bag, removed a yellow watermelon and laid the luscious ripe fruit on the bed.

He gripped one of the knitting needles, raised it above his head and stabbed the fruit. The needle slipped right through the melon's hard rind and came out the other side with barely any effort. The melon could just as easily have been a human heart. The needle was as sharp as a stiletto knife.

Perfect.

Next, he went into the bathroom and opened his washbag and removed the hypodermic and the two vials of Botox. He inserted the thin metal tip of the hypodermic into one of the vials, sucked out the colourless liquid and gripped a puckered fold of his forehead flesh.

Ouch.

He injected the shots at intervals, dabbing the pinpricks of blood away with a wad of cotton wool, and then worked on the skin at the sides of his eyes and the wrinkle creases in his cheeks. All part of his disguise.

He was done within ten minutes and looked at himself in the bathroom mirror. Wonderful stuff, Botox. By the time he flew out of the country, his forehead frown lines would be gone, his crow's-feet vanished and the creases in his jowls would mostly have disappeared. He'd have knocked close to ten years off his appearance, and he'd look like a new man.

Two hours later he headed out to the travel agent's in Arlington. He hated booking over the Net: there was nothing like the personal touch.

'Good evening, sir, how may I help you?'

The blonde young woman behind the counter had been busy serving someone, but when she came free she offered him a chair and he sat. 'I'd like to book a return ticket to Istanbul. With at least a two day stopover in Paris.'

'You want to fly from Baltimore?'

'If possible.'

The blonde tapped her computer. 'There may only be a connect from New York, JFK.'

'That would be fine.'

The blonde woman smiled enthusiastically. 'Istanbul, *wow*, that sounds exotic.'

'It's a truly incredible city. Very Byzantine, full of history and intrigue,' the Disciple enthused, his jaws still aching from the injections.

'Are you travelling on business or pleasure?'

The Disciple found it an effort to offer the blonde even a tiny smile. 'I think you could say both.'

She consulted her screen. 'When were you thinking of travelling?'

'Any time within the next couple of days would be perfect,' the Disciple replied.

The blonde looked up from her computer. 'Hey, you're in luck. I see there's an Air France combo from New York, for sixteen hundred bucks. It's a pretty good deal, flying business class, and allows you to make a stopover in Paris on your way to Istanbul. There are plenty of seats available and you could even fly tonight if you want. What do you think?'

The Disciple's face felt tight as a drum but there was no mistaking the gleam in his eyes. 'I think that sounds absolutely perfect.'

32

Angel Bay, Virginia

It was way past midnight when I lifted the front door latch. Hunger pangs gnawed at my stomach since my dinner had been interrupted, but it was too late to eat. Besides, my mind was plagued by the warden's words.

I knew I'd have difficulty sleeping and I hated taking pills of any kind, but tonight I took half an Ambien and swallowed the broken white capsule with a glass of water. I rarely used the Ambien, except if I'd been working erratic shifts or had major difficulty sleeping. It was supposed to kick in after ten minutes but sometimes it took longer, so I made a mug of steaming cocoa and took it up to my bedroom.

Something else niggled at me and I didn't know why. Lucius Clay had suggested I'd left my phone number when I'd called the prison, but the more I thought about it the more certain I was I hadn't done so. *Maybe I'm just too tired to remember?*

But I was convinced that he was hiding something from me and that my radar had picked up on it. He seemed uncomfortable talking about the deaths of David and Megan and Patrick. Why? What had he got to hide? I fretted over the questions for a while and then I let them go in frustration. *What if it's all my own imagination and I'm being paranoid?*

The photographs belonging to David and myself, and Megan's CD player, still lay on my bed, so I stashed them away in their box before I undressed, changed into my nightrobe and took off my engagement ring and placed it on the nightstand. I set my alarm for 7 a.m., finished my cocoa and turned off the light, then

I opened the window. I lay on my bed in the darkness and stared out at the lights on the bay, waiting for the Ambien to work.

The view was always spectacular, and I loved to wake in the morning with the sun streaming in through the bedroom window, especially when there was a cool breeze blowing in off the water. Tonight the sky was clear and starry, the water cold and calm. Gradually, I started to feel drowsy and the bay shore lights started to blur. As I stared sleepily out at the moonlit night, I thought about all the evenings on which David and I had shared the same view as we lay here on this bed. I remembered waking early some mornings and hearing the shrill sound of the wild geese passing overhead as we lay entwined in each other's arms.

'Don't you love that sound?' David would always say.

I grew to love it too because it reminded me of the peace I felt lying next to him. I remembered the comfort of David hugging me, the sometimes passionate, sometimes erotic, sometimes tender sex. I remembered the disagreements, the impassioned arguments, the jokes we shared, for it was a vivacious relationship. Mostly it was our future together that we talked about, and the memories of those times suddenly made me sad. But what I most remembered was that David always made me feel loved and fulfilled, *and* he made me laugh.

I have a theory that none of us escapes our share of unhappiness in this life. Either we suffer a lousy childhood, or crappy teens, or a tortuous adult life – but one way or another we always have to receive our quota of human pain. OK, so I'd had an imperfect childhood, and like most I'd survived. But when I met David, all my desires and hopes were answered – he was warm and kind, humorous and affectionate, and not afraid to show his feelings in public. All the things I'd longed for in a partner as I grew up.

There was only one memory that was kind of strange: I remembered the night he had given me the engagement ring. We had driven out to Virginia for the weekend and stayed in a rambling, romantic old B&B that had once been a plantation home. After a steak dinner cooked by the chef-host we'd gone for a walk in the grounds. It was a warm spring night, the sky clear, and David pulled me to him and kissed me and said, 'I've got something for you.'

I giggled because I'd had two glasses of wine and felt giddy. 'Let me guess?'

He smiled and showed me the ring. 'I'm being serious.'

I was stunned when he slipped the diamond-and-white-gold ring on my finger, and I admired the stones in the moonlight. 'I . . . I don't know what to say.'

'Just promise me one thing,' David said seriously.

'What?'

He put a hand to my face. 'If we ever part for whatever reason, just remember not to keep the ring. It's bad luck when a relationship's moved on, or didn't you know that?'

I was surprised by his words and I remember thinking: *David, what a strange thing to say*. 'You sound superstitious.'

'You want to hear a secret?' David said. 'Years ago my mom told me that after she and my father got engaged they began to argue a lot. He started to show his true colours and became possessive and domineering. They even broke up for a while, but she never gave him back his ring. Then he started calling on her again. Eventually he wheedled his way into her life and they married. But whenever she had a drink too many mom used to say that she came to regret that decision. She regretted not throwing away her ring and moving on with her life. I guess what I'm really trying to say is that if it goes wrong between us, or for some reason we part, don't be afraid to burn your bridges.'

I shook my head. 'I don't think it'll be like that with us. But if you want, I promise.'

Looking back, I often wondered whether David had had some kind of premonition that night. The way that sometimes it seems as if a window opens and we can see into our future.

As I dwelt on these thoughts the Ambien started to kick in, my eyelids began to flicker and I felt as if I was being sucked into a narcotic limbo. My brain became putty, but as I crumpled into a deep sleep I heard the telephone ringing on my nightstand. I *think* I forced myself to come awake, because what happened next had a dream-like quality. I fumbled for the receiver and put it to my ear. 'Hello?'

All I heard in reply was a stony silence.

'Hello?' I repeated.

No reply. I began to wonder whether the line had gone dead, or whether I had *dreamt* that the phone rang. 'Who's there?' I asked.

Silence. But seconds later I heard music. Very faint, very distant, but *definitely* music. Then it grew in volume. I recognised Megan's music and my body felt like ice.

It was Slipknot's 'Circle'.

It couldn't have played for more than five seconds and then the music faded and the line went dead. I felt numb, and a cold shiver rippled through my body. Had I *imagined* the music and the call? I was certain I'd heard both, but at that moment I was so drugged and overcome by exhaustion that I couldn't even say whether I was awake or asleep.

Suddenly it felt as if a giant hand were pressing down on me, smothering me, forcing me under a big black wave. I fought to stay awake but lost – the narcotic finally took hold and I was swallowed up in the depths of a powerful darkness.

33

I woke the next morning feeling groggy. The Ambien had worked its magic but I felt as if I was hung-over. So I climbed out of bed, ran the shower and put my head under a jet of ice-cold water.

And that's when it hit me. *The phone call.*

Had it really happened? Had I really heard the Slipknot music? I was so confused, I felt distressed. Maybe the sleeping pill had made me hallucinate and imagine the call? I turned the cold water to hot as my mind desperately sought reasonable answers.

Why would someone play Megan's favourite music to me down the phone line? *It doesn't make any kind of sense.* As I soaped myself under the steaming water jets a thought hit me. I grabbed a couple of fresh towels, traipsed back into the bedroom and checked under the bed. The cardboard box was still where I'd left it – and Megan's CD player was still inside.

I thought: *What if someone called me last night but had a wrong number and simply didn't reply to my question – while at the same time the CD player somehow started to play of its own accord?*

That sounded far too complex and coincidental. But to my fevered mind, anything seemed possible. For the CD to play, it would have to be faulty. I decided to check it out. I flicked on the switch and the music played immediately. Then I turned off the switch, jiggled it up and down and shook the player, but the music didn't play. I figured there wasn't anything mechanically wrong with the switch. I turned to the phone. I picked up the handset and punched in *69, to give me the number and time of the last caller. The number that appeared was for Lucius Clay's cell phone, which he'd given me when he'd called me at 7.20 the previous evening to arrange our diner meeting. I checked in my jeans pocket and found the slip of paper I'd written it on. It was definitely the same number.

Now my mind was turning cartwheels. Someone had called me in the early hours and played music down the line but the phone gave no record of it. That didn't make sense. There had to be a rational explanation for what I'd experienced last night. *There just has to be.* Then it struck me who could help unravel the mystery. I finished towelling myself, dressed, put on a little make-up and body lotion, and brushed my hair.

The office was already busy when I got there just before eight. A couple of agents stood around drinking coffee but most of them were on their phones or tapping away on computer keyboards. I headed to my cubicle, hung up my coat then rummaged in my desk Filo for Sterling Burke's extension number.

He was a Bureau tech expert I'd worked with on several cases that had required a lot of trawling through phone records. Sterling was a kindly, eccentric guy close to retirement and had once hit on me for a date – I politely declined – and he sometimes bugged me by calling me 'darling' or 'honey'. But he *was* helpful, and a sweetheart.

'Hey,' a voice said, and I looked up and saw Cooper standing there. He was dressed casually in jeans and leather loafers, and wore a waist-length tan suede jacket. He threw me a smile. 'You always in this early?'

'Usually. So you made it in time?'

'Been here since seven.'

'You looking to get a mention in dispatches or need the over-time?'

Cooper came to sit beside me. 'I could say it's on account of dedication and commitment but the truth is I didn't sleep all that well. I spent most of the night thinking about the case.'

'I wish I could say the same but I slept like I'd been hit by a train. Come up with any ideas?' I asked.

'Not a single one, I'm sorry to say. Anything I can help with?'

Cooper sounded as if he was trying to be extra-friendly. Maybe he was being genuine, but I still didn't entirely trust him. I checked my watch. Sterling Burke ought to be at his desk by now and I was itching to call him. 'Maybe. Where's Stone?'

'Last time I saw him, he was headed down to the lab to see if they've made any more progress,' Cooper answered.

I grabbed my cell phone. 'Do me a favour and hold the fort. I'll be back in ten minutes.'

34

I headed down the hall to the ladies' restroom. The cubicles were empty and I punched in Sterling's number. I didn't want to phone him from my desk in case anyone overheard me. As the number rang out, I kept wondering whether I should tell Lou Raines and Cooper about my late-night call. Or would they think I was crazy? Then a husky voice came on the line.

'Technical. Sterling Burke speaking.'

'Sterling, it's Kate Moran.'

'Kate! How are you, honey?'

'OK. You sound hoarse.'

'Got a damned bad cold. Some of the sons of bitches I work with are trying to nudge me into going home to bed and keeping my germs to myself, but like I always say, it's good to share.'

'I need a favour, Sterling. This time it's kind of personal. I need to run something technical by you.'

'Sure. Shoot.' Sterling sniffled.

'I got a call this morning, not long after midnight. I was almost asleep when the phone rang, but when I picked up the receiver the line clicked dead. I checked the last incoming call by hitting star sixty-nine and it gave me a phone number and time for a call I'd got at 7.20 the previous evening, but gave no record of the post-midnight call. My question is this, could the phone company computers have missed recording the call, or could my phone be faulty?'

I heard Sterling blow his nose and sniffle again. There was a silence and I began to wonder whether he was mulling over the technical problem I'd just posed him when finally he said, 'Have you got a problem with nuisance calls, Kate? Is that what this is about?'

The guy was on the ball, I'd give him that. *How much should I tell him? Keep it to yourself for now*, I warned myself. 'I guess I can't be really certain. But I'd sure like to check out the one last night. And you're the expert.'

'So they tell me. Outgoing calls are no problem. We can confirm those easily because you're always billed for them. Incoming can be a little more complex and take time, as you know. But give me your landline number and the name of your service provider and I can check with their computer records.'

I gave him the details and Sterling said, 'OK, let me see what I can do. I'll give you a call back just as soon as I can. It shouldn't take too long.'

'Thanks, Sterling. Could you call me back on my cell?'

'No prob,' he said, and hung up.

I freshened up in the restroom then went and bought myself a coffee and a Kellogg's breakfast cereal bar from a vending machine down the hall. Shortly after I had munched the bar and finished my coffee, Sterling rang me back.

'I'm sorry, sweetheart, but there's definitely no record of a call to your landline from any number after midnight. In fact, the only call was from a cell phone at seven-twenty p.m. in the evening.'

Sterling recited the number and I recognised it as Lucius Clay's. It was the call he'd made to arrange our meeting. 'You're sure that was the last incoming call?'

'Proof positive. Computers may glitch, but they don't often lie. Your service provider experienced no technical problems that would have caused no number to be displayed. If someone called you post-midnight, their number would have been trapped.'

'Is there any other way a caller's number wouldn't show up on their computer records?'

'It's highly unlikely, Kate. And it has me puzzled. But if you really think you're having a problem with malicious calls and want to make a formal complaint to the phone company I can point you in the right direction and have someone contact you, no trouble at all. I'll personally see that it's taken care of, straight away.'

147

'That won't be necessary.'

'You're sure?'

'For now, but if I have a problem again I'll get back to you. Is there any other way that I could have got a call at home without the number showing up?'

Sterling sighed and thought about it. 'The only situation that I can think of where it could happen is if you have an internal extension. Then you're offline and out of the phone company's loop.'

I thought about that. The cottage had three extensions: in the bedroom, the living room and David's studio. Some internal phones have a different ring but my old one didn't: it had the same irritating high-pitched electronic ring for external and internal calls. The thought of someone being *inside* the house and calling me freaked me out. *Could it have happened, or did I really imagine the call?* I convinced myself it had to be my imagination or the hallucinogenic effect of the sleeping pill I'd taken. An intruder wouldn't enter a house just to make a freaky call and then leave. Besides, the house was locked. Even the studio was always left locked. 'Thanks a bunch, Sterling. I really appreciate it.'

Sterling said, 'Sure. But if it happens again you call me and we'll do something officially.'

'I'll do that,' I answered.

'Take care, honey. And any time you're free for a coffee give me a bell.'

When I returned to the office, my phone was ringing. I picked up. 'Moran.'

'Kate? It's Paul.'

'Paul who?'

'Don't be funny, Kate. It's me, your husband. Or do you forget that fast?'

I sighed. '*Ex*-husband. What do you want?'

'Is that any way to talk to the man you were once married to?'

I'd had a couple of calls from Paul in the last few months, and each time he'd worn me down talking about what a good marriage we'd had. *If it was that good, why did he leave?* He was still working in Met homicide. I'd heard from a female Met officer I knew that Suzanne had dropped her assault charge, but the rumour was that Paul had threatened her into doing so.

'What do you want, Paul?'

'I hear you've got a double homicide on your hands. A Devil's Disciple copycat. Sounds weird. Think you'll be able to solve it?'

When David and Megan were killed, Paul had called to offer me his condolences, but I had got the feeling that his offer wasn't entirely genuine. Sure enough, about a month after the funerals he'd actually had the neck to call me up and ask me out to dinner to try to rekindle our 'relationship', as he called it. Paul was fast becoming impossible, and spinning out of control. I knew he needed therapy but he was in denial. 'Who told you about the case?'

'Hey, you know the way word travels in this business. Don't forget I worked on the Disciple's double homicide in the District years back, before you Feds got involved.'

'Is that why you called, about the homicide?'

'No, I've got tickets for a jazz concert on Tuesday night. I thought you could do with a night out and might like to join me and then have dinner afterwards.'

I sighed. 'Paul, all I'd like is to be left alone to get on with my life. Could you do that for me? What part of "we're divorced" do you not understand?'

His voice flared with bitterness. 'Don't you have even an ounce of feeling for me? We were married for five years, for Christ sakes. We've known each other a long time.'

'Look, Paul, you're becoming obsessive. If you need someone to talk with, I can help find you a good therapist. But you know what they're going to tell you? The same as I'm telling you, that you have to leave me alone and move on with your life.'

I heard his anger flare again. 'You know, you're going to be sorry some day, Kate. Really fucking sorry you and me didn't get back together.'

'What's that supposed to mean? Is that some kind of threat?'

'Some day you'll know what it meant, and then it'll be too late.' Paul's phone clicked dead.

It was obvious Paul was unhappy, but I didn't have time to reflect on his words because as I looked up Vance Stone walked into the office, deep in conversation with Cooper. Stone looked over at me with a smirk. 'Well, well, the dead arose and appeared to many.'

'I've been in since before eight, Stone.'

'Good for you.'

'I hear you two know each other, so there's no need for introductions,' I said.

Stone came over to join me. 'Sure, Coop and I used to work together.'

I noticed that Stone was clutching what looked like a lab report in his hand. 'What's that?' I asked.

He replied, 'Seems like you gave Diaz quite a challenge. He worked all through the night and managed to get a bead on the tag by getting a list of dry-cleaning requisite suppliers. He called a whole bunch of their sales reps and eventually found out that the batch of tags was sold to a store outside of DC.'

I felt my pulse race. 'That's good work.'

'Better than that,' said Cooper, 'the store's been open for business since seven-thirty and I just called and cross-referenced the tag. The owner says the skirt was picked up after being cleaned a month ago and the customer left a name, Fleist, a cell phone number and an address on the shop part of the tag.'

'What's the address?' My pulse was pounding.

Stone crumpled his paper cup and tossed it into the bin. 'A trailer park in Rockville. Let's get going, Moran.'

35

Ten minutes later we were heading north for 270. Cooper was in the passenger seat and I was in the back. 'Do we know exactly where we're going?' I asked.

Stone ignored me, but Cooper said, 'I checked with the Rockville police. The trailer park's outside of town, along Royston Avenue.'

I consulted the Tri-state map Cooper had handed me from the glove compartment and found Royston Avenue, just outside of Rockville. 'I guess if we keep on this route we should see it signposted.'

Stone sped out along the interstate. As I put aside the map my mind was on edge. Had I *really* received last night's call? *Maybe there was no call and I'm just going crazy?*

We made Rockville just after 10 a.m. and I gave Stone directions from the map. 'It should be coming up on the right.'

Sure enough, Royston Avenue appeared and Stone hung a right. It had started to rain, and I peered ahead through the drizzle and saw a trailer park packed with homes. A billboard said: FIRST CLASS FACILITIES AT BUDGET PRICES. The place didn't look first-class. It looked shabby. Inside the gate was a prefab hut that I guessed was the manager's office. Stone halted in front of it.

It was steaming hot when we opened the door and stepped inside, the windows fogged up and an electric air heater going full blast. A bulky, tough-looking guy with a bushy grey moustache and wearing a greasy baseball cap sat behind an office counter, polishing a silver trophy with a worn rag. He looked like an ageing biker, with a couple of tattoos on his beefy arms, and he cautiously assessed his three visitors. 'Howdy. Why do I get the feeling you folks ain't looking to rent a site?'

'You're right,' I told him, and showed my creds. 'FBI. You the manager?'

'Manager, handyman, rent collector, general dogsbody, you name it, that's me, the only guy who works here. Fact is, I consistently award myself employee of the month. I'm pretty proud of that. Name's Roy Jargo. What can I do for you?'

'Have you got anyone named Fleist staying here?'

Jargo's eyes narrowed with suspicion as he slowly got to his feet. 'There's a guy lives in a Suncruiser motor home near the end of the park. Goes by the name Otis Fleist.'

'Does he live alone?'

Jargo shook his head. 'No, with his daughter. Her name's Kimberly. At least, he said she was his daughter. But hey, these days you never know. The world's weird, or ain't you guys figured that out by now?'

'What age is the daughter?'

'Fourteen, fifteen, at a guess, maybe sixteen tops. Hey, what's this about? These folks in some kind of trouble with the Feds?'

'How long have the Fleists been here, Mr Jargo?' I asked.

''Bout three months.'

'You know where they're from?'

Jargo shook his head. 'No, I don't. I never asked and they never said. We keep paperwork to a minimum here. All we ask is that they pay their rent on time and don't cause no freakin' trouble.'

'Do the Fleists do that?'

'Yes, ma'am, so far.'

'What else can you tell me about them?'

'Ma'am, with respect, I don't know shit. I don't mean no offence, but that's just the way it is around here. Folks generally keep themselves to themselves and I don't get nosy. They could be building an H-bomb in their trailer and I wouldn't know about it.'

'But you'd know if there was anyone else living in their motor home apart from just Fleist and his daughter, wouldn't you, Roy?'

He shrugged. 'To tell the truth, I wouldn't. But I don't reckon there is. I reckon it's just Fleist and his girl. Why you ask?'

'When was the last time you saw them?'

'A few days ago, I reckon.'

Stone said, 'Anyone else by the same name living in the trailer park?'

'Fleist? Naw. Hey, you guys never told me what kind of trouble we're talking about here.'

'Do you have a spare key for the motor home?'

Roy Jargo shook his head at Stone. 'No, I don't. Some folks leave me a spare just in case, but some don't. And Fleist didn't.'

Stone said bullishly, 'Then you better find us a crowbar if you've got one.'

36

We walked to the end of the park and the manager pointed out the Suncruiser: a pale white-and-cream with a cherry-wood dado trim and an integrated awning. It looked a few years old. The windows appeared locked and the curtains were closed. Jargo said, 'Looks like there's no one home.'

Stone tried peering in through one of the curtained windows. 'When *exactly* was the last time you saw anyone in the motor home?'

Jargo thought about it and scratched his neck. 'Maybe four or five days ago. Can't say for certain. I can't watch every door. Got a busy social calendar.'

I tried the door handle but it was locked. So I rapped half a dozen times on the door while Cooper and Stone walked around the motor home, checking windows as they went. 'You're sure it was four or five days?' I asked Jargo.

'I reckon. But hey, I can't be a hundred per cent certain. Why?'

I tried pushing in the door but it felt rock solid. 'Did you see anyone other than the occupants enter or leave the motor home in the last few days? Or whenever?'

Jargo tugged at his beard. 'Don't believe I did. Hey, you folks ain't answering any of my questions.'

'I'll fill you in later. Any suspicious-looking characters hanging around the park recently?'

Jargo shrugged. 'That description covers pretty much half the folks living here.'

'Anyone who stood out? Or anyone new you didn't see before?'

'Nope, guess not.'

Cooper and Stone came back. 'The back door's locked,' Stone grunted. 'Same with the frigging windows.'

I banged on the door again. 'This is the FBI. If there's anyone in there, open up the door, please.'

No reply. I repeated the announcement and banged on the door twice more but got no response. I nodded to Cooper and Stone, took out my Glock and held it at the ready, and saw them do the same.

The manager looked worried. 'Hey, the fuck's going on here? I don't want no shooting in my park.'

'Mr Jargo, I've got some bad news. We're going to have to break down Fleist's door. You better go find that crowbar.'

Jargo was horrified and moved to stand in front of the door. 'Hey, now see here, who's going to pay for any damage? I could be liable.'

Stone forcibly moved him aside. 'Get out of the damned way,' he snarled. Jargo went to protest but Stone gave the door a savage kick. It didn't budge, so he lashed out again. This time there was a sound of splintering wood and the door hinges shattered. A final kick and Stone sent the door flying inwards. Then something happened none of us was expecting.

We all noticed the smell. *A sweet stench of rotting flesh.*

I put my hand over my mouth and turned to Cooper and Stone. They looked startled.

'Better not forget my manners – ladies first.' Stone sounded like he was mocking me as he covered his mouth.

Thanks. I moved into the Suncruiser, my gun at the ready, taking one cautious step at a time. I got another shock when I stepped inside the door. As my eyes flicked around the darkened home I noticed the dim outline of a figure lying on the bed. My heart raced as I swung my pistol round to aim. I inched my way forward, hoping that whoever the figure was they weren't armed and looking for a shoot-out. 'FBI,' I shouted. 'Get up off the bed and put your hands above your head!'

I reckoned that might be difficult in a low-ceilinged motor home, but the figure didn't attempt to move or reply, and the stench was suddenly so overpowering that I felt like throwing up. I squinted, but I could still hardly see. *Damn.* I was so wound up that it had never occurred to me to think of hitting the light switch. Stone was covering my back so I called over my shoulder, 'Give me some light here. Flick on the light or open the damned curtains.'

Stone hit the wall switch and a strip light flickered overhead, flooding the room with harsh neon. I blinked, blinded by the sudden burst, then opened my eyes again.

'*What the fuck . . . !*' mouthed Stone.

Cooper joined us, and now we could see the rotting corpse lying across the bed. It was a German shepherd dog, as dead as wood by the looks of it. The animal lay in a pool of dried blood, the smell so putrid that I had to cover my mouth with my sleeve. Stone and Cooper did the same.

'Smells like the mutt's been dead a couple of days.' Stone prodded the dog's carcass with the tip of his gun.

The animal's throat had been cut. Its black-and-tan coat was stained with congealed crimson and squadrons of flies buzzed around the wound. Now that I had some light, I looked around the motor home. It was a mess. Clothes lay tossed on the floor and unwashed dishes littered the kitchen sink. I saw no sign of any bloodied knife – I guessed a blade had been used to kill the German shepherd. In all probability whoever killed Fleist and his daughter killed the dog.

I turned to the kitchen area. On one of the shelves I noticed a photograph of a man. Then I saw another shot of him and a young woman: *Fleist and his daughter, Kimberly.* Neither of them looked very happy, especially the daughter, her sad face staring out at me. At the end of the room was a door that I figured led into the bathroom. I signalled for Cooper to check it out. His weapon at the ready, he cautiously approached the door, then wrenched it open, and I saw a toilet and shower area. 'It's an empty john,' Cooper called out.

I turned back as Stone put his weapon away, wrinkled his nose and studied the dead animal. 'Jeez, he's sure stinked up the place. Who's been a bad dog?'

I saw Stone smirk as he prodded the German shepherd with his shoe. 'I hate fucking shepherds. Give me a Dobermann any day, they're tougher.'

I fumbled for my cell phone. 'Anyone ever tell you that you're a sick bastard, Stone?'

'Yeah, all the time. Who you calling?'

'CS.' As I punched the number to contact the crime scene unit, I said to Cooper, 'Let's take a look around the place and see what we can find.'

'Sure. I'll get some gloves from the car.'

I got through to CS and told them to get their guys out to Royston Park, pronto. Then I did the next most important thing I could think of.

I called Lou.

37

I wanted us to carry out a visual search of the motor home while we waited for Lou and CS to arrive. But I figured three in the Suncruiser was a crowd and I didn't want a bunch of us tramping over evidence. So I left it to Stone and Cooper while I went to talk to the manager again.

The photograph on the kitchen shelf of Fleist with his daughter suggested to me that they didn't exactly look like the perfect family. In the snapshot both of them displayed bland stares – there were no hugs or beaming smiles even for the camera, and I was eager to find out as much as I could.

I found Roy Jargo back in the office, screwing a top on to a bottle of Red Star bourbon. He was as pale as death as he lifted his shot glass to me. 'Want one?'

'Roy, in case you hadn't noticed, I'm on duty.'

'So am I, but hey, sometimes you just need a jump start.' Jargo had a tear in his eye as he knocked back his glass.

I took out my notebook. 'You think you'll be OK?'

Jargo's hands shook. 'I've seen some weird shit as a trailer park manager, but this beats everything. I love animals. Had ten dogs when I was a kid. My mom bred pedigree Snow Bears. I even had one until a couple of years back when he got run over by a Mack, squashed him like he was a pumpkin. I loved that Snow Bear. Took me a full year to get over it.' He wiped his mouth, sniffled and poured himself another shot. 'How anyone could slaughter the Fleists' dog like that I just can't figure out. Sick bastards.'

I better not tell you what I think happened to the Fleists. So much for the tough-guy biker image and the tattoos. Roy was a wuss.

I decided I'd hold off telling him my suspicions about the Fleists for a little while longer. 'Maybe you better lay off the bottle until after I take your statement.'

'Hey, it's my bottle. And this whole thing has really upset me.'

For a moment I thought Roy was going to cry; he sounded like a troubled ten-year-old. 'Taking a statement while you're under the influence wouldn't be worth a whole lot of clout in court,' I suggested.

'You reckon that's where this'll go? For killing a dog?'

'I'd take a bet.' *If only you knew the rest.*

'You think someone will pay for what they did to that poor old mutt?'

'If we catch them, I can promise, but how about for now you just sit yourself down over there and try to take it easy.'

Roy's hand trembled as he put down his glass and eased himself into a chair.

I flicked open my notebook. 'Tell me more about Fleist and his daughter.'

'Like what?'

'Did they have the dog with them when they arrived here?'

'Yeah. Except I saw the dog about as much as I saw Fleist. Which wasn't all that often. They all kept indoors most of the time, him, the daughter and Reno. That's what they called the dog.'

'Why was that?' I asked.

'Why'd they call him Reno? Hell, I don't know.'

'I meant why did they stay inside so much?'

Roy picked up another glass from under the office counter, this time a big empty tumbler. I thought he was heading for the bourbon again but instead he filled it with water from a pitcher on the desk. 'To tell the truth Kimberly looked pretty sad most of the time. And I noticed she was always kinda cautious when- ever I spoke to her. But why she was like that, you'll have to ask Fleist.'

'To be honest, Roy, I don't think Mr Fleist will be answering any questions. Nor will his daughter.'

Roy frowned, took a sip of water. 'Yeah? How come?'

'We believe they may have been murdered.'

Roy sputtered a mouthful of water and it flew in a jet across the room and splashed the floor. He stared at me as he wiped his lips with his sleeve.

'*Jesus*, you ain't shitting me, are you?'

'No, I'm not. And maybe you can help me.'

'What in the hell that's supposed to mean? You thinking I'm a suspect?'

'Not yet. You can help by telling me everything you can recall about Fleist. And I mean *everything*. Right down to the smallest *little ol'* detail.'

For ten minutes I listened as Roy claimed that he hadn't seen Fleist a whole lot, and that the guy never had much to say. 'What about a wife or girlfriend?' I asked.

'Hey, all I know is that when he checked in here it was just him and his daughter. I didn't see no Mrs Fleist, or no girlfriend.'

There was a knock on the door and Cooper entered, his face serious. He jerked his thumb towards the Suncruiser. 'We found something. You better come take a look straight away.'

38

Cooper filled me in on the way to the motor home. When we got there Stone was chewing a matchstick as he leaned against the entrance door. 'Cooper tell you?'

'He told me you found a bunch of stuff,' I answered.

Stone nodded his head towards the Fleists' home. 'Come see. It's pretty fucking weird.'

I followed him back inside and saw that one of the wardrobe doors was open.

Stone had snapped on a pair of latex gloves from the box that Cooper had brought from the car. 'We checked around without disturbing too much. There's some scuff marks near the door that may be nothing, but I can also see what looks like some man-made fibres on the dog's claws. That may be nothing, of course. But take a gander at this, Moran.'

Stone crossed to the kitchen floor area where he carefully lifted a corner of the marble-blue linoleum and peeled it back about a yard. Underneath I saw a small flap. Stone lifted the flap to reveal a deep cubby-hole, about nine inches square, which had obviously been welded to the motor home's chassis. Inside was a clear plastic folder with some papers inside, and what looked like a package wrapped in newspaper. 'So what's in the folder?' I asked.

'A map of Greensville Correctional Centre.'

'What?'

'You heard me. And it looks legit. It's stamped by the Virginia State Corrections Board.'

I slipped on a pair of latex gloves and gingerly picked up the folder. It contained some architectural drawings and the blue-ink print in one corner read: GREENSVILLE CORRECTIONAL FACILITY.

I was puzzled and still trying to figure out the significance of the map as I said to Stone, 'What's in the wrapper?'

Stone picked up the wad and tapped it in his hands. 'I found this after Cooper left. Cash, all in hundred-dollar bills. About five grand's worth, I reckon.'

'What else have you found?'

Stone grinned. 'You're going to love this.'

He moved over to the open wardrobe and I followed. The clothes rails were packed so tightly that it looked as if the wardrobe might burst. Stone plucked out an ink-black garment that looked like a cape, which had a motif stitched on to the left breast. The motif had a grey background, overlaid with an image of a shattered black cross, broken jaggedly in the middle where the lines intersected. Beneath the cross was the image of a crimson teardrop.

'Recognise this, Moran?' Stone asked, fixing me with a stare.

I couldn't avoid his eyes, no more than I could avoid the icy chill that shot through me the second I saw the cape. I examined the garment as Cooper appeared behind me. 'What the hell's that?' he asked.

'Constantine Gamal would sometimes wear the same type of black robe when he butchered his victims,' I explained. 'We found two of them at his apartment. He devised those symbols himself – a black robe with a broken cross and blood teardrop motifs on the sleeve. The big question is what's the cape doing here? Did Gamal and Fleist have some connection?'

Cooper said, 'I read about that cape during the trial. The broken cross was supposed to symbolise the power of Satan's forces and the crimson droplet signified blood spilled in ritual sacrifice.'

'Go to the top of the class,' Stone said as he tucked the garment back in its place. 'But you wouldn't want to believe all that satanic black magic crap, Cooper. No more than Gamal really did, or Moran here believes it. Isn't that a fact, Moran? What does Lou's little girl have to say?'

I heard the niggling tone in Stone's voice and knew he was out to goad me, so I didn't even bother with a reply. I noticed that Cooper had a puzzled frown that seemed to say: *What the hell's going on between you two?* It was obvious no one had yet explained the rift between Stone and me. Or Stone's restrained suspicion that I had killed David and Megan. Everyone I knew figured his mistrust could easily be put down to professional envy. But I didn't want to get caught up in a public spat so I moved away.

But Stone wasn't satisfied to leave it there and wanted to goad me even more. 'Ain't you happy Lou's made you his number two on this case, Moran? I guess as far as Lou's concerned it matters if you're a woman.'

I fixed him with a look. 'When are you ever going to give your mouth a rest, Stone?'

His face broke into a snide grin. 'I'm beginning to wonder what you're doing with yours when no one's looking. You ever get down on your knees for Lou? Show him a very personal thank-you for all the help he's given your career? Give him a blow to show your gratitude?'

'How dare you.' Fury got the better of me and I slapped Stone across the face. He reeled back, clapping a hand to his jaw, amazed that I'd actually hit him.

'You fucking bitch . . . !'

I felt so damned good seeing the shock on Stone's face, but in an instant I knew I'd made a big mistake. I noticed Lou Raines standing in the doorway. He fixed me with a withering stare. 'Did I interrupt something, Agent Moran?'

39

Raines stepped into the motor home. He wrinkled his nose at the dead German shepherd. 'What the frig's going on here? And what's with the dead mutt?'

I flicked a look at Stone, whose hand slid away from his jaw to reveal an angry red welt on his cheek and a bloodstain on his lips.

Raines said, 'Do I have to ask the damned question again or are you all deaf? What have you got to say for yourself, Agent Moran?'

I felt such an idiot, like a schoolgirl in trouble with a teacher. 'Lou, it's not—'

His voice was brittle with anger. 'I'll tell you what it's not. It's not a proper investigation in progress. That's what I came here expecting to find, but instead I witness what looks like a kindergarten brawl. I'll talk to you later, Agent Moran. Stone, do you intend bringing disciplinary charges against Moran?'

Stone put his sleeve to his jaw to wipe away a trickle of blood. 'I'll think about it.'

Raines shook his head in dismay. 'Then while you're doing that, how about I get an update on what's happened here?' He pointed to the German shepherd. 'Let's start with the dead doggie.'

I gave the explanations and Raines glared. 'Let me see the robe. Gimme some spare gloves, Cooper.'

Cooper handed him a pair of latex gloves and I led Raines over to the wardrobe, where he examined the garment without comment. 'Where's the other stuff?'

Stone pulled back the linoleum to reveal the floor recess, the money and map. Raines knelt, and when he had examined the map he scowled. 'What the frig was the guy doing with a map of Greensville?'

'That's got us all stumped,' I answered.

'No kidding? So how come you and Stone can agree on that, yet you both end up in a fight?'

I didn't reply. What the hell could I say? Raines addressed Stone. 'Well, you got an answer, Vance? Or you stuck for words too?'

Stone dabbed his mouth. 'I guess.'

Raines stood. 'Any of you made any meaningful observations? Agent Moran, you look like you were about to say something.'

I looked down at the cubby-hole. 'Assuming the mine victims we found are Fleist and his daughter, whoever killed them probably didn't have robbery as a motive. They would have found the money stash as easily as we did.'

Raines didn't comment, removed his latex gloves. 'When CS get here I want every speck in this motor home examined, right down to the last frigging dust mite.'

Suddenly he fixed me with an ugly stare and nodded towards the door.

'Agent Moran, you and me need to have a talk.'

I followed him outside and he strode towards the manager's office, then turned on me with a scowl. 'What in the hell's the idea of sparring with Stone? You just hit the guy for the fun of it?'

'What do *you* think, Lou?'

'Don't get lippy, Kate. I'm asking *you*.'

'It wasn't like that.'

'Then what *was* it like? Did he goad you? Did you argue about something? What was it?'

I was tempted to explain but telling tales out of school wasn't my way. 'Let's just say that Stone and I had another difference of opinion.'

Raines exploded. '*Jesus*, Kate, you may be one of my best agents but I'm not going to have you assaulting one of your colleagues. Maybe if you won't answer me I should ask to hear

Stone's side of the story. Answer the frigging question. Did Stone provoke you, yes or no?'

'I really don't want to make this an issue, Lou. I can fight my own battles.'

Raines sounded even more vexed. 'Sure you can, which is why we're having this conversation.'

'Can't we just forget it?'

Raines pointed a finger at me. 'On one condition. You two make your peace. I don't want this thing between you two turning into a fight-club scene every other day. Or I'll damned well make it an issue if I have to, got that?'

Knowing Stone, making peace was going to be impossible. But judging by the mood Lou was in right now, it was better simply to agree with him. I bit back my own anger. 'Yes.'

'You look like there's still something bothering you,' Raines countered.

'Why didn't you tell me Cooper and Stone used to be partners?'

'What the hell's that got to do with anything?'

'It might have.'

'You're getting paranoid, Kate. There's nothing to it. Cooper's sound, he's not on Stone's side, in case that's what you think. Now, are you through in the motor home?'

'We've done all we can until CS arrive,' I answered.

'OK, then I want you to ride back to the District with me and Cooper. Stone can wait for the CS crew.'

'Any reason I get to go with you?'

Raines produced his car keys. 'Yeah, the old guy at the mine shaft, Billy Adams.'

'What about him?'

'He's come up with an E-fit of the suspect's face.'

40

Randy Rinaldi was one of the Bureau's best forensic artists. He was a handsome guy in his mid-fifties with a salt-and-pepper beard, cobalt-blue eyes and pencil-thin eyebrows that looked like they'd been put on with eyeliner. We were in his cubicle at the field office and I sat beside him in a borrowed chair. He was into family in a big way – a bunch of photos adorned the desk, of Randy's wife and their pretty young daughter on graduation day, and a couple of others of babies that were obviously grandchildren.

Randy said, 'I spent over two hours with Billy Adams, Kate. Believe me, it's about the best I could come up with.'

The image of the UNSUB – unknown subject – stared out at me from a flat LCD screen, the product of Billy Adams's memory, Randy's skill and his E-fit software. It was after three and I still hadn't had any lunch, just a cup of bitter black coffee, and I tried to ignore the hunger pangs gnawing at my insides.

Randy said, 'Billy was so traumatised it took a big effort even to get him to talk. Here, let me print you off some copies.'

Randy stabbed the print key with a finger and the HP colour printer spewed out a half-dozen A4-sized printed sheets. I picked one up and stared into the face of the suspect that Billy Adams had claimed he saw hanging around the mine. He had described the guy as having an oval, clean-shaven face and dark hair. With no really prominent characteristics – an unremarkable nose and eyes and chin – the unsub's face was of the bland Mr Man-in-the-Street variety. In other words, a nobody.

'What's the matter?' asked Randy. 'You don't look happy.'

I sighed with bitter disappointment. 'Am I supposed to be? Couldn't our witness say if the guy's features were even a *little* more distinguishing?'

Randy stroked his cropped beard. 'He was a distance away at the time, Kate, and he didn't exactly see the unsub's face in a floodlit stadium. I know it might not be much to go on, but I reckon we're lucky to get what we've got. At first, all Billy could say for certain was that the figure was a white guy, which sure was a big help.'

I had a feeling that the E-fit picture was going to be useless to the investigation. One of those composites that a witness some-times came up with if only to put flesh on the bones of an unseen perpetrator. All it usually meant was that the witness actually saw *nothing* worthwhile. 'Sorry, I'd been hoping for more.'

'It's a tough one, huh?' Randy raised an eyebrow in query.

'I've a feeling it's going to be.'

Randy saved the file to disk and the image disappeared off the screen. He consulted the wall clock, saw it was almost 3 p.m., rummaged in his desk drawer and found a clear plastic lunch box. 'Way past time to put on the nosebag. I'm gonna head down to the square for a half-hour, get some air. Got an extra salami on rye with wholegrain mustard if you're interested in joining me? You can even have my apple.' Randy offered me a cheesy grin. 'It's got no noticeable teeth marks.'

'Tempting, but I'll take a rain check.'

Randy stood and proudly picked up a shot of what looked like a newborn baby from his desk. 'You see the new ankle-biter? My daughter Dolores had a son last month. That's the sixth grand-child. Name's Christian. Cute, huh?'

I admired the shot. 'You're a lucky man, Randy.'

'Hey, you said it. Kids are everything. How're you getting on with the new guy, Cooper?'

'I guess we tolerate each other.'

'Tough about his kid, huh?'

'What do you mean?' I asked.

'You didn't know? He's got a seven-year-old son who needs specialist medical treatment. I hear that's why he transferred to the District. One of the best children's hospitals in the country is Johns Hopkins in Baltimore. He tried to get a transfer to the Baltimore office except they had no openings, but they offered him DC instead, which is near enough with a commute, I guess.'

'What's his son got?' I asked.

'SLE. That's systemic lupus erythematosus to you and me.'

'I've heard of it. Isn't it some kind of auto-immune disease?'

Rinaldi nodded. 'It pretty much affects every organ in the body. The problem is there's no known cause so all you can do is keep the disease at bay, but at least you can do that.'

I thought: *Boy, was I wrong about the nightclubs.* No wonder Cooper looked tired – coping with a sick child and trying to work a full-time job with the Bureau couldn't be easy.

Rinaldi returned the picture of his grandson to his desk. 'You eat today, Kate?'

'Breakfast at seven.'

'To hell with that. Hey, I didn't eat lunch for years on this damned job and ended up with ulcers the size of a pit bull's testicles. It ain't worth skipping meals, so listen to my advice and go take a break.'

'I've got too much on my mind right now.'

'We all have, but that's no excuse. Do yourself a favour, go nibble.'

41

Randy was right. I needed to grab a coffee and a bite to eat and unwind somewhere. I decided to visit my favourite coffee bar two blocks away for a sandwich. But as I sat in the lab on my own after Randy had gone to lunch I found myself staring down at an image of the unsub on the glossy paper. He didn't look like anyone, really. A neutral. A nobody. *One of twenty million joes you'd see on the street.*

And I'd been hoping for a breakthrough. *So much for hope.*

I lingered in front of Randy's empty computer screen. I knew the E-fit software, had toyed with it on several occasions, so I copied the file that Randy had named UNSUBIMAGE 819K, then brought my copy up on screen. My cell phone buzzed and I flicked it on. 'Moran.'

'Kate, it's Frank.'

My brother Frank had quit working for the Bureau eighteen months earlier with a booze problem. I'd tried to help him in any way I could, and so had a lot of his former colleagues, but after attempting rehab a couple of times he still couldn't leave the bottle alone. I'd called him two weeks back to see how he was doing but he was on a bender. When Frank was off the wagon it was impossible to talk to him, and after a rambling conversation I'd hung up. But this time he sounded sober. 'Welcome back to the land of the living,' I said.

'Hey, before you hit me with a stick, I'm truly sorry, I know I've been an asshole again.'

'You've been drunk.'

'Yeah, and now I'm sober.'

'For how long, Frank? You're killing yourself. It can't go on like this, you've got to lick this thing. You're breaking the heart of everybody who cares for you, and you know that.'

'Yeah, I know.'

'Is that all you've got to say?'

'I'm trying,' Frank said quietly.

'So you keep saying, but you still haven't quit. You've got to do it now, before it's too late.' Sometimes it almost felt as if Frank and I were acting out a scene in a disaster movie. I imagined him on the roof of a burning building with flames licking around his ass; I was in a helicopter overhead, throwing him down a rescue rope and telling him to grab hold, but he was saying, 'Can you give me a little time to think about this?'

Frank fell silent. He'd heard the sermons a million times before, as often as I'd given them to him, and I *kept* giving them to him because I loved him. As I waited for him to reply I toyed around with the suspect's bland face, first fleshing out his cheeks, then altering his hairstyle and the colour of his dark hair, to grey from brown. I was fooling around, just hoping to get a spark going, create *something* noticeable in the face. 'So what are you going to do about it, Frank?'

'I'm trying to kick the demons to hell, Kate, believe me. It's just that, well . . . sometimes when I get a curved ball that I can't handle I hit the chute and slide.'

After he'd sobered up, Frank usually became fragile, and he sounded that way right now. I knew that scolding him was pointless. 'So why'd you call?'

'I need to talk, Kate. If you've got ten minutes I'd sure appreciate it.'

From the E-kit menu I gave the suspect a beard, then took it away again and gave him some stubble. 'Talk about what?'

'Not over the phone. Could you call by my place some time today?'

'Frank, if you're behind with your bills I'm not loaning you, not again, and that's a definite. You've got to start standing on your own two feet and take responsibility for this mess you're in. *Tough love*, remember? No more crap, no more *poor me*.'

I'd loaned Frank five thousand dollars six months earlier to clear some debts and he'd paid back half of it but the remainder was proving a problem. *Except how come he always finds money for booze when he needs it?* But it wasn't the money, it was the principle.

'Kate, it's not about money, I give you my word. And I'll only take up five minutes of your time.'

Despite Frank's denial, I figured he was in financial trouble again. But I found it so hard to say no to him when he needed my help. I sighed. 'I've got a team meeting this afternoon, so it'll have to be later. I'll call by about six.'

'Thanks, Kate. See you, sis.'

I switched off my phone and turned back to face the computer. I had significantly altered the unsub's face, and as I stared at the LCD screen I shivered. A question shot through my mind. Was I subconsciously projecting my own bogeyman on to the screen or had I hit on something? By changing a few vital parameters – altering his hairstyle and its colour, filling out his cheeks, giving him stubble and changing the colour of his eyes – the screen image now looked disturbingly familiar.

The face that stared back at me was Constantine Gamal's.

42

When I pulled up at Frank's place in Springfield it was a quarter before six and growing dark. The bungalow belonged to a Bureau buddy of his who'd been posted overseas for a year, and Frank was house-sitting. I was still shaken as I went up the garden path to the bungalow – the image of Gamal on the screen had freaked me out, especially when I reminded myself that he had trained himself to become an expert at disguise. A chilling idea was beginning to form in the back of my mind that I didn't want to entertain.

I rang the doorbell and Frank finally answered the door with an attempt at a grin, wearing only jeans and towel-drying his sun-bleached hair. 'You're early, I was in the shower. Come on in.'

He was forty-three, but looked older, years of hard drinking leaving his skin pitted and craggy. My colleagues often said he looked like the actor Tommy Lee Jones, and it was true, but Frank wore his hair long and mostly in a ponytail, with an elastic band keeping it in place. Except a lot of times he looked like a bum, especially when he drank. I noticed that his eyes were heavily bloodshot, and his complexion was ruddy. 'Are you feeling any better?' I asked.

'To tell the truth, not a bit.'

'Serves you damned right.'

Frank led me into the front room. 'Yeah, well, the piper's got to be paid. Take a seat. Want some coffee?'

'I'll skip. What was it you wanted to talk about?'

173

'Slow down, little sis. I'm coming to it.'

I sat on the couch as Frank settled with a sigh on to the easy chair opposite. He finished towelling his hair and pulled on a scruffy grey T-shirt that looked like a dog had slept on it. It was hard to believe that Frank had once been one of the Investigative Science Unit's best agents, with a doctorate in criminal psychology. He'd worked out of Quantico, coordinating with the NCAVC – the National Center for the Analysis of Violent Crime – examining murder scenes, drawing up psychological assessments of the unsub and victim, trying to draw a profile of the killer. But witnessing too many brutal crime scenes and body dump sites, especially those involving children, had taken its toll.

Frank had always liked a drink, but soon he started to drink heavily, then his marriage fell apart, and the following year his eldest son was killed in a motorcycle accident in Baltimore. His life was ripped to shreds, and one day he just walked out of his office, hit the bottle hard, and never went back. The last eighteen months had consisted of cycles of drunkenness and sobriety, and he'd had a tough time keeping his head above water.

'This case you're working on,' he said, patting down his mussed hair and using his fingers to put on his elastic hair band.

'Which case are you talking about?'

'*The* case. The bodies in the disused mine out near Acre.'

That threw me. 'How'd *you* know about that?'

'Want some coffee?' Frank asked again.

'No, I want an answer.'

Frank poured himself black coffee from a pot on the table and grinned, that same Tommy Lee Jones grin. 'You think I'm dumb? I watch TV. A couple of the local channels had reports.'

'I meant how'd you know I was involved? My name hasn't been making headlines again, not that I know of.'

Frank sipped his coffee. 'I still hang out with most of the guys I worked with. Drunk or sober, I'm not deaf, sis.'

'Word's been travelling fast,' I answered. 'And what exactly did you hear?'

Frank put down his cup and sat back with another sigh. 'Two

bodies were discovered at the mine, mutilated and burned, Gamal-style. I hear some of the guys are even calling him another Kebab Killer, like they did Gamal. Because he'd cut and cook his victims, Middle Eastern style.'

'Knock it off, Frank. It still bothers me to even think about his MO.'

I could see that Frank was immediately regretful that he'd reminded me of Gamal's killing method. 'Hey, sometimes I've got a big, insensitive mouth I've got no control over. I'm really sorry, Kate. How'd your team meeting go?'

'There were no breakthroughs, if that's what you're asking. We're still at the starting line. So why are *you* interested?'

'I'd like to offer you my help.'

I raised my eyes in mock disbelief. 'Frank, no disrespect, but I figure you need to help yourself first.'

I noticed that Frank's hands were trembling. I figured he was itching for a drink but trying his damnedest to hang in there. He saw me notice the tremor and folded his hands on his lap. 'I didn't mean that to sound hurtful,' I said. 'I wasn't paying you back for your remark.'

'Sure, I know that, no offence taken. My hands are up and I'm pleading guilty. But we've worked together before, Kate, and worked pretty well.'

Aside from the Gamal manhunt, there had been a federal murder case in Baltimore eight months earlier when Frank had offered advice to me on the quiet, and I'd been very glad of his expertise. We'd occasionally worked together when he was still with the Bureau, but I was hesitant about involving him this time round because he hadn't stopped drinking.

He gave me a sort of pleading look. 'I haven't lost my touch. And it can be the same rule as before, meaning nobody has to know. Let me give it a shot.'

I could have done with someone like Frank to bounce ideas off about the case. He was still one of the most talented investigators I knew. They say that the best ones can see through a lie immediately, and on a good day, when he was sober, Frank could see through a brick wall. 'The question that springs to mind is *why*, Frank. What's in it for you?'

'Because you're my sister and I owe you.' Frank leaned forward and in an uncharacteristic gesture he put a hand on mine. He wasn't usually touchy-feely, but I got the impression he wanted me to know he truly cared. 'You've always been there for me, rain or shine. Most of the time I've been too drunk or self-pitying to even thank you. I guess I want to make a down payment on what I owe you.'

'Is that the only reason?'

Frank smiled. 'Heck, no, I need something to do to keep me busy, otherwise I'll go stir crazy here, Kate, honest to God I will. Another few days of doing nothing and I'll be chewing the carpet or drinking.'

'I get the feeling there's something else . . .'

Frank took a breath and looked at me. 'You want it from the hip?'

'Sure.'

'Take it from someone who's been there. I think you're tired, Kate. I can see it in your eyes. You're washed out. You *need* someone to lean on. Someone to unburden yourself on.'

'Thanks a bunch.'

'It's the truth. The Gamal case sucked a hell of a lot out of you. If you ask me, it damned near killed you, only you didn't want to give up. It was just like when we were kids and we had to solve the puzzle and find the last piece.'

One of the few abiding childhood memories I had of my father was of Sunday evenings when we were kids. While Mom visited her sisters, he and his buddies played some serious poker in the living room. He'd have consigned us kids to the old pine table in the kitchen and given us a big, thousand-piece jigsaw puzzle. Except beforehand he'd have removed a single piece of the puzzle and hidden it somewhere about the house. Once we completed the puzzle, minus one part, we still had to find the missing piece. Frank and I would never give up until we found it, even if we had to tear the house apart, and I could still remember the madcap exhilaration of the hunt. I often wondered whether our old man had deliberately set out to breed a couple of stubborn investigators. 'What are you trying to say?' I asked Frank.

'By my reckoning you needed some R and R to get yourself back on track. But no, Raines tosses you straight into the jaws of another investigation.'

'I had a few days off.'

'Big deal. And to make things even worse, the murders come across as copycat killings. Anyway, I've been such a scabby asshole lately that I want to make it up to you by giving you the benefit of my brilliant analytical mind.' Frank half smiled. 'Is all that reason enough?'

Frank was right about one thing: I needed to unburden myself to someone, tell them all the weird things that had been happening lately. His offer was tempting. Maybe because I was desperate for confirmation that I wasn't going crazy. But I was still wary of bringing him on board. Sober, he was a terrific investigator, but drunk he was a loose cannon who could get me in trouble. 'I appreciate the offer, I really do, Frank, but I can't accept, not this time.'

Frank rarely got angry, but I could see he was frustrated as he slapped the table and spilled his coffee. 'Damn it, Kate, I *know* you. You're itching to talk things through with someone. And once you do, you're going to feel a whole lot better.'

He was probably right. Then Frank got me in a clincher by saying, 'Besides, I've got some ideas on the kind of suspect you should be looking for.'

That got me interested. 'What ideas?'

'First, you count me in,' Frank insisted.

'You're not bullshitting me?'

'No way.'

I thought about it. 'There'd be a condition.'

'Name it,' he said.

'You quit boozing while you're helping me out. Not one alcoholic drink. Not even a Scope mouthwash or a candy liqueur. I mean it, Frank. Or else we part company.'

'You drive a hard bargain.'

'It's for your own good.'

Frank offered his hand, and stretched a smile. 'I'll do my very best. How's that?'

I held back my hand. 'Nope, it's all or nothing, Frank.'

'*OK! OK!* We've got a deal, now let's hear it all, everything you've got.'

43

I told him everything. Every damned thing that had happened in the last forty-eight hours, including the creepy midnight phone call, and Frank was right, I felt better immediately. Except that the joy lasted all of about five seconds. 'You think I'm crazy, don't you?'

'Never have done,' he said with a grin. 'But seeing as you might even be *considering* that Gamal could still be alive, I'm thinking about it. Get *real*, Kate. You saw the guy being executed, right? You saw the poison injected in his veins and you heard him pronounced dead, right?'

'Yes. But what if he somehow survived the execution? I've got this gut feeling there might be some kind of weird or supernatural aspect to it all. The murders at the mine have the same MO as Gamal's, the same signatures. Then there's the fact there were no footprints in the snow, and the image I came up with on the computer. It's all weird and I can't explain it . . .'

Frank shook his head. 'Then don't. Take a reality check. The Department of Corrections has never made a mistake like that. The guy's mouldering in his grave, so don't give your doubt another moment's thought. I bet no one's ever survived an injection of potassium chloride in their veins, let alone the other chemical stuff they use. As for a supernatural aspect to it, I'm not even going to dignify that absurdity by going down that road.'

I immediately felt better again. Frank had a way of cutting through the bullshit when he was sober and I was so glad I'd talked to him. 'You're right. I mean, the footprints thing. I keep thinking there's got to be a simple answer, and there probably is. Someone could have gone to great pains to brush them away.'

'Right,' Frank agreed.

I began to feel sane once more, until more thoughts hit me and my stomach turned. 'But there should have been *some* evidence of brush strokes. And what about the phone call I got last night? What about the music?'

'Either it was all in your mind, or someone *did* call you and play the music.'

'But why?'

'There you've got me. If it *did* happen . . .'

'It *did*, Frank. All day I've tried to convince myself it was the sleeping pill or my imagination. But the more I've thought about it, the more I'm certain I got the call.'

Frank said, 'Then it would suggest maybe that the perp knows a lot about you already. Maybe even has some kind of grudge against you and wants to taunt or upset you or both. But as to who they might be and why they'd commit murder using the same methods as Gamal, those are things we'll have to figure out. It stands to reason we've already got a possible option on the killer. It could have been some sicko who followed the media reports of the murders, and who gets off on the kind of crimes Gamal committed.'

I nodded. 'Someone who's decided to follow in Gamal's foot-steps now he's out of the game.'

'Exactly,' Frank agreed.

I was alarmed. 'If you're right, then they could have been in the house, using one of the phone extensions to call me. Sterling Burke suggested that was the only other way I could have got the call, because it wasn't in the phone company records.'

'You still keep that spare Glock pistol under your pillow?'

'Yes.'

'Keep it there for now, in case this is something personal. You know as well as I do there are wackos out there like the kind we've just talked about. So keep your doors locked and put your alarm on. Except it sure as hell couldn't have been Gamal himself in body or in spirit, so get that crazy notion out of your head.'

Frank was right again. He poured us each some coffee. 'It'll keep you awake. You sleeping OK?' he asked.

'Lousy.'

'Try half a bottle of Dewar's. Always works for me.'

'Funny. I'll stick with a sleeping pill. You said you had some ideas on the unsub.'

Frank swallowed his coffee, thought for a moment and then raised an eyebrow at me. 'OK, here's the way I see it. The kind of guy we're looking for – and I figure we're dealing with a guy – is someone with a psychiatric history, twenty-five to forty, physically fit, maybe even a powerful physique. To me it seems that, in all probability the killings were the work of a diagnosed paranoid schizophrenic. The crime scene reflects rage, over-control and overkill. The guy's either a psychopath or a borderline case, and he'll have the common traits of someone with psychopathic tendencies: controlling, manipulative, a powerful desire to win, and in his mind he's always right.'

Frank paused, thought some more and added, 'However, he's also of above-average intelligence, and so he's probably got a college degree. He's someone who's able to turn on the charm when they need to. Maybe he's got a prison record. Maybe it's someone who knew Gamal on the inside, who served time with him, and admired him. Also, they've got that old reliable, a van, or maybe an SUV, probably the usual high-mileage variety. But I figure that while he's probably killed or maimed before, he's been out of the game for some time.'

'Except you could be wrong.'

'Sure I could be. This ain't an infallible science. I can only go on fact and instinct. But I figure that whoever it is, you better find them fast.'

'Why?'

'Because I'm pretty convinced that this is just the beginning. The chances are he's going to kill again. I'd even take a bet it's going to be soon.'

44

I spent another half-hour going through the case with Frank and by then I was beat. Frank led me to his front door. He had given me some things to think about. 'I know you said you're sure about the phone call, but are you *absolutely* sure you couldn't have been dreaming?' he asked.

'I *heard* the phone, Frank. I took the call – I wasn't dreaming or having a nightmare. I heard the Slipknot music. It was so damned scary. You do believe me, don't you?'

'If you're that convinced it happened, then sure I do. What about any leads from the mine or the trailer?'

'All we've got so far has been the dry-cleaning stub that led us to the trailer park. And some cloth or wool fibres we found under the girl's nails and on the dog's claws that may or may not be relevant.'

'No confirmation yet on the bodies?'

'Not yet, but I'm hoping we should have that soon, either from DNA or dental records.'

'What about the drawings of Greensville prison you found in the trailer?' Frank asked.

'That's the weird one. That and the cape that turned up in the closet kind of suggests to me there may be some link between Fleist and Gamal. But what it is we can't figure, at least not yet.'

'Did Forensics examine the cape and the drawings?'

I nodded. 'Your old friend Diaz tells me he found no usable prints on either. Just some smudges that were indistinguishable. He's checking out the cape but so far he says he's found no human contamination, which seems pretty odd to me. I thought

Diaz would at least have found hair from either Fleist or his daughter.'

Frank's brow creased in thought. 'Maybe neither of them ever wore the cape.'

'Then what was it doing in the trailer?'

Frank smiled. 'Hey, you're the investigator, that's something you're going to have to find an answer to. Do you know of any other link between this guy Fleist or his daughter and Gamal?'

I was finding it hard to keep my eyes open. 'No, but I'll be doing my damnedest to check it out.'

'Anything else you ought to tell me?'

I explained about Warden Clay and Frank raised an eyebrow. 'What do you think he was trying to hide from you?'

'I don't know. Call it investigator's instinct but the more I think about it the more I'm convinced that Clay was uncomfortable around me. As if he knew something that I didn't and he intended to keep it from me. He's too clean, too sugary, like maybe it's part of an act. I don't trust him.' I half smiled. 'Of course, I could be misjudging the poor guy. I've been wrong before.'

'How about I do a little background digging on Clay for a start? I still got some friends working in the Department of Corrections I can talk with.'

'Just be careful, OK? I don't want word getting back to the warden.'

'You bet.' Frank saw I was exhausted and patted my arm. 'Leave it there for now. You need sleep. Go rest, sis.'

'This time I won't argue.'

'It'll be good to be working together again, Kate.'

I turned to leave. 'Just remember to stick to your part of the bargain.'

Frank let me out. 'Scout's honour. You take care of yourself.'

I walked out to the car, climbed in. Frank waited at the door and waved.

As I drove away I felt better knowing that he was in my corner.

Twenty minutes later, as I turned on to the Eisenhower Freeway, I wondered whether my imagination was working overtime. I caught a glimpse of a black Ford van in my rear-view mirror. I was pretty sure it had followed me all the way from Frank's home. It was too far behind to see the driver or the plate but the Ford stayed behind me for at least three miles, then suddenly peeled away and disappeared into the night-time traffic.

45

Angel Bay, Virginia

I was still thinking about the van as I turned the key in my front door. I was exhausted and I wanted to run the bath, knowing I needed to soak, but first I made sure I'd locked the front door. Then I checked the back one too, and all the windows, before I walked out to the study and found it locked as well. I walked back into the cottage and put on the house alarm. It wasn't wired into the studio, but knowing that the cottage was protected was enough.

While I waited for the hot water to fill the tub I lit the fire. Then I made a chicken salad sandwich with a light mayonnaise dressing, poured myself a glass of Napa Valley Merlot and flicked on the TV. I was really too tired to watch, but I needed some distraction from the case and to catch up with the world. But after ten minutes of flicking between the news and Jay Leno, I'd had enough and my bath was ready. I undressed, poured in some orange blossom and jojoba cream and stepped into the hot, sudsy water.

I felt better immediately. I soaked for fifteen minutes, the fragrant steaming water almost sending me to sleep. By now I had convinced myself that the Ford van I *thought* I saw behind me was a product of my imagination.

When I finally stepped out of the bath, I dragged on my bathrobe and sipped another glass of Merlot by the fireplace until I was ready for sleep. I set my alarm for 6.30 and opened the bedroom window. A cold breeze floated in, lifting the curtains as I lay on the bed. I loved cold nights like this, the kind of nights

I'd enjoyed with David, when he'd put on a Norah Jones CD and we'd lie in the darkness, touching and talking and laughing.

But I couldn't play Norah Jones – that would surely have torn my heart to pieces. Besides, I was so exhausted that I didn't need music to send me to sleep, I was dropping already, my eyelids heavy. I closed my eyes to the darkness, listening to the cold claws of the wind sweeping across the shore, and then the distant sound of the wild geese out in the bay.

I don't know how long it was before I drifted into a deep sleep but the next thing I knew a noise like a fire-bell alarm woke me. My heart began to pound as I came awake, and I fumbled in the darkness to grasp my nightstand clock: the green numerals read 4.01 a.m. I'd been asleep for four hours. But the noise didn't stop. Then I realised that the shrill rumpus I'd heard was the phone ringing. I felt drugged, unable to lift myself off the bed, and I struggled to haul myself from under the sheets and lift the receiver.

My first thought was that it might be either the office or Frank calling me, but then for some reason caution kicked in and I tried to focus on the lit panel that showed the incoming number.

There's no number.

I flicked on the phone, put my ear to the receiver and distinctly heard the Slipknot music – heard it as clear as crystal. An icy feeling spread through my body as I recognised the lyrics of a track that Megan used to play: I was sure it was called 'Killers Are Quiet' because she and her friends often used to sing the words when they hung out in her room.

I remembered the track – like most teenagers trying to find themselves, Megan was into poetry and lyrics in a big way, and as I tried to get to know her we'd discussed her current favourite songs. It hadn't occurred to me that the previous night's caller might attempt a repeat performance. The shock hit me like a hammer blow and I sat up in bed. '*Who is this? Who is it? Answer me!*' I screamed.

A couple of seconds later the music faded and I heard a voice that chilled me to the bone. 'Can you hear me, honey?'

The voice sounded otherwordly, and then a snatch of the Slipknot music played again in the background before the voice repeated: 'Can you hear me, honey?'

I thought: *Oh my God! I don't believe this. It sounds just like David's voice.* I almost fainted. *I'm going insane.* I felt sure that I was going to pass out, but instead panic set in and I slammed down the phone and I slid my hand under the pillow and grabbed my spare Glock. I climbed out of bed and tugged on my bathrobe. Perspiration drenched my face and fear and panic gripped me.

No incoming number had come up on the handset. *What if the call was from one of the phone extensions?* I moved out into the living room, holding my Glock at the ready. I stepped into the hall and checked the alarm. It was still armed. I had the extension in the study to check, so I punched in the disabling code, then took my keys and moved to the rear of the cottage and unlocked the back door.

It felt cold outside, an icy wind coming up from the water. It blew around my bathrobe and my bare legs felt like ice. I heard a noise, like a tree branch scraping. *Was that the wind or is someone out there?* I kept my Glock at arm's length, crossed the gravel and tried the study door. It was locked, the lights out. I unlocked and opened the door quietly, then hit the light switch. The study lights sprang on and the room looked just as I had left it: cold and empty, the floor spattered with dried paint. I stared at the phone. It was still in its cradle. At that moment I suddenly felt that maybe I *was* going crazy after all. Had I imagined the whole episode?

And then the phone in the study rang.

46

This time I was fully awake. This time I was ready for the caller and not half asleep. But the phone must have rung a half-dozen times before I could overcome my fear and grasp the receiver. I raised it slowly to my ear and heard a faint buzz of static on the line.

But no voices. *Nothing.*

Was someone listening in at the other end? Were they deliberately trying to drive me crazy? A split second later a voice spoke so loudly that my heart skipped: '*Kate?* Are you there?'

I jumped. It was Lou Raines. Hearing his voice gave me such a tremendous sense of relief I almost felt like crying. 'Lou . . .'

He must have recognised the panic in my tone because he said with concern, 'Hey, is everything OK? Is anything wrong?'

'No . . . nothing's wrong.' My eyes moistened and I suddenly felt on the verge of breaking down. I desperately wanted to tell Lou about the call but thought: *I'll feel such a fool if he doesn't believe me.* I had no logical explanation for the call.

'Are you still there, Kate?'

'Yes . . . I'm here.'

'Hey, are you *sure* you're OK?'

'I . . . I was fast asleep. I'm just surprised by the a.m. call. What's the matter, Lou?'

'Sorry to wake you but something important came up and it couldn't wait.'

'Sounds serious.'

I heard a sharp intake of breath and a second later Lou exhaled a heavy sigh.

'I got a call from Bob Dixon minutes ago. He was working late.'

Bob 'Whistler' Dixon was one of our team, an experienced agent with over twenty-five years' service. He was also a night owl who enjoyed working into the late hours, usually whistling away like a happy canary. Rumour had it that he and his ball-breaker wife hadn't slept together in years and that was why Bob was so chirpy. 'I'm listening.'

'About three-thirty a.m. he came across an interesting wire from an old buddy of ours, Inspector Maurice Delon in Paris. It seems that the French Sûreté have got a fresh murder case on their hands. The bodies of a couple of American tourists, a father and daughter, were found butchered in a section of the Paris sewers about four-teen hours ago after an anonymous caller claimed to have found the bodies. Delon wanted us to help confirm the victims' ID, and he also remarked on the strong similarity between the killings and those Gamal carried out in the Paris catacombs five years back.'

I knew the details of the case Lou was referring to. Gamal had been attending an international conference of psychiatrists in Paris when he went on a killing spree. And where better to slake his morbid thirst for murder than in the city's ancient sewers? He'd abducted and killed an American tourist and his seventeen-year-old daughter and disposed of them in the catacombs that formed a warren of tunnels beneath the Paris streets. The victims had been identified through DNA evidence. Inspector Delon had been in charge of the investigation, which had only been solved after we apprehended Gamal in the US. I felt my heart begin to race. 'Go on.'

'According to Delon, the murders bear all the hallmarks of Gamal-type killings – the bodies dismembered and the remains torched. They even found a crucifix at the scene. All of which has Delon puzzled, not to mention me.'

I was dazed. Raines sighed again. 'It sounds so damned familiar, Kate. It's weird. Which is why I want us to take a look.'

'You mean travel to *Paris*?'

'Yeah, with Cooper. It's best if you and Stone stay out of each other's hair for a couple of days. It's obvious as hell that he's got a bug up his ass about you.'

'You told Cooper about this?'

'I called him five minutes ago.'

'When do we leave?'

'You're both booked on an Air France flight to Paris, leaving Baltimore International at six-thirty p.m. today. So start packing.'

PART THREE

47

S pecial Agent Gus Norton used his sleeve to wipe the conden-
sation from the windscreen. He was in the passenger seat as
the Taurus sped towards Rockville, and he shot a look at Stone,
who was busy driving. 'You want to tell me again what the hell
we're supposed to be doing out in the sticks?'

Stone said, 'I told you, I got a call this morning from someone
at the trailer park.'

'And I heard you, but who called you and about what? That's
the part you haven't explained,' Norton grumbled.

'A broad by the name of Emily Jenks. She said she had some
information about Otis Fleist that might interest us.'

'Yeah? Any particular reason why she called *you*?'

Stone plucked a pack of cigarettes from his door's side pocket
and selected one. 'Because after I checked out the motor home
with Moran and Cooper yesterday, I knocked on some doors in
the park and handed out my card. No one I spoke with seemed
to recall anything about the Fleists but then this dame Jenks calls
me back this morning. I checked up on her with the park manager.
She's retired, touching seventy, lives alone.'

Norton was a tough-looking guy with the muscled body of a
weightlifter. He had been Stone's sidekick for two years but he still
wrinkled his nose in protest as his buddy touched a lighter flame
to the tip of his cigarette. 'Hey, you still trying to kill me, Vance?
If you're gonna smoke, crack open a window, for *Chrissakes*.'

Stone hit the window switch until the glass was half down.
'Happy now?'

'I'd be happier if you didn't give me lung cancer. So what exactly did the old lady see?'

'She didn't want to talk over the phone. Wants to discuss it in private.'

Norton grinned and flicked a look at Stone. 'I once knew an old lady who used to say that. Old bird was eighty if she was a day and had a thing about cops. She'd call the precinct every once in a while, pretending she was being bothered by a stalker. Except as soon as she got a cop alone inside her house she'd suggest he might come back later for some cupcakes and a blowjob, gratis. You believe that? Maybe old lady Jenks is just after a little excitement in her life?'

'Yeah, sure,' Stone answered.

'Take the next right.'

Stone hung a right and they saw the trailer park up ahead. Norton said, 'Hey, you hear that stuff about Gamal putting the hocus-pocus on Moran before he got the needle?'

Stone raised a sceptical eyebrow. 'You don't believe in that mumbo-jumbo shit any more than I do.'

Norton grinned. 'Hey, but how about her and Cooper getting a jolly to Paris?'

'Fuck them.'

'You really hate her, don't you, Vance?'

Stone flicked a sour glance at Norton. 'Listen, if you ask me I happen to think Gamal was telling the truth for once when he said he wasn't responsible for the Bryce murders.'

'Since when would you believe a shitbag like Gamal? Get real, Vance.'

Stone drove into the trailer park, pulled up outside an older-style trailer that looked like it needed some refurbishment, and jerked on the handbrake. 'You know my feelings about Moran. I don't have to spell them out.'

Norton sighed. 'Vance, you're the only one in the department who could even think she might have murdered her fiancé and his child for financial gain. Not a single colleague I know could take it seriously, and that includes me. The fact is, most people

I know suspect maybe you're crazy for even thinking it. They know the rivalry between you and Moran, for fuck sake. You're forever tearing strips off each other. But suggesting that a fellow agent may have committed murder, even when you make out it's just a professional intuition you've got, that's some heavy shit you're laying down, man. You know what people say behind your back? Everyone thinks you've gone too far. Me, I've got to admire Moran's restraint. I'm surprised she hasn't filed a complaint against you. And like I said before, where's your fucking proof?'

'I've been in this business fifteen years and my instinct's never been wrong, Gus. *Never*. I told you what I heard her say on the phone a week before Bryce was killed. You know about the misplacement of the crucifix and the fact that David Bryce was shot to death, unlike any of Gamal's other victims.'

'Yeah, you told me, you told me a hundred times, but you'll need more than that and instinct. You'll need granite-hard evidence to back it up.'

Stone jerked on the handbrake and said bitterly, 'Mark my words, it's only a question of time before I find the proof I need. Now let's go hear what this old broad has to say.'

48

Stone knocked on the trailer door and an elderly woman wearing a floral nightdress and rollers appeared. 'Yes?'

Stone flashed his ID. 'Emily Jenks? I'm Federal Agent Stone, and this is my colleague Agent Norton. I believe we spoke on the phone, ma'am.'

The woman studied Stone's creds. 'My, I wasn't expecting you so soon.'

'We beat the traffic.'

'Come inside, please.' The woman opened her screen door and led the way into the trailer's living room. An easel was erected in a corner and a bunch of artist's requisites were laid out on a small, paint-stained table: brushes and pots.

As the woman led them in, Stone studied a dozen or so framed paintings hanging on the walls, most of them scenes of Mexican peasants toiling in maize fields, or Native Americans. 'You an artist, ma'am?' he asked.

'Kind of. It's really just a hobby. Currency forgery is my main interest. I can do an excellent twenty-dollar bill. But I'm having trouble with the fifty note. Getting Grant's beard right and the security thread have been big problems.'

Stone gaped at her. 'Ma'am?'

'Can't you Feds take a joke? Grab a seat.'

Norton studied a painting of Native American children on a reservation and said admiringly, 'Hey, that's good. Used to paint myself, oils too, but nothing as good as this. You've got talent to burn.'

'Why, thank you, young man, you're far too kind.'

'No, I mean it.'

'Most of my work you see is for sale,' the woman said hopefully.

'No kidding.' Norton coughed. 'Yeah, well, who knows? Maybe next time I'm passing.'

Stone gave Norton a look to cut the chit-chat and then directed his attention back to his elderly host. 'How about you explain why exactly you called me, Miss Jenks?'

Jenks hesitated, as if unsure how to begin, and Stone said encouragingly, 'Take your time, ma'am. In your own words.'

'You said if I recalled anything at all. Well, about four nights ago I saw someone leaving Mr Fleist's trailer. I only remembered the incident last night, long after you'd gone.'

'*Who* left his trailer?'

'A visitor. I remember I'd just switched off my TV and was getting ready for bed when I heard voices and crossed to the window and saw the visitor talking heatedly outside Mr Fleist's trailer.'

Stone flicked open his notebook. 'Yeah? Go on.'

'There seemed to be some kind of disagreement going on between them.'

Norton said, 'A disagreement about what, Miss Jenks?'

'I didn't hear exactly. I just overheard a few words here and there. Hardly anything. But I'm pretty sure there was an argument taking place.'

'Then what did you see?' prompted Stone.

'Well, it was too dark to make out anything clearly because there was only moonlight, but I'm reasonably certain the visitor was a woman.'

'How's that?' Stone asked.

'I caught a glimpse of the outfit she was wearing when the reading light in her car came on as she climbed into her vehicle. She wore a box-cut navy two-piece, a kind of officey outfit, with pants. There was a silver motif on the sleeves, kind of like a twisting vine, halfway up each arm of the outfit. The reason I noticed the outfit so distinctly is that my daughter wears a similar one which she bought at Jasmine's Boutique over in Bethesda.'

'What's the address of the boutique?'

'I don't know exactly, but I think it's on Main Street.'

197

'You said you heard a couple of words here and there. What exactly *did* you hear?' Stone pressed.

'As the woman was leaving, she said, "You open your mouth and there'll be trouble." Those were her words, as far as I recall.' Emily Jenks smiled. 'Except there may have been an F word in there somewhere. In fact, I'm certain there was. As in . . . there'll be *fucking* trouble . . .'

Norton smiled. 'You can just say it was the F word, if it bothers you, Miss Jenks.'

'Oh no, it doesn't bother me at all,' Jenks responded. 'My deceased husband Newt used the F word all the time. He was quite partial to it, especially in the bedroom.'

Norton coughed again and said with a frown, 'Have you got any idea what the woman might have meant?'

'None at all. And I hardly know Mr Fleist or his daughter. They always keep to themselves.'

Norton threw a look at Stone, who turned back to Emily Jenks and said, 'But you're sure about the words you heard?'

'Yes, I'm very sure. I may be seventy-two next birthday but my doctor says I've got excellent hearing and my eyesight's pretty damned good too.'

'Did Fleist reply?'

'No, I didn't hear what he said, or if he did say anything. I didn't really see him either, because he remained inside the doorway.'

'Is there anything else that you overheard? Anything that might be important?'

Jenks considered, before she said, 'Well, yes, as the woman left, I saw the vehicle she drove.'

'What was it?'

'A dark blue Bronco with Virginia plates, but I didn't take note of the numbers.'

Stone frowned and glanced at Norton, who looked just as perplexed. Stone turned back to Jenks. 'You're *certain* about that? Dark blue, with Virginian plates?'

'Yes, absolutely. And it was definitely a Bronco.'

★   ★   ★

Ten minutes later, as they climbed into the Taurus, Stone looked back at Emily Jenks's trailer. 'What the fuck do you make of that?'

Norton shrugged. 'You got me there. But as a fellow artist, I could tell she liked you, Vance. At one point she had a certain look in her eye.'

'What the fuck are you talking about?'

'I reckon she was sizing you up for a nude portrait, imagining how she'd like to paint you in the buff.'

'Very fucking funny. How about being serious for a while?'

Norton grinned, then said more seriously, 'What are the chances that the old bird could have been mistaken about the Bronco?'

'She seemed pretty certain about it to me.' Stone was resolute as he looked Norton in the eye. 'I told you Moran was up to her ass in it.'

'Granted, it sounds fishy. But what some old lady thinks she saw and heard from a distance and on a moonlit night ain't exactly concrete evidence, Vance. Me, I wouldn't put a lot of store by what she said, not legally. She's raised some serious questions, that's for sure, but she sure as hell hasn't helped answer any.'

Stone started the engine. 'Then I've got an idea how we might get some answers.'

49

France

I'd always dreamt of seeing Paris, ever since I was a gawky teenager. And now it was finally happening. The only problem was my visit seemed more like a nightmare than a dream. It was 7 a.m. as I peered sleepily out of the window of the American Airlines 767.

We had started our descent over the French coast and far below me I saw crumbling sandstone cliffs and a headland of irregular, box-shaped green fields. I guessed we were somewhere over Normandy. Beside me, Cooper yawned and stretched as he opened his eyes. 'Morning,' he said. 'Or should I say *bonjour*?'

'You sleep like a two-year-old, Cooper, you know that?' I answered. He'd been zonked for most of the journey across the pond – some of it through heavy turbulence – and now he blinked and stretched some more.

'Always do when I fly. The sign of an untroubled conscience. You?'

I said, 'Almost never. I hate flying. I guess it's the feeling of not being in control. But I managed to doze for about twenty minutes. By the way, maybe I owe you an apology.'

'About what?'

'Those late nights I slated you about. I hear you have a son who's got lupus.'

Cooper nodded, but said nothing. I thought I saw pain in his eyes.

'Do you have a picture of him?' I asked.

Cooper flipped out his wallet and proudly handed me a colour pic. 'That's Neal. Light of my life.'

I saw an attractive-looking kid with dark hair, a quirky-shy smile and pale skin, who looked younger than seven. His face appeared bloated. From the background, he looked like he was in a hospital room. 'When was this taken?'

'A couple of weeks ago. He'd been having a check-up at Johns Hopkins and getting some steroid shots, that's why he looks so swollen in the photo. Neal started to show some of the symptoms of lupus about four years ago. He suffered from fatigue and breathing problems, and inflamed and swollen joints and stomach cramps. It took a while to get to the bottom of it. Treatment's a long-term thing but we've found a good local doc to call on when we need him to give his steroid shots, and the hospital looks after the broader picture. With a little luck Neal can still lead a reasonably OK life. How'd you know about lupus? It isn't that common.'

'A relative of my mom's suffered from it, years back.'

Cooper was surprised. 'No kidding? By the way, isn't it about time you called me by my first name?'

'You think so?'

Cooper offered me a smile and I saw that glint of his. 'I think so.'

'In that case, we're about to land in fifteen, Josh.'

'Yeah?' He rubbed his eyes and craned his neck to see what he could of our approach into Paris as the belly of the aircraft shuddered and we heard the whirr of the flaps being lowered. Suddenly in the distance I saw the Eiffel Tower jutting up through a thin layer of wispy cloud.

'Isn't that something,' Josh remarked, as wide eyed as a ten-year-old.

I noticed the River Seine, a grey ribbon of water that snaked across the countryside below us. 'I've always wanted to visit Paris, ever since I was a kid,' I admitted. 'What about you?'

Josh turned back from the window. 'I've been here before, in my teens. As a backpacker.'

'There's something else I ought to say. I'm sorry you had to witness the spat between Stone and me the other day. It shouldn't have happened.'

'That's OK. It's no big deal,' he replied.

'But it is. I guess it's no secret that Stone and I have had our differences.'

Josh put up a hand. 'Hey, you don't have to explain. After yesterday, I made it my business to learn about the rumours. Everybody in the office seems to know about his issues and why he's got a plank on his shoulder. The word is, the guy's resentful of you.'

'That doesn't bother you? I thought you and he were friends?'

'Stone and me? The truth is, we never really hit it off as partners,' Josh confessed.

'Really?'

'Really. Just in case you thought we might have.'

'Maybe I did.'

'Well, you're wrong.'

It was gradually dawning on me that Cooper wasn't the enemy. On top of that, he seemed like a nice guy. And I could actually see him as a pretty good dad. To cap it all the guy had considerate eyes. I saw him glance out of the window. 'So what do you think?' he asked.

'About Paris?'

He looked back at me. 'I meant about this whole damned case. It's taking on a complete other dimension. If someone had said to me twelve hours ago I'd be winging my way to France with this investigation I'd have said they were nuts.'

'That makes two of us.'

Josh said earnestly, 'Gamal's death is not in doubt, but what's getting to me is who in the hell is the sicko who's mimicking his MO, and *why* would anyone want to do that?'

I had no answer. Suddenly the seat belt lights flashed and the chime sounded. I felt a tiny flutter of excitement in my stomach that I was finally about to land, but my mind returned to Josh's question. *Who would want to mimic Gamal's MO?* As I stared out of the window I prayed that somewhere down there in Baron Haussmann's Paris we'd discover the reason why.

★   ★   ★

The aircraft touched down with a heavy bump and fifteen minutes later we disembarked. Once we had passed through Customs and baggage claim we stepped out into the arrivals area. I noticed two men standing by a pillar and carrying a placard that said 'MORAN+COOPER'.

One of the men was tall and dressed in a navy reefer jacket with the collar up. His companion was shorter and smoked an unfiltered cigarette. Josh and I approached them. 'I think you guys are looking for us.'

'Agent Moran? Agent Cooper?' the man in the reefer jacket said. Except it sounded more like *More-Ann* and *Cooo-per*. It was the first time I'd heard my surname pronounced with a French accent and it sounded a tad sexy. 'That's me, I'm Moran. This is Agent Cooper.'

'*Bonjour, madame, monsieur,*' his companion said politely. 'May I welcome you both. I am Inspector Delon, and this is my colleague Detective François Laval. We have a car outside. Please allow me to carry your baggage, madame.'

'*Merci beaucoup.*'

The inspector had a bushy moustache and a silver earring in his right lobe, and he raised an eyebrow as he led us from the terminal. 'You speak French, madame?'

'You've just heard the only two words I know, Inspector.'

A smile flickered on Delon's lips, but then suddenly Josh spoke something rapidly in what sounded like fluent French.

The inspector looked impressed. '*Mais très bien, monsieur.*'

I gave Josh a look as we followed Delon outside the arrivals building. 'You never told me you spoke the language.'

'Don't get too excited. I speak just enough to get by – and that's what I told the inspector.'

'It sounded pretty fluent to me,' I said.

'My mom was French-Canadian so we used to spend most of our summers in Quebec when we were kids. My French *grand-mère* always insisted we spoke French.'

'Any other secrets you'd care to confide?'

Josh offered me a grin. 'Maybe. But I think I'll keep them in reserve.'

The inspector led us to a navy-blue Renault parked at the kerb and Laval stashed our bags in the trunk. Delon opened the rear doors and ushered us into the back. Then he sat in the front passenger seat and turned to face us. 'There has been a development in the case, so if you don't mind we will drive straight to Sûreté headquarters.'

I felt my heart quicken as Laval started the Renault. 'What kind of development?' I asked.

Delon was grave. 'A very curious one. I received the forensic reports on the murders. All the evidence suggests that they are of the exact same nature as those committed by Constantine Gamal in Paris five years ago, except of course they were committed in the sewers and not the catacombs. In fact, even the minor details are the same. And only the police knew the crucifix was placed between the bodies because we never disclosed that exact detail to the press. Apart from the locations, you could say we're dealing with identical cases of murder.'

50

The Disciple entered an alleyway off the Rue Boulard. It was his second morning in Paris and already he was enjoying himself. Yesterday he had killed two more victims in the sewers, then made his phone call from a public phone box to sewer maintenance, which would tip off the police. All part of his strategy to lure Kate Moran.

Now he had a fantasy to act out. He really wanted to know what it was going to feel like to kill her. But first he wanted to ravage her. And he needed to act out his fantasy to perfection so that when the moment came it would all go according to plan. Which meant he needed a substitute victim. And he knew exactly where he was going to find one.

This wasn't the area around the Boulevard de Sébastopol, famous for its brothels, a colourful red-light area that buzzed with pimps, hookers and their patrons, the tenements bursting with native French and Arab and black immigrants. Instead it was a maze of alleyways in the Denfert Rochereau district, home to the Paris catacombs. The Disciple entered a hallway through a double oak door, climbed a metal staircase up to the second floor and buzzed an apartment.

The woman who came to the door was in her early thirties and very pretty. She was fair haired and wore a skimpy skirt and had terrific legs. Her short top showed off her midriff. There was a diamond stud in her belly button and another tiny one in her nose, and with her Cupid lips and firm breasts she oozed sexuality. He had spotted her the previous night on the street and finally decided that she would be perfect for what he had in mind. A change of make-up and blonde hair and she might almost look like Kate Moran.

'Monsieur?' The door was still held firmly in place by a security chain.

The Disciple spoke a little French. 'How . . . how much to spend some time with you?' He added the hesitancy for effect, making it sound as if he were a timid customer.

She smiled, as if glad to have a client at such an early hour. 'That depends on monsieur. Do you have any special desires?'

He nodded shyly. 'Just . . . just some games.'

But the woman was suddenly more wary. He guessed she'd met some weirdos in her day. And now she was about to experience her worst nightmare.

'What games had monsieur got in mind?' she asked.

He held up a small overnight bag, and said shyly in French, 'Nothing rough. Just a little game of dressing up. I . . . I have some clothes I'd like you to wear.'

'I charge three hundred euros for an hour.'

He feigned a frown. 'That . . . that's expensive.'

Suddenly the young woman had the security chain off its latch and was looking him up and down as she ran a pair of crimson manicured fingernails down his lapel and winked at him. 'Maybe. But I'm worth it.'

He swallowed nervously, which added a naive touch. 'OK. I'll pay three hundred.'

The woman stepped back to admit him. Her flat was pleasantly decorated – brushed steel lamps, soft lighting, a stone-white vase with some fresh lilies on a Scandinavian coffee table – and everything was much cleaner than he had expected. Now for the fun and games.

'The bathroom is that way, monsieur. Please take a shower first. And then I promise that you will enjoy an exquisite experience.'

The Disciple checked his watch. He just had enough time to complete his fantasy before he had to leave. The killings he had committed the previous day in the sewers were just the beginning. Because once he was done with the prostitute he had some more killing to do underground.

51

As we drove through the Paris suburbs I remembered the Constantine Gamal murders in the city five years earlier. He had attended a week-long psychiatry conference at the Paris Hilton hotel. Ironically, as it turned out, the paper Gamal wrote for the conference was entitled 'Exploring the Killer's Mind'. Which was a pretty sick joke considering that in the space of the week Gamal managed to butcher two people.

A father and his daughter – Walther J. Liephart and his seventeen-year-old daughter, Becky, both from Ohio. They were first-time tourists in Paris, celebrating Becky's high-school graduation. Their abduction and deaths were a classic case of how gullible some murder victims can be.

Gamal had managed to pick them up at a Paris metro station – overhearing their American accents, he had followed them secretly and carefully evaluated his prey before deciding the father and daughter would become his next victims. When the Liepharts appeared to lose their way, Gamal bluffed them into believing that he was an American historian working in France and proceeded to charm the hell out of the naive father and daughter. Later that afternoon he drove them around Paris to sightsee.

Then, following a pre-planned strategy, and carrying a back-pack in which he had hidden the murderous butcher's knife-belt of his trade and a lethal axe, he lured them into the catacombs below the streets of Paris on the pretext of giving them a guided tour. What Gamal did to those two victims horrified even the most hardened of the Sûreté's homicide detectives – Becky's head was axed from her body with such brute force that shards from her neck bones were embedded in the catacomb floor. The mutilated corpses were eventually discovered a week later, a small wooden crucifix lying between the bodies. A container of petroleum spirit had been discovered near by but the corpses hadn't been burned.

The assumption was that Gamal may have fled without completing that part of his ritual because the catacombs were full of tour groups and by going through with it he might have drawn attention to his crime and lessened his chance of escape.

I knew from researching Gamal's Paris murders that the catacombs stretched for almost two kilometres under the city streets. They were a maze of vaulted tunnels that contained the bones and skeletal remains of over six million Parisians. During the reconstruction of the French capital by Baron Haussmann in the late seventeenth century, entire neighbourhoods had had to be razed to the ground. Church graveyards had to be emptied, and to house the remains the catacombs were constructed deep under the city. Now they had become a tourist attraction. Parisians called the tunnels the Empire of the Dead. The eerie crypts were the perfect setting for Gamal's killings.

Inspector Delon lit a reeking French cigarette and rolled down the window as we sped over a Seine bridge. 'As far as we can determine, the murders occurred over thirty-six hours ago. The bodies were discovered by engineers working for the municipality's sewers maintenance department, very soon after the crime was committed, perhaps less than half an hour. An anonymous male caller telephoned their office and reported seeing the corpses, then hung up.'

'Could you trace the call, or was it recorded?'

'Unfortunately not. And he has not made himself known to us, despite a plea we have made through the media.'

'Who were the victims?' I asked.

Delon blew out a cloud of smoke which was vacuumed away through the open window. 'A father and his teenage daughter from Kansas. As far as we know, they were not seen in the company of anyone suspicious at their Left Bank hotel. It appears they were both butchered with a knife and an axe and their corpses placed on a small, hastily made funeral pyre and set on fire with petroleum. We found a wooden cross placed midway between the bodies.'

I shuddered. 'What else do you know about the crime scene?'

'Fortunately the bodies didn't completely burn – the engineers called the police and managed to put out the fire. We also recovered their passports and belongings, which had not been placed on the pyre. The scene is well preserved.'

Suddenly the musical tone of Delon's cell phone interrupted us and he answered the call. He spoke rapidly into his phone before he turned back to us, his face sombre. 'That was headquarters. It seems there has been an attempt to abduct and kill two more victims.'

'Where?'

'In the catacombs in the Denfert Rochereau district, where Gamal killed his Paris victims five years ago. The site is about a kilometre from the sewer tunnels where we found the other two yesterday. It seems we have witnesses.'

I felt my pulse quicken. 'Who are they?'

'A female tourist and her daughter spotted a man wielding a knife in one of the tunnels. He tried to attack them but fled the scene when the other members of the tour interrupted his attack.'

'When did this happen?' I asked.

'Less than ten minutes ago.' Delon reached under his seat and plucked out a blue light. He stuck it on the roof then hit a switch, and the *nee-naw* of the siren pierced our ears. The inspector's eyes sparked with the prospect of the challenge. 'The catacombs are no more than five minutes from here. Gendarmes are sealing off the entire area above and below ground, so there can be no escape. If the killer's down there, we will find him.'

52

My heart raced as the Renault sped through the streets of Paris and the siren wailed. The catacombs may have been no more than five minutes by car, but the journey seemed to take an eternity.

'Paris hasn't changed much,' Josh announced as we hurled along a busy tree-lined avenue with cute little pastry shops, restaurants, tiny tobacconist's shops and bars with small round tables outside.

'When exactly were you last here?'

'When I was a baby-faced freshman of nineteen.'

'Don't tell me – you had a terrific time, most of it spent chasing seventeen-year-old female students?'

Josh shook his head and his lips parted in a smile. 'Sorry to disappoint you, but younger women never did it for me, even back then. I like to stick around my own age group, it's a lot more comfortable.'

I thought: *Is he jibing me, or trying to tell me something?* But I didn't have time to dwell on it because we screeched to a halt at the end of an imposing street that was peppered with dozens of police vehicles. Traffic had been blocked off at both ends and dozens of armed gendarmes were jumping down from police vans, racing along the pavements and darting down side streets.

'We're here,' Delon announced as we pulled up in front of a centuries-old, solid-looking stone building with the French tricolour fluttering from a wall-mounted pole. The building formed part of a square containing a tiny park with a few clusters of trees. The nearby benches were home to sad-looking groups of bemused winos and the homeless.

Delon climbed out and we followed him and his colleague over to where a clutch of plainclothes police and uniformed gendarmes were receiving a briefing as they stood beside a black steel entrance door. It was open to reveal a flight of yellowed limestone steps that led down a stairwell.

Delon lit a cigarette and took an angry drag as he spoke to the cop in charge, then finally came back to join us, carrying a map protected by a sealed plastic cover. '*Voilà!* A diagram of the catacombs. So far we have the tunnels sealed off between here and here – the Boulevard de Port Royal and the Rue Dareau.'

Delon jabbed his finger at the map and Josh and I studied the diagram. I figured we were talking about an area many times the size of a football pitch, criss-crossed with tunnels, and which probably resembled an underground maze.

Delon went on, 'The officer in charge feels certain the killer is still in there somewhere.'

'How come he's so sure?' I asked.

Delon jabbed at the map. 'Because there are only a certain number of exits. And we have each one sealed off and gendarmes posted at the steel doors. No one has tried to pass up through them yet.'

'You're saying you've got the killer boxed in?' Josh suggested.

Delon's tone was confident. '*Oui*, I believe he's trapped.'

The inspector seemed pretty sure of himself, but I didn't believe in that kind of attitude unless you had the culprit handcuffed in front of you. *Especially in Gamal's case – he's as wily as a fox*. I suddenly realised the absurdity of what I'd just thought: *I'm thinking as if Gamal is still alive. Am I crazy?* Suddenly a cop with a hand-held radio raced up to Delon and spoke in an agitated manner.

'What's going on?' I asked Josh, who had listened to their heated conversation.

'From the sounds of it, the unsub's been spotted again,' he replied.

'*Where?*'

'They're jabbering so fast I can't figure out what they're saying exactly.'

I felt excited as Delon turned back to us. 'There has been another sighting by two of our officers guarding a stone staircase leading down to the catacombs, next to the old hospital of St-Vincent de Paul, a street away. They saw a man armed with a knife come up the stairs and challenged him but the man ran back down into the catacombs again and disappeared.'

'Did your officers get a look at his face?'

Delon nodded. 'The suspect was in his thirties, or early forties. Dark haired, Mediterranean looking, with tattooed arms.'

Again I could hardly believe what I was hearing. *It sounds like Gamal.* The inspector scratched his head, as if bemused. I wondered whether he was thinking the same as me. I felt a chill go through me but didn't comment. *What's the point?* Josh gave me a look, then Delon said, 'Our killer is obviously looking for a way of escape. He's probably desperate and will kill again if he feels he has to.' He removed an automatic pistol from his waist holster and stepped over to the catacombs' entrance. 'You'd both better wait above ground.'

'No way, Inspector. I'm going down with you,' I said, and immediately I thought: *Am I crazy?* I felt my palms begin to perspire, my heart drumming in my chest.

'We're both going,' Josh added.

'I'm sorry but this is a very dangerous situation,' Delon advised.

'We're still coming with you, Inspector,' Josh insisted. 'And there's no way you're going to stop us.'

Just then Detective Laval appeared, carrying two rubber-encased torches and a couple of communications radios. He started towards the door and Delon stared back at us and emitted a heavy sigh. 'Very well. But I must warn you that you do so at your own risk.'

53

I felt my legs go weak as Delon and Laval led us down the winding stone staircase to the catacombs. My heartbeat quickened at the prospect of going deep into the bowels of Paris. *What have I let myself in for?*

'It's easy to get lost in the catacombs, so stay near me,' Delon advised us, clutching the map. 'Once, a tourist got lost down here and his body wasn't found for eleven years.'

'You're kidding?' I said, alarmed, and already I felt as if the walls were closing in on me. I didn't want to take another step but I forced myself to stay as close to Josh as I could.

'Pardon?'

'I mean, you're joking.'

Delon shook his head vigorously and turned down the volume on his radio.

'No, madame, I am not. And just remember, if there's the slightest threat of any danger, keep well out of the way and leave any trouble to me and my men.'

Of course I'll keep out of the damned way – I'm not armed and I don't have a death wish.

The stairwell's limestone walls were illuminated by Delon's torch. By now we were deep underground. The air smelled damp and I couldn't stop myself shaking. I guessed we had descended well over a hundred steps, and as we came to the bottom of the staircase I saw the mouth of a tunnel with a barrel ceiling. Neon strip lights were fastened to the ceiling arches, protected by wiremesh bulkheads, and they illuminated the damp walls, which dripped water. The ground was covered with gravel chips.

And then I got one of the biggest shocks of my life. On either side of the tunnel were recessed archways that resembled church cloisters, and they were stacked high with densely packed human skulls and bones, solid mounds that were two metres high and three or four metres deep.

There were *thousands* of dead – *hundreds of thousands* – and the grim archways seemed to go on for ever. These were subterranean crypts on a massive scale, and I'd never seen such a sight. '*My God.*'

Delon shone his torch into one of the gruesome archways. 'Some of the skeletons belong to victims of the street riots during the French Revolution, over two centuries ago. You can see bullet holes in the skulls of those who were shot.'

'*Jesus.*' Josh studied the macabre mounds of bones, then laid a fingertip on one of the skulls. 'I'm touching history.'

'Up ahead you'll see what we Parisians call the Crossroads of Death,' Delon informed us.

'Why's it called that?'

'You'll see,' Delon said mysteriously, and followed Laval.

I shivered. *Why in God's name did I want to come down here?* Was I subconsciously trying to face up to my fear, or was I just being really dumb? I didn't know the answer, but my fear was alive now, and I froze with panic as the two Frenchmen moved on ahead. Josh said, 'Hey, are you OK? You seem a little shaky.'

'I . . . I'm OK.'

'Enclosed spaces bother you?'

I guessed Josh had me figured out but I shook my head. 'No, I'm fine, really.' But I wasn't fine. I was almost freaking out. To distract myself I pointed to a black granite slab above the tunnel archway, which had four short lines of an inscription in French. 'What does it say?'

Josh's eyes narrowed as he read. '"Crazy that you are, why do you promise yourself to live a long time, you who cannot count on a single day."'

'What does it mean?' I knew in my heart that I was only trying to buy time – I was *dreading* having to enter the catacomb tunnels. *Anything* to distract me.

Josh said, 'Kate, this isn't exactly the moment for poetry appreciation. But if you really need to know I think it's a line from Dante, though maybe I'm wrong.'

Up ahead, Delon waved his torch impatiently. 'Madame, monsieur. Please keep up with me. It will be safer.'

I could feel my fear growing by the second, as was my reluctance to move into the tunnel. I looked again at the lines on the black granite slab. 'Don't you think it sounds vaguely like a warning?'

'I'm damned if I know. Come on, we better catch up.' And with that Josh grabbed my arm and ushered me into the jaws of the tunnel.

54

'Stay close,' Josh whispered, and held my hand. His grip was reassuring, but with every step my sense of panic grew and my breath came in short rapid throbs. Ahead of us Delon and Laval led the way, playing their torchlight on the slimy walls. The air was damp and the ceiling dripped water. At every turn we saw ancient street signs in black slate, cemented into the walls.

'What you see are the original street names from old Paris. They were placed here along with the corpses,' Delon said as he checked the map. 'The passageway where the suspect was seen should be about two hundred metres ahead of us.'

'You're sure our man's trapped?' I asked, trying to deflect my terror. 'He can't escape the catacombs?'

Delon looked up from the map. 'Officially, the catacombs are an enclosed series of tunnels. However, I have heard rumours that they contain a number of steel doors that lead to the city's sewers, which is a separate tunnel system. But some years ago the doors were meant to have been sealed up by municipal engineers, to protect the city against a possible terrorist attack.'

'You're certain that they're still sealed, Inspector?' Josh asked.

Delon nodded. 'So Laval was informed by the engineers. But of course, there is always a chance that one of the sewers' inhabitants managed to break through the seals.'

'*Inhabitants?*' I asked.

'Drug dealers and criminals wanted by the police often make the sewers their home. They know they are safe from the law and so they hide in makeshift underground rooms. In fact, I wondered if our anonymous caller who reported seeing the bodies is one of them. It might explain why he hasn't contacted the police.'

Josh added, 'The other thing is, these places attract certain types on the fringes of society – transvestites, sadomasochists, to name but a few.'

'You're joking?' I said.

'You name it, all human life is there,' Josh remarked. 'I read about the sewers and they're a pretty weird place. Seems there's a whole underground culture going on down there. Not the kind of thing that gets mentioned in the best guidebooks.'

'Exactly,' Delon responded with a wry smile. 'Come, let us not delay.'

We passed cavernous archways stacked with skulls and bones. The sight made my claustrophobia worse and I felt a rush of blood to my head. I was feeling faint and didn't know whether I could take another step.

'Which way, Inspector?' Josh asked.

Delon consulted his map and shone his torch to the left. 'That way, I think. Stay near me, please. This part of the catacombs is extremely dangerous. The tunnels branch off in many different directions.'

Suddenly a brief shadow fell across the walls ahead of us, and then disappeared. The sound of scurrying footsteps echoed. 'There's someone up ahead,' I whispered, my heart pounding.

Delon was already readying his weapon, a glaze of perspiration on his face. 'Stay close behind me,' he urged as we moved forward carefully.

We rounded a bend and then saw that the tunnel split into two passageways.

'Which way?' Josh whispered.

Delon was sweating heavily and couldn't seem to make up his mind as he studied the map. 'I'm not sure, so I think we had better split up. Mademoiselle, may I suggest you go with Laval. Monsieur, you come with me. And please be careful. If you see anything, we can make contact on the radio.'

I didn't like the thought of going deeper into the tunnel, even with Laval for company. I was barely hanging in there as it was – really I wanted to find an exit, fast, and had the terrifying feeling that we were being watched from the shadows. I tried to tell myself that it was my own irrational mind at work. Suddenly Delon's radio squeaked and he put the mouthpiece to his lips and answered in a whisper, '*Oui?*'

As Delon listened and replied in rapid French, Josh shone his torch at me.

'You don't look too good. You sure you're OK?'

'I . . . I don't know.' I was perspiring and sensed my fear becoming more rabid by the second. I was losing it completely and felt close to collapse.

Delon finished his conversation and said, 'The suspect has been spotted again.'

'Where?' Josh asked.

I was so scared I couldn't even speak as Delon said, 'A hundred yards from here, heading in this direction. We'd better split up. The suspect will be coming towards us using one of these two passageways. Madame, if you would go with Laval and the monsieur will come with me. And for God's sake be careful.'

Delon moved right, and Josh gave me a wave before he and Delon vanished into the tunnel.

Detective Laval regarded me. 'Ready, madame?'

No, I wanted to scream. *I can't move an inch. I'm scared out of my mind and think I'm about to break down.* That's what I wanted to scream. But instead I offered the detective a tight smile. 'Sure. After you.'

Laval didn't look all that convinced, but he shrugged. Then he readied his pistol and moved into the tunnel, and I followed him.

From behind an archway, the attacker watched the woman follow the detective and swore to himself. Sweat dripped from his face. He was breathless after racing through the catacombs, trying to avoid capture. The police had blocked off every exit.

In his left hand he grasped a knife with a jagged blade. He knew he was trapped unless he could kill his pursuers. His eyes were accustomed to darkness, and as he watched from behind the pillar he saw the woman move past him after the detective and his face lit up.

He noticed that she had no gun. She'd be the first to die. As the pair moved on, he heard their footsteps fade. He wiped the knife on his jacket and grinned to himself: he felt confident he could handle them both. He looked forward to plunging his knife into their flesh, longed to see them squirm and shriek in agony.

But first he needed to get close to his victims – and he knew exactly how he was going to gain the element of surprise. Next to him on the wall was an electrical circuit box that supplied power for the bulkhead lighting. Using the metal blade of the knife he could short out the lights. He placed the tip of the knife into the screw slot and began to open the box cover.

55

I felt like a sleepwalker, dumbly trying to negotiate my way through a darkened room with nothing but my own irrational fear for company. No matter how many times I told myself that there was nothing to worry about, that I *wasn't* trapped here, that I could leave any time I wanted, it didn't help. I was still as scared as hell.

My body was bathed in perspiration, my legs trembling, and I wondered whether Detective Laval was aware that I was cracking up. I had to get to an exit *now* – it was the only way I could stay sane. And then something truly scary happened. After three or four minutes of turning corners and moving deeper into the tunnel maze, I got the feeling that Laval was lost.

He checked his map by a bulkhead light and I saw droplets of sweat drip from the end of his nose. 'Are . . . are you OK?' I asked, trying to stop my own voice trembling. I was desperately trying to conquer my fear and knew that my fight or flight instinct was kicking in, a rush of adrenalin flooding my veins.

Laval looked at me with a pair of big, brown, French eyes that reminded me of a sad dachshund. 'I . . . I am not sure, madame.'

'Let me see the map.'

'I'm certain I can find a way out eventually . . .'

Eventually? I thought: *Jesus, Laval, this isn't some country garden maze we're ambling through.* Now I *really* began to panic. My hand shook as I held it out to Laval, fear braiding my voice. 'Please . . . two heads are better.'

'Two heads?' Laval responded, confused.

'I meant we have a better chance of figuring out where we are if we work together.'

'But of course.' Laval handed me the torch and I studied the map and thought: *No wonder the guy's confused.* The drawing resembled an engineer's blueprint and was covered in tiny symbols that were impossible to understand: lines and boxes, odd little triangles, all joined up by a lattice of thick, erratic lines that resembled a web made by a drunken spider. Here and there a few typed words in French adorned the drawings, just to confuse me even more. 'What do the boxes and symbols mean?'

'I'm really not sure,' Laval confessed.

'You're not sure?'

Laval scratched his head. 'There wasn't time to consult with the engineers. I thought I could follow the map, but now it has me confused, madame.'

'Terrific.'

I heard a soft *plop*, and when I looked down I saw that water was dripping from the roof and landing in a large pool in front of my feet. *Maybe the roof is going to cave in and flood the tunnel?* My feeling of panic was beyond reason now. *My God, get me out of here, now . . .*

And then the worst thing that I could imagine happened. I heard a scraping noise and sensed a *presence* somewhere behind me. I turned and saw a spray of electrical sparks ignite in the shadows.

A split second later the tunnel was plunged into darkness.

56

I panicked, dropped my torch and the light went out. I wanted to reach down to find it, but I was riveted to the spot. I could barely muster the courage to flail my hands in the darkness in front of my face, and when I did all I touched was a damp wall. 'Laval . . . ?' I whispered, and I was tempted to scream.

'I'm here, madame,' his voice answered.

Thank God. 'Where are you?'

'Close by, madame. Please stay where you are and I'll come to you.'

'The torch!'

'I'll find it,' he answered.

I must have sounded terrified. Laval's voice was near, but not near enough for me to distinguish his location. He sounded in control and unafraid, which helped keep me from losing my mind. I was sure I saw sparks before the lights popped. I also had the weird feeling that there was someone out there in the blackness, but all I heard was my own laboured breathing and Laval's smoker's wheeze. Then something touched me and I jumped.

'It is me,' Laval said huskily. 'Are you all right, madame?'

'Did . . . did you hear a noise and see sparks before the light went out?' I whispered.

'A noise?' Laval queried. 'Sparks? No, madame. I heard and saw nothing.'

I felt relieved. Maybe I'd only imagined the noise. But I'd definitely seen the sparks. 'What . . . what could have caused the lights to go out?'

'God knows. But these things happen. Where's the torch?'

'I dropped it. I'm going to try to feel for it on the ground.'

Mustering all my courage, I dropped down to my knees. From out in the darkness around me I thought I heard a faint sound like shoes scraping and then a tiny grunt. 'Laval, is that you? Are you still there?'

'Yes, madame.'

Thank God. 'Don't move a centimetre.'

'Of course.'

I ran my hands over the puddled ground. It was covered with bits of rock and stone, pebbles and grime – I dreaded to think what else I might be laying my hands upon, but I had to find the torch. *Where the hell is it?* I moved to my left, my hands shaking as they searched – I was so damned scared that I might grab hold of a rat. My imagination was in overdrive in a darkness that felt as oppressive as the inside of a coffin. *I feel as if I'm being buried alive.*

And then my fingers touched something hard. I recoiled in fear before I prodded the object with a finger. *The torch. Thank God.*

'I've found it,' I told Laval, and grasped the torch. The glass didn't feel broken and the switch was still on. I flicked it several times but the torch wouldn't light. *Damn. Maybe the bulb shattered? Or the batteries have come loose?* A second later I heard a clatter behind me – it sounded like a metal object hitting the floor.

I jumped in fear, my heart pounding again. 'Laval? Is that you? What's wrong?'

But no one answered. I frantically tightened my grip on the butt of the torch, and suddenly the light sprang on.

Thank God.

I blinked as the tunnel was swamped in illumination. Then came the next gut-wrenching shock, which set my heart hammering wildly. The chamber was completely empty.

Laval had vanished.

57

My breathing came in rapid spasms. I was alone in the cavern. *Or am I?* I had a weird feeling that *someone* was near by. I couldn't see them but I could *sense* their presence. Then I spotted Laval's automatic pistol lying in a shallow puddle. He must have dropped his gun – that explained the metallic sound I'd heard. *But where the hell is Laval?*

'Laval? Are you there? Answer me, *please* . . .'

No one replied. I wanted to scream the question. Had Laval moved off into the darkness? *But why would he do that?* And even if he had moved he would have answered me by now. There had to be a more sinister reason for his disappearance. My legs trembled as I knelt to pick up his gun.

And then I saw something.

A black shoe.

It stuck out from behind a pillar, fifteen feet away.

Was Laval hiding behind the pillar? But why would he *hide*? I was gripped by an ice-cold terror, and as I frantically grabbed for Laval's gun I saw the foot move from behind the pillar and then suddenly Laval stepped out.

I stood, panting with relief. 'Thank God. What were you doing there . . . ?'

I saw that an arm was locked around Laval's neck. Another hand held a frightening-looking butcher's knife pressed against his throat. I couldn't see the face of the detective's captor – it was in shadow – but Laval was terrified. Sweat glistened on his forehead and he spoke in a choked voice. 'Please, madame, don't do anything unwise . . .'

I didn't intend to, but as I stared numbly at the hostage scene unfolding before my eyes I said to Laval's unseen abductor, 'Who are you . . . ?'

He ignored me, but I saw his grip tighten around Laval's throat and the detective's voice became a strangled whisper. 'Please, madame . . . put down the gun or he really will kill me.'

I shone the torchlight on Laval's face, then flicked it towards the killer. He was well hidden behind the pillar. I caught only the briefest glimpse of the shadowed side of his head and then he disappeared again. *Who is he?* Suddenly he pressed the blade against Laval's throat and a trickle of blood appeared.

'Please, madame . . .' Laval begged in a strangled voice.

I knew that if I dropped the gun the killer would finish us both. I heard his laboured breathing as he whispered something into Laval's ear.

The detective said hoarsely, 'He said if you don't put the gun down this *second* he'll cut my throat . . .'

I saw a livid fear in Laval's face, but I also saw a grim resolve, and I was about to learn just how brave the Frenchman was.

'OK, I'm putting the gun down,' I announced.

As I slowly placed the gun on the ground I kept the torch trained on Laval's face and saw him give a tiny shake of his head, his eyes saying no, as if he was willing me *not* to obey the command I'd been given. *Don't put down the gun*, he seemed to say. I knew he was right – the only chance we both had was if I remained armed. And then it happened, so quickly that I barely had time to react.

Laval grunted and with a supreme effort he attempted to grasp his assailant's hand and free himself. 'Shoot him!' he screamed hoarsely.

The warning died in Laval's throat. His attacker slashed with the blade and a fountain of blood stained the detective's neck. But at that precise moment the attacker was caught in my torch-light and I saw that he wore a black ski mask. I aimed for a head shot. I fired twice and Laval's attacker was punched back into the shadows.

I fired again and again, hammering him back into the tunnel, one of the shots snapping his head back with such ferocity that his skull cracked off the wall. Then he slumped down in a heap and lay still.

58

I was jubilant. *I've killed Gamal's copycat.*
But my jubilation died when I shone my torch back at Laval. Blood streamed from the gash in his throat; his shirt and jacket were drenched in crimson. The detective was still alive – a gurgling sound came from his lips – but I knew that if I didn't act fast he'd bleed to death. I tore off my scarf and pressed it against his neck to try to stem the bleeding. 'Can you hear me, Laval?'

His eyelids flickered and he grunted a faint reply. I thought I heard a sound behind me and gripped the pistol and spun round, shining the torch at the killer's body. He didn't move. *Is he really dead?* My heart wavered, but my fear of dark and confined spaces was momentarily forgotten – I wanted to see the killer's face close up, wanted to see who had tried to murder Laval and me.

I took the Frenchman's right hand and kept it pressed against the scarf. 'Hold it against your neck, it'll stop the bleeding. Do you understand me?'

Laval's eyes closed but he kept his hand pressed against his throat. I inched closer to the body, playing the torchlight into the shadows. I washed the light over the still form until it settled on the masked man's face, only the eyeholes visible in the mask. I felt bile rise in my throat. There was a gunshot entry wound above his left eye and his left jaw was a bleeding pulp of shattered bone and flesh, where one of my shots had drilled through the woollen mask. Suddenly the killer's right hand jerked in a tiny spasm.

My heart jumped as I aimed my gun at him and then I heard a rush of air escape from his lips and his chest deflated. His hand fell still, hung there limply like a twisted claw. Echoing footfalls charged down one of the tunnels.

I spun round as Delon appeared, Josh behind him, along with three other armed gendarmes. I was still in shock, but the next thing I knew Josh was by my side, his arm around my shoulder. 'Hey, take it easy.'

'I got him, Josh. I got him!' I said hoarsely. Then reality kicked in as I stared over at Laval. 'We need an ambulance and paramedics right away. Laval's bleeding badly.'

Delon rushed to Laval's aid and felt for a pulse. One of the gendarmes shouted into his radio and within minutes another uniformed gendarme appeared from one of the other tunnels, escorting two paramedics. They attended to Laval and finally Delon came over and put a hand on my arm.

'Are you OK, Madame Moran?'

'I'll be fine. It's Laval I'm worried about. Will he live?'

Delon looked worried as the paramedics gingerly loaded Laval on to their stretcher and carried him away, guided by the gendarmes carrying torches. 'I can only pray. He's one of my best detectives. What happened here?'

I told Delon. Beads of sweat glistened on his forehead as he stared over at the masked body sprawled in the shadows. He hadn't yet put away his gun. 'Let's take a look at him.'

Josh and I followed Delon. He shone his torch at the killer and started to pull off the bloodied ski mask. I didn't know what to expect, but suddenly I had a completely irrational thought: *Will I see Gamal's face?*

Delon removed the mask. The left side of the killer's skull was mangled by my gunshots. He had the same black hair and Mediterranean olive complexion as Gamal but that was where the similarity ended. The dead man was older, more heavily built, and his shoulders were broader. He also had two long crude tattoos on each of his forearms, of naked women with their legs splayed.

'Interesting,' Delon remarked, examining the killer's face.

'You know this guy?' Josh asked.

Delon nodded. 'Yes, I know him.'

'Who was he?' I asked.

Delon was grim as he looked around the catacombs. Suddenly it seemed as if the grisly sight of rotting bones was too much. He put away his gun. 'Come, I think we all need some fresh air.'

59

Five minutes later we climbed up a stone stairwell into the chilly Parisian sunshine. I saw an ambulance speeding away, presumably with Laval, its sirens blaring, as Delon stared after it. I realised I still had Laval's pistol and I removed the magazine, made sure the safety catch was on and handed the weapon over to the inspector. 'What happens next?'

Delon slipped the pistol and mag into his pocket. 'Naturally there will have to be a formal investigation into the shooting. This should not affect your freedom to leave France, but it must be done, you understand?'

'Of course.'

'Laval is a married man with three children, it would be a tragedy if he died. We were lucky you managed to shoot his attacker.' Delon took a packet of Gauloises from his pocket and offered one to Josh and me. 'Cigarette?'

We both shook our heads. 'Who was the man I just shot?' I asked.

Delon lit his cigarette with a cheap plastic lighter and blew out a cloud of smoke. He sighed and gestured to a bench across the street. 'Let's sit down.'

We walked ten yards across the street and sat. Near by was a gathering of drunken winos, chatting and rolling their own cigarettes, oblivious to the bustling police presence.

Delon took a drag on his Gauloise. 'His name was Pierre Jupe, an escaped killer. A year ago he was found guilty of the savage rape and murder of two women and sentenced to life imprisonment. Then a month ago he managed to escape from a high-security prison on the outskirts of Paris. The alarm was raised and a massive police search was carried out but Jupe was not found. I believe now that he may have taken refuge underground. You have helped us to put an end to a brutal career.'

'Why would he kill in the same fashion as Constantine Gamal?' Josh asked.

Delon shrugged. 'Are we really certain that he did? As I told you, criminals wanted by the police often hide out in the sewers. I suspect that yesterday our searches underground for the killer got too close, and maybe Jupe found a way into the catacombs for his own safety. God knows why he tried to attack the two women. Perhaps he saw it as an opportunity not to be missed. Unlucky for him, but lucky for us.'

'You don't think Jupe is the same killer who murdered the couple in the sewers?' I suggested.

Delon considered. 'It's impossible to answer your question without seeing the complete forensic evidence. But I have my doubts. Jupe wouldn't be the kind to kill his victims in the same manner as the two Americans killed yesterday. May I ask why the FBI sent two of its agents to Paris so quickly? I get the feeling that you are both especially interested in these crimes.'

Josh said, 'We think there's a Gamal copycat at work. He's already killed two people in the US in the last week.'

Delon stared back at us with raised eyebrows. 'I see. Most curious.'

'We wanted to find out if there were any links between our case and yours. It seems there may be. The position of the crucifix suggests we're dealing with the same killer.'

Delon stood and crushed out his cigarette with his shoe. 'So it would appear. And unfortunately a killer who is still at large. But I can assure you that we will use every resource we have to catch whoever is responsible. I will make sure we liaise with the FBI.'

I pulled up my collar as a gust of bitterly cold wind slashed at my face. Delon sounded bullish but I didn't feel so confident of finding our killer. 'I'd like to see the murder scene in the sewers,' I told him.

'You're sure you feel up to it after what happened?' Josh enquired.

'Yes, I'm fine. If it's OK with you, Inspector?'

Delon nodded. 'Of course. It's not far, about a kilometre away. We can go there now.'

Josh and I followed Delon to his Renault and a few minutes later we trundled into a quiet cobbled alleyway in a commercial area that was dominated by sturdy old granite buildings. Halfway down the alleyway two uniformed gendarmes stood guard beside a squared-off section of crime scene tape and saluted us as we climbed out of the car.

Delon said, 'Unfortunately there are mostly offices in this area, empty in the evening, so we have had no luck in finding witnesses who saw anything suspicious. The bodies were found directly beneath this street, over there.'

The inspector pointed to a heavy metal grille set in the cobbles. He still had his torch and he handed Josh and me one each before he spoke to the gendarmes, who unlocked and lifted the grille, exposing a set of granite steps that led downwards. Delon said, 'It's a maintenance entrance to the sewers. According to the engineers, the grille lock mechanism is quite simple and would not have been difficult to open.'

We followed Delon down the steps into a darkness filled with the stench of sewage and a faint whiff of petroleum. We were in a huge sewer tunnel below the alleyway, with ancient stone walkways on either side. A filthy river of raw sewage rushed past in a deep rutted channel in the middle. When I flashed my torch I saw slimy brown walls and a barrel ceiling that glistened with moisture.

We were only steps away from the granite stairway leading above ground, and I could see the blue light of the sky, which helped to calm my claustrophobia. We were on the left-hand walkway, and I studied the site as Josh did the same a couple of steps behind me, holding a paper tissue to his mouth to mask the stench. But there wasn't much to see. The area where the bodies had been burned was squared off with portable metre-high metal poles embedded in concrete weights to keep them upright, and protected with more crime scene tape, the stone ground blackened by the fire the killer had set encircled by a chalk mark. Part of the blackened ground looked like a patch of congealed tar. As I flashed my torch around the stinking darkness I confirmed with Delon that several other chalk markings inside the circle indicated where shards of the victims' bones had been found, the result of their bodies being hacked with an axe.

The scene was much the same as the Gamal murder sites I'd witnessed, but that still didn't fail to send a chill through me. After five more minutes of observing my silent inspection, Delon seemed barely able to endure the terrible stench and asked, 'Have you seen enough?'

'I think so. Josh?'

Josh nodded and took the tissue from his mouth. 'I guess.'

'Now, I should take you both to your hotel, *non*?' Delon suggested.

I took a long look around the sewer and was tortured by a couple of familiar questions: *Who killed here and why?* Up above me I could hear the faint sounds of the busting streets of traffic-clogged Paris. Our killer was still on the loose in a massive city of over six million souls, and for some reason I had a strange feeling that we were being toyed with, as if this was all part of some evil game plan.

Josh took hold of my arm, jolting me from my reverie, and wrinkled his nose. 'I think the inspector's right about heading back to our hotel, Kate. After visiting this place I reckon we could both do with a hot shower.'

60

The Disciple sat on the bed, watching the woman undress. The dimly lit room was clean, the sheets fresh, and the air smelled of lavender. The woman was quite ravishing, and he studied her as she slipped off her dress and top and stood in front of him in panties and bra. He said in French, 'Remove the rest.'

The woman gave him a smile as she unhooked her bra. Her swollen breasts looked luscious – just the way he liked them.

'Remove *everything*,' he ordered, his breath quickening. He adored seeing a woman strip, and he watched with pleasure as she slowly peeled off her flimsy panties and tossed both bra and panties on to the bed.

'Exactly what kind of games had you got in mind, monsieur?'

The Disciple took his rucksack from the floor and slowly removed the items: a blond wig, a pastel cream nightdress, a roll of Clinique No. 31 pink 'style' lipstick, a pair of black lacy panties and a fake gold chain. They were all duplicates of items that he'd seen in Kate Moran's cottage, except the wig. The other things he left hidden in the backpack.

The woman studied the items and smiled, as if she already knew the script – he was like all the other johns who got a perverse kick out of her dressing up as a neighbour's wife they lusted after, or just some bitch they worked with who they'd like to fuck. *Whatever turns you on, moron.* She nodded to the things he'd placed on the bed and plucked the wig from the pile. 'You want me to wear all these?'

'Yes.' The Disciple closed the backpack. The remaining items were for the big finale. He watched as the woman made a show of putting on the nightdress, then the underclothes and chain, before she crossed to a mirror, slipped on the wig and applied the pink lipstick. She placed her hands on her hips and leaned forward, displaying her breasts. 'Now do you want to fuck me, *chéri?*'

No doubt about it, the bitch did the trick. *She's fucking perfect.* With the dim lighting and his vivid imagination she could resemble Kate Moran. 'Yes. Come here,' he ordered hoarsely.

She sashayed over, flicked her fingers through his hair and stared him in the eye. 'You better fuck me good, *chéri.*'

'Don't . . . don't worry, I will,' he promised. 'But I'd like to be a little rough.'

'Hey, I don't go in for anything *too* weird or heavy, OK?'

In an instant, he changed. The rage that exploded from him was like an eruption of lava as he grabbed the woman's arms, spun her round and entered her savagely from behind, gripping her hair. She seemed a little frightened but she didn't complain – she was obviously used to rough sex. It was all over in less than five minutes, and when he was spent he lay back on the bed.

'Good?' she asked, turning to him and tidying her hair.

'Sure.' Not that he thought the bitch gave a shit. She was just making chit-chat. He nodded. 'You said an hour. I'd like to do it once more.'

The woman shrugged, gave a tiny sigh and looked as if she had been hoping he'd already had enough. 'As you wish.'

'Bend down. I want to take you again from behind,' the Disciple ordered.

As the woman bent over he quickly reached into the rucksack and took out the slim, three-inch hypodermic needle. He plunged it into her right buttock and then struck her a blow across the back of the head that sent her reeling on to the bed. She moaned in pain, paralysed by the blow. In an instant he had taken out the gag and the rope. The woman was still conscious and she attempted to scream but he struck her again.

Her head slumped to one side and her body fell still. A minute later he had her trussed up, the gag tight around her mouth and a thick rope tying her hands and feet together. He slapped her awake. This time he'd deliberately used a smaller dose. He wanted to see the whites of the woman's eyes when he killed her, just like he intended with Kate Moran. She was groggy from the drug but she stared at him in horror, as if hardly believing that her mild-mannered customer had turned into a savage beast.

This was the part he enjoyed the most, seeing his victims paralysed with terror. The frightened look in their pleading eyes turned him on, made him feel like God. He grinned. 'You said I'd enjoy it. You were *so* right, *chérie*. This is where the fun begins.'

Raw panic erupted in the woman's face and she tried to scream behind the gag. All of his furies emerged now as he saw her face turn red, as if she was going to burst a blood vessel. But it was useless. No one could hear her cries for help.

The Disciple plucked the leather belt of butcher's knives from his rucksack.

Just before noon the Disciple was a passenger on the Air France bus to Charles de Gaulle that left from the Arc de Triomphe. He felt invigorated, as if he were a new man – freshly disguised and clean shaven, his hair coloured grey and gelled back off his face, his eyes tinted aquamarine blue with contact lenses. He wore a smart linen suit and carried expensive leather baggage. No one would ever recognise him as the backpacker who'd entered the Rue Boulard in search of sex.

When the bus pulled up outside Charles de Gaulle Departures, he climbed down with the other passengers and made his way across the road to the terminal entrance. He approached an Air France reservations desk, and a stunning young woman of Moroccan extraction wearing a luscious cherry lipstick smiled up at him with huge brown eyes. 'Monsieur?'

'I'd like to check in for my flight. I have a business-class ticket.'

The woman frowned. 'Your flight to where, monsieur?'

'Istanbul.'

61

Our hotel was on the Left Bank. For once we didn't get stuck with some lousy budget motel but a decent four-star. We each had pleasant rooms with Egyptian cotton sheets, double-sized beds, a complimentary tea and coffee tray and a mini-bar. There were even views of the Seine and the Eiffel Tower, and under different circumstances the Normandy Hotel might have been the perfect romantic retreat.

Josh came with me into my room and we both stared in awe at the stunning views that went all the way to the white-stone cathedral of Montmartre. I wanted to say *wow* but resisted.

'Is it anything like you imagined it to be?' Josh asked.

'Even better.' I wanted to add: *All that's missing is a lover to share it with*.

When I looked back, Josh put a hand on my shoulder. 'You reckon you're OK after the shooting?'

His touch felt like a tiny jolt of electricity. 'Positive,' I lied, but I didn't want to dwell on it. His touch felt good, but then his hand slid away.

'The tunnels seemed to bother you.'

I glossed over Josh's observation. 'They made me feel a little nervous, but I'm fine now. So what you want to do about tonight?'

Our return flight was open – we could sort out the details later with Delon – but right now we had an evening in Paris ahead of us, and it might even be pleasant if only I could stop thinking about the man I'd just killed. The only consolation was that Jupe was a brutal killer who had inflicted horrific torture on his innocent victims. But that didn't diminish the heavy guilt I felt at taking a human life.

Josh said, 'I guess you're pretty exhausted seeing as you didn't sleep much on the flight. I could do with some rest myself. How about we have a nap, then meet at seven?'

'Sounds fine to me.' Delon had invited us to dinner that evening, and we'd agreed to meet in the lobby at 7.15, but I got the feeling he'd probably be preoccupied with Laval's condition and was just trying to be sociable to his visitors.

'See you at seven, then.' Josh headed for the door but suddenly turned back. 'You mind if I ask you a question?' His eyes lingered on my face.

'Ask away.'

'Did you ever shoot anyone dead before?'

'No. I wounded a guy once. You?'

Josh nodded. 'Seven years ago. It's not an easy thing to cope with if you're halfways human. It took me months to get over it. You dream about it, have nightmares for a time, even begin to have all kinds of doubts about yourself, your abilities, your motives.'

I nodded. 'I think I know what to expect, Josh.'

'Then that's half the battle. I guess what I'm saying is, if you feel the need to talk, I'm only two doors away. I know we're colleagues but I'd like to think we can also be friends.'

I touched his arm and looked into his eyes. He really sounded thoughtful and caring. 'Thanks, I appreciate that.'

And then Josh did something totally unexpected. He reached out and gently touched my cheek with the palm of his hand. I was surprised by his gesture, and when his eyes stared into mine I felt so tempted to move into the comfort zone of his body and kiss him. But suddenly the shrieking sound of a barge horn out on the Seine broke the spell and we both stood there, staring awkwardly at each other. 'You need me, just holler,' Josh said quietly.

I squeezed his hand before he let it fall away. 'Thanks, Josh.'

'Get some sleep, OK?'

I stood at the window after Josh had gone and stared out at the Seine. Barges drifted by on the cold green river. It had started to rain, a raw drizzle that licked the streets. It was barely noon, but so much had happened in the last four hours since I'd landed in Paris that I had to pinch myself to ensure that I wasn't dreaming.

Yes, I'm in Paris. And yes, I've just shot a man dead.

But what bugged me most was the thought that our copycat killer was probably still out there. I wondered what he'd get up to next. Sleep was going to be difficult. I had memory flashes of the darkened catacombs, and I still didn't know how I'd got through the tunnel experience. But I knew I didn't want to *ever* do it again. *Work on the fear*, my mind told me. *Use fear to your own advantage*. Sure, it all sounded terrific until you had to do it. My mind felt tortured as I recalled the masked man holding the knife to Laval's throat, and relived the moment when I had shot him in the head.

I came away from the window, feeling shattered as I collapsed on the bed. Another five minutes and I was starting to doze. For some reason, I kept thinking of Josh's hand touching my face. *What would have happened if I'd allowed it to go farther?*

I tried not to even go there. Eventually I drifted off to sleep, my mind swirling with the images of the darkened tunnels and the bullet-shattered face of the man I'd just killed.

62

Angel Bay, Virginia

Stone turned his car into the driveway of Kate Moran's cottage. Gus Norton took one look at the immaculately landscaped gardens, the upmarket view and the main house and whistled. 'Hey, nice place. How long's Moran been living here?'

'Since about six months after they met. Then Bryce went and left her the property in his will.'

Norton whistled again. 'This place must be worth well over a mill, at least. How come you know so much about Moran's personal life?'

'Because I've made it my business to know. Three months ago a Victorian farther along the Bay went for a million and a half. You credit that?'

'So Moran did OK for herself.'

Stone's face had a look of resentment. 'When you add in the half-million dollars and the paintings Bryce left her I'd say she's only biding her time before she quits the Bureau. If you ask me, the bitch is a gold-digger.' He unbuckled his seat belt, ready to step out of the car.

'You really think this is wise, Vance?' Norton asked.

'She's out of the country. It's the best opportunity we've got.'

Norton looked uncertain. 'That wasn't what I meant. What you've got in mind to do isn't exactly legit.'

Stone sighed. 'Listen, don't be a dickhead. So far Moran's boxed us clever. Now we've got a chance to get even.'

'Except it's highly fucking illegal, Vance. We're breaking and entering, for Christ sakes.'

Stone smiled tightly. 'And no one's going to know about it but us, so long as you keep your trap shut. OK? Now let's get up to the cottage.'

Norton sighed and gave a reluctant nod. Stone handed him a pair of latex evidence gloves and slipped another pair in his pocket as he went up to the cottage front door and rang the intercom.

'Why are you ringing if Moran's in Paris?' Norton pulled on his gloves. 'She lives alone, right?'

'She's got a cleaning lady comes in twice a week, and today's one of her days. Except she's usually gone by now, but better safe than sorry. If she answers, we tell her we got the wrong address and come back later.'

'What about an alarm?'

'The code is David Bryce's birth date.'

'How the fuck do you know all this?' Norton asked.

Stone tapped his nose with an index finger. 'I've been doing my homework.'

'Now you've got me worried. Sounds to me like you've been doing a lot of fucking homework, Vance.'

'OK, so I took a look in her desk drawers a while back. I saw the code written down in her notebook. I also found a spare set of her house keys and got a copy made. Happy now?'

'No, I ain't, Vance. Aren't you going over the top searching through her stuff? That could be construed as tampering. If Lou finds out he'll bust your balls. What the hell else have you been up to?'

Stone suddenly turned on his colleague and gave him a menacing stare. 'Nothing, you hear? And Lou ain't going to find out so long as you keep your mouth shut. I thought we were partners, Norton. Whose fucking side are you on?'

'Sure we're partners, but—'

'Then trust me. I told you, Moran's as guilty as sin and I'll prove it yet, no matter what it fucking takes.' Stone looked across the empty grounds as he pressed the buzzer a couple more times. No one answered. Then he slipped a hand into his jacket pocket and took out a set of keys and said to Norton, 'Time we took a look around Moran's lair.'

63

They stepped into the cottage hallway, Stone using the set of copied keys. Norton closed the door while Stone disabled the alarm. They moved into the front room. A panoramic window looked out across the bay shore. '*Jeez*, terrific view,' Norton remarked.

'We came here to work, not admire the damned bay, so get to it,' Stone responded. 'And be extra careful, Gus. I don't want her to know someone's been here.'

'Sure. I'll leave everything as it was.'

'You take downstairs, I'll take the bedrooms.'

Five minutes later, Norton was checking the kitchen drawers, searching among a pile of letters and bills, when he heard Stone call out from the upstairs landing, 'Get your ass up here, quick.'

Norton climbed the stairs. When he entered Kate Moran's bedroom, Stone was standing by one of the closets, tiny beads of perspiration beading his face. 'Take a good look at this,' he announced.

He held up a navy two-piece outfit on a wooden hanger. Norton saw a spiral of silver brocade on the jacket's arms and he whistled. '*Shit.*'

'Just like Emily Jenks said. A navy two-piece with a silver brocade.'

'What are we going to do with it?' Norton asked uncertainly.

'Pop it in an evidence bag and take it with us. Have Diaz take a look at it and check the fibres to see if they match the fibres we found under the Fleist girl's nails and on the dog. I don't have to tell Diaz who the outfit belongs to.'

'*What?* We didn't even have a fucking warrant to get in here, Vance. It wouldn't be admissible.'

Stone carefully removed an evidence bag from his pocket, then rolled up the outfit and popped it inside. 'We've no choice. Moran might try to get rid of it. Keep looking a little longer.'

'For what?'

'Anything that looks interesting. Then we'll get the hell out of here.'

Twenty minutes later they reset the house alarm and climbed into the Taurus.

'What now?' Norton asked.

Their only discovery had been the two-piece, but Stone seemed bullish as he started the ignition. 'Remember we talked with Brogan Lacy after the killings of her daughter and her ex?'

'Sure.'

'I figure I ought to have a talk with her again, this time with specific reference to Moran. Maybe it's time I heard what she has to say about the woman who wanted to marry her ex-husband. And maybe I'll bring Lou along.'

'Yeah?'

'Yeah. And then I'll tell him what we've found.'

64

Paris, France

I woke to the sound of a barge horn on the Seine. It was dark outside and I was groggy as I fumbled to see my watch. Six p.m. I'd closed the curtains in the hope that I'd get some sleep, but after tossing and turning I had dozed for barely three hours.

I knew I'd have to call Lou soon, so after I had made myself a cup of Nescafé instant I dialled his direct line. I got his voice-mail on the third ring. So I left a message to say I'd try calling him again but that if he needed to talk urgently he could contact me on my cell phone. I didn't mention what had happened in the catacombs: I'd explain when we spoke in person. I dreaded having to tell him that the French would hold an inquiry: Lou *hated* any kind of inquiry involving his agents, and I figured this one would have him snarling.

Next, I checked my cell phone for messages. There were three, all from Paul, my ex, and I figured they had been sent while I was on my way across the Atlantic and my cell had been switched off. *'Look, I'm sorry about the other day. I was being an asshole.'* He didn't sound to me in any way sorry, except for himself. *'How about we meet and talk this through, Kate? The truth is, I can't seem to live without you. Besides, I know now we ought to have stayed together and the divorce was a mistake.'*

His next message was more brief, and had been sent two hours later, after I hadn't replied to his first call. *'What's the matter, why won't you talk? Just call me, for Christ sakes.'*

The third one had come three hours later and was abusive. *'Why the fuck won't you call, Kate? Are you ignoring me? Well,*

245

you're not going to ignore me for ever, you hear? Fuck you.'

What was happening to Paul? He'd become so bitter towards women since Suzanne had walked out on him. It worried me that he couldn't control his temper – his behaviour was getting worse. If he wasn't careful he'd get himself in trouble. I decided it would be pointless to call him back.

By a quarter before seven I had showered, washed my hair, dressed in a cream trouser suit for dinner and put on make-up. Five minutes later I knocked on Josh's door. He opened it wearing a pale grey sweatshirt that was cut off at the elbows, and I had to admit he looked good in casuals: the grey showed off his tanned, muscled arms, and his day-old stubble was definitely kind of burly.

'You're early. Didn't you sleep much?' he asked.

'Nope. I was beat as hell but only managed three hours. You? Don't tell me, you slept like a day-old baby?'

Josh smiled back at me as he led me inside. 'Pretty much. I'll just shower and shave and I'll be ready to go in fifteen minutes.'

True to his word, fifteen minutes later we were in the elevator travelling down to the lobby. Josh was dressed in a pair of casual pale chinos, black leather loafers, a navy blazer and an open-necked pale blue cotton shirt, and the aftershave balm he'd rubbed on his face smelled good. 'You hungry?' he asked.

'Not really. I think the shooting's taken the edge off my appetite. So anywhere's fine with me, even a burger-and-fries joint.' With all that was going on in my mind the last thing I was thinking about was food.

Josh smiled as we stepped out into the lobby. 'Better not mention burgers and fries to Delon, or he'll probably have a fit. You know the French, they take their cuisine pretty seriously. Did you call Lou?'

'Yes, except he wasn't at his desk.'

'Did you leave a message about the shooting?'

'I said I had something important to tell him and asked him to call me as soon as he got a chance.'

There was no sign of Delon in the lobby and after ten minutes

246

we decided to head out into the street and wait there. 'I've been wondering if Stone's made any progress,' Josh remarked.

I didn't even want to *think* about Stone. I just hoped he kept out of my way in future. But I didn't have a chance to reply to Josh because as we hit the pavement a white Citroën pulled up in front of us and Delon jumped out of the passenger side. He offered us his hand before he held open the rear door for us. 'My apologies for being late, but I was at the hospital checking on Laval.'

'How is he?'

'Alive, thankfully, and the doctors are hopeful, which is good news.' Delon ushered us into the back seats. The restaurant was in the Latin Quarter, less than five minutes away by car, and on the short journey the inspector wove the tiny Citroën in and out of traffic like a man possessed – but then everyone in Paris seemed to drive as if they were high on crack. 'I'm afraid I have no more news, except to say that we are still searching the catacombs and the sewers for our killer and for any evidence. I have over twenty search teams working around the clock. But with such a large area to inspect, it will take time.'

'Do you have results from the crime scene of the two victims?' I asked.

'We are still working on it. In fact, if it interests you it might be better if you remained in Paris an extra day or two until we have something.'

Josh said, 'Inspector, if our boss agrees we'd be happy to take you up on that.'

But I could imagine Lou's response to a request for an extra couple of days in Paris: *Get your asses back here, pronto.* We pulled up outside a cosy, well-lit restaurant overlooking the Seine. Delon parked the Citroën out front and led us inside. My appetite returned, and in the course of the next two hours I enjoyed a delicious meal of fresh crab salad, red snapper and steamed vegetables, followed by a crème brûlée dessert. The mood was lightened by the half-bottle of white wine and the glass of cognac I drank with dinner. And despite his preoccupation with Laval's health, Delon turned out to be an entertaining host.

As we left the restaurant, he offered to drive us back to our hotel, but Josh said to me, 'How about a walk along the river? The fresh air will do us some good. We can always grab a cab later.'

The Seine's bridges were lit up by soft green lighting and some steps led down to a pedestrian walkway along the river. A tourist barge drifted past, and a bank of powerful halogen lamps positioned on its decks suddenly sprang to life and illuminated the twelfth-century Notre Dame cathedral. I agreed with Josh and said to Delon, 'If you don't mind we're going to take a walk, Inspector. We'll make our own way back to our hotel.'

Delon shrugged and offered us a handshake. 'As you wish. You have my number if you need to contact me. Let us talk tomorrow.'

I shook Delon's hand. 'Thanks for all your help, Inspector.'

'Goodnight, madame, monsieur.' Delon gave a polite bow, climbed into his Citroën and waved us farewell as he drove away.

I looked at Josh. He stared back at me with what I thought was meaningful intent, then he kindly offered me his arm. 'Let's go take that walk.'

65

Richmond, Virginia

Stone drove into the public parking lot across the street from the Medical Examiner's office. 'Lacy says she can only spare us fifteen minutes – she's back on duty at two.'

Lou Raines finished the chicken tikka sandwich that he'd bought for lunch and wiped his mouth with a paper napkin. 'What you haven't told me is why the frig you want to talk with her? What's your angle?'

Stone reversed into a parking space. 'Maybe Brogan Lacy can shed some light on why her ex-husband drew up his will so that Kate Moran would be the sole beneficiary if Megan died.'

Raines rolled the cellophane sandwich wrapper into a ball, popped it in the ashtray and exhaled a deep sigh. 'I thought I told you to lay off Moran. The last thing I want is this thing between you two turning into a frigging vendetta. I can't give your theory any credence, Vance. I know Kate. She's not a schemer, or worse a killer, for Christ sakes. I'll make a bet right now your theory's off the wall.'

Stone bit back his temper as he opened his door. 'We can't ignore the fact that Gamal claimed he didn't do the Bryce killings. Or that we've got another copycat killer on the loose that could be anyone. So how about you just bear with me on this one, Lou? Who knows what we might hear?'

'A hundred to one says this is a waste of time,' Raines grunted, and they crossed the street and entered the ME's office. Stone led the way to a suite of rooms and rapped on the door.

'Come in,' a female voice said.

Brogan Lacy looked up from a laptop as the two men entered her office. An uneaten sandwich and a bottle of spring water stood on her desk, along with some notepads and pens, and she didn't look happy to see her visitors. Stone said, 'Promise you we'll be out of your hair before you know it.'

Lacy looked resentful as she placed some papers in a file and removed her glasses. 'As I explained when you called, Agent Stone, I have an autopsy to attend at two o'clock.'

'Yes, ma'am, I understand. This won't take long.' He introduced Raines. 'I think you already met my superior, Senior Agent Raines.'

'Yes, we met before and during the trial.' Brogan Lacy shook Raines' hand and gestured to some chairs. 'Take a seat, gentlemen.'

Stone took a seat but Raines remained standing and said, 'We're truly sorry to have to bother you, Miss Lacy. How've you've been since we last met?'

Suddenly the businesslike mask slipped and Brogan Lacy's face took on a tortured look. 'I'm getting by, Mr Raines. Most people must imagine that doctors are more easily able to cope with death because they often deal with it on a daily basis. But I'm afraid no amount of training can ever prepare you for losing your only child.'

'I'm sure not. That kind of loss is hell to deal with,' Raines said genuinely.

'I think I accepted the loss of David a little more easily because we'd already divorced and moved on, but you never divorce yourself from your children.'

Raines answered, 'No, of course. I'm sorry, perhaps I shouldn't have asked. I'm sure the pain is still a constant.'

Lacy said, 'Actually, maybe now is the time to say I'm grateful that your department did a fine job of catching David and Megan's killer.'

'Thank you,' Raines replied.

'Now, how can I help you both?'

Stone said, 'It's about your ex-husband's will. When we spoke this morning you explained that David had bequeathed his entire estate to Megan. But that in the event of Megan's death, the sole beneficiary would be Kate Moran.'

'Yes, that's correct.'

Stone said earnestly, 'Miss Lacy, did it strike you in any way strange that David would make Kate Moran such a beneficiary, even though he had only known her a relatively short time, just over a year?'

'What do you mean by strange?'

'I guess I mean suspicious,' Stone answered.

Brogan Lacy looked from Raines to Stone, and frowned. 'Am I allowed to ask where this conversation is leading?'

Stone said, 'We can cover the explanations later, Miss Lacy. If you would just answer the question for now, we'd appreciate it.'

Brogan Lacy frowned. 'Are you in any way suggesting that Kate Moran may have done something *wrong* by benefiting from my ex-husband's will? That you're suspicious of her because she profited from my husband's death?'

'Nobody said that, Dr Lacy,' Raines answered.

'They didn't have to, but unless I'm deaf it's what is being implied.'

Lacy looked from Raines to Stone, waiting for an answer.

Stone obliged. 'Let's just say we're trying to tie up some loose ends, Doc.'

Lacy scowled. 'What loose ends? I thought the investigation was closed. The man who killed my ex-husband and daughter has been executed.'

'Yes he has, Miss Lacy, but if you could just answer the question. Did you think it strange?' Stone asked again.

Lacy replied, 'Look, I really don't know what this is all about but let me make one thing clear. David loved Kate. He felt that he had at last found a soulmate and I was happy that he'd got together with someone who could love him. In my experience, he could be a very difficult man to live with. Like most artists he was temperamental, and especially so since he'd become successful. But I'm certain Kate Moran didn't want to marry my ex-husband for money. Does that answer your question?'

'You sound pretty sure of that.'

'Agent Stone, I'd know a gold-digger, and Kate Moran was most definitely not one, in case that suspicion crossed your mind.'

Stone placed his hands on the desk and leaned forward to ask his next question.

'It didn't *ever* bug you that she and David had a relationship?'

Lacy frowned. 'I'm wondering why you ask me that.'

Stone offered a flicker of a smile in return. 'No reason, other than my own curiosity.'

'The truth is, David and I had a tempestuous union at the best of times. But thankfully, after our divorce we discovered we were better friends than marriage partners. And of course we had Megan. We were both always so grateful for that. She was a wonderful child, who seemed to have inherited the best characteristics of both of us. And I loved her *deeply*. So very deeply.'

'Of course,' Raines said quietly.

Lacy took a moment to reflect. 'You know what's strange? I deal with death and homicides on a daily basis in the autopsy room. I've seen every kind of death imaginable in the course of my work, but I couldn't bring myself to see the bodies of David and Megan the day they were brought in. It would have cut my heart out. But what's strange is that there are all kinds of terms for those who lose loved ones, Agent Raines. When a child loses a parent, we call them an orphan. When a wife loses a husband, they're widowed. But I don't know of any term for a parent losing a child, do you?'

Raines shook his head. He heard the naked emotion in Brogan Lacy's voice and saw her wet eyes and was certain the doctor was about to break down. He noticed a bookshelf behind her and almost to distract her he went over to the shelf and plucked down a book entitled *Poisons and Their Treatments*. 'You deal with many poison cases, Doctor?'

'What?'

Raines held up the book. 'Poison cases. You deal with many?'

Lacy was diverted by the change of subject and wiped her eyes with a tissue. 'I'm sorry. Yes, they're not uncommon. Children swallow dangerous household cleaners or medications by accident. Unfortunately, some cases are fatal.'

'Are you an expert on poisons?'

'No, I'm not a toxicologist, but I've dealt with my fair share in the autopsy room. Why do you ask?'

'No reason.' Raines replaced the book on the shelf.

Lacy said impatiently, 'You gentlemen both seem to be asking me questions that have no reason. Are we finished yet?'

Stone said, 'Almost done. I'd like to go back to my original question. You really don't think it was in any way strange that your husband made Kate Moran the beneficiary of his will after only knowing her a relatively short time?'

Lacy shook her head in mild frustration. 'No, I don't. In fact, I'd have been surprised if he *hadn't* made her a beneficiary. David was a kind man, one of the kindest I ever knew, especially about money. And personally, I didn't need his money, I had my own. But what interests me is why I get the feeling that you think Kate Moran may have had something to do with David and Megan's deaths.'

'We never said that,' Raines answered. 'We never said that at all.'

Lacy looked at Stone, as if seeking confirmation of the answer she'd been given, but Stone remained tight lipped. 'You don't look like you agree, Agent Stone.'

Stone's mouth was still pursed as he gave Raines a hard look. 'I think my boss already answered your question, Miss Lacy.'

'I'm sensing a mixed message from you, Agent Stone,' Lacy responded.

Stone remained silent. For no evident reason, Lacy became flustered and consulted her watch. 'If . . . if you'll both excuse me, I have an autopsy to perform. I usually try and set aside a little time to gather my thoughts beforehand, so if you don't mind, I'd appreciate it if you left.'

'Thanks for your time, Doctor,' Stone acknowledged, but he looked frustrated.

Lacy led her visitors to the door and Raines offered his hand and said with genuine sympathy, 'I want to wish you all the best, Miss Lacy. I'll keep you in my prayers.'

He saw Brogan Lacy struggle to keep back her emotions. 'Thank you, Mr Raines. But if there's one thing I've learned it's that prayer changes nothing.'

66

Brogan Lacy waited until her visitors had left and then stepped over to the window. Minutes later she saw the two agents exit the building and head towards the car park. She wondered what their real motive was for questioning her. Maybe she was being overly suspicious. She could determine nothing specific behind their questions, as if they were trying to feel their way blindly, in the dark.

She came away from the window and tossed her uneaten sandwich in the corner wastepaper bin. She had little appetite these days. She'd lost thirty pounds in the last eighteen months and would probably lose another thirty if she wasn't careful. But she knew she had to keep up her strength, owed it to the memory of her daughter not to allow herself to slide all the way into the abyss. Except each day was getting harder and harder to get through without her darling Megan.

She had learned the real meaning of grief in losing her only child. It was truly hell on earth. Real, raw pain that felt like a thousand daggers piercing her heart. *Nothing will ever fill the haunting absence that her death has left behind. A young life is so precious.*

She would be forty-eight next birthday, and it was really far too late for her to ever hope to have another child – and besides, how could she ever hope to replace beautiful Megan? Sometimes, when she remembered her daughter's smile and her laughter, her good humour and her many tendernesses, remembered holding her as a baby and soothing her to sleep in her arms, she felt like ending it all by kneeling beside Megan's grave and simply blowing her own brains out. Constantine Gamal's cruel legacy of pain hadn't gone away and it never would. She knew exactly who to blame for that.

Why don't people who inflict grief ever stop and think about the wrong they are about to do? Why don't they consider the chronic misery they cause? As she started to move from the window, she saw a middle-aged woman come up the hospital path, arm in arm with a young girl who looked as if she might be her daughter.

The girl was pretty, in her early teens, and her blonde hair was long and tousled the way Megan's hair used to be. Brogan Lacy felt tears well up and turned away from the window, barely able to control her distress. Her hands shook and she felt tortured by memories. She was tempted to take her medication, the uppers that kept her head afloat, because the ache in her heart was so powerful. Except she had work to keep herself occupied that afternoon, and had to remain alert. But when she returned home she knew she'd have to take her pills to get through the evening.

Suddenly the door opened without a knock. A young woman carrying a clipboard entered the office, and said with concern, 'Are you OK, Dr Lacy?'

'Y-yes, Anne. I just had something in my eye. But I'm fine now. Thank you.'

The woman said, 'We're ready for the autopsy.'

Brogan Lacy thought: *No matter what, I have to keep up my strength. I have to maintain appearances.* It was all part of her strategy for coping, even if at times she felt she was fighting a losing battle with her sanity. In truth, as every day went by she felt she was losing her mind a little bit more.

She wiped her eyes, her hand shaking. 'Thank you, Anne. I'll be right there.'

67

Paris, France

Josh led the way across the street and down a flight of stone steps to a walkway. We passed a couple of lovers kissing on a riverside bench. I almost felt envious. *It's been such a long time since I kissed a man, since I was caressed and felt wanted.*

It was a surprisingly mild evening, and as we walked I was acutely conscious that Paris was where David and I had intended to spend our honeymoon. I remembered the excitement in his voice as he told me: *'We'll be staying at the Ritz, Kate. You'll love it.'*

'You still upset about killing Jupe?'

Josh interrupted my thoughts, and I crossed my arms to keep out the chill of a sudden cold gust from the river. 'I think I'm almost over that hurdle.'

He nodded. 'Good. But there must be something else on your mind. You look miles away.'

I told myself: *I don't want to talk about the pain in my past.* But despite myself, I *did* talk. I'd had a little too much alcohol, and I suddenly found myself opening up. I told Josh about David and our plans for our honeymoon, and I felt a little better for having talked about it.

'Mending yourself after a death is pretty slow going,' Josh offered. 'It can't be rushed. But I think the real trick to surviving bereavement is just to carry on blindly and try to ignore the pain. It's all you can do.'

I looked out at the river. 'Sometimes it feels as if I'll never get over it. There are days when I manage to lock my grief away in

257

a special little compartment inside my head. I try to keep it there, and I can even manage to fool myself into thinking that the ache has disappeared, but every now and then it somehow manages to reach out and grab me by the throat. You know the way it is when you fall in love with someone and then you lose them.'

'Tell me.'

'The way sometimes it can shatter your soul, and leave you trying to pick up the pieces for the rest of your life. I felt that way about David.'

Josh sounded sympathetic. 'If I'm to be honest I thought that way about my ex-wife, Carla, too. I sort of know how you must feel at times. I guess there are some wounds that never really heal. I had a younger sister who died when I was twelve. She was a great kid and I loved her a lot. That was over twenty years ago, but I pretty much think about her every day and it still gives me a twinge.' He suddenly stopped walking and put a hand gently on my arm. 'I guess the truth is that deep inside we're all hurt beings and haunted souls and we keep so much of our grief hidden. But if you ever feel the need for someone to talk to, don't be a stranger. Talking helps. Makes it feel like someone is sharing the load.'

Josh's tender manner made me feel closer to him, and sent a tingle down my spine. The episode in the catacombs, too, had brought us closer, but I almost felt guilty for experiencing that feeling. 'That's kind of you, Josh.'

His hand lingered for a moment, as if he was going to say something else, but he changed his mind, and let it fall away. I got the feeling that he cared, and I was touched. We walked farther along the path, both of us silent, until I said, 'Tell me about yourself.'

Josh shrugged. 'Hey, there's not really much to tell. My life's been pretty boring.'

'Then you have my permission to bore the hell out of me.'

'OK, you asked for it.' Josh smiled. For the next five minutes he told me about his background. He'd been born in New York, and his parents were still happily married after almost forty years.

His father was a TV scriptwriter, and his mom a retired legal secretary. He had two brothers who also worked in TV, and his youngest sister, Marcie, was a production assistant. At first he didn't offer much about his marriage, except that it had lasted two years before he and Carla had divorced. 'Why the divorce?' I asked.

'Lots of reasons. Carla mostly, but I also had an affair.'

I stopped walking. True, I didn't like the sound of *that* admission, but I sort of admired him for telling the truth.

Josh said, 'You looked shocked. Hey, it wasn't for the reason you might think.'

'You don't have to explain.'

'Kate, the reality is that people have affairs for all kinds of different reasons. Some of them are selfish, and some of them are valid. It probably sounds like I'm making excuses but I'm not. I know I did wrong. But at the time I needed to connect to someone emotionally, which is why I had the affair. Carla had quit the marriage for a time and walked out, but we were still legally married. The lady I met was a good woman. Divorced, with a couple of kids. Our affair didn't last longer than a few months but I reckon it saved me from going crazy. That's how bad my married life was.'

'How come?'

Josh shrugged. 'Carla never allowed me to get really close. She just wasn't the "get close" kind. Even with Neal. It used to drive me nuts that she wasn't at all maternal. I guess the honest truth is that Carla married me on the rebound, never really loved me and couldn't hack marriage, or even motherhood. The fact she didn't want custody of Neal proves that.'

'But *you* had the affair.'

Josh put his hand up. 'I plead guilty on that count. But I believe I did the right thing at the time, for my own sanity's sake. I told Carla the truth about what had happened and she used it to get her divorce.'

Suddenly my cell phone vibrated twice. I plucked it from my bag, checked the screen and saw I had a voice message. It was from Lou. '*It's Lou returning your call, Kate. I've got a couple of important meetings to attend to right now but I'll call you again later. There are a few matters I need us to talk about. We'll speak then.*'

'You want to call him now?' Josh asked, when I told him about the message.

'I'll wait until we get back to the hotel.' I sensed from Lou's tone that he wanted our conversation to be private. I wondered why.

I turned to Josh. 'Let's go grab a cab.'

68

Twenty minutes later we pulled up outside the Normandy Hotel. As we went up in the elevator I suddenly felt I didn't want to be alone: I had enjoyed Josh's company and I wanted our time to continue, but when we came to my door he turned to me and said, 'Well, I better say goodnight, Kate.'

I lingered, and I knew Josh sensed my reluctance to leave. Then he leaned over and gently kissed my cheek. I flushed. It felt so good to feel his skin brush my face. His cologne smelled of vanilla and lemon. Then his mouth found mine and we kissed, a slow, deep kiss that went on for a long time.

Finally, I pulled away gently, and he looked straight at me, one of those eye-to-eye looks that hide nothing and say everything. He seemed to read my mind. His hand came up and with one finger he traced the outline of my jaw.

He said, 'Can I tell you something? For some reason I don't want to go.'

'For some reason I don't want to go, either,' I responded.

'You want to come inside and I'll hold you? Just hold you.'

I was tempted to smile. 'Where have I heard that line before?'

'I mean it. Just hold you.'

I actually saw him blush, and for some reason that made me want him to hold me even more. 'It's been a long time since someone's done that. Except I . . .'

'Except what? Regulations?' Josh smiled and said quietly, 'I don't recall reading any regulation that says I can't offer a fellow agent comfort and solace.'

'Is that what it'll be?'

He looked at me seriously. 'Honest? I think you need to be

held. And if I'm truthful, maybe I do too.'

I didn't answer. Instead I let Josh lead me into his room. He closed the door. A soft light was on by his bed. He didn't let go of my hand as he sat down on the bed and I sat down beside him. Then his arms came up and swept around me. It felt so comforting, so very comforting. *Josh, the truth is I don't just want to be held . . .*

I looked into his face and tried to tell him that. I still felt so guilty. David had been dead less than eighteen months and I found myself attracted to another man. Josh didn't speak, not a word, but I felt his breath on my neck as he moved closer to me, and it felt good. Finally he kissed my forehead, then my eyelids, my cheeks, his mouth moving down as he placed tiny, flicking kisses on my neck. 'You smell good,' he said, and his mouth moved down to kiss the tip of my chin, then down my neck. I felt a rush of pleasure and I moaned, which only encouraged Josh even more. He kissed me on the lips and I felt his tongue touch mine. *I like the way he kisses. He kisses beautifully.*

His hands moved over my body and I shuddered with the genuine pleasure of his touch, and then one hand slipped under my blouse and cupped my breast. I tried to pull away but I couldn't. *I can't shut my feelings off for ever. I can't spend my life afraid, even if I am.*

He rolled my nipple between his fingers, and when I put my hand on his chest I could feel his heart beating and I liked the feeling. And then suddenly we were lying on the bed and his hand moved gently to open my blouse. Very softly he kissed my breasts, taking my nipples in his mouth and sucking them.

Josh stopped, looked into my face. 'We don't have to do anything, not unless you want to.'

'I want to.' I trusted him. *I like these feelings. He's a considerate, loving man.* He drew me to him, his mouth met mine again, and this time we kissed long and hard, then his lips moved down over my belly. I reached down and felt his erection as I fondled him through his pants. *He feels so hard, so manly.*

I couldn't wait any longer. We undressed each other with a

sudden wild passion, and then with a slow and deliberate tenderness Josh moved on top of me and I took his tongue in my mouth and guided him inside me.

69

I heard the bleating of an ambulance siren outside the hotel window and came awake. Five hours had passed – it was almost 5 a.m. Josh lay beside me, in a deep sleep. I loved the clean, fresh smell of him. The light was still on and his body was naked. It turned me on to look at him. His broad chest, his soft but muscled stomach, his thick hair, his athelete's legs. And then I saw his penis, no longer hard. I resisted the urge to touch him and make him hard again.

It feels so good to feel a man's body against mine. To smell his masculine scent. I guess I wanted this to happen. To feel desired again. To be held. Then I felt a wave of guilt as I thought of David. *I'm still wearing his ring.*

And then another thought intruded: Lou hadn't called my cell phone, but what if he'd tried calling my room? Maybe I should check or try phoning him again? I was anxious for him to know about the shooting. I climbed out of bed, kissed Josh's neck, dressed and let myself out of the room. Once in my own room I got through to Lou's cell on the second ring.

'Sorry I didn't get back to you, it's been a busy day,' Lou said tiredly.

'Are you at home?'

'No, still in the office. I was just about to call. I've got some news for you.'

It sounded good to hear Lou's voice, but what he told me next chilled me to the bone.

'Kate, a double murder's been committed in Istanbul, an old stomping ground of Gamal's. The victims were an uncle and his niece, and both had been savagely knifed to death in a well-

264

known tourist venue called the Sunken Palace. A wooden crucifix was discovered lying between their bodies.'

I felt so dazed that I had to sit down on the bed. I'd read about the palace – it was an ancient underground cistern built by the Romans and had been the scene of another of Gamal's killings.

'When did this happen?' I asked.

Lou's voice echoed down the line. 'About eight hours ago.'

I was speechless. Finally Lou said, 'Are you still there?'

'Y . . . yes, I'm here.' Alarm bells rang inside my head. Istanbul was the site of Gamal's first killings – of his father and sister – and the coincidence of the fresh murders in Paris and Istanbul set my mind on fire. 'How did you find this out?'

'Delon's boss called me less than half an hour ago. He'd flagged the catacomb murders on Interpol's 24–7 database and the Turks picked up on it immediately and started to ask questions. It seems they had their own underground double homicide last evening. The victims were discovered very soon after they were killed and Delon's boss has learned that a butcher's knife or cleaver was used on both victims,' Lou said.

I felt sickened. How long could this savagery go on? *As long as it takes to catch the killer*, I told myself. 'What are we going to do?' I asked Lou.

'*We?* We're doing nothing.'

'But look at the MO, the location, the victims' profiles, the signature crucifix. It's got Gamal trademarks written all over. It's got to be our copycat.'

'Maybe it is, but for now this one's for the Turkish police to investigate,' Lou insisted. 'It's too early for us to be sticking our noses in. We better wait and see what develops.'

'But we can't ignore this when it could give us a lead.'

Lou sounded annoyed. 'We're not ignoring it, but you're not going to Istanbul, Kate, and that's final. Especially not after what happened today in Paris.'

'Did Delon slate me?'

'The opposite. I reckon he covered your ass. But you can tell me your side of the story when you get home.'

I felt deflated and angry, and then to make things worse Lou dropped a bombshell.

'And I do want you home. There's something we have to talk about in private once you get back,' he said. 'It's a sensitive issue and I hate to have to be the one to say it, but Stone's been sniffing pretty hard and he's come up with some questions regarding the Fleists' deaths that may need answering on your part.'

I felt my heart quicken. 'What's *that* supposed to mean?'

Lou said abruptly, 'I'm not prepared to talk about it over the phone, Kate.'

'Stone's out to ruin my name because he despises me, Lou. I thought you of all people knew that. What are you trying to imply? What's he been saying?'

'We'll discuss it when you get home.'

I felt suddenly desperate – it seemed I was losing the one strong ally I thought I had. 'What's going on, Lou? Why can't you just give it to me straight?'

Lou was silent, then he gave a sigh that echoed down the line. 'Kate, until I learn otherwise I believe that you're innocent of any accusation Stone might throw at you.'

'What accusation is he throwing at me now?'

'We'll talk when you get back. But I honestly think you need to help clear the air on a few issues, and that's about as much as I'm saying, so don't push it.'

I let out a breath in frustration. 'OK, we'll play it your way, Lou. But Turkey isn't even a four-hour flight away. Let me at least check out the murders, *please*.'

'*No*,' he insisted. 'I told you, forget it. And that's a firm frigging order.'

I was surprised by the ferocity in Lou's voice. Before I had a chance to speak again, he said, 'I've organised your seats back on Wednesday morning on an Air France flight to Dulles. When you get to the office we'll talk this thing through.'

I was seething. 'I have to tell you that right this minute I'm finding it very hard to like you, Lou.'

'Tough.'

I gave it one last attempt. 'Lou, for God sakes, I think we're making a big mistake by ignoring Istanbul.'

But my pleading fell on deaf ears. Lou snapped back, 'No dice. We're not ignoring it, we're just leaving it to the Turkish authorities. Meanwhile you just get yourself home on Wednesday, you hear?'

70

I sat on my bed for almost ten minutes considering all that Lou had just said. I felt hurt and stunned and furious. Something about the drift of Lou's conversation had me worried, and I had the feeling that despite his reassurance he wasn't completely on my side. *Stone's been sniffing pretty hard and he's come up with some questions regarding the Fleists' deaths that may need answering on your part.* What the hell did Lou mean? Had Stone been bad-mouthing me again or casting doubt on the way I was carrying out the investigation?

I felt determined to try to solve this case. I knew Lou said Istanbul was off the cards, but the more I thought about it, the more I felt it was a vital part of the investigation. Except it meant I'd have to defy Lou's orders, and that kind of defiance could mean instant dismissal.

Istanbul was almost four hours away by air. I began to calculate. *What if I flew there and back on the same day? Lou need not know about it.* I reckoned I'd have to endure close to eleven hours' travelling time, including getting to and from the airports. But I could try to grab some sleep on the aircraft and have the rest of the day to investigate the killings, then be back in time for my return flight to New York with Josh.

The more I thought about it, the more I convinced myself it could be done. I decided to call the information desk at Charles de Gaulle airport. My French was non-existent, but the man who answered spoke English. 'Madame, how many I help?' he enquired.

I explained that I needed to fly to Istanbul that day, and then fly back to Paris the same night. 'Is that possible?'

'Certainly there are flights, madame. But the airline sales offices are not yet open.'

'You're saying there's no way I can book a ticket right now, for a flight today?'

'This is the information desk, we don't handle bookings. You could always try booking online.'

I'd noticed that the hotel room had a computer keyboard attached to the TV. 'Can you tell me when the first flight leaves for Istanbul this morning?'

The man sighed. 'One moment, please.' I heard him tapping away on a computer. Finally he said, 'Turkish Airlines flies from Charles de Gaulle to Istanbul this morning at eight-thirty a.m., arriving just before twelve-thirty p.m. local time.'

'When's the last return flight back?'

'The last flight to Paris departs Istanbul this evening at eight-forty-five p.m. local time, arriving Charles de Gaulle at midnight local. I can see on my screen that both flights are wide open – only half full – so there are plenty of seats available. You will have no problem if you arrive at the airport and wish to buy a ticket. The Turkish Airlines ticket desk will be open from five-thirty a.m.'

'You've been a big help, thanks.' I figured I had about two hours to get to the airport if I decided to fly.

As soon as I put down my phone, Josh rang me. 'Hey, how are you? I heard you closing my door and tried to call you on your phone but it was engaged. I figured maybe you were calling Lou.'

'I just got off the phone to him.'

'Want to come back in here and tell me all about it?' Josh suggested.

I was tempted to resist but knew I had to face Josh before I got a cab to the airport. 'I'll be right there.'

As I left my room I wondered how I'd explain my absence the next day. I didn't want to admit to Josh that I intended flying to Istanbul or the reasons why. That way, if the dirt hit the fan, he was in the clear. But when he eventually found out, he was going to wonder why the hell I hadn't told him about the murders. But I'd face that hurdle when I came to it.

I knocked on Josh's door. This time he was wearing a T-shirt and shorts and drinking an instant coffee he'd made using the complimentary tea service. 'Name your beverage,' he said with a smile. 'Fine old cognac? A ten-year-old port?'

'If Lou spotted those on our expenses he'd have us hung from the Washington Monument.'

'Be a devil. You'll need something to help you get back to sleep.'

'I'll have a hot chocolate, that's help enough.'

'Hot chocolate it is.'

As Josh made my drink I kept reminding myself that this was the first time since David had died that I'd allowed another man get in any way close to me. Josh was kind, sensitive and tactile. He was everything I liked in a guy. But then I started to remind myself that he was my partner. I was beginning to feel guilty that I'd enjoyed his company. And *very* guilty that I was about to mislead him.

Josh handed me my drink and said, 'Well, don't keep me in suspense. What did Lou have to say?'

'Delon cleaned my slate on the tunnel shooting.'

'Good for him. See, I told you. What about flights?'

'Lou booked us a return flight for tomorrow morning, ten a.m. That was the earliest he could get.'

Josh said with a touch of excitement, 'It seems we've got another twenty-four hours in Paris. Maybe we could do the Louvre, or Napoleon's tomb at Les Invalides? Or how about we do the wild thing and go visit Père Lachaise cemetery where Jim Morrison is buried? Then we could head up to Montmartre and the Arab Quarter and find a neat little Moroccan restaurant . . .'

This is the part I'm dreading. I hated myself for lying – for keeping back the truth about Istanbul – but I had no option. 'I'm really sorry, Josh, but you see there's a girlfriend of mine who lives in Paris. I was hoping to catch up with her and her French husband. I called her yesterday and mentioned if I had time I'd meet her this morning. We'll probably spend the day together.'

I saw the disappointment register instantly in Josh's face. 'Well . . . sure, that's OK,' he said.

'What will you do?'

Josh gave a valiant shrug. 'Don't worry about me, I've got plenty to keep me busy. I'll go see how Laval's doing. And if I've got time there's a whole bunch of tourist places I can visit. Who knows, we might even bump into each other. Or maybe we could all meet up for lunch someplace?'

I felt my face flush. 'I . . . I think Beth was making some plans. I hope you don't mind, Josh?'

'Hey, no problem, I understand. You don't feel sorry for what happened between us?'

'No, of course not.' I touched his arm and felt a twinge of guilt, but I couldn't tell Josh that.

'I guess I better let you get some sleep,' he said.

He led me to the door. I hated myself for deceiving him. *This isn't me.* 'Thanks for offering to show me Paris. I really appreciate it. I mean that.'

Josh said graciously, 'Sure, maybe we'll do it again some other time, and it's no problem. You get some sleep. And I hope you and your friends have a good day.'

PART FOUR

71

Charles de Gaulle Airport, Paris, France

Seven-ten a.m. and I felt bleary eyed. The airport was buzzing despite the early hour, and there was already a queue at the Turkish Airlines ticket desk. When my turn came I bought a same-day return.

The flight made a major dent in my MasterCard – I just hoped the trip proved to be worth it. An hour later I boarded the flight, carrying just my oversized handbag as hand luggage, complete with make-up and a change of underwear – I'd left my suitcase in my hotel room. I was just about to switch off my cell phone when I noticed I had a voice message. It was from Frank: '*Kate, it's me. I've got some news, so call me when you can.*'

I wondered what the news was, but just then a stewardess went through the pre-flight safety procedures and instructed all passengers to switch off their cell phones. Before I flicked mine off I texted back: '*Busy for next 4 hrs. Call u soon as I can.*'

Fifteen minutes later the aircraft was already taxiing towards the runway for take-off. Once it reached cruising altitude and I'd finished breakfast I watched half an hour of the in-flight movie, then surprised myself by managing to grab a couple of hours' sleep. When I woke I found the restroom and freshened up, and the next thing I knew a steward's announcement was requesting that passengers return to their seats – we were about to begin our descent into Istanbul. I walked back to my window seat thinking: *If Josh and Lou only knew where I was.*

Lou would probably have an instant coronary. Josh would be . . . I didn't know what. *I just hope he understands when I finally tell him the truth.* I buckled myself into my seat. The rainy skies of Europe were no more; now sunlight sparkled on the blue waters of the Sea of Marmara. We descended across the Bosporus waterway that links Europe with Asia, and I saw the morning rays glinting off the golden domes of countless beautiful mosques.

Istanbul was a sprawling tapestry of thirteen million souls. *And somewhere down there might be Gamal's copycat killer.*

Five minutes later, when the Airbus brushed the runway to make a perfect touchdown, I felt a tingle of anticipation. I had arrived in Istanbul, one-time killing ground of Constantine Gamal, and ancient city of Byzantine intrigue.

I passed through Immigration and Customs without any problems. But I knew I faced an obstacle: *How am I going to inspect the murder site and victims' bodies without official police clearance?*

I remembered Lou telling me something that Einstein had once said: Look at a problem for long enough and an answer will present itself. Well, I'd been racking my mind since early that morning and now the answer came to me. I knew *exactly* how I was going to overcome the obstacle.

In the arrivals terminal I switched on my cell phone and got a message from a service provider – at least my phone worked in Istanbul. I found a currency exchange kiosk and changed two hundred dollars into Turkish notes and some small change. But instead of using my cell I headed for a payphone across the hall to call Frank.

The arrivals terminal had that strange mix of frantic and calm you get in Mediterranean cities. As if the world were about to end and half the folks needed to get someplace fast and the other half had resigned themselves to impending doom. The terminal was a crush as people rushed past and others strolled at a snail's pace. When I reached the phone booth I had to wait several minutes until an elderly woman dressed in a black robe had finished her high-pitched, squealing conversation. She eventually slammed down the phone, smiled politely at me and tottered off.

I picked up the handset and first tried to call Frank, but the line was busy. Then I found the number for Inspector Ahmet Uzun at Istanbul police headquarters in my Filofax and punched the keypad. A second later the line clicked and I heard a voice say, 'Uzun.'

'Inspector Ahmet Uzun?'

'Yes, this is Ahmet Uzun. Who is this?'

'Inspector, this is Kate Moran of the FBI. I hope you remember me?'

'Kate Moran!' Uzun's surprised voice exploded in my ear.

I'd met Uzun at Quantico when he had attended a specialist training course. He was one of Turkey's top homicide detectives. 'Of course, I remember. How are you? To what do I owe this pleasure?'

'I was wondering if you'd have a little spare time this afternoon?'

'Time, for you? But of course. And please, call me Ahmet. Where are you calling from?'

'Istanbul airport.'

A silence followed, in which I could imagine a bemused Uzun wrinkling his forehead. 'You are in Turkey on *holidays*?'

'I wish. No, I'm here about the double murder yesterday at the Sunken Palace, and I need your help, Ahmet. Can we talk somewhere private?'

Uzun fell silent for a few moments, as if considering all I'd said. 'Very well, I know a nice hotel. Very historic, and very agreeable for a lunchtime chat.'

'Why don't you just give me directions to police headquarters and I'll meet you there?'

Uzun sounded cautious. 'No, better if I meet you at the hotel. It would be more convenient. The hotel is called the Pera Palace. I'll see you there in an hour.' He gave me directions before he dropped a bombshell. 'And by the way, your boss Lou Raines just called me half an hour ago.'

72

Istanbul

The yellow taxi dropped me right outside the Pera Palace Hotel, overlooking the Golden Horn. I stepped into an ornate lobby with marble floors and soaring columns. I needed to quickly familiarise myself with the city so I'd bought a guide-book as I left the airport. As I flicked through the pages in the taxi I found a mention of the Pera Palace – it was once one of the grand old hotels on the Orient Express route, famously known as the hotel where Agatha Christie stayed as a guest when she visited Istanbul. The management had even turned her favourite bedroom into a miniature museum, complete with some of her personal belongings.

But I wasn't here to visit museums. After five minutes of hanging out in the lobby I was about to resume my browsing in the guidebook to pass the time when Inspector Ahmet Uzun strolled in. He was a tall, greying, handsome Turk with an immaculate smile. He shook my hand. 'It's a pleasant surprise to see you again, Kate. You should have told me you were visiting Istanbul and I could have had a driver meet you at the airport.'

'To tell the truth, it was a last-minute decision. And it's supposed to be a secret visit, Ahmet.'

'Secret?' Uzun frowned and nodded towards a marbled archway. 'Come, let's have some coffee in the lounge and you can tell me all about it.'

The inspector hadn't yet explained why Lou Raines had called him – but I had a feeling I was soon going to find out. The guidebook had mentioned that the Pera Palace Hotel was over a hundred and fifty years old, and once I saw the lounge I wouldn't have disagreed. I felt as if I were stepping back into the Victorian era – it was all dark panelled mahogany, soaring marble columns and red velvet drapes. 'Thanks for agreeing to meet me at such short notice,' I said gratefully.

'My pleasure. Let me order some refreshments.' Uzun smiled and lit a cigarette – in Turkey, almost everyone seemed to smoke; even old men in their eighties I'd seen on street corners and who should have been dead years ago from the habit still puffed away merrily.

Uzun said, 'You want to try the local coffee? It's strong but I promise it won't kill you unless you drink at least six cups.'

'I'll give it a shot.'

Uzun ordered two coffees and sandwiches from a white-coated waiter. The Pera had a stunning view of the Golden Horn, the famous Blue Mosque visible in the distance, fishing boats tossing on the choppy waters. The waiter returned with a silver tray containing two plates of neatly trimmed sandwiches and two tiny glass cups of treacly coffee, and the inspector handed me one of the cups. In between sips of his own he devoured one of the sandwiches. 'So tell me why you're in Istanbul.'

I explained how I'd heard about the Sunken Palace murders, and then I told Uzun about the copycat killing in Virginia and Paris. He put down the remains of his sandwich and frowned with sudden interest. 'It certainly sounds incredible. But why is your visit meant to be secret?'

'To tell the truth, Ahmet, I'm here unofficially, of my own accord.'

Uzun was puzzled. 'I don't understand.'

I sipped the sweet, velvet coffee. 'I thought the Istanbul killings might in some way be linked to the Virginia murders and the others in Paris. But I didn't have a clue as to how or why. That's why I flew here. I need to see the murder site and review what evidence or leads you have. I was hoping I might find some connection.'

'I see,' Uzun replied, but he didn't look at all certain about my motives.

'I can answer any questions you may want to ask me, Ahmet, but maybe first you could tell me about the killings. I'm booked on a return flight to Paris later this evening and my time is tight.'

Uzun frowned again. '*This evening?*'

'I've only got four hours before I have to head back to the airport. It's complicated, Ahmet, but please try and trust me on this. I need as much information as you can give me about the case.'

Uzun brushed crumbs from his jacket and shrugged. 'The case is one of mine. What exactly is it you need?'

'To see the crime scene and the bodies. And I'd like my visit kept unofficial.'

Uzun thought for a moment, then pursed his lips before he summoned the waiter and asked for the bill. 'Very well. My car's parked outside, so just as soon as you finish your coffee I can take you to the morgue and then the murder site.'

I put down my cup. Uzun settled the bill and put away his wallet.

'What about the murders?' I asked.

Uzun picked up his car keys. 'I can tell you this much – it's a bizarre case that's got everyone in the homicide department completely puzzled.'

73

Uzun sped through frantic, crowded streets, past colourful bazaars and markets, then turned down towards the waterfront, with a view of the magnificent Topkapi palace. Under different circumstances, he would no doubt have been proud to point out places of interest in this ancient city, but now he looked serious. 'What did you mean by bizarre?' I asked.

'You know about the murder site, the city's famous Sunken Palace, sometimes called the Underground Basilica?'

I nodded. 'Yes, it was where Gamal committed one of his earlier double homicides. I've read about the palace but I've never seen it.'

'Perhaps you have. Have you ever watched the James Bond movies *The World Is Not Enough* or *From Russia with Love*?'

I couldn't see the connection but said, 'Sure, why?'

Uzun suddenly swung round a corner and I held on for dear life as he answered, 'The Sunken Palace was used in scenes in both movies. You don't remember?'

'No,' I confessed. But the inspector obviously did and warmed to his subject.

'It's called the Sunken Palace because that's exactly what it looks like. An underground citadel. It's located not far from Istanbul's famous St Sophia's Church.'

The church I had read about in the guidebook. St Sophia's was built in the fourth century AD, during the Roman tenure of Constantinople, a stunning piece of ancient architecture that had survived the centuries.

Uzun said, 'Despite being called a palace, it's actually a vast underground cistern which once served as Istanbul's water reservoir, and was built by the Emperor Constantine in the fourth century. It's enormous, all below ground.'

He went on to describe the cistern as a web of underground passageways with soaring columns and carved stone Medusa heads. I shivered just thinking about all those creepy passageways.

Uzun added, 'The bodies were found by a caretaker in one of the caverns last evening. They were of an uncle and his niece and were found soon after they were killed, probably less than half an hour after their deaths, when a fire alarm was set off in the Sunken Palace. A security inspection revealed the victims. There were no witnesses to the crime, but as soon as I saw the corpses I knew we had an interesting case on our hands.'

'Go on.'

'The bodies were disembowelled and an attempt was made to burn them after death, just like many of Gamal's victims. The smoke from the fire had set off the alarm. We also found a wooden crucifix placed between the corpses but it didn't reveal any fingerprints. Nor do we know how the killer managed to gain entry to the palace, or if he did so with his victims. It may well have been by using an entrance not usually used by the tourists, but we're not sure. However, the murders were so remarkably similar to Gamal's that I thought we had a copycat killer.'

I felt another shiver. *This sounds just like Virginia and Paris.*

Uzun continued, 'So this morning I decided to call on Gamal's surviving sister, Yeta, and ask her if she knew of anyone who had been close to her brother – an acquaintance or relative, perhaps, or someone she knew of who might have admired him. In that way I hoped we might be able to get a lead to our copycat. I felt I was clutching at straws perhaps, but in this business you will clutch at anything to solve a case.'

I'd never met Gamal's sister, and she was something of a mystery woman. She hadn't appeared at his trial, refusing to travel from Istanbul to testify.

'What did Yeta have to say?'

'That's what's so bizarre.'

'*What* is?'

Uzun looked baffled, and his next words sent a shock wave through me. 'Yeta was already traumatised. She claimed that she had just received a phone call from her dead brother.'

74

I was disturbed by Uzun's revelation. Suddenly it seemed as if my own suspicions were valid but I tried to remain composed. 'But Gamal's dead. I *saw* him executed,' I said.

Uzun said, 'I know it seems incredible and I don't doubt for a second that he isn't dead. But Yeta claimed the caller sounded *exactly* like her brother. When I arrived at her home she was so distressed she was about to phone the police.'

I felt my pulse quicken. 'What did the caller say?'

'He claimed that he was Gamal and he was back in Istanbul to attend to some unfinished business and that he wanted to meet with Yeta. Those were almost the exact words he used, apparently.'

Blood raced in my temples, and I felt the beginnings of a pounding headache.

'*What business?*'

Uzun shook his head. 'He didn't say. But whoever he was he obviously intended to unsettle Yeta. She's not the kind of woman who gets easily upset – she's a tough and capable person who held her life together despite having to endure a homicidal brother. But she was definitely shaken, and puzzled.'

'What else did the caller say?'

'Yeta was so shocked she says she can't remember anything else. She claims that he remained on the line for no more than a minute before he hung up. The caller spoke in English, and with an American accent, just like Constantine's.'

'She's absolutely *sure* that the caller sounded like her brother?'

'I asked her the same question. She mentioned she hadn't spoken with him in at least ten years, so I asked how could she be so certain. But she has convinced herself it was Constantine's voice she heard.'

'I'd like to meet and talk with her.'

Uzun shrugged. 'I can only ask. But the woman's so upset, don't be surprised if she refuses to speak with you.'

'Tell her who I am. Tell her I *really* need to see her. Please do your best to convince her, Ahmet.'

'I'll try.'

We trundled across a bridge, past a Turkish bathhouse, and slowed in front of a granite building with massive oak entrance doors, a sign overhead in red Turkish lettering. 'Where are we?'

'The police morgue.' Our taxi halted and Uzun told the driver to wait for us. We stepped through the oak doors into a long, sterile hallway covered with chequerboard blue-and-white tiles.

I knew that in Muslim countries the dead are buried quickly, usually by sundown, certainly at the latest by the next day. As absurd as it sounds, autopsies are not always performed in murder cases, or are perfunctory at best. But Turkey was more enlightened, and Uzun explained that the police followed best international practice. At the end of the corridor we paused outside a grey door with more Turkish lettering.

'The pathologist's name is Hakan Sayin. Prepare yourself, Kate. What you're about to see is not pleasant.' Uzun pushed the door open and I followed him through.

On one side of the morgue were some steel freezer cabinets. Near the sinks was a metal butcher's block, complete with the frightening instruments of the pathologist's trade: scalpels, knives, stainless-steel basins and various electric saws. Two metal trolleys with blood gullies were positioned in the middle of the room, and on top lay two bodies covered by white plastic sheets. A bald man with glasses and a heavily scarred jaw was scrubbing his hands at a washbasin. As he finished drying himself he turned to us and Uzun said, 'Kate, meet Professor Hakan Sayin. He autopsied the victims.'

Sayin offered his hand and said in perfect English, 'Ahmet tells me you're an American, with the FBI.'

'Yes.'

'Follow me, please.' The professor led the way to the trolleys, took a grip of one of the sheets and said to me, 'I'm afraid these two are particularly bad. Are you ready?'

'Yes.'

The professor pulled back the sheet and I saw that the corpse lying on the trolley was of a man whose body had been burned, like the corpse in Virginia, much of his flesh blackened charcoal. In the centre of his chest was a cavity where the heart and organs had been removed. The professor said, 'You wish to see the other victim?'

I nodded. He pulled back the second sheet. I almost wept as Uzun said, 'The man's niece. She was about fifteen. She suffered the same fate as the uncle.' I saw the gaping hole in the victim's scorched chest cavity and felt bile rise in my throat. I never seemed to get over the shocking sight of these victims, especially the younger ones, no matter how often I saw them. Uzun said, 'You've seen enough?'

'I think so.'

We left the professor. Uzun led me outside and lit a cigarette. 'You still want to see the Sunken Palace?'

I felt my blood run cold. *No, I don't. I hate to even think of going into that underground death chamber.* But I knew I had to see the murder scene, even if I was convinced that once I stepped inside the place I was going to panic. I checked my watch: I had barely three hours left before I headed for the airport. Time was flying. 'Yes, I want to see it.'

75

As Uzun drove me through the city his cell phone buzzed. He pulled over to the kerb to answer the call, and spoke rapidly in Turkish. When he frowned and gave me the occasional glance I started to get worried. *Who's he talking to?*

After several minutes he flipped shut his phone and gave me a look. 'I've just had a surprising conversation.'

I felt apprehensive. 'What do you mean?'

Uzun looked bemused as he put away his cell phone and pulled out into the traffic again. 'That was Gamal's sister. It seems you're in luck after all. She's agreed to your request. In fact, it's most strange, but I got the feeling she was eagerly looking forward to meeting you. I've arranged for us to rendezvous outside the Sunken Palace in ten minutes. Her apartment's not far from there.'

I felt relieved. As we drove along a broad street, Uzun pointed to an enormous, magnificent church that seemed to be twenty storeys high. 'St Sophia's, the oldest cathedral in the world, and a miracle of Roman engineering. It dates from the fourth century AD.' He smiled. 'Actually, it was built by local slave labour, but the Romans provided the architects.'

The cathedral was stunning, as awe-inspiring as Rome's Colosseum, and even better preserved. Uzun gestured ahead. 'The Sunken Palace is not far.'

Minutes later he pulled up outside a single-storey granite building with a sturdy oak entrance door and said, 'The public entrance. Usually at this time of day you'd see queues of tourists, but since the murders it's closed to visitors, and will remain that way for at least several more days.'

We stepped out on to the pavement and Uzun's cell phone rang again.

'Please excuse me,' he said as he checked the incoming number. 'Of course.'

He moved away to take the call in private, and I strolled up to study the underground entrance. As I got closer I realised that there wasn't just one door but a pair, and one of the doors was already open. The way inside was barred by a sturdy metal trellis. A short hallway lay beyond the trellis, and granite steps the colour of worn ivory led down into the bowels of the building. I felt my palms moisten as my claustrophobia returned. My heartbeat quickened; my old fears were back. *God, I really don't want to do this again. Do I really have to go down there?*

I saw Uzun put his phone away and fix me with a worried stare. 'I'm afraid our visit's off.'

I was surprised by his abrupt tone. 'Why, what's the matter?'

Uzun said in a firm voice, 'Kate, that was my boss. He just had Lou Raines on the phone.'

My spirits sank. I felt my face flush and knew the game was up. 'What . . . what did he say?'

'He knows you're in Istanbul and he wants you arrested.'

His words sank in. '*Arrested?* For what reason?'

Uzun was perplexed. 'My boss didn't say. Only that he wants me to take you into custody, by force if necessary, and I'm to put you on the first plane leaving for the US. What's going on, Kate?'

'Raines didn't explain to your superiors?'

'If he did, I haven't been told. All my boss said was that you had defied orders and come to Istanbul without FBI permission.'

How does Lou know I'm in Istanbul? Did Josh figure it out and tell him, or did Lou manage to reason it out for himself? I felt suddenly angry.

'Does that justify my arrest?'

'I have my orders, Kate.'

'Do I *need* Raines' permission to visit your country?'

Uzun was still confused. 'You tell me. What's going on?'

288

I sighed. 'To be honest, I don't know where to begin. It's all very weird, Ahmet.'

Uzun put a hand on my shoulder in a gesture that gave me the feeling that he was trying to help me. 'I'm sure it is, but why don't you start at the beginning? Come, sit down.'

He led me to a bench across the street that faced St Sophia's. For the next few minutes I tried to explain everything. 'I told you it was weird. Are you still going to arrest me?'

Uzun's brow puckered. 'I don't understand any of it, but I'm afraid I must still take you into custody. I'm sorry.'

'Ahmet, I *have* to speak with Yeta. What harm can it do? At least just let me do that.'

'Orders are orders,' Uzun said firmly. 'And disobeying them would be more than my career is worth.'

I felt desperate, and then I saw Uzun chew his bottom lip, as if he was having difficulty with his own decision. 'However, there is something I neglected to mention,' he said.

'What?'

'I didn't tell my boss that I had met you,' Uzun admitted. 'The truth is, he never asked. He obviously assumed that you hadn't yet tried to contact me. So it seems you're ahead of the game, but only by a whisker.'

I got the feeling Uzun was trying to tell me something. 'What are you saying, Ahmet?'

He stood. 'Between you and me, I never saw you. And if I was you, I'd leave Istanbul, *now*. I will have to put out an alert for your arrest to cover myself. And that means sending my men here, to the Sunken Palace, as part of any search. Raines suggested that you'd want to visit the murder site.'

'First I have to talk with Yeta and then I have to see the site. I didn't travel all this way for nothing.'

'That would be crazy. You risk being arrested and then there would be nothing I could do to help you.'

I was obstinate. 'I know that. But my mind's made up, Ahmet.'

Uzun sighed. 'Very well, I'll give you thirty minutes before I alert my officers. And not a second more.'

'Thank you.'

He nodded towards the entrance with its metal trellis. 'That's the entrance to the basilica. There's a security room just inside the door and there should be two policemen on duty at the scene. I can call there from a payphone down the street. I won't say who I am, just that I'm from HQ. I'll tell them that you're a foreign police officer who's interested in the case and ask them to let you down to see the murder site. But you'll have to go without me. I can't risk being seen in your company.'

I looked at the entrance with growing fear. 'You think that the police will do as you ask?'

Uzun shrugged. 'It's worth a try. Forensics have finished all their work so there really shouldn't be a problem.'

'And Yeta?'

He glanced at his watch. 'She agreed to meet us here in five minutes. But I'd better move if I'm to make that call.'

'How will I talk with Yeta? I don't speak Turkish,' I reminded Uzun.

'Don't worry, she speaks excellent English. She's a lecturer in biochemistry at Istanbul University.'

'How will I recognise her?'

'I don't think you'll have any problem. She bears a striking resemblance to her dead brother.'

That sounded almost eerie. I touched Uzun's arm. 'Thanks again.'

He studied my face earnestly. 'From now on, you're on your own, Kate. Try to take care. And good luck with sorting out your problems with Raines.'

If they ever can be sorted out, I thought. I nodded my gratitude, then Uzun slid into his Renault and started the engine. 'Remember, you have thirty minutes, no more.'

76

I suddenly felt alone and vulnerable as Uzun's car disappeared into the stream of traffic. I also felt damned angry about Lou wanting me arrested. I never imagined that he would do such a thing. It couldn't have been just because I'd breached discipline. There had to be a more compelling reason.

Whatever it was, I knew it had to be serious, and I figured that Stone had dragged up something spurious from God knew where. I reckoned that the warped bastard was up to no good again.

'Miss Moran?'

I spun round. People brushed past me on the busy pavement but I immediately noticed a woman standing five feet away and got a shock. She had salt-and-pepper hair, wore a dark woollen jacket and pants, and her skin was bare of make-up to reveal the pale colour of someone who avoids the sun. The likeness was remarkable. *I'm staring at Gamal.*

'Y . . . yes, I'm Kate Moran,' I stammered.

'I'm Yeta,' she said almost shyly, offering her hand. Her accent sounded faintly American. She had exactly the same deep-set eyes, high cheekbones and piercing stare as her brother. It was unsettling. But instead of callousness in Yeta Gamal's eyes I was sure I saw pain. Instead of hatred, I saw compassion. I guessed she was no more than forty-five, but with her grey-flecked hair and deep-set worry lines, she looked prematurely aged.

I offered my hand. 'How do you do. It's good of you to meet me.'

Yeta accepted my handshake and stared back at me. 'I have heard much about you from Inspector Uzun, Miss Moran.'

I wonder how she feels now that she's face to face with the person who helped send her only brother to his death? Does she hate me and want revenge?

I searched her eyes and saw no sign of revulsion. But I reminded myself that here was a woman who had refused to appear at her brother's trial as a witness. Who had never spoken ill or otherwise about him, no matter how callous his crimes. Had Yeta Gamal had a close relationship with her brother? Another question niggled me: *Why has she agreed to meet me here?* 'I guess we better try to go inside.' I rattled the gate and called out, 'Hello, is anybody there?'

As pedestrians hurried past, I peered into the hallway and saw an open door off to the right. What looked like the flickering blue shadows of a TV splashed the walls and I heard what sounded like a football game playing, then moments later two police officers, one in his fifties, the other a fresh-faced recruit, appeared from an office in the entrance hallway to the Sunken Palace. They came towards us, the older man smiling as he unlocked the trellis gate with a key attached to a long chain which he took from his pocket. He spoke rapidly in Turkish.

Yeta answered, then she said to me, 'He wants to know which one of us is Madame Moran. I told him it was you. He said someone just rang from headquarters to say that you'd be arriving to visit the murder site.'

I looked into Yeta's face. 'I have a favour to ask.'

'Pardon?'

'Will you accompany me down to the Sunken Palace?'

She looked over at the steps leading down, as if this wasn't part of the deal.

'I . . . I didn't intend to.'

'I know, but I have a fear of enclosed spaces and it would help me so much,' I said honestly, and indicated the policemen. 'Besides, I don't speak a word of Turkish. I'll need someone to translate. *Please*.'

She hesitated for a long time, and looked unwilling, but then finally she said, 'Very well. I'll go with you.'

I could see that for some reason she was still reluctant. She said something to the older cop and he admitted us. Yeta entered first, and the older cop beckoned for me to enter the hallway. The sound of cheering erupted from the office TV and the cop barked an order to his younger companion, who disappeared back into the room.

'What did he say?' I asked Yeta.

'He wants to know who scored. It seems there's a football game he has an interest in.'

The cop was suddenly all business as he beckoned us towards the stairwell.

The thought of going down into the bowels of the earth again filled me with dread, and I was so overcome by a surge of fear that it made my palms sweat.

Yeta stared at me, puzzled. 'What's the matter? You look unwell.'

'Nothing. I . . . I'm fine.'

And with that I forced myself to follow her and the cop down the stairs, taking one slow step at a time.

Across the street the Disciple studied Kate Moran and Yeta as they entered the Sunken Palace. He wore Aviator Ray-Bans and a motorcycle helmet, and he dismounted from his dark blue Yamaha 250cc.

He had followed Yeta from her apartment, keeping at a safe distance, and his planning had paid off. He had figured it was only a question of time before Moran learned of the murders he'd committed in the Sunken Palace and his call to Yeta, and that she would show up in Istanbul.

It was another strand of his strategy to lure Moran into his trap. Setting fire to his dead victims near a fire alarm had been deliberate, ensuring that the police quickly found the bodies. And now Moran had taken the bait, just as he'd hoped.

He felt the anger boil inside him as he locked his motorcycle. Everything he needed was in the small rucksack on his back, including the butcher's knives. He'd give it a couple of minutes and then he'd make his move and cross the crowded street to the Sunken Palace. With a little luck, and if everything went according to plan, he was going to kill again.

77

We moved down and our footsteps echoed on the stairwell's ancient stone walls. The policeman and Yeta were silent, and I shuddered as we descended, despite the fact that the palace was well lit. 'Have you ever visited the Sunken Palace before?' I asked Yeta. I *needed* to talk, needed to know that there was someone near me to help keep my fear under control.

'Yes, when I was a child,' she answered, deadpan. She didn't elaborate, and I had the feeling that for some reason she was as scared as I was of being underground.

The air became cooler the deeper we descended and then suddenly we came to a landing and there it was – one of the most incredible sights I have ever witnessed. A vast chamber, so massive that it looked like a colossal cathedral. An enormous corridor stretched before us, lined with hundreds of thick, gigantic stone columns at least forty feet high, which extended as far as the eye could see. I was stunned. 'I . . . I'd no idea the palace was so enormous.'

'During the Roman period, this was Constantinople's reservoir which supplied the entire city with fresh water,' Yeta explained.

The reservoir still contained water – dozens of huge rectangular pools lit by powerful arc lights anchored to the limestone ceiling. Yellow light bathed the palace in a golden tint. Water dripped from the damp stone walls, and wooden walkways crisscrossed the water pools. I could understand why it was called the Sunken Palace – it resembled an ancient citadel that had been flooded. The policeman gestured towards a corner and spoke, and Yeta translated again. 'He says that the crime scene has been marked off and we are not to pass the police tape. It's right over there.'

'Isn't he coming with us?'

'He says we can go alone, that it isn't far,' Yeta answered with a shrug.

I saw the cop glance back towards the steps, as if he was anxious to return to his TV. I had momentarily forgotten my claustrophobia but now it returned and I felt tremors of fear. 'Tell him thanks.'

Yeta translated and the man nodded and left us, his footsteps slapping up the stone steps. I didn't want to descend any farther into the chamber but what choice did I have? I turned to Yeta and looked for reassurance that we could safely find the steps again. 'You said you'd been here before. Can you find your way out?'

'Of course. Perhaps I should tell you that my brother Constantine had a fascination with the Sunken Palace.'

Considering the menacing atmosphere, I was hardly surprised. 'Tell me.'

'There are stories that ritual murders took place here in Byzantine times, and the stories intrigued him. In fact, this is where Constantine carried out two brutal killings, but no doubt you are aware of that?'

'Yes, I knew.'

I wanted to ask Yeta to tell me about the phone call she'd received, but she gestured to the last few steps. 'Follow me, and be careful. With all this water about, the steps can be slippery. The last thing we want is for an accident to happen.'

We reached the bottom of the stairwell and the awesome sight of the floodlit palace. 'Tell me about your brother's childhood,' I said.

So little was known about Gamal's private life, and he had refused to talk about it during his interrogation and trial. What little the Bureau knew had been gleaned from Inspector Uzun's investigations.

Yeta's mouth tightened. 'I have heard people talk about Constantine with almost a sense of tragedy. How such a gifted psychiatrist should himself turn into a sadistic killer. But there was no tragedy. The answer is simple. Constantine had an evil streak even when he was very young. He began with killing and torturing small animals. First it was frogs and mice. Then it progressed to butchering cats and dogs in bizarre, meaningless rituals, until finally he killed my father and my sister. I would even say that my brother studied psychiatry simply to try to understand his own sick behaviour. Not that it did him much good. He never changed.'

I figured that Constantine Gamal had probably exhibited the other two predominant traits common to almost every serial killer – apart from inflicting cruelty on small animals or childhood peers, he would have started malicious fires and have been a bed-wetter way past the normal age for kids. What we *didn't* know was why he'd killed his father and sister. His motives had never been fully explained. I made a mental note to come back to that question. We walked across a section of wooden boardwalk towards the crime scene, our footsteps echoing around the ancient walls. 'You say your brother had a fascination with the palace?'

Yeta nodded. 'When he was eleven our father brought him

here on a visit. Constantine liked the sinister atmosphere and was already obsessed by death, even at that age, and was drawn to dark, underground places. Not long afterwards he bundled my pet puppy down here under his coat and butchered the animal in one of his rituals. I always thought that the puppy had strayed, but years later Gamal took pleasure in telling me what he had done. I despised him for that.'

Yeta's mouth tightened at the gruesome memory. As we rounded a corner I saw several limp strings of luminous yellow crime scene tape that marked off the murder site. We were in a dark, remote corner of the Sunken Palace. 'Were you and your brother ever close?'

Yeta gave a snort of derision. 'No. Constantine wasn't exactly a lovable child. Looking back, I can see that he was always different and took perverse pleasure in inflicting pain.'

I remembered my mental note to ask about her brother's motives. 'Why do you think he killed your father and sister?'

Yeta shook her head. 'At first, I thought it had to do with the fact that my father often beat him. My mother died when we were young, which didn't help, but I'm convinced that there was an evil streak in Constantine's nature, almost from birth.'

'Was your father a brutal man?'

'He was sometimes harsh. But he wasn't depraved, like Constantine.'

'In what way harsh?'

'Constantine was highly intelligent but he was a difficult child and wilful, and often as punishment for a misdemeanour my father would lock him in the basement cold room where he kept freshly killed meat. Other times Constantine would watch my father at work, slaughtering the animals, with a morbid fascination. My brother seemed to take perverted pleasure in seeing the animals being butchered.'

I knew about the cold room, one of the chilling facts that Inspector Uzun had unearthed about Constantine Gamal's past life, but I listened with interest as his sister told me her story in person. 'What about their relationship?'

Yeta shrugged. 'It was always an uneasy one. Constantine despised my father, and considered him stupid. They argued constantly. Then one day there was a fire in the basement of the butcher shop. Neighbours helped put out the blaze and that's when my father and my sister were found in the cold room, their bodies badly burned and slashed to pieces in a frenzied attack. My sister was dead but my father clung to life for a few hours in a coma. The killings had the appearance of a robbery gone wrong – money was stolen from the shop and some personal valuables were missing. No suspicion fell on Gamal, but he was questioned by the police in the course of their investigation, just as I was. The killings were never solved, not until Constantine's murder spree was brought to an end in America. But I have a theory about his later killings.'

'Tell me.'

'I think that he got sick pleasure from butchering my father and sister. I also think that he sought to repeat that pleasure by killing other victims with a similar profile in a similar environment. It's as if all his crimes were echoes of that first crime. Do you agree?'

I nodded. 'It's classic serial-killer behaviour – repeating a crime, perfecting it if you like, to heighten the killer's original enjoyment of the act.'

We had come to the crime scene. I saw an ancient block of weathered granite that served as a seat. Splashes of crimson stained the block. I turned to Yeta and saw her wipe her eye. 'Are you all right?' I asked.

'Yes. I'm sorry. I was just thinking about the pain the victims must have suffered. When Inspector Uzun told me I was horrified. It's so disturbing.'

I touched her arm. 'It sounds like the phone call you received was also pretty disturbing?'

Yeta was unsettled. 'It was so bizarre, I just couldn't believe it. The caller sounded so like Constantine.'

'But you hadn't heard from your brother in more than a decade. How could you be certain you knew what he sounded like?'

Yeta considered before she replied. 'You're right, I couldn't be. It was uncanny but I felt I could actually *sense* his evil down the phone line and I so convinced myself that it was Constantine I was almost hysterical. But the more I thought about it afterwards the more rational I became. Constantine is dead, so it had to be someone else who made the call. Someone with a grudge, perhaps.'

'A grudge?'

'The caller had to be a crank, or a sick person. Someone playing tricks on me for some warped reason.'

'Why would they do that?' I asked.

'Constantine caused so much grief that I can understand a family member of one of his victims wanting to upset me. There can be no other explanation, Miss Moran.'

'You really think that someone would taunt you by pretending your brother was still alive?'

Yeta nodded. 'Yes, I do.' She turned her attention to the crime scene. 'You came all the way to Istanbul because of this murder?'

'It's more complex than that.'

'What do you mean?'

I decided to tell Yeta everything, and when I finished she was mystified. 'Why would *anyone* want to copy my brother's crimes?'

'I'm not sure.' I tried to brace myself before I made my next statement. 'I know this is going to sound totally absurd, but after all that's happened there's the unlikely possibility that your brother survived his execution.'

I saw Yeta's face turn ashen as she registered my words. 'You can't be serious?'

'I said it's an *unlikely* possibility. I know I saw him die. I heard him pronounced dead. But these fresh murders have left me baffled. I began to wonder if your brother had managed to avoid death with some kind of antidote. I know it sounds crazy. You're a biochemist. Do you think it's in any way possible? What's the matter? You're frowning.'

Yeta was still pale. 'Yes, there are antidotes even to the most lethal of poisons.'

'You mean your brother *could* have survived?'

Yeta reflected on my words as she looked towards the water pools. 'Now you're frightening me, Miss Moran. I'm only telling you what I know is technically possible – that antidotes can be manufactured.' She considered again, and said with a frown, 'There's something perhaps you ought to know. When we were children, Constantine had an ability to slow down his heartbeat until it appeared as if he was almost dead.'

Now it was my turn to register shock. 'What do you mean?'

'He was very fit and swam every day in the Bosporus. He used to boast that he had developed a breathing technique that allowed him to hold his breath underwater for more than five minutes. In the process, he would slow down his heartbeat until he was almost clinically dead. I think it was all part of the fascination he had with death – he enjoyed taking himself to the edge of mortality.'

I was dumbstruck, and more deeply worried than ever. A shiver went through me. Right at that moment I felt that the first thing I had to do when I got back to DC was to seek a court order to exhume Gamal's body. It was the only way I could prove his death. 'What you've told me is disturbing. I'm starting to wonder if I could be right about your brother surviving his execution.'

Yeta's face was drawn as she buttoned her coat. 'Personally, unless I saw Constantine dead and buried with my own eyes, I would believe nothing. Now, I must go. I have a lecture to give in half an hour, if I can manage to hold my sanity together.'

'No, please wait, Yeta . . .'

'I'm sorry, I really must go. I'm already late. You better come with me now.'

Yeta was already moving towards the stairs, her footsteps echoing on the boardwalk. I began to follow her, overcome by terror at the thought of being left alone for even a moment in such an eerie place.

But a split second later my worst nightmare became reality. The lights were extinguished and the entire palace was plunged into blackness.

* * *

Pop.

The Disciple flicked off the circuit breaker and grinned to himself. He'd just shut off the electricity for the entire lower floor of the Sunken Palace. But the lights were still on where he stood in the security room upstairs, and he stepped back from the circuit panel. On the floor lay the body of the young cop whose heart he'd stabbed with a knitting needle.

The idiot had admitted him when he'd pretended to play the lost tourist, jabbing a finger at his street map in search of directions. The older cop lay slumped in a chair. He had met the same fate as his colleague, stabbed through the heart. The Disciple stepped over the body on the floor and removed the pair of Electra night-vision goggles from his backpack. Time to have some fun.

He moved towards the steps leading down to the Sunken Palace, paused at the top of the darkened stairwell, slipped on the night-vision goggles and switched them on.

Now he could see through the blackness below, except that everything had a lime-green tint. *Magic.* Night becomes day.

As he moved downstairs his rubber-soled sneakers didn't even squeak.

79

I wanted to scream in the pitch blackness. I was frozen with fear, too scared to move, and all I could think was: *God, this can't be happening to me.*

I was too frightened to risk even a single step. *What if I strayed off the walkway and slipped into the water?* My heart drummed against my ribcage. It felt just like the catacombs all over again. *What the hell caused the power to go out?* I had a terrible premonition that something bad was about to happen.

'Yeta? Where are you?'

'I . . . I'm over here.'

Thank God I'm not alone. The sound of another voice was a tiny comfort.

'Miss Moran, I . . . I have a confession to make. I have a fear of the dark.'

I heard a nervous tremor in Yeta's voice. *Terrific. And I have a fear of confined spaces. What a pair we make.* 'Just take slow, deep breaths, it always helps if you feel panic coming on. Do you feel panicked?'

'Y . . . yes.'

'We ought to try calling out. The police should hear us.'

'If . . . if you think so.'

Yeta sounded too petrified to do anything so I called out at the top of my voice: '*Hello? Can you hear me? Is anybody there?*'

My voice echoed in the hollow darkness, but no reply came. 'We need to find the nearest light switch, or a torch.'

'I . . . I have a cigarette lighter in my handbag.'

'Where's your handbag?'

'On the floor. I dropped it when the lights went out.'

'Stay exactly where you are, Yeta. I'm going to come to you. I'll try to find it.'

'I won't move,' she promised.

It was difficult to judge distance in the dark, but her voice sounded near, perhaps only yards away. I knelt down on the walkway and inched forward, scrabbling at the ground in front of me, extending my fingers.

'Did you find the bag yet?' Yeta asked, anguish evident in her voice.

'No, not yet.' I splayed my fingers wide as I searched the ground to left and right, but I found nothing. Then I heard a sound like a scurrying rat.

Oh, Jesus, that's all I need, rats. I fought my temptation to panic, knowing that if I lost it Yeta would go to pieces. I searched some more. The scraping sound got louder, then I heard what sounded like a sharp intake of breath. I thought: *Yeta must be hyperventilating.* 'Try and hold on. Your bag has got to be here somewhere,' I told her.

No reply.

'Yeta . . . ?'

Still no reply. Primal fear pounded through my veins. 'YETA!' My voice resounded as a frightening echo in the pitch black. My stomach felt knotted as hard as steel. *What the hell is wrong with Yeta? Is she so scared she can't reply?*

I crawled forward and suddenly felt something soft under my hand. It felt like leather. *The bag.* I clutched it in the darkness. *Thank God.*

'I've got it,' I said aloud. Still no reply came from Yeta. In panic I fumbled around inside the bag until eventually my fingers found what felt like a cigarette lighter.

I managed to flick it on and a burst of light exploded in front of my face. Immediately I wanted to cry out but my scream was trapped in my throat. Ten yards in front of me Yeta lay on the boardwalk, blood pumping from a wound in her throat.

80

For a couple of seconds I froze in alarm. Then I heard a gurgling sound from Yeta's lips and saw her eyelids flicker – she was still alive. But I could see that she was bleeding to death.

What could I do? Panic overcame me and my mind was assailed by questions. Yeta's assault had happened so quickly and in complete darkness. Her attacker had to be out there in the blackness. And then it hit me like a blow from a baseball bat. *I'm alone and unarmed and I'm the next victim.*

I held up the lighter flame in the dark. I saw water and soaring pillars and shadowy wet stone walls. But not a single person. Where was the killer?

My heart pounded so fast that I felt it was going to explode. My mind was swamped with fright and I was barely able to function. Yeta's eyelids hardly flickered now and her breathing was shallow. A stream of blood seeped from a small puncture hole in her neck. I noticed another puncture wound over her heart, a circle of blood staining her blouse. Both wounds looked like they could have been inflicted by a stiletto knife. My hands were shaking so much that I could barely hold the lighter, but I knew that if I didn't do something fast she'd bleed to death.

I crawled over to her, but almost the moment I reached her side I heard a soft gush of air escape from her lips and her head rolled to one side. I grabbed her wrist and felt for her pulse. Yeta was dead.

A scraping noise sounded behind me and I spun round, sensing that something was moving out in the darkness. I held the lighter higher but all I could make out were shadows and stone pillars.

The flame weakened. I was terrified the lighter would go out. The thought of being alone in hostile darkness with a killer petrified me. I had no weapon, I was vulnerable and terrified, and I had to get out of there before it was too late. Yeta was beyond help, and I didn't intend to be the killer's next victim.

I let go of Yeta's limp hand, and as I pushed myself to my feet I heard the noise again. A soft sound, like a sandal brushing on wood. Or a rat. But instinct told me it wasn't a rat.

It's Yeta's killer, waiting to strike. What if Constantine Gamal really is alive and he's hidden behind one of the stone pillars? That thought sent me into a panic. If I was right he'd kill me. I remembered his hate-filled eyes, could still feel his teeth biting savagely into my flesh.

Fear swamped me as I heard another scraping sound to my left and held the lighter in that direction.

Nothing. Or did I see a shadow flit behind one of the pillars?

I didn't wait to find out. I cupped the lighter flame with my hand and ran like hell towards the stairwell.

The Disciple watched from behind a massive stone pillar. He clutched the knitting needle in his hand. Suddenly, through his night vision goggles, he saw Moran run towards the stairwell. He was having fun, toying with her the way a cat might play with a mouse. The stupid bitch was trying to get away, running in blind panic. She looked scared and confused, which was *exactly* how he enjoyed seeing her. *All part of the game.*

She bounded up the stairs, taking them two at a time, but he didn't have to run after her. Tucked in his pocket were the guard's set of keys. He had locked the metal exit trellis. *Let's see if the bitch can still find a way out.* He wanted to pit his mind against hers and enjoy the exquisite pleasure of her fear for as long as he could. He grinned, then stepped out from behind the pillar and moved after her.

81

I raced up the stairs and reached the top. The flame had gone out and I tossed away the lighter. I was torn between trying to find the policemen and my urge to flee the building. My gut instinct was to head straight for the exit and that's what I did, but when I tried to open the trellis gate it was locked.

I'd heard no one follow me up the stairs but I was convinced that Constantine Gamal was after me and that it was only a matter of time before he came up the stairwell. I panicked and looked back towards the guard's room. I noticed that the door was open and the light from the TV still flickered. 'Hello!' I called out. 'Is anybody there?'

No reply. I reached the doorway and saw the policemen's bodies, one on the floor, the other slumped in a chair. Pools of blood puddled the tiled floor beneath them. My pulse went off the scale.

I stared down at the older man and saw that the bunch of keys was gone from his belt, and at that moment I felt certain I was about to die. *Someone's taken the keys and I can't escape.*

I didn't know of any exit except through the front door. Then I noticed that the door on the electricity circuit panel door was wide open and a bank of circuit breakers had popped. Someone had cut the electricity to the basement.

And I know who that someone is.

A second later I thought I heard distant footsteps. *Is there really someone on the stairs, or was it just my fevered imagination?* My mind was so stressed I couldn't tell. Panic gripped me. *I'm trapped with no way out.*

Reason told me there had to be a spare set of keys somewhere, so I started to frantically search the room. It was about ten feet square, with a table and two chairs, and an old gas stove which the guards obviously used for cooking. I tried not to look down but I couldn't avoid stepping in the cops' blood as I crossed to check the table's drawers.

I found no keys. I scoured the room for a hiding place that might contain a spare set and noticed a wooden cabinet in a corner. I tore open the door and found a food cupboard used by the guards, lined with shelves of tinned food, jars of condiments, tea and coffee, pots and pans, and at the bottom a dented five-litre can of cooking oil. I ran my hands over the shelves but found nothing until I touched something on the cabinet's left side. It felt like a hook with a set of keys. *Please God, let it be a spare one for the gate . . .*

I plucked down a metal ring with five keys. *But what if none of the keys fits the lock?* I had to buy time and slow up the killer. An idea struck me and I hauled out the can of cooking oil. It felt pretty full and I heaved it out into the hall. The footsteps on the stairs sounded like they were getting closer. I unscrewed the plastic top and tilted the can, and the oil gushed down the stairway.

When I'd emptied the can I darted towards the trellis, my heart beating so furiously that my chest hurt. I inserted one of the keys into the trellis lock but it wouldn't fit.

I swore.

I tried another.

It didn't fit.

I tried the next – this time the key went in but it wouldn't budge.

Jesus.

The footsteps sounded close. Moments later they halted. In the silence that followed I could hear heavy breathing. By now my heartbeat was hammering in my ears, and when I tried to listen again I heard nothing. Then suddenly I heard another slow, measured footstep that slapped on the stairs, followed by a thumping sound, and then silence once more. It sounded as if the killer had encountered the oil and was having difficulty climbing the stairway or had slipped. But then the slapping noise started up again, more slowly. The killer was still coming up the stairs.

Oh God.

I inserted the next key, and the next, but neither worked.

When I tried the last key, the lock sprang open. I almost collapsed with relief. My hands trembled as I tugged the trellis across and yanked open the metal door. A rush of traffic noise greeted me. Seconds later I heard more footsteps slapping on the marble steps and I darted into the crowded street.

82

I ran frantically as curious pedestrians stared at me. Then I realised I was being stupid – fleeing a crime scene would only attract attention and make me look like a criminal.

I slowed to a walking pace and pretended to peer into shop windows. It took a few more minutes before my breathing returned to normal, but the relief didn't last long. I realised that Gamal might be in disguise, anywhere in the crowds around me.

I kept checking over my shoulder, but with so many people on the streets it would be easy for a killer to choose his moment to slip a knife between my ribs. I searched the faces in the passing crowds, looking for anyone resembling Gamal, and got a massive shock when I spotted a dark-haired man wearing sunglasses and carrying a rucksack on his back, strolling ten yards behind me. He looked about the same height and build as Gamal.

I noticed him avert his gaze to stare into a shop window. *Is it Gamal, or am I being paranoid?* I knew there and then the only way I was going to put my mind at rest as to whether Gamal was alive or dead was to open his coffin. And the sooner the better. But first I had to get home.

Moments later I heard the shrieks of police sirens. *Are Inspector Uzun's men on their way to the Sunken Palace to find me, at Lou's request?* If I went back and told them what had happened, would they believe in my innocence or would I end up in worse trouble? I couldn't wait to take that risk – at least for now I'd feel safer on the move. I walked for ten minutes and didn't see the man follow me. I saw an archway leading into a marketplace. A sign overhead had words painted in gold lettering: KAPALI CARSI. I remembered from my guidebook that this was Istanbul's famous

Grand Bazaar, and that it dated from the fifteenth century. I darted under the archway and entered the bazaar.

It was a noisy and dazzling marketplace, an overcrowded maze crammed with tiny stores, the air smelling of exotic perfumes and spices. As I moved deeper into the passageways I saw that the bazaar was lined with every type of store imaginable: glittering jewellery shops, heavily laden food stalls, leatherware outlets and stores selling bales of brightly coloured material. Merchants, some wearing traditional gowns and clutching prayer beads, sat hunched over silver trays of tea or coffee and tried to coax passers-by inside their shops.

My mind returned to the fix I was in. I was innocent and wasn't scared of cooperating with the Turkish police, but I figured that if I allowed myself to be detained by them I'd be sucked into their investigation and could be stuck in Istanbul for weeks until I'd ironed out the mess. At worst, I might even be accused of the murders of Yeta and the guards. It was no reflection on Inspector Uzun, but I preferred to do my explaining to Lou, and my gut instinct told me to get the hell out of Istanbul. I didn't feel safe on Gamal's home turf, and Yeta's death had proved that I wasn't. Running might make me look guilty but my intuition told me it might keep me alive. Besides, I wanted to open that damned coffin.

First, I needed to make it to the airport. Public transport would be safer – a cab driver might remember me. I searched the guidebook's back pages and found mention of an airport bus service – according to the map, the street wasn't more than a ten-minute walk away.

The enclosed bazaar was beginning to make me feel claustrophobic. I felt I had to get out before I got lost in the passageways. Traders pushed their wares under my nose, trying to sell me everything from a pair of silvered kitchen taps to a leather jacket. I couldn't see the dark-haired man with the sunglasses. *But that doesn't mean he isn't out there.* At any moment I might get a knife stuck in my back.

A stallholder I passed urged me to buy some sugared almonds, but I had to cut him short. 'Where's the nearest exit? The way out.'

He uttered something in Turkish which I couldn't understand, but another stallholder pointed towards the next corner. 'Exit is that way, madame.'

'Thank you.'

'Would pretty lady like some leather shoes at a very good price?'

I couldn't blame the guy for trying, but now wasn't the time. Then I noticed that his stall had several racks of sunglasses and another one of headscarves. I plucked down one of each. 'How much for a pair sunglasses and the scarf?'

'For you, madame, I give you a bargain.'

I wasn't in the mood for haggling. 'I'll take them.'

The merchant started to wrap the items but I said, 'No, I'll wear them now.'

'As madame wishes.'

I paid the merchant and slipped on the black headscarf and dark glasses, but as I turned to go I noticed a man lounging by a gold merchant's shop, twenty yards away. He wore a rimmed dark hat, black scarf and Ray-Bans. I wasn't certain that he was the same man I'd seen in the street, but I was *sure* that he was observing me. I wasn't going to wait to find out whether he was Gamal. I plunged through the swarms of customers and hurried towards the exit.

Hidden in the crowded bazaar, the Disciple observed Kate don the headscarf and dark glasses. He had ditched his motorcycle and tailed her on foot from the Sunken Palace. He got such a kick out of seeing the bitch so scared it didn't matter that she had slowed him up and somehow found a spare set of keys and escaped. Or that he had slipped on the oiled stairs, fallen down a couple of steps and cracked his right elbow against a wall. His bone still hurt as he rubbed his arm. *All part of the risks of the game*. He still felt the greasy oil on his hands and clothes, despite using a T-shirt from his backpack to clean himself. The bitch was pretty clever, he had to admit that. *But not as clever as me.* Right now, he was feeding off her fear, getting high on it, but if she thought she could flee from him for ever she had another thing coming. He had plans for Kate Moran. He was going to make her suffer dearly for what she had done to him.

He saw her hurry towards one of the bazaar's exits and followed.

I found the street with the Turkish Airlines bus stop. Two buses had pulled up, passengers boarding and disembarking. I made my way along the queue behind a group of Swedish backpackers and bought a ticket to board, then took a seat midway down the carriage.

I had checked behind me all the way to the station but I saw no one following. The mysterious stranger in the hat and sunglasses was nowhere to be seen. But as I studied my fellow passengers, just to be certain that he wasn't on the bus, a terrifying thought struck me. Like any investigator worth his salt, Uzun would have his men covering the airport. *And if the airport is being watched, my passport will be tagged in Istanbul. Once I try to check in I'll be a marked woman.*

I felt trapped, but it was too late to change my mind – the driver was already pulling out into the flow of traffic. Five minutes later the bus was speeding out of the city towards the airport. I was certain now that the police would be watching out for me. I estimated that I had less than an hour to figure a way out of this mess, or else the moment I stepped into the departures terminal I was a goner.

83

Alexandria, Virginia

Lou Raines crashed the phone down on his nightstand and climbed out of bed. He pulled on his dressing gown and with an angry sigh strode over to his bedroom window. His wife was staying with their daughter in Baltimore, which was just as well considering the shitty mood he was in.

The rain was coming down in sheets, the District alive with the glow of an electrical storm, lightning flickering on the skyline and rainwater drenching the window. A whole bunch of questions that needed answering rattled around in his mind, but after the phone call he'd just received he really only had *one* question: *What in the name of fuck is going on with Kate Moran?*

This was Raines' first day off in a week, and he hated being disturbed at home, but the call he'd received from Inspector Ahmet Uzun had been urgent. It had also deeply troubled him. Three more people had been murdered in Istanbul: one of them was Constantine Gamal's sister, Yeta, and the other two were cops, all three victims killed at the Sunken Palace. In the case of Yeta the MO was typically Gamal: a dark, underground site and the weapon of choice a blade of some kind. A lightning flash illuminated the window and Raines gritted his teeth and shook his head fiercely as he stared out at nature's light show.

He'd tried calling Moran on her cell phone almost a dozen times before he'd finally given up and slammed down his receiver, his frustration at boiling point. Her cellular was on call-answering. He couldn't fathom what was going on in the absence of any contact from her. According to Inspector Uzun, Kate Moran had completely disappeared. Witnesses had seen a woman matching her description fleeing the Sunken Palace.

Raines considered that she might have fled because she was under threat. But Uzun claimed she was spotted fleeing down a main street and with no sign of anyone pursuing her. Raines thought: *Something about all this doesn't make any sense. Kate's been behaving strangely since this whole frigging business began.*

He reminded himself she had even suggested that Gamal may have survived his execution. *I mean, how frigging crazy is that?* Executed men don't come back from the dead. The murders had to be the work of a copycat, period.

But who, and why? And here was a weird question that he figured might be posed by some people: *How come Kate Moran has the awkward knack of turning up most places there's a killing?*

As he threw off his pyjamas and began to dress before heading to the office, something else niggled him, big time. The fact that Moran had directly disobeyed his orders and flown to Istanbul. If there was one thing that got right up his butt it was his team disobeying orders. Discipline was the keystone of a well-run department. He expected to be obeyed or else there was hell to pay.

He sighed again. *What the hell have you gone and done by vanishing, Kate? People are going to start thinking you're implicated in these murders.*

Raines couldn't remotely figure out how or why. But somehow he had the feeling that Stone might try to sort that one out for him.

84

Istanbul

As I travelled in the bus towards the airport a shriek of sirens sounded and a convoy of police cars overtook us. I sank down in my seat as the procession flashed past, heading in the direction of the airport. That was when I got a shock – I glimpsed Inspector Uzun in the back seat of one of the cars. He was busy speaking on his cell phone and he didn't look thrilled.

Damn.

I knew instantly that even if I made it to the airport I didn't stand a chance of escaping. With Uzun there to identify me, I was finished. I seemed to be running from one set of troubles to another with no way out of the mess.

I half expected a police checkpoint even before I reached the airport, but ten minutes later the bus drove up a sloping road and pulled up outside the departures area. The passengers disembarked but I was rooted to my seat. I knew that I might as well have a 'catch me' sign stuck on my back if I left the vehicle.

As the last of the bus passengers climbed off, myself and a young woman dressed in some sort of airport uniform with an ID badge around her neck were the last on board. She wasn't budging either, which suggested to me that maybe the bus still had another stop to make.

The driver fixed me with a stare and babbled in Turkish, as if suggesting that I might like to get off. I shook my head, indicating I was staying put. With a shrug, he turned round in his seat and pulled out into the traffic again. I watched as he swung left into a lane that sloped downwards. And then our destination dawned on me. *We're heading for the arrivals terminal.*

It was only an elevator ride to Departures, but what was the point? I'd still be caught by Uzun. The driver halted and I finally stepped off the bus, following the uniformed young woman into the crowded arrivals terminal. But there were no hordes of police – Uzun was obviously concentrating his forces on the departures level.

I still couldn't relax, a black cloud of anxiety hovering over me. *Should I risk attempting to fly out of Istanbul or just give myself up?* But all I could think of was staying ahead of the posse for just long enough to open Gamal's coffin and prove my own sanity. I looked up at the arrivals/departures screens and saw that there was a flight to New York leaving in three hours. But New York had tough immigration procedures, and even assuming I could buy a ticket for the flight I'd face insurmountable problems.

I needed somewhere quiet to think things through so I found the restrooms around a corner, stepped into an empty cubicle, locked the door and sat down. I felt emotionally drained and physically exhausted. I was still free but I was convinced that Uzun was covering the departures terminal upstairs. If I showed my face he'd recognise me a mile off. Besides, the police would have my passport flagged. I'd be apprehended the moment I appeared at a ticket desk. I'd have to keep well away from the departures area.

But then an idea came to me. *Maybe there is a way out of this mess.* My black cloud lifted a little. I had the beginnings of a plan to get out of Istanbul. But would it work?

85

Washington, DC

Raines was behind his desk at 9.30 a.m., sipping hot black coffee, when there was a knock on his door and Stone entered. 'You wanted to see me, Lou?'

'Yeah. You'll be glad to know that Moran's gone missing.'

Stone frowned. 'In Paris?'

'No, Istanbul,' Raines answered. 'She's completely disappeared.'

'*What?* I thought you said you gave her direct orders not to go there?'

'I did,' Raines answered, and explained to Stone everything he'd learned about what had happened in Istanbul.

Stone gritted his teeth. 'What the fuck's she up to? My gut instinct tells me that bitch is somehow playing us all for fools.'

Raines sounded irritated. 'Watch your tongue, Stone. And don't give me gut instinct.'

Stone said with unconcealed rage, 'What the hell more do you want, Lou, a signed confession? I've got incriminating evidence, the clothes from her cottage – Diaz is checking them out now. And I've got a description of her and her Bronco from the old lady at the trailer park.'

Raines shook his head. 'Ain't that terrific. A pity you didn't have a search warrant for the clothes. And the lady at the trailer park's over seventy with poor eyesight, and from what Norton says there might be a doubt about her sanity.'

'What about the other stuff you just told me? That Moran's been at the scene of three murders in Istanbul and witnesses *saw* her flee. That the Turkish police want to question her. You telling me that's no big deal?'

Raines said, 'Don't try to colour things, Stone. And there are a couple of things about your suspicion that don't add up. The E-fit, for one. It was of a man, not a woman. And two, the evidence is that a woman shouted outside the trailer. Would a woman have been strong enough to carry two bodies fifty yards into the mines?'

'You're saying it couldn't have been Moran in disguise at that mine, to mislead us? And don't tell me she isn't strong enough to carry a body. I've seen her in the gym, and she's about fit enough to do it at a push.'

Raines shook his head. 'All that aside, Kate Moran's in enough trouble, and she's got no motive for any of the other killings. Besides, we know there's a copycat killer out there. All the Turkish police want to do right now is talk to her. All she's done in Istanbul is behave irrationally.'

Stone's tone was accusing. 'Sounds to me like you're having doubts about this, Lou. To tell the truth I'm more concerned about the other facts. I mean the clothes and the Bronco. From where I'm sitting, we've got more than enough circumstantial and solid evidence to arrest her. So let's stick to the rules, follow protocol and arrest her.'

'Have you got any other advice you'd like to give me, Stone?' Raines said drily.

'Yeah, sometimes irrational people do crazy things.' Stone leaned forward and placed his fingertips on Raines' desk. 'So the only way we're going to get to the bottom of this is to pull her in and lean heavy on her. Of course, I can't ignore the fact that you and she are buddies. Or maybe I'm missing something there?'

Raines was defensive. 'Like what?'

'That maybe you have something going on with Moran and that you're letting it cloud your judgement? Or maybe you haven't got the guts to do what you have to do because she's a close friend?'

Raines jumped to his feet, red faced. 'Don't *ever* imply that there's anything other than a professional relationship between Moran and me, or so help me, Stone, I'll haul you bare assed over hot coals.'

'You're going easy on her. I can't ignore that.' Stone drew back but was unrepentant.

'That's your opinion.' Raines crossed to the window and looked out at the rain sheeting down, his hands on his hips, fury on his face as he said, without turning back, 'Get the fuck out of my office. *Now!*'

Stone crossed to the door and said sullenly, 'I'm going to nail her, Lou. I've got more evidence to gather, more bones to pick over, but I *will* nail her in the end. You and she may be buddies but I reckon she's just a conniving, murdering bitch, and I'm going to prove it. Did it occur to you that she might flee Istanbul and go on the run? Have you thought of that?'

Raines turned back from the window and said fiercely, 'For your information, that's a no-hoper, Stone. Inspector Uzun's alerted all border exits, set up roadblocks out of the city, and he's got the airport covered. He's there right now himself, and he's personally watching every departing passenger. He's confident there isn't a hope in hell that Moran will escape from Istanbul.'

86

I left the restroom and stepped back into the arrivals hall. I was certain that if I presented my passport to buy an airline ticket I'd be arrested, which meant that if I was to have any hope of leaving Turkey then I had to get myself both a disguise and a false passport.

That part of the plan I'd sort of figured out, but it was going to be tough and probably dangerous. I slipped on my sunglasses, wrapped the scarf around my head, Turkish style, walked across the arrivals hall to a beverage stand and bought myself a cup of coffee. Then I found an empty seat and sat. I scanned the passing crowds and prayed that I'd spot what I was looking for.

I'd spent a couple of months on a dipper detail at Dulles as a cop so I knew the signs to look out for, and after about twenty minutes I spotted a pickpocket. A guy about thirty, baby faced, with a slight limp. He looked like a respectable young professional in a dark business suit and carried a leather briefcase in his right hand and a Gladstone bag over his left shoulder. Baby-face was also one of the slickest pickpockets I'd ever seen in action – so fast he was almost undetectable.

I noticed that every time the airside doors opened and a thick stream of passengers flooded into the arrivals area from their flights, Baby-face would slide into action. He'd mingle with the surge of passengers, then step away towards the exit doors. Then he'd reappear a little later and perform the same ritual on a fresh batch of passengers. I hardly saw his hands move under the Gladstone bag but I knew by instinct that every time he melted

321

into the stream of passengers, he'd go 'fishing' – stealing wallets, purses, personal belongings, anything he could get his slick fingers on. Airports were the ideal haunt for pickpockets – busy passengers were the perfect targets, usually in fast transit and with their guard down. And Baby-face was a first-class operator, so I knew he wouldn't risk his luck and buzz around the honey pot for ever. He'd high-tail it out of the airport before he was nailed by Security. Sure enough, a minute later I saw him walk towards the exit doors.

I tossed my coffee cup into a garbage bin and followed him outside as he walked towards a well-polished black Mercedes parked about thirty yards past the taxi ranks. A beefy, tough-looking guy with a shaven head and a gold earring sat in the driver's seat. He was smoking a cigarette, and I saw Baby-face lean into the passenger window for a couple of minutes and chat. Then I saw him slip the driver his briefcase.

I figured the bald driver was Baby-face's relay man. He'd hoard the stolen goods and be ready to effect their escape just as soon as their work was done. Sure enough, the driver moved the brief-case on to the back seat and handed Baby-face another identical briefcase. I guessed this one was empty, and that Baby-face was about to fill it with another stash. With all the cops and security men upstairs in departures, I reckoned these two guys were having a field day.

Baby-face finished his drop, then left the driver and disappeared back inside the terminal for another fishing run. I let him go – I knew that it was his bald accomplice I had to deal with. My big fear was that the driver was armed. He was at least a hundred pounds heavier than me, rugged built, and he sure *looked* dangerous. I figured on him not speaking English – he didn't look like the kind of guy with a mastery of foreign languages. A pity because, knowing what I had to do, this would make my job even harder.

But I had no choice. If I wanted to get out of Istanbul I had to take this guy on. I braced myself by taking a deep breath, then started to walk towards the black Mercedes.

87

I reached the Mercedes just as the driver lit a cigarette. I yanked open the rear door and jumped into the back seat next to the leather briefcase. 'Taxi?' I said as the driver spun round.

He looked completely dumbfounded and put away his lighter, his eyes wide as he mouthed something in Turkish and waved for me to get out of his car. I didn't budge and said, 'Do you speak English? I need a taxi to take me to my hotel.'

The guy gave me an appraising look and relaxed just a fraction before he displayed a gap between his thumb and forefinger. 'Little English. But this is no taxi, lady. Go! Leave!'

I thought: *At least he speaks English.*

'Taxi over there.' The driver indicated the cab rank thirty yards away, then his stare settled guardedly on his black briefcase nestled beside me. He waved me away impatiently. 'Go, go! Out!'

I eyed the case. 'It looks to me like you and your friend had a good day. Did you steal much?'

The guy's jaw dropped as I flashed my ID in his face and said, 'See those doors into arrivals? Any minute now the police are going to come to arrest you so you better get out of here, fast.'

I wasn't sure whether the driver understood what I was saying or whether he could even read my FBI creds, but I didn't wait to find out – I grabbed the briefcase. But I'd made a big mistake if I thought he was going to allow himself to be easily duped. His eyes ignited with rage as he lunged for me, and I jumped out of the Mercedes.

I had gone barely ten yards when I glanced back and saw the driver clamber out of his seat. His face was scarlet with anger and he was even bigger and more muscular than I'd thought. He was mouthing what I guessed were obscenities as he shoved past passengers and came at me like an enraged bear.

Hell.

I pushed my way into the crowded terminal.

The Disciple watched from outside the arrivals entrance door and saw Kate Moran jump out of the Mercedes grasping a black leather briefcase. The bitch had a nerve, he'd give her that.

He'd followed her in a cab from the bus station, and once she reached the airport he'd tailed her and saw her stalking the baby-faced guy with the limp. It took him a while to piece it all together, but he was pretty sure what Moran was up to. He reckoned the guy she had marked was a pickpocket and Moran needed to get her hands on a stolen passport.

He almost laughed to himself – it was fun watching her try to stay alive and one step ahead of the law. He watched the enraged driver jump out after her and push his way into the crowded terminal. The Disciple saw the driver reach into his pocket. He guessed he had a gun or a knife, and from the furious look on his face he intended to inflict serious damage on Kate Moran.

The dumb fuck – he couldn't allow that. *Sorry, pal, the bitch is mine.*

The Disciple gripped a knitting needle in his right hand as he moved after the driver, who was jostling through the crowd. He caught up with him and slipped the needle in below the guy's third rib, puncturing his heart. The big Turk stiffened and gasped.

The Disciple kept moving even as his victim collapsed in the middle of the crowd. In one swift movement he had wiped the needle clean and tucked it back inside his sleeve. He heard a scream from someone in the crowd when they saw the driver hit the ground, blood spraying from his chest wound.

By then the Disciple was already ten yards away, striding after Moran.

88

I heard a commotion behind me, looked back and saw a sea of bobbing heads and faces. I was sure I'd heard a scream from somewhere in the crowd but I couldn't see the driver. *Maybe he's given up?*

I didn't intend to find out what the commotion was about. At the far end of the terminal I entered the ladies' restrooms. I found a cubicle, opened the leather case and examined my stash. Inside was a jumble of stolen goods – a bunch of wallets and purses containing banknotes in at least four different currencies, two cell phones and five passports.

I opened the first passport, belonging to a German teenage male. I put it aside and flicked through the others: another German, this time a dark-haired, bespectacled female aged thirty-five but with a Turkish surname. I figured she was probably an emigrant. The others belonged to a twenty-year-old British man, a blonde-haired Italian woman aged forty-five, and an elderly American male professor.

This wasn't exactly the mother lode that I'd hoped for. I had to pick one of the women – the Italian or the German-Turkish lady. *What if the passports have already been reported missing or stolen?* I figured it was probably too soon after the thefts – but I couldn't be sure.

I studied the passport photos and settled on the German-Turkish woman: she was closer to my own age. Her name was Sevim Yaver. Her hair was darker than mine but I figured I could cover my head and face with the scarf, Muslim style. I slipped her passport into my pocket and examined some other personal items in the purses: among them a pair of black-framed woman's glasses, a couple of sticks of lipstick and a make-up compact with mirror. I pocketed the cell phones – the remaining passports and belongings I'd pop in the first postbox I saw in the terminal and hope that they'd eventually be returned to their owners. I slipped my own passport in my hand luggage, and tucked my wallet and personal cell phone into my jeans pocket.

Next, I used the compact and put on as much make-up as I dared, and applied one of the lipsticks – a bright scarlet, not exactly my colour, but hopefully it would draw attention away from the rest of my face. Then I adjusted my headscarf so that it entirely covered my hair and put on the glasses.

Everything's a foggy blur. How the hell am I supposed to see anything?

I adjusted the glasses on to the bridge of my nose so that at least I could peer over them and see where I was going. I looked in the make-up mirror and compared myself to the passport photograph of the woman. The resemblance wasn't too hot, but so long as no one looked too closely maybe I had a chance.

It was time to test the water.

89

I took the elevator up to Departures. As soon as I stepped out I noticed that uniformed and plainclothes police officers were everywhere.

My spirits sank. *They're out to find me with a vengeance.*

I saw no sign of Ahmet Uzun. *Please God he's not in the airport.*

I noticed a postbox near by and slid the other passports and belongings into the slot.

Then I checked the departure screens. I figured I couldn't fly directly to the US with Sevim Yaver's passport because US Immigration required visas and did passenger fingerprint checks. I thought about flying via Canada, but their airport Immigration had a meticulous reputation, and anyway there were no direct flights to Canada listed. I noticed a Lufthansa flight to Frankfurt departing in something over an hour. It might be better for me to fly there considering that Sevim Yaver was a German citizen, and then I could try to make a stateside connection from Frankfurt, but using my own passport. That leg of the trip would be fraught with risk, but I had no other option that I could think of.

I approached the Lufthansa ticket desk. A young female clerk was serving a customer, and when my turn came I said in English, 'I'd like a one-way ticket on the next flight to Frankfurt. Do you have a seat available?'

The clerk studied me with curiosity, as if she expected me to speak Turkish because of the headscarf, but then she simply said, 'Yes, madam, I believe there are seats, but let me just check.'

Five minutes later I had bought myself a business-class ticket. I handed over the lady's credit card, praying it hadn't been reported lost or stolen, but the sales clerk swiped it on her machine without any problem and asked me to sign the slip. She didn't bat an eyelid as she handed back my card and ticket and directed me towards check-in. 'Boarding will commence in twenty minutes. Do you have baggage, madam?'

'Only hand luggage.'

'Then I can check you in here.' She tapped her keyboard and handed me a boarding slip. 'Have a good flight, madam.'

It all seems too easy. I felt a pang of guilt for using Sevim Yaver's credit card, but took comfort in the fact that the credit card company would probably have to reimburse her. My heart was thumping as I joined the queue for the passport check. I knew that by buying a one-way ticket at short notice I had probably already alerted the authorities: now I fitted a drug smuggler's profile. But there was no going back. Twenty yards away dozens of people were lined up in front of a string of booths manned by passport officers.

Uniformed policemen stood guard beside each booth, closely scrutinising the faces of departing passengers. *If they compare my face closely with the passport I'm carrying, I'm a goner.*

Seconds later a man stepped out of a nearby office and joined one of the cops standing guard beside the passport booth. And that's when I knew I was finished even before I started.

It was Inspector Ahmet Uzun.

328

90

P anic set in and my palms began to sweat. I was having trouble breathing and thinking straight. But I had enough sense to know that if I turned and ran I'd be noticed. *And if I remain in the queue, Uzun will recognise me. Either way, I'm finished.*

The line moved up. I noticed that Uzun was intently studying the faces of every passenger who passed in front of him. I thought hard but saw no way of escape. I finally resolved to give myself up. It was crazy behaving like a wanted criminal when I knew that I had done nothing wrong.

But try telling that to the police. I had steeled myself to approach Uzun when I noticed a bank of phone booths thirty yards away and a thought struck me. Uzun was absorbed studying the departing passengers and no one else was paying me any attention. I fumbled through my Filofax pages and found the number I needed. I took one of the cell phones from my hand luggage, flicked it on and punched the numbers.

As my call rang out I looked ahead and saw Uzun pull out his cell phone. I saw his lips move. 'Uzun,' he answered.

I wanted to keep our conversation short and sweet. Any announcement over the airport PA might alert him that I was in the building. 'Ahmet, this is Kate Moran.'

As I watched from thirty yards away I could see him stiffen with shock. 'Kate, where are you calling from?'

'First you have to believe me when I tell you that I had nothing to do with Yeta Gamal's death.'

I saw Uzun swallow hard. 'I believe what you say, but why are you running?'

'It's a long story. But for one, I don't feel safe, Ahmet. What happened to Yeta could happen to me.'

'Then let me protect you.'

'With all respect, I've got a feeling that wouldn't make a lot of difference. As bizarre as this sounds, I'm beginning to convince myself that the person who killed Yeta may have some kind of paranormal power. I'd feel safer watching my own back. You think I've gone crazy, don't you?'

'I think you're under stress and still in shock after Yeta's death. But shock can make us do illogical things, such as running away. Where are you? We need to talk, Kate.'

He sounded anxious and I saw him begin to pace up and down as he listened. 'Ahmet, the bottom line is I think someone is trying to set me up. That's the honest truth,' I replied.

'I said I believe you, Kate. But we *must* talk. You must give yourself up for questioning.'

'What reasons did Raines give for wanting me arrested?'

'At first he said you disobeyed orders. Now he says that evidence has been discovered by your FBI colleagues linking you with a more serious charge.'

It was my turn to be shaken. I was going over my self-imposed time limit on the phone but I couldn't help it, my curiosity overwhelming. *'What evidence? What charge?'*

'I don't know, Kate. All I do know is that you have to give yourself up.'

I bet Stone's behind this. I took a deep breath and said, 'I'll meet you in the Pera Palace Hotel in one hour.' I flicked off the cell phone.

I saw Uzun gather his men together, and within less than a minute they were bundling towards the exit. I turned away as Uzun hurried past me.

My ruse worked.

Uzun was going to be furious when he found out he'd been conned – but I'd had no choice. I remained in the queue. The uniforms checking passports were more relaxed now that the police had disappeared. When my turn came the guard barely

330

gave my document a second glance and waved me on.

Fifteen minutes later I boarded my Lufthansa flight to Frankfurt.

The Disciple watched Kate Moran as she moved towards passport control. What a clever bitch she was, but then he'd always known that. He was standing only yards behind her in the queue, clutching his own boarding card and passport for the Frankfurt flight. He'd approached the Lufthansa desk immediately after he saw Moran buy a ticket – a quick check on the departures screen had told him that the only Lufthansa flight leaving that evening was to Frankfurt – so he bought a seat on the same flight.

He'd witnessed her making a call on her cell phone and watching the cops, and then he saw the cops hastily depart. He saw Moran's reaction and he figured out what had happened. *Very fucking clever – drawing the cops away with a phone call. But she won't stay clever for much longer.* Right now she was free only because he had chosen to allow her to remain free. It was all part of his game, enjoying her terror to the maximum, because it gave him such exquisite pleasure to see Kate Moran in mortal fear and running for her life. But the moment when he would finally take his revenge was coming very soon. And when it came he had something very special planned.

He was close enough to touch her. He reached out, tempted to grip the bitch by the hair, but he bit back his fury and withdrew his hand. *Revenge is a dish best served cold.* He watched as Moran stepped up to passport control and was waved on by the Turkish official. When his turn came, the Disciple presented one of his passports and smiled politely at the officer. The man gave the document a careful glance and ushered him through.

This time the Disciple had disguised himself as a backpacker, with a grey woollen hat and dark grey chino combats and a windcheater. He wore tinted designer glasses and the tiny clump of false blond beard in the middle of his chin added a hip, youthful touch.

He was ten paces behind Moran, watching her figure and

331

grinning to himself. More than any of his victims, he was going to enjoy making her suffer because of all the torment she had caused him. Killing her was going to be the absolute climax of his murder spree.

Now wasn't that something to look forward to?

PART FIVE

91

Washington, DC

'Well, what have we got, Diaz?' Stone unfolded a piece of Juicy Fruit from its wrapper and stared down at Armando Diaz. They were in the lab, Diaz wearing his white coat and thick aluminium-rimmed glasses and hunched over a microscope as he rubbed the gold stud in his left ear.

Stone hated shit like that – earrings and body piercings. They suggested to him that the wearer was either a weirdo or a masochist, or both. Diaz was certainly a tad weird – he'd seen him skating into work wearing glove-tight Speedo gear. He was wearing Speedo now under his lab coat, for Christ sakes. A luminous green-and-black one-piece. The guy had to be a borderline fruitcake. 'You ever buy yourself some decent clothes, Diaz?'

Diaz looked up from the microscope. 'What?'

'You deaf? That stuff you got on ain't exactly regular office wear, more like a dance outfit,' Stone suggested.

'Hey, don't knock it, man. No one can wear Speedo the way a Latino can. And the girls love it. They can see the complete package you got to offer. You ought to try it. Might improve your chances.'

Stone grunted. 'So what have we got, Diaz, you going to tell me?'

'We've been working together five years now, maybe it's about time you called me Armando.' Diaz looked back into his microscope.

He sounded tetchy, and considering the guy's piercings and

his Speedo gear, Stone figured he expected to be noticed. 'OK, Armando, give it to me.'

'I've got something interesting. In fact, it's *really* interesting, man.'

'Yeah? I'm listening,' Stone slipped the stick of Juicy Fruit between his lips and chewed.

Diaz looked up. 'The fibres we found on the dog Fleist's trailer and the ones under the girl's fingernails match the fibre in the pants outfit you gave me to look at, the one with the silver brocade.'

Stone stopped chewing and grinned. 'You're sure about this? No mistakes?'

'Take a look in the scope if don't believe me. It's a perfect match. But I can get another opinion if you want to nail it on the head?'

'Do it.' Stone squinted into the scope and saw two highly magnified fibres that looked like flaky ropes. They appeared similar but for now he would have to take Diaz's word for it. 'How long's the confirmation going to take?'

'I can get it done within half an hour.'

'Diaz, baby, you've just made my fucking day.'

'So who does the pants outfit belong to?'

'Wait for it – your friend Kate Moran.'

Diaz was confused. 'We're talking scene contamination here, right?'

'No, with luck we're talking murder or accessory to murder,' Stone answered, and hurried out of the lab, leaving Diaz open mouthed.

Stone still had a smug grin on his face as he took the elevator up to his office. When he stepped out he saw Lou Raines coming down the hallway towards him, carrying a sheet of paper, an infuriated look on his face as he beckoned Stone to follow him into his office.

'I've got some news for you, Lou.'

'So have I. Sit down,' said Raines bluntly.

Stone sat, sensing trouble. 'What's up? You don't mind me

336

saying so, you look like you've got an ass full of haemorrhoids, Lou.'

Raines flapped the sheet of paper in his hand. 'No, but I got a mother of a headache. I just got another call from Istanbul.'

Stone said eagerly, 'Go ahead, I'm listening.'

'Uzun had cops all over the airport, thinking she might make an appearance, then surprise, surprise, he gets a call from Moran. She tells him she'll explain what happened when she meets him at an Istanbul hotel. Except when Uzun gets there she doesn't show up. Either she changed her mind or she deliberately sent Uzun on a wild-goose chase.'

Stone was jubilant. 'I told you she's up to something, Lou. And what she's done proves she's in shit, right up to her neck.'

Raines said bitterly, 'Whatever it is she's doing she's chafing my ass.'

'Has Uzun got any ideas where she might be?' Stone asked.

Raines slumped into his desk, opened a drawer and rummaged until he found a large plastic bottle of Tylenol. 'No, but I'll take a guess she'll be trying to quit town. Except Uzun had her passport tagged at his end so if she attempts to leave Turkey she'll be arrested. He checked all the passenger names on flights out of Istanbul, even the private and chartered variety, but her name didn't turn up on any manifest. She didn't board any of the aircraft.'

'He's saying she's still in Istanbul?'

Raines popped two of the pills into his mouth and threw back his head as he washed them down with a slug of water from a bottle of Aquafina on his desk. 'Uzun's saying nothing, except he can't find her. He's going to check the security videos of departing passengers just in case she managed to get aboard a flight in disguise. If she did, there might still be time to catch her before she lands. Meanwhile, we better consider having Moran's name bulletined and her photograph circulated to Immigration in case she shows her face at a US airport. Now, what's this frigging news you've got to tell me?'

* * *

Stone slid behind his desk and made the call to Immigration, and when he had finished he had a self-satisfied grin on his face. *As soon as Moran puts a foot on US soil she'll be arrested on suspicion of conspiracy to murder. And about damned time.* He was finally going to nail her.

Even Raines had at last started to get suspicious when he'd learned the news about the fibre match from Moran's pants suit.

Stone had just finished his call when Norton burst into his office. 'Better grab your coat, Vance, and we ought to see Lou. I just got a call from the search team over at the Chinatown metro tunnel.'

'They turned up something?'

Norton flicked a nod. 'Yep, a couple of bodies. It seems Gamal might have told the truth after all.'

92

I stared out of the aircraft window at snowcapped mountains below. We were midway over the Austrian Alps. The Lufthansa captain announced that we would soon begin our descent into Frankfurt. I was tormented with worries.

What if the Turkish police discover the passports I abandoned? Uzun is no fool – he'll figure out what I've done, run a check on stolen passports and maybe he'll get lucky and flag the one I've used. The German authorities may already be waiting to arrest me at Frankfurt airport.

I hadn't been able to relax during the entire flight, the tension racking me. I heard the aircraft engine noise change pitch and moments later felt a sinking sensation as the plane began its descent.

Ten rows away the Disciple sipped a cup of hot coffee and stared at the back of Kate Moran's head. He felt a delicious sensation of pleasure. Moran hadn't a clue he was tailing her. He wanted to rub his hands with glee but instead he sniggered out loud.

He wasn't watching the in-flight entertainment – the Tom Cruise movie was crap – and he hadn't got his earphones on, which was probably why the elderly grey-haired lady seated next to him looked up from her book when she heard him laughing to himself. She looked at him as if he were mad.

The Disciple eyeballed her with a wild stare. *Hey, I am mad, lady. You keep looking at me like that and I'll rip your fucking eyes out.*

The terrified woman averted her gaze and returned to her book. The Disciple again turned his attention to the back of Kate Moran's head. Very soon he was finally going to have his revenge.

He could hardly wait.

Ten minutes after my flight touched down at Frankfurt I boarded a transit bus with the other passengers and it drove us towards the main terminal.

So far, so good.

If my escape had been discovered in Istanbul I'd have been met on the tarmac by the German cops. *But what if they were waiting to arrest me in Arrivals?*

Seconds later my fears were heightened when the bus drew up outside the terminal and the hydraulic doors opened with a hiss. As the crowd surged forward I spotted a couple of uniformed and plainclothes police officers waiting to meet the disembarking passengers.

The Disciple had his eyes firmly on Kate Moran. She was fifteen feet away and twice she'd looked towards the rear of the bus, but he still hadn't been spotted. And why should he? His array of disguises was so damned good – he was convinced she would never recognise him. As the bus doors hissed open he saw the plainclothes and uniformed cops waiting just inside the terminal and his heart flipped. But only for a second, and then his confidence was restored. *There's no fucking way they can identify me. But what if they're waiting for Kate Moran?*

He saw her hesitate before she was jostled along by the surge of passengers.

He waited for a couple of seconds and quickly followed her.

93

Frankfurt, Germany

One of the German uniformed police officers caught my eye as I moved forward with the surging crowd. The cop was tall, blond and good looking in his green uniform, and I noticed his eyes following me from the moment I spotted him.

I thought: *He's suspicious about me.* He gave me a long, penetrating stare and I felt my stomach churn. *Any moment now he'll arrest me.*

But then the cop diverted his eyes past me, his attention focused elsewhere in the crowd. I felt a rush of relief and followed the flow of human traffic into the baggage hall and the passport lanes. Fifty yards on, I glanced back – the cop was busily observing other passengers and no longer paying me any attention. For once I was glad my instincts had been wrong.

With only hand baggage, I was one of the first passengers in the queue for Immigration. My nerves felt on edge as I waited to present my passport. It was finally my turn and the uniformed officer inspected my document, scanned it on his computer and compared my face to the passport photograph. Something must have made him unsure, because he looked again at the snapshot and then up once more at my face. But a second later he nodded politely and handed back my document. *'Danke Sehr, Fräulein. Nächst, bitte!'*

I passed into the arrivals hall, found a coffee bar and ordered a double espresso. As I sipped it I began to relax. *If I've got this far, maybe I can make it to DC.*

But I knew that the longer my ordeal went on the greater the chances that I'd be caught. I scanned the electronic departure boards and saw several flights bound for the US: two to New York, and one each to Atlanta and Miami.

There was also a Lufthansa flight to Baltimore-Washington, an hour from DC.

The problem was I'd have to purchase a ticket using my own passport and credit card. That was the tricky part – it meant I'd leave myself wide open to being caught once I landed in the US. But I had no choice. If I flew via Canada I'd still have to pass through US border Immigration to get home. And I couldn't use the German passport – even if it had a US visa there were finger-print checks to confirm the owner's identity.

For some reason I thought of Josh and felt guilty. *He'll never trust me again after the way I've behaved towards him.* I wondered whether he was still in Paris? I was tempted to call his cell phone, but that would only risk exposing me. And right now I needed a ticket to Baltimore-Washington, pronto, so I finished my coffee, picked up my bag and went to find the Lufthansa ticket desk.

The male ticket clerk smiled. 'Fräulein?'

'I'd like to book a one-way seat on the next departing flight to Baltimore.'

The clerk tapped at his keyboard. 'I'm afraid the only seats left are in business class.'

'I bet this is going to cost me an arm and a leg?'

The clerk spoke immaculate English and smiled sympathetic-ally. 'At least an arm, I'm afraid.' He did a quick check on his computer and told me the price.

I started. 'You're kidding me? For a *one-way* ticket?'

'Unfortunately so, Fräulein. And there are just ten seats left. But perhaps you'd like to try for an alternative flight?'

'No, I'll take Baltimore.'

Istanbul

Ahmet Uzun sat in the tiny airport police office and watched the TV monitor. For three hours he'd reviewed security footage of the thousands of passengers who had departed Istanbul since late that morning. He rubbed his gritty eyes and exhaled with tired frustration. The order from his superior had been explicit: *Find Kate Moran.*

But he was getting nowhere. This was the sixth tape he'd watched and he still had another four to go. Every now and then he had freeze-framed when he felt the urge to closely study a passenger's face, but so far he hadn't had a shred of luck. No sign of anyone resembling Kate Moran. *Where has she disappeared to?*

He was convinced she had already left Istanbul and that the call from her asking him to meet her at the hotel was a ploy – probably to get him away from the airport while she made her escape. *So how did she escape?* The TV screen went blank as the tape came to an end.

Uzun yawned and rubbed his eyes again. After studying so many tapes, the passengers' faces were beginning to blur. *This is driving me crazy.*

The sergeant by his side popped out the tape. Uzun nodded to him. 'Slide in the next one, please.'

The guard popped in a fresh cassette and Uzun turned back to study the monitor. *Sooner or later I have to spot Kate Moran. And I'll bet a month's salary she's somewhere on one of these tapes.*

But could he find her in time?

94

I stepped into the departure lounge and rummaged for my cell phone. I'd passed through the ticket and passport checks without any hitches, which gave me hope. I figured the real problems would start once I landed on home soil – there was a good chance that by then Lou would have bulletined my US passport and I'd be tagged for sure. I had no option except to take the chance.

The flight to Baltimore-Washington had already been announced but I wanted to make my calls. I punched in my home number and checked my messages. There were another two abusive calls from Paul. He sounded pissed off and angry. In the second he said, *'I guess you're not going to call me back, are you? You're really something else, you know that, Kate? You don't give a frig about me. I guess I was right all along and our marriage is really over. I thought I'd offer you a second chance to get back together, but no, you're too dumb to take it. But don't worry, every dog has its day. You'll be sorry.'*

I hadn't a clue what Paul meant, but clearly he was becoming bitter and hateful. He even sounded unbalanced. I decided to put in a quick call to Metropolitan Homicide and talk to him. Not that I loved him any more, but I cared that he was veering out of control. 'Detective Paul Malone, please.'

A familiar voice said, 'Detective Malone's on leave. Who is this?'

'Is that Sergeant Kowalski?'

'Kate? How are you doing, honey?'

'Getting by. I was looking for Paul, Sarge. You know where he is?'

'Yeah, he took some leave and left town. Said he needed a break.'

'He told you that?'

'Yeah. You ask me the guy hasn't been the same since you two split. He's not himself any more, can't even settle himself into a decent relationship. You want to know what else I think? The guy's burning himself out with work since his private life went belly up. He's still a good cop, Kate, but mentally he's driving himself downhill.'

'You know where he is?'

'Haven't a clue. You know Paul, he won't tell you everything. But one of the guys was on an airport detail and saw him checking in at Dulles a couple of days ago. Like he was flying somewhere.'

I thanked the sarge and put Paul out of my mind for now. I had two more messages from Frank, telling me to call him. I guess he'd left messages on my cell, too. I called his cell phone and heard his familiar voice answer on the second ring. 'Yeah?'

'Frank, it's Kate.'

An empty silence filled the line and then Frank said, 'I've been trying to call you all day. I'm being killed with worry. Where the hell have you been?'

'Frank, if I told you, you'd never believe me.'

'Try me.'

'Paris, Istanbul, Frankfurt. That's Frankfurt, Germany.'

'You're waiting for me to laugh, right?'

'I'm not kidding. Right this minute I'm in Frankfurt airport, but that's strictly between you and me. Especially don't tell anyone from the Bureau.'

'The devil are you up to?' Frank asked.

'You'll have to let it wait until I get back home. *If* I get back home. Was that the only reason you called, because you were worried about your kid sister?'

'Mostly, because you didn't return my calls, but hey, listen, I

345

also did some digging on Lucius Clay. Asked my buddies in the Department of Corrections about the warden. It seems he's got himself in trouble with his department bosses on account of his views.'

'What do you mean?'

'Rumour has it that Clay's become a closet liberal in recent years and had some unease about several executions he was charged with carrying out. He gave an interview to the *Richmond Times-Dispatch* soon after one of them and the tone of the piece was that Clay was a reluctant state executioner. It caused the shit to fly in the department and he got his ass hauled over the coals for making his views public.'

'Anything else?' I asked.

'In his defence Clay claimed that he was misquoted in the article. But the feeling among his peers is that he was pissed off big time with being dressed down by the department. Not that you'd ever know it. Since then Clay's kept his mouth zipped and his opinions out of the newspapers. It seems he's got a cautious disrespect for journalists.'

'What else did you learn?'

Frank said, 'Nothing much. Except that he's away at a conference and should be back tomorrow. Maybe I ought to talk with him?'

I mulled over everything Frank had told me and said, 'Just be discreet. You can tell him you're my brother, that ought to get you a foot in the front door, but don't mention anything about the copycat case. I'm in enough trouble.'

'How come?'

'Frank, I can't tell you everything right now, but trust me, you're the only one I can turn to.'

'It sounds serious.'

'It is. I'm working on an idea that may help get me out of my fix, but only so long as I can avoid getting myself arrested when I land home.'

'*Arrested?*'

'Don't even go there, Frank, that story's for another time.

Please, listen up, I need you to ask some questions for me in Greensville Correctional Center . . .'

The Disciple watched as Kate Moran finished her call and started to board the Baltimore-Washington flight. He was twenty yards away, observing her from behind an open newspaper. He had already bought a ticket on the same flight – he had seen Moran step up to the Lufthansa ticket desk, then waited until she had finished her business before he headed straight for the same desk. 'Hope I'm not too late?' He smiled at the Lufthansa clerk.

'Sir?'

'I need a ticket on the same flight as my friend you just served, Miss Moran.'

'You need a one-way ticket to Baltimore-Washington?'

'That's right.' The Disciple handed over his credit card and opted for a seat eight rows behind Moran. Now, as he watched her start to board the flight, he wondered who she had phoned. Did it really matter? *No one can save her.* He admired her body: neat ass, curvy figure. He was looking forward to having some fun with her before he tortured and killed her.

He saw Moran being checked through the departure gate for final boarding. Minutes later he presented his ticket and passport at the same gate, and smiled at the pretty female Lufthansa official who scrutinised his travel documents. 'Thank you,' he said politely.

She returned his smile as she handed him his seat stub. 'Have a pleasant flight, sir.'

'Hey, I'm sure I will.'

95

Istanbul

U zun felt like banging his head on the wall. He never wanted to look at another videotape again – *not ever* – for as long as he lived. Six hours of continuously studying the security tapes and it felt as if every ounce of energy had been sucked out of him. His eyes were sore from focusing on the screen and he had a splitting headache.

When he began looking at the tapes a disturbing thought struck him: *What if Kate Moran wore a Muslim veil to disguise herself?* He still hadn't seen one female resembling Moran. *Not a single damned one.* But he knew that fatigue had set in, which could lead to mistakes. *Perhaps I simply missed her?*

And Uzun was torn. He didn't *want* to find her, but he knew he had a job to do. He took a mouthful of the cold, gritty Turkish coffee in front of him and let out a yawn that sounded like a cry of pain. The sergeant beside him said, 'Are you OK, Inspector?'

Uzun was tired. 'No, I'm not OK. We're going to have to start looking at the tapes all over again.'

'*Again?*'

'You heard me, Sergeant.'

'Yes, sir.'

After another hour Uzun had spotted several women, one wearing a black headdress, who boarded a flight for Frankfurt. She may have been Kate Moran in disguise. But the truth was, he really couldn't be certain.

He was about to rewind the tape in question and check the woman's appearance again when the door burst open and one of his corporals appeared, carrying a white plastic grocery bag. 'My apologies, sir, but something urgent has come up.'

'What?' Uzun barked with irritation.

'It's about four stolen passports that have been found in a postbox in the departures area, sir.'

Uzun was suddenly interested. 'I'm listening.'

The corporal explained about the discovery and said, 'The airport police tell me that most of the passports they found had been reported missing by their owners in the last four hours. However, it seems a fifth foreign passport was reported lost or stolen in the airport but it was not among the ones we found.'

'Who does it belong to?'

'A German citizen, a lady of Turkish extraction.'

'Her name?' Uzun snapped.

'Sevim Yaver, age thirty-seven.'

Uzun felt his pulse quicken when he heard the profile. 'Did you check to see if anyone boarded a flight using any of the names since the passports were reported?'

'Yes, sir. That's why I thought you'd like to know. The lady's document was used to board a Lufthansa flight to Frankfurt that departed at six p.m.'

Uzun's eyes sparked as he turned back to the tape. He rewound to the portion that showed the woman in the black headdress who interested him. *Damn.* Her face was too well covered for him to clearly distinguish her features. But the time recorded on the tape was 5.34 p.m. Twenty-six minutes before the flight departed.

His gut instinct told him it had to be Kate Moran.

96

Greensville, Virginia

Frank Moran turned off Interstate 95 and drove up to the razor-wire walls and the necklace of watchtowers surrounding Greensville Correctional Centre. He pulled his Camarro into the visitor's parking lot and walked towards the prison entrance. A female guard brandishing a clipboard was seated behind the reception desk and she looked up. 'Hi, how can I help you, sir?'

'Got a noon appointment with Captain Gary Tate. The name's Dr Frank Moran.'

'May I see some ID?'

'Surely.' Moran offered his driver's licence.

The guard studied the licence, then handed it back. 'Captain Tate's expecting you, Dr Moran. Go take a seat and I'll tell him you're here.'

Captain Gary Tate was a tall, imposing black man with a powerful physique and a respectful manner. As he led Moran along a corridor to his office he said in a measured drawl, 'I believe you're doing some research, Dr Moran?'

'That's right. You mind if I ask you a couple of questions, Captain?'

Tate shrugged. 'Ask away, Doctor. Your buddy in the Department of Corrections who phoned me asked that you be given all the help possible.'

'How long have you worked at Greensville, Captain?'

'Ten years next month. Why?'

'I hear you've taken part in quite a few executions?'

Tate nodded. 'You heard right.'

'You mind me asking how many executions you had to help carry out?'

'Eighty-nine to be exact,' Tate replied calmly.

'How many of those were by lethal injection?'

'Pretty much all of them. Six were by electric chair, old Sparky.'

Moran said, 'Then I guess you're the man I need to talk to. Tell me, Captain, in your expert opinion, is it possible for a condemned prisoner to survive an execution by lethal injection?'

97

Off the US East Coast

I felt a hand on my shoulder and awoke with a fright. I looked up and saw a slim guy in a navy blue suit standing over me. I almost panicked, but then he said, 'Something to drink, madam?'

The guy was a steward pushing a drinks trolley, but he'd frightened the hell out of me. 'A . . . a glass of water, please.'

'Ice and lemon, madam?'

'Yes, thank you.'

The steward poured me the water, added chunks of ice and a slice of lemon and moved on. I swallowed the cold water but I still felt groggy and wondered how long I'd slept. I checked my watch: almost *six hours*. I'd been so exhausted that I'd slept through most of the flight. I visited the bathroom to freshen up, and when I returned to my seat the pilot announced that we'd be landing at Baltimore in forty-five minutes. I looked out of the window and saw that we were over the US mainland.

At that moment, I felt my anxiety return. *Will Lou Raines be waiting for me at the airport?* What I'd told Frank was true: I had the beginnings of an idea to get me out of the mess I was in but I needed to remain free to put my idea to work. With shaking hands I buckled my seat belt and prepared myself for landing.

The Disciple thought: *It won't be long now.*

He was still eight rows behind Kate Moran and he had it all planned. He even knew the location of their final showdown. Not a natural cave or a tunnel, but something more appropriate, closer to home. Getting her there was going to be the big problem, but he had already figured that one out. He pushed the call button and a few moments later a stewardess appeared. 'Sir?'

'I'd like some whisky on the rocks. A couple of those miniature bottles. Pour one but leave the other unopened.'

'Yes, sir.'

A few minutes later the woman returned and set his miniature drinks down. When she had gone he put the unopened bottle in his pocket. *For later*. All part of his plan. As he poured his whisky it excited him to think that Kate Moran was barely ten yards away and completely unaware of his presence.

If only the stupid bitch knew the torture that I'm about to inflict on her. It's payback time, baby.

When he finally felt the big aircraft lurch and begin its descent, he finished his drink, sat back and buckled his belt as a smirk spread across his face. *Very soon I'll have her all to myself to do as I want.* He could hardly fucking wait.

98

Greensville, Virginia

'Let me get this right. You're asking me if anyone could survive an execution by lethal injection?' Tate's eyebrows were knitted in puzzlement.

'That's right,' Moran answered. 'I've been thinking of writing a paper on the subject. So, is it possible?'

'You a medical doctor?'

'My doctorate's in criminal psychology,' Moran replied. 'But looking at it from your perspective, I was wondering if there might be anything that could go technically wrong to disrupt the execution?'

Tate shrugged, removed his officer's hat and ran a hand through his thinning hair. 'Lots of things can go wrong, Doc, but they rarely do. The fact is, it's highly unlikely a condemned prisoner could survive an execution. And I mean *highly*.'

'But it *could* happen?' Moran persisted.

'It could. But there'd have to be a whole lot of things getting messed up.'

'Such as the chemicals being tampered with or the wrong ones being used?'

Tate shook his head and replaced his hat. 'That really can't happen. The drugs used in the execution are supplied by the Department of Corrections. They're sealed and kept under lock and key until right before they're used, and there's no way they could be substituted or tampered with.'

'Three chemicals are used, right? Sodium thiopental, pancuronium bromide, and potassium chloride, which is the one that finally stops the heart.'

Tate nodded. 'You've done your homework, Doc. Once the inmate is hooked up to the saline drip and covered up to his chest with a sheet, the chemicals are then administered. Why?'

Moran frowned as he considered. 'I just wondered, what if antidotes to the chemicals were mixed in with the saline?'

Tate smiled. 'You've been reading too many novels. I couldn't even say for sure if there *is* an antidote for the chemicals.'

'Captain, I can tell you that pretty much *all* toxic chemicals have an antidote. Even the most deadly nerve agents like VX and sarin. Poisons so strong that just a spoonful could wipe out an entire village.'

Tate considered and gave a shrug. 'I'll have to take your word for it. But for any kind of antidote to be given to a condemned prisoner there would have to be collusion with someone in authority working inside the facility.'

'How high an authority are we talking here? As high as Warden Clay, maybe?'

Tate shrugged. 'I guess you can't go much higher. Another way for things to go screwy would be if the wrong drug were to be deliberately administered. You know what I'm saying? But we're straying into the realms of fiction here, Doc. I can't imagine that kind of an inside job. Not unless the prison official had a pretty powerful motive.'

'So what *would* need to go wrong?' Moran asked.

Tate gave the question some thought. 'A bad batch of chemicals, maybe. But I've never actually heard of that happening. Or if the prisoner had a very strong constitution and was somehow immune to the poisons. But again, that's highly unlikely. The only thing I can think of is that sometimes chemical crystals can build up in the tube lines from residue and block the flow. But we always check the lines before an execution.'

Moran digested the information. 'What about *during* the execution? Do you monitor the lines in case they crystallise then?'

'Not really. But we've never had a problem in that way.'

'Anything else that could go wrong?'

Tate thought for a moment and shrugged. 'Every prisoner has a different body weight and tolerance to the chemicals. By tolerance I mean if a prisoner had a long history of using barbiturates, then his body would have a higher resistance to the drug, and so he would need more poison to kill him than usual. I guess if the executioner misjudged the amount of chemicals to be used, that might be a factor. But then again, the prisoner ain't leaving the chamber without having been pronounced dead, so we'd just keep pumping him with chemicals until the sentence had been carried out.'

'Have you ever heard of an apnoeist, Captain?'

'Ap-what?'

'An apnoeist is someone who can hold their breath for an extraordinarily long period, up to eight minutes in some cases. There's a woman called Audrey Ferrera, a free diver, who holds the official world record for diving down to one hundred and twenty-five metres and holding her breath while her heart rate also slows down. And the Sadhu holy men of India have the ability to induce full autonomic control of their metabolism through meditation. They can use mind control to lower their respiration and bowel function and bring their heartbeat almost to a standstill.'

Tate was impressed. 'You don't say.'

Moran smiled. 'I've been doing a little research.'

'And I appreciate the lecture, Doc. But are you asking me if a condemned prisoner did something like that during his execution would we notice it?'

'You took the words right out of my mouth.'

Tate mulled this over. 'Now that's different. If they slowed their heart rate right down to almost zero then the guys administering the drugs would spot the rate drop on their ECG monitor, see a flat line that signified myocardial death, and maybe think the prisoner was already on his way and had been dosed enough, so they just might cut off the feed lines early.'

'So the prisoner *could* survive the execution?'

'Yeah, I guess it could happen in that instance,' Tate admitted with a shrug, and then grinned. 'But at some stage down the line someone's going to notice. I mean, the guy's got to be body-bagged and autopsied, right?' He consulted his watch, as if he had business elsewhere to attend to.

'By the way, are executions videotaped?' Moran asked.

'No, sir, they're not.'

'What about Constantine Gamal's? I believe there was video equipment in operation during his execution.'

Tate said suspiciously, 'Who told you that?'

'One of the witnesses. I've chosen Gamal's execution as one of my studies.'

Tate considered, then said candidly, 'That was an exception.'

'Why?'

'The Medical Examiner's office asked to be allowed make a video of the execution. I believe for research purposes. It was a one-off situation.'

Moran pondered his answer. 'So what precisely happens after the prisoner is pronounced dead?'

Tate said, 'We shift the body out of here even before it's had a chance to go cold. One minute he's here, next minute he's zipped up in a white body bag, his toe is tagged and he's in the meat van, bound for the Medical Examiner's office in Richmond, sixty miles away.'

'Is the autopsy carried out right away?'

Tate shook his head. 'No, it isn't. The prisoner doesn't get zipped out of the bag until seven a.m. the next morning and then they're autopsied.'

'By a Medical Examiner?'

'Not always.'

Moran frowned. 'What do you mean?'

'You'd really need to check with the ME's office in Richmond to be certain, but I hear they often use juniors to perform the autopsy. By that I mean medical grads who are training to be MEs. Ain't no big deal in a prisoner's case. We *know* how he died. The examiner's just got to be content that death is due to the method of execution.'

357

Moran let the information sink in. 'One other question, Captain. Did anyone ever escape from Greensville?'

Tate smiled. 'One guy, a few years back. He got out at night through one of the sally ports. Despite the fact that it was the middle of winter and he was dressed in orange prison overalls, he managed to get himself down to the main road.'

'What happened to him?'

'The dumb son of a bitch stopped a pick-up driver and asked the way to Vermont. Didn't even try to hijack the vehicle, just thanked the driver and started walking north. We caught him within an hour.'

Moran said, 'I appreciate your time, Captain. But I just realised I've got a couple more questions.'

'Fire away.'

'When does Warden Clay get back from attending his conference?'

'I believe he's back home today. But he isn't on duty until the day after tomorrow. Why?'

'I may need to talk with him. Do you know his home address?'

Tate eyeballed his visitor. 'That kind of information can't be given to the public for security reasons.'

Moran smiled. 'Sure, I understand. One last thing. Do you know who exactly in the Medical Examiner's office requested the video of Gamal's execution?'

'No, sir, I do not,' Tate answered.

'But the request would have come from high up? I mean, for something like that to be allowed happen we're talking about the Chief Medical Examiner, right? Or maybe one of the senior medical assistants. Someone pretty close to the top.'

'Yes, sir, I believe so.'

99

Chinatown, Washington, DC

Stone shone an electric torch over the two shallow graves. The smell of human decay filled his nostrils. He and Raines were in one of the maintenance tunnels eighty yards from the Chinatown station. A pair of powerful halogen lamps illuminated the crime scene. Near by was a storm drain. It was pouring with rain above ground, water dripping through the metal ventilation grilles over their heads and on to the chips of shale rock that covered the tunnel floor.

Diaz said to Raines, 'They're buried almost three feet deep, and side by side. Whoever did it had to remove six inches of rock shale, then dig down a couple of feet into the earth before covering the bodies again with the shale.'

Raines examined the pathetic sight of two sets of skeletal remains lying side by side in their shallow graves. Near the bodies was a rotting mound of rags and other shreds of evidence, waiting to be examined and bagged. He studied the surroundings, and peered up and down the tunnel. 'The ground beneath the loose rocks is pretty hard, so it couldn't have been an easy job. The killer would have needed a pick and shovel and plenty of time to finish the dirty work. That means it had to happen when there were no maintenance crews about and no subway trains running.'

Diaz nodded agreement. 'It figures, otherwise the killer would have risked being seen.'

'Did you determine their sex?' Raines pulled up his coat collar. His clothes were drenched after he had got caught in the downpour as he raced into the subway station from the car, and now he wiped his wet face with his hand. The remains had mostly decayed, but he figured that one victim was certainly an adult; the second skeleton looked like it might belong to a young adult or teenager.

Diaz answered, 'A male, thirty-five to fifty, and a pubescent female, fifteen to twenty. That's the best I can offer until we've done our lab work.' He gestured to the clear-plastic evidence bags. 'The clothes they're wearing were mostly rotted because of the high moisture content down here, but I'd say they weren't exactly high fashion to begin with. The male's coat had a charity shop docket in one of the pockets. A Baptist charity clothes store in the District. See it there?'

Raines knelt to get a closer look at one of the evidence bags, which contained a scrap of sepia-stained paper with a faded imprint. He recognised the Baptist charity shop logo. He was confident they had found Gamal's victims and he felt anger boil inside. 'Only an evil monster would want to kill a homeless father and his child. May God have mercy on their souls.'

Stone turned to Diaz, who wore waterproof nylon pants and an FBI rain jacket with gold lettering on the back, and he wondered whether the guy had a Speedo outfit on underneath. 'Anything else that grabbed your attention?'

Diaz winked. 'You mean apart from that shitty-looking jacket you're wearing?'

'That's real funny, Armando.'

'These caught my eye.' Diaz knelt and used tweezers to pluck the remains of two pieces of soggy paper from the rotting mound waiting to be stored in evidence bags. He laid them on top of a square sheet of white plastic for easier viewing.

'What have we got here?' Raines asked.

'A couple of chits for a Salvation Army hostel. They're for two beds, the night before Gamal claimed he killed his victims. So I figure we're in the ballpark, time-wise. November twenty-third, almost fifteen months ago. Thanksgiving, if I remember.'

Raines sucked in a deep breath between clenched teeth and let it out in a gesture of despair. 'The metro wouldn't have been running that regularly which made the work of burying the victims easier.'

Stone looked satisfied. 'I guess we have to face up to the fact that Gamal may have told the truth, Lou. He sure was right about the bodies.'

Raines ignored the comment and nodded to Diaz. 'Thanks, Armando.'

'Hey, any of you guys going to tell me what the story is with the pants outfit I've got in the lab? Stone here says it belongs to Kate. I'm kinda confused.'

Stone started to say something but Raines gave him a look and got in first. 'So are we, so let's keep this between ourselves for now, Armando. We've got some issues that need to be cleared up first with Kate, OK?'

'Whatever you say.' Diaz frowned, a look that said the answer he'd been given wasn't satisfying enough, but he shrugged and went back to work.

Raines stared up at the water dripping from the storm drain overhead, an absent look on his face, as if his mind was far away.

Stone joined him. 'I know we've got some more investigating to do before we can be certain, but I'm betting someone else killed the Bryces. And maybe I'll take another bet while I'm at it, about where the finger might end up pointing. What do you think, Lou?'

'You know I'm not a betting man. I think you're jumping the gun, Stone. You're convinced that you're right on all counts in the Bryce case but you can't just go on strong instinct. Though seeing as you could at least have been right all along about Gamal not killing the Bryces, maybe I owe it to you to listen.'

Raines' cell phone chimed. He stepped away to take the call, and when he had finished and put away his phone Stone came over. 'Problems?'

Raines looked strained as he searched his pockets for his car keys. 'That was Inspector Uzun in Istanbul. He's got a bead on Moran. She's on a flight back home.'

Stone's face sparked. 'To where?'

'She's flying into Baltimore International. Let's get moving.'

100

I sat rigid in my seat as the plane touched down. Five minutes later, as the aircraft taxied to a halt at the gate, my body felt as tense as a coiled spring. I thought about Josh. I felt I owed him an explanation and apology, and I was tempted to call him the moment I stepped off the aircraft, but I risked getting caught if my call was traced.

The crew members pushed open the cabin exit doors. Passengers started to rise out of their seats and grab luggage from the storage lockers overhead. But I was frozen to my seat. *What if armed cops are already waiting to arrest me when I disembark? Or maybe I'll be tailed to the arrivals area and overpowered and cuffed?*

I knew one thing. If I was arrested now, it would ruin whatever hope I had of finally proving whether Gamal was alive or dead. I *had* to stay free. I could handle facing Lou – our meeting was inevitable – but I wanted to do it on my terms. Passengers filed down the aisle past me. I took a deep breath and forced myself to stand and grab my overnight bag from the storage locker. I saw a movement out of the corner of my eye and looked back down the aircraft. I wasn't the last passenger. A man wearing sunglasses was seated about eight rows back. Clumps of blond hair stuck out from under a grey woollen hat pulled down over his head, and he had a trimmed strip of blond designer beard down the middle of his chin. He was dressed in a grey nylon Reebok windcheater, and appeared to be the backpacker-tourist type. He gave me a quick smile then his head disappeared behind the seat as he fumbled to get his belongings together.

I turned back to face the exit door. Three cabin crew waited patiently for me to disembark. I felt a flutter of fear as I grabbed my holdall and walked up the aisle.

The Disciple observed Kate Moran leave the aircraft, but not before she had glanced at him and he had smiled back. *Stupid bitch! I can see you, but you can't see me. Isn't it amazing what a disguise can do?*

The moment when she would no longer remain free had finally arrived. He grabbed his bag from the seat beside him and rummaged in it until he found the hypodermic. He had already filled the syringe with benzo – the shot was powerful enough to fell a two-hundred-pound man. A female with Moran's body mass would pose no problem. Next, he removed two plastic knitting needles from the lining of his bag. He slipped one of the needles in his inside pocket and the other up his right sleeve. He stood and followed his next victim.

101

Washington–Baltimore Interstate Highway

Stone had his foot hard to the floor and the Ford's engine snarled like an enraged animal. The siren wailed. The speedo was pushing a hundred and ten – they'd covered twenty-five miles in fifteen minutes. 'Another five minutes and we're there,' Stone announced as a sign for BWI airport flashed past and he spotted an aircraft coming in to land in the distance.

In the passenger seat Raines finished his call and flicked off his cell phone. 'The airport police commander is sending all his available men to cover the arrivals terminal. He says the Lufthansa flight landed twenty minutes ago and some passengers may already have passed through Immigration.'

'*Shit*. Could they have missed her?' Stone said anxiously.

'It's possible. The commander's about to alert them. But he's confident that if Moran's in the terminal he'll find her.'

Baltimore International Airport, Maryland

My heart beat like a piston as I joined the queue for Immigration. I noticed the usual officials hanging around, along with clusters of armed airport police. *Are they waiting to pounce on me?* I was too scared to make eye contact with any of the officers in case I provoked suspicion.

Several passengers were waiting just ahead of me in the queue: a frail, elderly couple and a teenage girl wearing torn jeans and sneakers and carrying a backpack. The couple quickly finished their business and the female immigration officer beckoned the

364

young backpacker forward. As the girl showed the official her documents my palms began to sweat – I had a terrible dread that I'd be arrested once I showed my passport.

I couldn't see any cops behind me but I spotted the passenger I'd noticed on board the aircraft – the guy with the blond hair, the tiny blond beard and woollen hat. He was next in the queue adjacent to mine, but this time he didn't acknowledge my glance. I didn't know why but a voice inside my head said: *There's something odd about that guy*. But I couldn't put my finger on it.

'*Next please!*'

I spun back round and saw the immigration officer beckon me with a wave of her hand. I felt my legs shake as I clutched my passport and stepped forward.

102

I handed my documents to the immigration officer and waited as she scrutinised my passport. I felt scared as hell. She studied my photo and stared up at me before she scanned the document into a computer. *Am I about to be arrested?* A couple of seconds later the officer gave me a sharp nod, handed me back my passport and said brightly, 'Welcome home, Miss Moran. *Next!*'

The Disciple saw Kate Moran pass through Immigration. He was in the next queue, and the officer processing his passport was taking for ever. He was a big, heavy-set guy with a mountain for a belly. The Disciple sweated as he saw Moran heading towards the Customs aisles – he didn't want to let her out of his sight. He flicked an impatient glance at the officer slowly scanning his passport into a computer. *Get a move on, for fuck sake.* But the officer took his time. Finally he closed the passport and handed it back to him. '*Next!*'

'Lazy asshole,' the Disciple muttered under his breath.

The officer turned red faced. 'Did you say something, buddy?'

'*Me?* You must be hearing things, Officer.' The Disciple grabbed his hand luggage from the floor and followed Kate Moran towards Customs.

103

Stone jerked to a halt outside the arrivals terminal with a squeal of tyres. He and Raines jumped out of the Ford as an airport cop appeared out of nowhere. 'Hey, you can't park there, buddy. It's a restricted zone. Shift that car *now!*'

Raines ignored the order. 'That radio of yours work?'

The cop took no notice of the question. 'I thought I told you – *move it!*'

'Get on to the airport police commander. Tell him I want confirmation that the entire arrivals terminal is sealed off.'

The cop placed his hands on his hips in a gesture of authority. 'And just who the hell are you, mister?'

Raines shoved his ID in the man's face. 'The man who's gonna bust your frigging ass if you don't do as I tell you *pronto*. There's a woman by the name of Kate Moran who just arrived off a flight from Frankfurt and I want her arrested on sight.'

I felt another surge of fear as I moved towards Customs. A half-dozen uniformed officers stood by the aisles. I couldn't believe my luck as I walked right through without being stopped.

My heart soared with a sudden feeling of hope. No one was waiting to arrest me. *Or maybe they're in Arrivals ready to pounce?* The doors into Arrivals parted and I saw a sea of waiting faces in front of me – chauffeurs, limo drivers, company reps, most of them holding up name placards – but I didn't see a single uniformed cop. A sense of relief washed over me.

Maybe Uzun didn't cotton on to my deception in Istanbul? But Uzun was as shrewd a cop as they come. He'd have figured it out. Which meant he'd have informed Lou Raines, who'd surely have decided by now to have the airports watched. As I filed out into Arrivals among the crowd of passengers my fears were realised and I froze in my tracks.

Right in front of me, less than twenty yards away, was a bunch of six uniformed airport cops waiting either side of the passenger enclosure. A couple of them held radios, while others had their hands readied on their holstered weapons. I tried to force myself to remain calm but my legs began to shake and I was overcome by a morbid feeling of defeat.

This is it, I'm caught.

I had no doubt in my mind that the cops were there to arrest me. *I have to remain free.* One of them frowned as he suddenly spotted my face in the crowd. He nudged a colleague, then the two cops mouthed something to their companions and stepped towards me. 'Kate Moran?' one of them said aloud. I didn't reply but forced my way through a wall of passengers, ducked under the enclosure barrier and ran through the crowded terminal.

104

The Disciple stayed behind Kate Moran as she moved through the crowd. He had the slim hypodermic in his left pocket and the whisky miniature in his right. All he needed was the right moment to strike.

Damn.

The second he noticed the waiting cops he knew that he was sunk. He saw Moran stiffen as she came to a sudden halt yards in front of a phalanx of airport police.

He'd had his plan all worked out: follow her to the exit doors, stick her with the hypodermic and douse her clothes with the whisky. In seconds she'd be like a zombie, almost out cold. Then he'd play the pissed-off husband whose wife had drunk too much on the flight and needed to be taken home in a cab. He even had it planned that once he got her outside he'd give the cabbie an embarrassed sigh and say: *My wife's had a few too many whiskies 'cause she hates flying.*

He imagined the cabbie's sympathetic nod and unspoken response: *Sure, your wife's a fucking lush.*

Except his plan was screwed up and he was furious. Moran had obviously fallen under suspicion for the Istanbul murders but he wasn't expecting the cops to be waiting to arrest her at Baltimore. He swore – maybe he should have stuck with his original plan? But it was too late now. He saw Moran hesitate for a second, then one of the uniforms stepped forward, saying, 'Kate Moran?'

As the cop lunged towards her, the Disciple saw Moran duck

under the metal barrier and weave through the crowd. She ran like hell, and the cops ran after her.

Damn. I've got to get her before the police do.

He pursued the cops.

105

I pushed through the crowds. When I'd gone at least fifty yards I dared glance back. Two cops were twenty yards behind me, forcing their way through the mill of passengers. The leading cop was tall and muscular, and he was bulldozing his way through the crowds. People had begun to scream as they saw the cops brandishing their handguns.

Suddenly I heard a shout: '*Halt or I fire!*'

I waited for the bullet but it never came. I figured the cop was hoping to stop me with a bluff threat. No officer with any sense would fire at an unarmed suspect in a crowd. I looked back again. Now the cops were thirty yards behind me. I was gaining ground, getting into my stride as I picked up speed. I kept zigzagging, ducking down, darting wildly through the crowd. '*Get out of the way!*' I screamed.

People stepped aside and the way ahead cleared. Another fifty yards on I glanced back again but couldn't see my pursuers' heads above the swarms of milling passengers. I looked ahead and suddenly off to my right I saw a long, broad corridor with doors either side. Breathless, I turned into the corridor. Halfway down I realised I was in a dead end.

I tried to open the doors either side. They were locked. One had a sign that said: JANITORIAL SUPPLIES.

The last door had a symbol for a men's restroom. Not a Ladies in sight. I found the door unlocked. I had nowhere else to go so I went in, passing the washbasins, the cubicles and urinals, desperately hoping that somewhere there might be a window wide enough for me to crawl through and make an escape.

The restroom appeared empty. I saw a window high up. It was

371

covered by a metal grille and half open, but I didn't get a chance to try to climb up because just then I heard footsteps race down the corridor.

I darted into one of the cubicles and locked the door. A second later I heard footsteps enter the restroom. They clicked on the tiled floor and I heard a squeak of shoe leather. Then came the sound of someone trying to catch their breath. I swore and gritted my teeth. I had been so damned close to escaping through the window – another ten seconds and I might have got away.

Now the room fell still. There was a slim crack between the cubicle door and the frame and I tried to peer through. At first I saw just a blur of white tile, but after a few more seconds I glimpsed a flash of blue uniform and my heart sank. I had half expected that I'd be caught, but now that it was happening I felt overcome by despair. *Once I'm found I'm finished.*

I peered again through the crack and glimpsed the cop's outstretched arm, the dark shape of a gun, and then I momentarily saw his face: he was the big guy I'd seen earlier, the one who'd been bulldozing through the crowds. He moved away, but seconds later I heard one of the doors to my left start to rattle and I knew I hadn't a hope in hell of escaping.

The cop's trying the doors. I retreated further into the cubicle and started to pray.

106

Officer Chuck Delano was breathless as he entered the restroom with his Glock pistol drawn. He sweated as he scanned the washbasin area, the urinals and cubicles.

Delano noticed the partly open window midway up the end wall. He was tempted to check the window but instinct told him to finish searching the restroom first. If the woman had come in here he doubted she would have had time to flee through the window – more likely she'd be hiding in one of the cubicles.

Delano had left his buddy Maguire trailing behind him when he'd seen a woman dart down the corridor and had beckoned Maguire to follow him. Where the hell was Maguire now? As he kept his gun gripped in both hands and advanced into the room, he suddenly heard a noise and spun round.

He expected to see Maguire but instead he saw a man enter the restroom. He had a tiny blond beard, his head was covered by a grey woollen hat, and he wore a backpack. The man grinned and suddenly jerked out his hand. Delano grunted as he felt something sharp pierce his flesh.

Jesus!

When he looked down he saw to his horror that a slim needle was embedded between his ribs. He felt an excruciating pain spread across his chest, gave a tiny cry and slumped to the floor.

The Disciple left the needle in the wound, knelt down and prised the Glock from the cop's grasp. *Where the hell has Moran gone? I know she's in here somewhere.* He moved to the cubicles and carefully pushed open a door.

107

I heard a grunt that sounded like a stifled cry of pain. It came from somewhere in the restroom.

Puzzled, I risked peering out again through the crack in the door. I couldn't believe what I saw: the cop's body lay on the floor. A long thin needle was stuck in his chest and a thin rivulet of blood trickled across the white tiles towards the cubicles.

Oh my God . . .

I saw the crimson flowing across the floor between my feet. Then I heard another noise that sounded like one of the cubicle doors creaking open. My next thought stunned me with the force of a sledgehammer – *the killer's in the restroom!*

I wanted to scream but a second later the cubicle panels rattled as the killer tried one of the doors. *How? How did he know I was here?* I tried desperately to control my panicked breathing. I had no weapon. *Nothing.* I felt vulnerable – I didn't even know how to begin to protect myself. But I knew I couldn't just wait for the killer to burst into the cubicle. *What can I do?* If I barged out I risked being killed.

Squeak.

I heard another cubicle door yawn open, followed by a long silence.

Squeak.

Another cubicle opening.

Squeak. And then something weird happened. I was sure that I heard what sounded like distant voices, growing louder. Then I heard more noises – this time from inside the restroom – the sounds of quickly moving feet, a grunt or two and a creaking noise. I couldn't figure out what was happening so I plucked up the nerve to peer through the crack in the door.

I saw the cop still lying on the floor, blood spewing from the needle stuck in his chest. His eyelids flickered and I was sure that I heard him breathing. *He's still alive.* I mustered enough courage to stand on the toilet seat and peer over the cubicle door. I noticed that the window I'd seen was wide open.

Has the killer gone? Or is he playing with me, trying to fool me into thinking that he's left the room? Why would he leave through the window?

I stepped down, opened the door and cautiously peered out. The restroom seemed empty. *What if he's hiding in one of the cubicles, ready to pounce?* But as the seconds passed and no one appeared, I began to doubt that he was still in the room. I checked the other cubicles. They were empty. I didn't understand it. *Why would the killer leave when he almost had me?*

I heard a gurgling sound from the cop's lips and knelt beside him. His breathing was shallow and it was pretty obvious that he'd die unless he got urgent medical help. Suddenly his left hand came up to grasp the needle embedded in his chest.

I gripped his hand. 'Please, don't touch it! Just stay still and don't even try to move.'

'It . . . it hurts. Hurts . . . real bad. *Oh, Jesus . . . !*' The cop's voice was hoarse with pain, and then suddenly his body jerked and his mouth opened as if he was going to throw up, but instead blood gushed from his throat. I saw his eyelids start to flicker, his hands shook, and I knew he was on the verge of death.

'Don't die. *Please!*' I begged.

Seconds later his eyes rolled and a rush of air escaped his lips as death claimed him. I felt so helpless. Then a clatter of footsteps sounded behind me and I jerked round. 'Get your hands in the air and don't move an inch!' A cop pointed his pistol at me.

And then another cop appeared, his gun drawn. 'We've got her!' someone roared.

I felt light headed. Raised voices echoed in the corridor. *Now I know why the killer left – he'd heard reinforcements.* Four more men with their guns drawn rushed into the restroom. Two were airport police, the other two were Raines and Stone. They looked shocked when they saw me kneeling over the dead cop, the floor awash with blood. 'Get up!' Stone shouted.

I attempted to stand but I didn't move fast enough because Stone grabbed me painfully by the hair and dragged me to my feet, triumph in his face as he pulled out a pair of cuffs. 'Kate Moran, I'm arresting you on suspicion of murdering Otis and Kimberly Fleist.'

108

Virginia

Frank Moran halted the rented pick-up truck in the grounds of Bellevue psychiatric hospital. He slipped on a pair of glasses then pulled a pair of theatrical teeth caps from his pocket, stuck them in his mouth and grinned at his reflection in the rearview mirror. 'Hey, I think the overbite suits me.'

He looked towards Bellevue and hesitated, then stared again at his reflection and scolded himself. 'Will you stop agonising over the fucking thing, man. Be brave and just go do it.'

Gary Vasem was a tall, muscled, good-looking guy with a permatan, highlights in his hair and bleached-white teeth. He was the late-shift supervisor at the Bellevue Mental Health Institute that evening, and he was browsing through some files when the middle-aged guy in blue overalls came in. Vasem glanced up and smiled. The guy in front of him kind of looked like a taller version of Tommy Lee Jones, except he had more prominent teeth. 'Sir?'

The man looked at Vasem's name badge. 'You the senior in charge, Gary?'

'Yes, sir, I am.'

'Professor Jenks around?'

'No, sir. He's gone home.'

The visitor flashed his ID. 'Lucky man he ain't crucified by shift work. The name's Moran. I'm an engineer with the phone company. Fact is, I put in the original PABX myself. But that was years back. Long before your time, young man.'

Vasem flashed a smile, pleased to be called *young man* when in fact he was close to forty. The eight hundred bucks he'd recently spent on Botox had obviously been worth it. 'I think you'll find there's been some major changes since then, sir.'

Moran nodded. 'Yeah, I can see that the board finally shelled out for a fresh lick of paint. Hey, you look like a fit young man, Gary. You work out?'

Vasem beamed. 'Pretty much every day.' He took great pride in his physique, did at least two hundred ab crunches a day, and his buns were as hard as mahogany.

Moran said admiringly, 'You look in great shape. But hey, you got a phone problem that I got to fix. It's supposed to be urgent.'

The nurse frowned. 'The lines seem to be working OK. Who reported the fault?'

Moran consulted his clipboard. 'It says here Professor Hicks wanted it rectified. He reported an intermittent hum on a couple of the lines. We've had a busy day and we're only getting round to it now.'

Gary looked doubtful. 'I'm not really sure I've got the authority to allow you to work on the phone lines, sir.'

Moran raised his shoulders and said brazenly, 'Hey, it's all the same to me, Gary, but you still get charged for the call-out. The junction box is in the basement, right? Maybe Dr Hodge can OK it for you? I remember her from my last visit. You could call her and tell her Moran's here.'

'Dr Hodge is in Vegas for the week, attending a medical conference, sir.'

Moran grinned. 'Lucky bitch. Bet she's doing the slots in her spare time.'

Vasem smiled back. 'You reckon, sir?'

'For sure. So what you want me to do, Gary? Go or stay? You're the shift head honcho. It's your call.'

The nurse shrugged. 'Well, I sort of guess it's OK.'

Moran nodded. 'That's what I like, Gary, decisiveness. Let me go check out the wiring.'

109

Baltimore International Airport, Maryland

F ive minutes after my arrest I was being led to an unmarked green Ford parked outside Arrivals. My hands were still cuffed as Stone and Raines escorted me out through the exit doors.

I felt uncomfortable with Raines. He'd taken away my hand luggage, searched through it and confiscated my badge, as if he was letting me know that any friendship between us was gone. But I had a powerful need to explain everything. 'Lou, we have to talk . . .'

He gave me an icy look. 'You're sure right about that, Kate. Boy, have you got some questions to answer. We'll talk in the car.'

We reached the Ford and Stone pushed me into the rear seat and jumped in beside me, while Raines climbed into the driver's seat. 'Do we really need the cuffs?' I pleaded.

Raines fixed me with a stare. 'What do you think, Kate? We've got evidence linking you to the Fleist crime scene. And I haven't even come to what we just saw in the restroom.'

'*What* evidence?'

Stone said, 'Don't come the innocent, Moran. We found fibres from a pants suit belonging to you in the Fleists' trailer. And a witness heard you argue with Fleist the night he died. The question is, why did you kill him and his daughter and stage it to look like copycat murders?'

I was dumbfounded. 'That's insane. I didn't kill Fleist and his daughter, or anyone else.'

Stone said, 'We'll see about that. What about the airport cop?'

'I didn't see his killer's face, he escaped through the restroom window just before you arrived. But I *know* it's the same murderer who killed in Istanbul.'

Stone said with contempt, 'Ain't that convenient. Why have I got trouble believing you, Moran? You're telling us somebody's on an international murder spree and setting it up to have you blamed for some of the killings?'

'That's exactly what I'm telling you. And you have to believe me, Stone.'

'No, I don't. All I've got to believe is the evidence. So tell me, Moran, what have you got to say about the deaths of Otis and Kimberly Fleist?'

I was enraged. 'Stone, if your mind wasn't so clouded by the fact that you despise me then you'd know I could never have killed the Fleists.'

'Tell that to the public prosecutor when the evidence is staring him in the face. This has gone way beyond reasonable doubt, Moran.'

I turned to Raines. 'Lou . . . I'm asking you to listen to me.'

Raines looked angry as he started the car. 'You're right, we have to talk. And you've got a hell of a lot of explaining to do, so how about you start right now?'

The Disciple stood outside the arrivals concourse and saw Kate Moran being led away in handcuffs. The stupid bitch had got herself caught and fucked up his plans.

He'd barely had time to escape through the restroom window – seconds more and he'd have been in deep trouble. The window had led out to a narrow alley between buildings, and minutes later he found himself walking out through a staff exit at the side of the terminal.

Bingo. He had figured the cops would take Moran out the front way, and he was right. But now how could he get his hands on her?

He saw two Feds put her into the back of the car and knew he had to act fast. He crossed smartly to the cab rank, where a black cabbie wearing a flashy red bow tie was sitting in the first vehicle, and said, 'Hey, you – I'll give you a two-hundred-dollar tip if you do what I tell you.'

The driver said cautiously, 'I think you got the wrong man, buddy. I really ain't that kind of guy.'

'I want you to follow a car.' The cab was ancient, and the Disciple guessed it had been around the clock a couple of times at least, the red seat leather cracked and worn. He just hoped it was up to the job.

The driver's eyes sparked. 'Now that's different. You said a *two*-hundred-buck tip? Get the hell in.'

The Disciple climbed into the back of the cab, noticed the green Ford pull out across the road and said to the driver, 'See that green Ford that just pulled out?'

The driver swung back round in his seat and saw the car moving away.

'Sure. This some kind of eye test? I ain't blind, you know, mister.'

'Forget the two hundred. Don't lose the Ford and I'll make it five hundred bucks.'

110

Frank Moran spent an hour searching through the files in the basement. The Bellevue trip was his own idea and he hadn't told Kate, but he hoped it would be worth the visit.

Some of the files he'd taken from their boxes and spread out on the table, but the dim and dirty neon strips overhead didn't help much. He had left the front cover off the phone system junction box, exposing a mass of coloured wires, just in case the male nurse got suspicious and came down to check.

He was riffling through another box of files when he heard footsteps descending the stairs. He frantically gathered up the documents and stashed them under the table. The permatanned Gary appeared on the steps; he halted halfway down and called out, 'Are you OK down there?'

Moran offered a buck-toothed smile and gestured towards a dark corner. 'Never better. Kinda poor light down here, but hey, you'd never guess what I saw?'

'What?'

'A rat, right over there.'

'A *rat*?'

'Yes, sir. I figure there must be more of 'em around so you need to call in pest control. Hate those damned little mothers, they give me the creeps. Always afraid I'll get bitten and end up with one of those nasty diseases you get from rodents. The one I saw was pretty big.'

Gary started to move nervously back up the stairs. 'I . . . I just wanted to make sure you were OK.'

Moran flashed another toothy smile. 'Don't you fret about me, son. I'll be up as soon as I'm done.'

'That . . . that's OK.' The male nurse retreated up the steps and gave a limp, uncertain smile before he closed the door after him.

Moran plucked an old, thick brown folder from the pile, began to flick through it and frowned. He laid the file on the table and began to scan the pages with the torch. He spent the next twenty minutes going through the documents inside and stiffened when he spotted a sheet from a yellow notepad tucked behind one of the pages. He read the handwriting on it and turned ashen. '*Jesus H. Christ.*'

With a glazed look on his face Moran stared at the notepad page and said to himself, 'Frank, old buddy, on a scale of one to ten, I'd say what you've found is fucking mind-blowing.'

III

I told Lou Raines everything, from start to finish, and why I'd ignored his orders. Raines flicked looks at me in the driver's rear-view mirror. Stone listened too, but I guessed he really wasn't interested in a single thing I had to say: I figured his mind was already made up that I was guilty as sin.

'You done now, Moran?' Stone asked matter-of-factly.

'I've told you everything I know. I don't understand how a witness could have seen me at the trailer park. I've got no answer, except it has to be a set-up.' I eyeballed Raines in the rear-view mirror but he ignored my stare. I felt close to breaking point. 'Why do I get the feeling that even you don't believe me, Lou?'

Raines avoided the question. 'Do I get to hear your theories as to who the culprit might be?'

I heard the despair in my own voice. 'All I'm certain of is that someone's trying to set me up for the Fleist murders. But why they'd do that I don't have one single clue, apart from the suspicion I've had about Gamal.'

Raines gave me a look of dismissal. 'That's totally insane. I don't buy it. Have you ever heard of even *one* person who survived a lethal-injection execution?'

'That doesn't mean it couldn't happen, Lou.'

'It's a bullshit theory,' commented Stone, and he added to Lou, 'I told you she was loopy. What more confirmation do you want?'

Raines eyed me in the mirror. 'I'd suggest you don't even go there, Kate, 'cause it ain't worth the talking. Gamal was autopsied, pronounced dead, and buried.'

I persisted. 'How do we know for certain his body was buried? How will we know *anything* unless we have Gamal exhumed?'

Raines let out a frustrated sigh. 'Don't try my patience. I told you, he's dead.'

'What about the spooky phone calls I received at the cottage?'

'From what you told us, you weren't completely sure at first if you did get the calls, or if it was your own imagination.'

'But I'm sure about the second call . . .' I argued.

'Maybe you are, but right now I'm more concerned that you ignored my orders and lied through your teeth to Cooper.'

'I didn't mean to but I *had* to see the Istanbul site, Lou.'

'You got Cooper in trouble, too. He got back home today, managed to get an earlier flight.'

I was about to ask what kind of trouble when Stone chipped in, 'You can't argue with the facts, Moran – the fibres we found and our witness.'

I fixed him with a firm stare. 'I'm an investigator, Stone. I know the way forensic evidence is gathered at a crime scene. Do you really think that if I wanted to kill the Fleists, for whatever insane reason you can think of, I'd be dumb enough to leave evidence behind?'

Stone said, 'I don't have to answer anything, Moran, *you* do. But give me time and I'll find the answer to the big question – why you killed David and Megan and staged it to look like a copycat killing.'

I almost lost it, and if I hadn't been cuffed I'd have punched Stone in the mouth. He looked smug. 'I've got you, Moran. You're going down so why not confess? We've even got a potential big cherry on the cake.'

'*What* cherry?'

Stone said, 'It's looking like Gamal did the other two murders, just like he claimed. And we've got proof.'

I felt my heart quicken as I said to Raines, 'What proof's he talking about?'

Raines said flatly, 'Gamal told the truth about the bodies. We found them in the Chinatown tunnel, where he said they'd be, and we're still working on the forensic evidence. But it's looking like he may have killed both victims about the same time he was supposed to have murdered David and Megan.'

112

'Hey, you're *sure* you got the five hundred in cash, mister?' After following the Ford for six miles on the Baltimore–DC interstate the cab driver glanced back at his passenger with a hint of doubt.

'I certainly am.'

'Mind if I see? Just that I get all kinds in this cab, mister. Man's gotta be careful he ain't being scammed. Not that I'm suggesting *you're* that kind, but it would help if I saw those greenbacks, you know what I mean?'

The Disciple was engrossed in thought as he stared beyond the windscreen.

The cab was about a hundred yards behind the Ford and he was convinced that the two men escorting Kate Moran were taking her to DC, and probably to the FBI field office by Judiciary Square. He *had* to stop her. But how?

'Mister, you listening to me?' the cabbie said.

'Yes, I've got the cash and yes you'll see it. Overtake the Ford and pull in at the next lay-by,' he instructed the driver. He took his wallet from his pocket and started to peel off a wad of notes.

'*Overtake* it?'

'That's what I said. Do it *now*, fast,' the Disciple said impatiently.

The driver hit the accelerator and the cab shot into the fast lane and overtook the Ford. The Disciple glanced into the car as he went past. He saw Moran in the back seat with one Fed, the other driving. The cab began to slow down again. 'Keep going!' he urged the driver.

'Can't, mister, we got lights.'

The Disciple looked ahead and saw a set of traffic lights just turning amber. *Shit.* He didn't want to be caught side by side with the Ford. The driver continued to brake but the Disciple screamed, '*Keep going.* Ignore the lights!'

'Mister, if a cop sees me doing that I'm fucked . . .'

'Break them, *goddammit,* and I'll make it the even thousand.'

'*Thousand?*'

'You heard me. Do as I say!'

The driver's greed got the better of him and he put his foot down hard, crossing the junction as the lights turned red. The Disciple saw a lay-by a hundred yards farther on and pointed. 'Pull in there.'

'Hey, you've got me breaking the damned law, mister, what the *hell's* going on?' the driver asked.

The Disciple replaced his wallet in his pocket. 'A slight change of plan. You're letting me out here.'

'Mister, I'll let you out in Kentucky if that's what you want, just so long as you pay me the grand you promised.'

The Disciple stepped out of the cab and handed a wad of banknotes through the driver's window. 'Thanks a lot.'

'Thank *you.*' The driver beamed at the wad.

In an instant the Disciple's free hand had come up holding the hypodermic and he plunged the needle deep into the driver's neck.

'*What the fuckin' hell . . .*' the driver managed to gasp, and then suddenly his head fell to one side and his eyes rolled back in their sockets.

The Disciple opened the driver's door. The front of the big old cab had bench seating but still it was an effort to manoeuvre the man's unconscious body across to the passenger side before he could slide in next to him. He turned to look out through the rear window and saw that the traffic lights had turned green. Seconds later the Ford passed him. Kate Moran was staring straight ahead, stone faced in the back seat. 'This is where you get yours, *bitch,*' the Disciple spat, and he pulled out into the traffic and sped after the Ford.

113

I couldn't take in what Raines had told me. *Gamal told the truth about the bodies. We found them in the Chinatown tunnel, where he said they'd be.* My head spun and I felt like passing out.

'Have you been listening to me?' Raines said.

'Y . . . Yes.'

'The victims were a homeless black man and his twelve-year-old daughter, missing from a Salvation Army shelter. They had been seen in the Chinatown district and disappeared around the time David and Megan were killed.

The shock of hearing Raines' revelation made me want to throw up. 'I . . . I don't feel well. Can we pull over?'

Stone was firm. 'You stay in the car until we get to headquarters. We're not falling for any scams, Moran.'

'It's not a scam. I feel ill.'

Stone was resolute. 'Then throw up if you have to, because this car ain't stopping until we get to DC.'

When Raines didn't intervene I felt completely alone. I said to him, 'I . . . I was convinced Gamal was lying. I never thought we'd find anything at the metro.'

Raines responded, 'Well, we did. The forensic prelims and the killer's MO suggest it was Gamal who killed the victims, and that he was in Chinatown when David and Megan were killed.'

I felt a growing sense of panic, and I could hardly breathe. 'But he . . . he could have carried out both sets of murders.'

'He could have,' Lou Raines acknowledged. 'That's always possible. But I'm not so sure. Tell her, Stone.'

Stone said, 'When Gamal covered up the burial site he was spotted by a metro worker. The worker backs up Gamal's claim that he was in the tunnel in the afternoon. So it's unlikely he could have killed David and Megan around the same time. But *someone* did.'

I heard the unveiled accusation in Stone's voice. I was fast losing any vain hope I had of convincing Raines of my innocence. 'Lou, for God's sake, you *know* I loved David and Megan. I couldn't have killed them.'

Stone butted in, sounding like he was enjoying my dilemma. 'Yeah? What about motive?'

'*What* motive?'

'Money, for one. You got a big inheritance.'

'I've never touched a penny of that money. And it was David's idea to make me a beneficiary of his will.'

Stone smirked as he jabbed a finger at me. 'You're sure *you* didn't encourage him, Moran.'

'Go to hell.' I was wasting my time with Stone, so I pleaded with Raines. 'Lou, I *saw* the killer back in the restroom. I'm not mistaken.'

Raines looked at me in the rear-view mirror. 'I'm not saying you didn't, but the airport cops searched the area around the restrooms and found nothing. And they saw no one suspicious trying to flee.'

'Baltimore International's a big, busy place. The killer could easily have got away.'

'All airport security staff have been alerted to what happened and they've been issued with the description of the man you claimed you saw. The watch commander will let us know if they turn up anything. Listen to me, Kate. We've been friends a long time but I can't ignore the fact that there are some pretty serious unanswered questions where you're concerned that could mean big trouble. I also can't ignore the fact that your job's made you some enemies over the years, so maybe someone *is* trying to set you up. I'll admit that's a possibility, so don't think I'm abandoning you. But let's get to the bottom of this back at the office. Hey, Stone, give it a rest and keep that mouth of yours shut, OK?'

Stone sat back, the smirk still on his face. 'Whatever you say.'

'Lou, I want you to know I'm telling you the honest truth.'

'Drop it for now, Kate. I'd appreciate if we could all take the rest of the ride in peace.'

Raines concentrated on driving. He had said he wasn't abandoning me, but I didn't exactly get the feeling that he was in my corner either. I felt helpless and betrayed, and Raines' revelation was too much. My stomach turned, bile rose in my throat and I made a retching sound.

'*Jesus*, Moran,' shouted Stone, and turned away.

Raines recognised my distress and started to pull in. 'Let her out of the car, Stone, for Christ sakes! Let her out before she throws up all over the damned seats.'

114

The Disciple was doing a steady seventy-five and keeping a hundred yards behind the Ford. He had peeled off the tiny blond beard and removed his glasses. Now he slipped on the cab driver's hat and picked up the hypodermic again. Using his elbows to control the steering wheel, he slipped the needle tip into the rubber-topped vial and pulled back on the plunger, filling the hypodermic with benzo.

All he had to do now was get close to the Ford and put his plan into action.

When he'd filled the hypodermic he tucked the vial in his pocket, then laid the hypo on his lap and got both his hands back on the steering wheel. He figured how he'd do it was like this – pull ahead of the Ford once it left the interstate and tail-end the motherfuckers, then get out of the cab doing the big apologetic act and saying his passenger was ill. He'd ask for their help with the sick passenger and then *wham*, as soon as the two Feds started to help him lift the cabbie out of the seat he'd stick one of them with the needle, grab his gun and shoot the Fed's buddy. It might be tricky to pull off but he felt confident he could do it. Then he'd deal with Moran.

He heard heavy snoring from the driver, still out cold. Maybe he'd used too much benzo and caused the guy to have a stroke? Not that he really gave a fuck. He slid his hand across and felt the driver's pulse. Weak. And getting weaker.

He sat back in the driver's seat. *Hey . . . what's that?*

He caught sight of a slim black object lying on the floor. He recognised it as a metal nightstick – the kind that worked with a swish of the wrist and expanded to become a hard, springy metal cosh. He figured the driver had kept it for protection. The Disciple pocketed the nightstick. It might come in useful when he dealt with the Feds.

He glanced at a road sign as it flashed past. Claremont Crossroads was straight ahead, and then came a shopping mall at a turn-off before the Eisenhower Freeway. He'd have to act fast. But suddenly his heart skipped as the Ford braked hard and slowed, then hung a sharp right into the shopping mall. The car raced to a vacant part of the parking lot and the doors sprang open.

He saw Moran climb out and bend over, as if she was about to throw up. One of the Feds was getting out beside her. This was perfect. He slammed on the brakes, hung a right and drove into the parking lot.

Almost a hundred yards from the Ford he slowed down. His brain was racing now, on fire, trying to modify his plan, and then *wham*, he had it, knew *exactly* what he was going to do, the whole thing coming together. Moran was still bending over, like she was throwing up, one of the Feds standing next to her.

He made sure his seat belt was snapped shut, then he kicked down on the accelerator, the engine snarled and he sped towards Moran. Within seconds he was less than fifty yards from his target. Now she wouldn't have time to move. He grinned as Moran looked up in horror and noticed the car speeding towards her. *Too late, bitch.*

The Disciple stuck his foot hard to the floor and the cab roared forward.

115

No matter how hard I tried I couldn't throw up. I was dry-retching, the impulse brought on by my anxiety and fear all rolled into one. I felt on the verge of tears. I knew I hadn't been able to totally convince Lou Raines that I wasn't a murderer.

'Are you going to throw up, or are you gonna stand there all day?' Stone jabbed me with a finger.

He was right beside me, his hand resting on the rear door, which was hanging open. Raines was in the driver's seat, waiting impatiently, tapping his fingers on the steering wheel.

'I . . . I'm not finished,' I said.

Stone was agitated. 'Then get a fucking move on, Moran.'

I glanced towards the mall and a thought crossed my mind. *What if I make a run for it?*

Raines called out, 'How is she?'

Stone didn't even answer, but jabbed me again, this time with his balled knuckles. 'Come on, Moran. Puke or get back in the fucking car.'

I was about two yards from Stone, who was still resting his arm on the rear door. He was over two hundred pounds and a touch overweight. The mall was two hundred yards away and I reckoned I'd beat him in a sprint. But I was wearing cuffs and I'd witnessed Stone firing on the range: he was an excellent shot. He'd take me down before I got fifty yards.

As I got ready to move back into the car something weird happened. I saw an old grey cab hurtling towards us at high speed from across the lot. The driver's face was a blur behind the windscreen. I couldn't believe what I was seeing – the cab was on a collision course with the Ford.

'Stone! *Behind you!*' I shouted.

Stone instantly put a hand on his side holster. 'Don't fuck with me, Moran.'

I wanted to scream at him to get out of the way, but Stone must have heard the growl of the cab's engine because suddenly he snapped his head round to look, but by then the cab was right on top of us. I flung myself to the ground and rolled away. A second later I heard a screech of brakes and the cab slammed into the Ford with a terrifying crash of metal.

116

Three seconds before crashing into the Ford, the Disciple slammed his foot on the brakes. The action slowed his speed but he was still touching thirty-five when he felt the impact.

BANG!

The crash sounded like a clap of thunder. He felt himself being lifted up bodily, his seat belt snapping him back just in time as the cab smashed into the Ford's rear.

A second later, steam started to plume from under the cab's hood. The Disciple had figured the ancient taxi hadn't got an air bag and he was right. His body felt shaken by the smash but he was still in one piece.

Terrific! He'd done it!

Moran had rolled away at the last moment, but he saw that one of the Feds had been propelled by the force of the crash into the side of the Ford. He had bounced off and slid to the ground. The other had been trapped in the driver's seat when his air bag had deployed and he was struggling to free himself.

The Disciple jumped out of the cab as the Fed on the ground tried to raise himself. He looked dazed, barely conscious, blood streaming from his nose. The Disciple grinned as he came up behind him. 'And where the hell do you think you're going?'

Before his victim could look round the Disciple had snapped out the spring-loaded metal cosh and whacked him hard across the base of the skull. He struck him twice more for good measure. The Fed grunted and his lifeless body collapsed. A thick stream of blood seeped from a deep wound in the back of his skull and gathered in an oily, crimson pool.

The Disciple saw Moran stagger from the scene in disbelief.

He'd deal with her soon – first he had business to finish. He knelt and opened the Fed's jacket and saw his Glock pistol. He removed the weapon and wrenched two spare ammo clips from his holster belt, then grabbed his FBI badge. He stood and walked over to the Ford.

He sniggered when he recognised Lou Raines through the driver's window. The air bag had expanded, contorting Raines' face, pushing it against the side of the window so that one of his eyes was half open and the other shut, his lips pressed hard against the glass as he struggled to free himself. *Funny. Like you'd see in a movie. Except this scene is going to end in tragedy.*

The Disciple said with a grin, 'Hey, Lou. We meet again. Are you ready to say hello to the Devil?'

Raines looked up, eyes wide in stark horror as he recognised his assailant. The Disciple raised the Glock and shot Raines twice in the head, shattering the glass and the air bag. The bag made a hissing sound as it deflated and the cream-coloured canvas was spattered with crimson.

The Disciple spun round and saw that Moran was a good seventy yards away, running for her life towards the mall. She was moving fast, but he could run too.

He started to chase after her.

117

I ran towards the mall in shock. I kept replaying the crash in my mind: the cab smashing into the Ford, Stone flying through the air, bouncing off the side of the car, his body hurled to the ground.

Then the cab driver's door burst open. Disoriented, my eyesight blurred, I saw a man step out. He wore a cab driver's hat and walked smartly over to Stone and whacked him on the head with a cosh.

Alarm bells were going off in my head: *This is no freak accident*. I staggered back, barely able to stand as I witnessed what happened next: the cold-blooded murder of Lou Raines. Then the killer turned to stare at me, and that was when I got my next big shock. *It's the guy I saw on the airplane*. I was sure of it. The guy I'd spotted with the grey woollen hat and a beard, but now the beard and the hat were gone. He'd been using disguises. And then it hit me with the force of a bullet. *It has to be Gamal in disguise. Or is it my paranoia making that assumption?* I didn't think so. I couldn't be sure but the guy had proved his talent for disguise and was about the same height and build as Gamal. The killer stepped towards me.

I ran towards the mall.

The Disciple quickened his pace as he raced across the parking lot. His body was in peak condition and his powerful lungs had no trouble keeping up the pace. He saw Moran dart in through the mall entrance lobby.

A few people in the parking lot turned to look at him but he'd already stuffed the gun into his jacket. He knew he had to act fast: it wouldn't be long before the cops or mall security appeared.

Seconds later he stepped in through the main entrance doors and a warm blast of air greeted him. He scanned the mall and saw Moran running fifty yards ahead before she veered off to the left and disappeared.

Like a hunter, he carefully surveyed his surroundings before proceeding. Only a few customers were scattered around the mall and no security was noticeable – a couple of mothers with strollers, a smattering of elderly folk, some teenage mall workers standing outside their storefronts, looking bored as hell. He was beginning to enjoy the hunt, confident that he'd locate Moran. He tapped the Glock, snug in his pocket, and felt the hypodermic in another. This time he had her.

118

Stone became conscious with a groan. He staggered to his feet, his vision blurred. Finally he managed to stay upright by leaning on the Ford. His skull felt as if he'd been hit with a tyre iron and his headache made him want to throw up. Then he felt liquid drip from his head and saw clots of his own blood spatter on the ground.

Jesus. He gingerly put a hand to the back of his skull. The flesh felt pulped and agonising to touch and he could barely turn his head. He hoped his skull wasn't fractured. Slowly, the fog inside his head began to clear and he turned round and blinked.

Lou Raines' bloodied face hung half out of the shattered driver's window. Two bullet holes were drilled into his head, one above the left eye, another just above his nose, and blood and brain matter were spattered all over the car's interior and the deflated air bag.

Stone staggered over to the car in disbelief. He knew it was a waste of time but he felt Raines' pulse anyway. Dead. *What the hell happened?* He remembered being struck from behind and then must have blacked out. He made his way over to the mangled remains of a grey cab, its bonnet and engine a tangle of crunched metal.

The body of a middle-aged black man lay slumped in the passenger's seat.

Stone felt for a pulse but found none. He noticed the dead guy's photo ID on the dash. *Did the cabbie have a heart attack and crash? But what the fuck is his body doing in the passenger seat?*

Who had shot Raines? Some instinct made him reach for his gun. It was gone. He searched the ground but saw no sign of his weapon anywhere.

His head was ablaze with pain but he managed to fumble for his cell phone and punch in a number. A nasal voice answered. 'Norton.'

'Gus, it's me, Stone.'

'The hell are you, Vance? You sound kind of funny.'

'Well, I ain't fucking laughing, Gus, that's for fucking sure. Raines has just been shot dead. I reckon Moran killed him and now she's on the run. She's armed, dangerous and desperate.'

'*Moran?*'

'You heard me. She was the only one around who could have pulled the trigger. I'm figuring the bitch even used my own gun. It's missing.'

'She shot Lou *dead*?'

Anger erupted in Stone's voice. 'Are you deaf? How many times do I have to say it?'

'Where the heck are you?'

Stone told him. 'There's a mall right in front of me. She may have headed inside. Get on to everyone you can, the local cops and any of our guys in the area. And try and get in touch with mall security. I want the place scoured. And I want Moran, dead or alive.'

'Hey, steady on, Vance.'

'Just do what I fucking say. I'll hold the line. And get me a fucking ambulance.'

'You hurt?'

Of course I'm fucking hurt! I got hit on the noggin by Moran. Now do what I told you!'

Stone kept the phone cradled to his ear as he looked towards the mall, then with a great effort he sank down on one knee. *Christ*, his head hurt like hell. He pulled up his right trouser leg and reached for a snub-nosed .38 revolver. His ace in the hole, for emergencies.

Once he found Moran he intended to use the .38, no warnings, no chances. It had gone beyond all that. He got to his feet and staggered towards the mall. Every step was an effort as the pounding in his skull got worse. He saw an elderly lady with a pink rinse drive slowly past him in an ancient, metallic blue GM, its paintwork rusted and flaking. Stone put up his hand, pointing his gun at the car, but when he reached for his badge he discovered it too was gone. *Shit*.

'FBI. Stop, lady!'

The lady braked to a halt, one hand going to her mouth in fright. Stone yanked open the passenger door with such force that the elderly woman let out a piercing scream – as if his fucking head didn't hurt badly enough already. He climbed into the car and saw a clutch of Wal-Mart shopping bags on the back seat. '*Calm down, ma'am!* I'm an FBI agent. I want you to drive me up to the mall.'

The woman gave him a confused look. 'W . . . why? Can't . . . can't you walk?'

Stone lost it completely then, his hand going up to touch the back of his skull, blood sticky on his fingers. 'Of course I can *walk*, but I just got a fucking hole in the back of my head, lady, and I'm chasing a wanted felon. Now drive me to the fucking mall!'

119

I entered the mall and risked a look back. I spotted the killer about a hundred yards across the lot. He was running towards me fast.

My heart sank. I looked around but couldn't see a security guard – the mall was almost empty – but then I figured it was pointless trying to alert a guard because I'd be giving myself away, so I kept moving. All I knew was that I had to get away from there *fast*, and I had to call Frank. I tried my cell phone but I couldn't get a signal. Ten yards past a Toys 'Я' Us I saw a sign pointing to the right for the restrooms and the phone booths. I followed the sign and found the phones halfway down a corridor, under an escalator.

I fumbled in my wallet for some coins, then looked back over my shoulder, but I saw no sign of my pursuer. I called Frank's cell phone after I had checked the number in my cell's address book. It rang, but there was no answer. Since Frank had quit the Bureau he'd stopped taking his cell phone everywhere with him. I called his home number. It rang unanswered too. *Damn, where the hell is he? I hope he hasn't gone on a bender.*

This time I left a message saying that I'd landed, it was urgent I reached him and I'd call him back on his cell phone. Then I thought about calling the only other person I could think of who could help me. Josh. I found his number in my cell address book.

How will he react? Will he be furious and slam down his phone or will he believe what I have to say? There was only one way to find out. I hesitated, almost frightened to make the call, and then I punched in his cell phone number.

Josh's voice answered on the second ring. 'Cooper.'

'Josh, it's Kate.'

A long silence followed. 'So, you finally decided to call. Where are you?'

I could tell by Josh's tone that I was definitely out of favour. I wondered whether Raines and Stone had already told him that they suspected I was a killer. 'A place called Claremont Mall, off Ninety-five. Ever hear of it?'

'Sure, it's where I often shop with Neal. What are you doing *there?*'

'Josh, before you say anything, I'm going to ask you to please listen carefully to what I'm going to say, because it's important. I landed at Baltimore airport about an hour ago.'

I was desperate to tell him everything that had happened, especially about Raines' death, but I was racked by guilt and for some reason the words just wouldn't come. I knew I'd have to ease my way into it. I waited for Josh's reaction but the line was silent. I guessed he must have known about my imminent arrest. 'I . . . I need to talk to you, Josh. I need to explain what's been happening. Are you still there?'

'Yeah, I'm still here,' Josh answered flatly.

He sounded distant, almost cold. Or maybe he was at HQ and couldn't talk? 'Are you in the office?'

'No, I'm at home. I don't get it. Did Lou tell you to call me? Because if you're looking for the luggage you left in Paris, I took it back on the flight with me and left it in the office, on Lou's instructions.'

At home. His home was in Gretchen Woods, maybe three miles away. I blurted out the truth. 'That wasn't why I called. I was arrested at the airport by Lou and Stone but I escaped.'

'*Escaped?* You're kidding me? Are you crazy? What's got into you?'

'I'll explain when I see you. I need your help, Josh, or I'm in even deeper trouble. All the things you've probably heard about me lately, they're not true. Someone's trying to set me up and I don't understand why. I don't understand any of it. But please accept that I'm innocent.'

Another pause, then Josh said quietly, 'I don't know what you're talking about, Kate. Listen, I don't mean for this to sound accusing, but you sure left me in the lurch when you fled Paris. Lou has suspended me. He wants an investigation.'

'I'm so sorry, Josh. I really didn't mean to get you into trouble.'

If Josh was suspended he was probably unaware of what had been happening. I thought: *At least he called me by my first name, that's something.* But the moment I heard him mention Lou's name, I cringed. No matter how hard I tried I still didn't have the heart to tell him about Lou's death. 'I know the apology's late but I had to go to Istanbul to see the murder scene for myself. I hoped I might find some clue to help me figure out the killings. Instead, things just got worse. And I need your help now, Josh. I really do. I need you to come to the mall and pick me up. Could you do that for me? I need to talk about the case, see if we can come up with any angles together.'

I heard a pause down the line, and then a sigh. 'There's another reason I'm at home, Kate. Neal's ill. He's feeling really bad with stomach cramps and sweats. That's pretty common with lupus and the doc's with him now, giving him some shots. I can't get out to meet you.'

'I . . . I'm sorry about Neal.' I knew at that moment that there was nothing Josh could do to save me, that I was completely alone. 'You're right, you better stay there and be with your son. That's where you should be.'

'Kate, do yourself a big favour – do everyone a favour, including me – and give yourself up. Will you do that for me?'

I heard the concern in his voice and I knew for sure that he cared, but I knew too that I'd blown what could have been a pretty good relationship. Right there and then I wanted to tell him about Lou's death, wanted him to know everything. *I saw Lou being shot point blank in the head by a man I believe to be Gamal.* But what was the point of telling him? Josh couldn't help. He'd probably even have difficulty believing me. 'I . . . I'll think about it,' I lied, and felt like crying.

'I mean it,' Josh said. 'For everyone's sake it's the best thing to do.'

'You truly can't help me?' I must have sounded desperate.

'I'm sorry, Kate, I really am, but I can't leave my son right now. Not for anything or anyone.'

'I . . . I understand.' In my heart I knew it was unreasonable to have asked him again. I couldn't expect Josh to leave his son and risk getting himself in worse trouble.

'Give yourself up to the nearest cop, Kate. Just do it. Please.'

Oh, Josh, why did it have to turn out this way? 'I . . . I hope Neal's OK.'

'So do I. I hear the doc calling me. I've got to go.'

'Take care, Josh.'

'You too,' came the reply, and a second later the line clicked dead.

120

I put down the phone and whatever hope I'd harboured about a relationship with Josh evaporated. There was an awful lot about him I liked, but maybe I was simply expecting too much. A voice inside my head told me: *Forget about Josh, the relationship's not going anywhere. And you're not going anywhere except prison if you can't prove your innocence.*

I ran a hand through my hair in desperation and tried to figure out what to do next. *I don't have many options. Maybe I could try and sneak on to a delivery truck leaving the mall, or steal an automobile?* I could wind up getting caught doing either. I was about to try Frank's number again when a sense of reality hit me like a ton of bricks. *Maybe Josh is right? Maybe it's time to give myself up?*

I heard footsteps, looked behind me, and my worst nightmare paralysed me with shock. Standing thirty yards away, staring me in the eye, was the killer.

The Disciple came to a Toys 'Я' Us store and turned right. He found himself in a corridor. He'd seen Kate Moran head this way. He came to a junction with a couple more corridors heading off in each direction.

Fuck.

Moran could have gone down either one of them. He'd have to try them one by one. He took the FBI badge from his pocket, and then the gun. Suddenly his luck changed. As he turned to his right he saw her, standing in front of a payphone under an escalator, thirty yards away.

She looked desperate, her hair messed, her eyes smudged. A

second later she looked up and their eyes locked. He saw her mouth open in terror and he sniggered. It gave him such a big thrill to see her fear.

She backed away, turned on her heels and ran down the corridor.

The Disciple ran after her.

121

I glanced back as I ran, trying to glimpse my assailant's features. I couldn't be sure, but my instincts convinced me it had to be Gamal in disguise. *Except who's going to believe me?*

He was no more than forty yards behind me and trying to gain ground, but then I saw him slowed up by a couple of mothers with strollers who crossed his path. I was in the main stretch of the mall now and staff and customers stopped to stare as I ran past, but no one intervened. I put on a burst of speed, dashed up an escalator, ran across a broad hallway and finally descended another escalator. I didn't know where the hell I was going. But I didn't have to glance back to know I was still being followed – I could hear his footsteps.

I raced to the bottom of the escalator and saw a big security guard built like a pro wrestler step out of nowhere and try to block my path. He held his hands out wide. '*Hey! Lady!* Stop, you hear?'

I tried to dart past him as he shouted, 'Hold on, there! Hold on, lady!'

He managed to grab my jacket but I instantly broke free and kept running, and then I heard a man's voice shout, 'FBI. That woman's a dangerous felon!'

I looked back and saw the killer clutching a gun and flashing a badge at the guard. *Was it Stone's Glock?*

Now the guard and the killer *both* took up the chase. *Jesus*, it was absurd. I couldn't believe that in a public mall I was being chased by a deranged killer *and* security as if I was the criminal.

Suddenly two more security guards stepped out in front of

me to block my path. But I was travelling so fast I darted right past them, avoiding their clutches. I reached the mall exit ten seconds later, almost out of breath as I rushed out through the automatic doors, and then to my shock I saw Stone. He was having difficulty climbing out of a dented blue car driven by an elderly lady, his left hand clutching the back of his skull. I didn't stop, and he stared at me wide eyed. Seconds later I heard him shout, 'Moran!'

By then I was thirty yards away, weaving in and out of parked cars, my lungs burning and my legs aching.

Suddenly two shots detonated.

Crack!

Crack!

I heard the rounds whistle past me, one of them smacking into the asphalt ahead, but I kept running, ducking and weaving, ignoring the pain in my lungs, until I came to an open patch of the parking lot and slowed my pace. I looked back, gasping as I tried to catch my breath. There was no sign of the killer and the security guard but Stone was limping towards me crazily.

I ran on for a hundred yards, until I knew he was too far away to get a clear shot. But by then something had snapped inside me and I felt as if all my will had gone.

Why? Why the hell am I doing this to myself? Why risk getting myself killed?

I made up my mind right there and then that I was going to give myself up to Stone. I collapsed in a heap on the asphalt, perspiration running down my face as I sucked in lungfuls of air and waited for Stone to come and arrest me. As I sat there feeling miserable I heard a vehicle approach. I figured: *Mall security. But what if the killer is in the vehicle?* I looked round as a navy blue Landcruiser halted. 'Get in,' the driver said.

I could hardly believe it. I stared open mouthed at Josh in the driver's seat.

'Are you deaf? I've bust my ass getting here, Kate. *Get in now.* If Stone gets any closer he'll recognise me.'

Without a word I dragged myself up off the ground, climbed

in and slammed the door. Josh reversed with a wild screech of rubber, spun the Landcruiser 180 degrees, and we sped away from the mall.

122

Six minutes later we pulled up outside a neat dormer in Gretchen Woods. Josh pressed a remote control. His garage door opened and he drove the Landcruiser inside. Shelves of paint and tools lined the breeze-block walls and an old dented food freezer languished in a corner.

Josh said, 'The Landcruiser's a loan from my sister while my car's in the garage being repaired. But in case you're worried, I figure Stone was too far away to see the licence plate.'

'What if he saw the driver?' I heard the garage door whirr shut but we remained in the Landcruiser.

'Then we'll find out soon enough. But I doubt it. And I didn't see any police choppers in the air either, so relax. Care to tell me what the deal was back there? It seemed to me Stone was out to kill you.'

'Not only Stone.' I suddenly felt emotionally and physically drained and close to breaking point. 'It's a long, bizarre story, Josh, that I'm not sure you'll believe. But I honestly didn't mean to drag you away from your son. He really ought to come first, but I appreciate what you've done. How is he?'

Josh ran a hand tiredly over his face. 'The doc had finished just as I put down the phone on you. Neal improved big time once he got his steroid shots and the doc seems to think he'll be OK. My sister Marcie had called by to see if she could help, and she's upstairs looking after him. She lives just round the block.'

'Close family, huh?'

Josh broke into a grin. 'Not always. But at least they're there when your back's against a wall.'

'Why did you change your mind and come rescue me?'

He looked straight ahead, thought about it, then turned to face me. 'I can't honestly answer that question, not right yet. I know I could get myself in deep trouble and mess up my career, as if it isn't messed up already. Maybe it had something to do with what happened between us in Paris. I figured it meant something. I trust you and I want you to tell me everything. Right from after you ditched me in Paris. OK?'

Ditched. It made it sound as if I'd abandoned Josh, and I guess I *had*, but I hated to think of it that way. 'How about we agree on *left* instead of ditched. That doesn't make me out to be such a bitch.'

Josh smiled and moved to climb out of the Landcruiser. 'OK, *left* me in Paris. Happy now?'

I held up my cuffed hands. 'Except for these.'

'I've got some tools in the garage that ought to solve that problem. Then we'll go inside. You've sure got some explaining to do.'

123

Ten minutes later Josh had removed my cuffs with a hacksaw and a pair of heavy-duty cutters, then he opened a door in the garage and we stepped into the kitchen. Pictures of Josh and Neal hung on the walls, one taken at a school baseball game, another at Disneyland. Neal definitely had his dad's dark hair and brown eyes. I saw a sturdy eucalyptus tree at the bottom of the well-kept back lawn, a home-made swing rigged up on one of the branches and a worn yellow plastic kiddie slide.

Josh took off his jacket. 'I guess Marcie's still upstairs. Come on up and I'll introduce you.'

I followed him upstairs to a bedroom off the landing. Neal lay in a single bed and looked much like he did in his photographs, except a little filled out by the steroids. An attractive woman in her early thirties with auburn hair sat beside him on the bed. She stood up as we entered.

'Hey, Marcie. And how's my boy?' Josh said to Neal as he joined him.

The bedroom walls were plastered with posters of football teams, and there was a picture of Neal dressed in an FBI baseball cap. There were other Bureau trinkets on the shelves, like an imitation ID badge, and I guessed Neal thought it pretty neat that his dad was a special agent. But in pride of place was a framed shot of Josh and his son on Bureau graduation day, taken with the FBI Director.

Neal gave me a hesitant look before he answered, 'I'm OK, Dad.'

Josh gave his son a hug and his sister offered me a friendly smile before she touched Josh's arm and said quietly, 'He's fine.

The doc said to keep an eye on his temperature and he'll call by again later. But he's over the worst, so you can relax.'

I saw immense relief on Josh's face and I realised the enormous sacrifice he had made to come and get me. He must have been worried sick.

'Thanks, Marcie, I appreciate you staying. I'd like you guys to meet my colleague, Kate Moran.'

Marcie offered her hand. 'Josh told me about you.'

'It's good to meet you, Marcie.' I wondered how much he had told her. 'I bet it wasn't all good?'

Marcie smiled. 'To tell the truth, he didn't say much. Just that you both worked together. And believe me, it's a compliment just to hear that from Josh. It's hard enough to get a word out of him at the best of times.'

I was almost tempted to say: '*Your brother's a good guy and I owe him,*' but I figured that would have sounded crass, so I kept shtumm.

'Don't you girls start beating up on me,' Josh said as he sat by Neal. He stroked his hair and leaned over to kiss his cheek. 'How's my man? What's the matter, lost your tongue? Say hello to Miss Moran.'

Neal looked up warily at the stranger in his room but didn't speak, just nodded.

I said, 'Call me Kate. I see you're a football fan, Neal. What do you think you'll be when you grow up? A player or an FBI agent?'

Neal's eyes came alive as if I'd mentioned his favourite topics and he said innocently, 'I think I'd really like to be both. If I was an agent and a Redskins player, that would be really cool.'

'Why's that?'

'I could fight baddies *and* play ball.'

I looked over at Josh. 'It sounds like your son's got a great career ahead of him.'

'Unlike his father,' Josh said drily.

'Do you like being a special agent, Kate?' Neal asked earnestly.

'It certainly has its moments.'

I saw Neal frown, as if he didn't understand, and I tried to explain. 'I guess what I'm saying is that I like my job most of the time, Neal. But some days, the work can be pretty difficult.'

Neal nodded agreement. 'That's what my dad says, sometimes.'

'Really? Well, your dad's a *very* special agent. Isn't he?'

Neal nodded solemnly and Josh raised his eyebrows to me in a half-smile. Marcie said, 'How about Daddy spends a little time alone with Neal while I take Kate downstairs for some coffee?'

'Coffee would be good, thank you.'

Marcie went out. I was about to follow her when Josh winked at me. 'Thanks for the vote of confidence. I'll be down in a little while. By the way, the bathroom is down the hall in case you need to freshen up.'

I must have looked dishevelled. 'Thanks for everything, Josh. I really mean that. Coming out when Neal was ill . . . I don't know what to say.'

'We'll talk in a little while.' His eyes fixed on mine and lingered meaningfully for a couple of seconds. He stroked Neal's hair again. 'Go get some coffee.'

124

When I'd freshened myself up and brushed my hair I went down to the kitchen. Marcie had made coffee and I joined her at the table. 'Help yourself to cream and sugar,' she offered.

Fresh coffee was exactly what I needed to perk me up and I took mine black with a spoon of sugar. 'I'm sorry for dragging your brother away at such a difficult time, with Neal being ill.'

I didn't mention *why* I'd dragged Josh away, and I was guessing he hadn't told his sister the *real* reason. In any case, Marcie didn't comment, except to give a tiny nod. 'Neal will be fine. He takes these turns now and then, and sometimes things get a little worrying, but he's always pulled through.'

'Have you children, Marcie?'

'Two, a boy and a girl, five and eight,' Marcie said. 'Best things that ever happened to me, even if they sure know how to infuriate their mom at times. My husband Dean had a week off work and flew with them up to New York to visit his folks for a couple of days while I stayed behind to oversee some redecorating we're having done. You have any kids?'

Her face darkened the instant she asked the question, one hand going to her mouth as her other touched mine in a consoling gesture. 'I'm sorry, Kate. I remembered just as I spoke. Josh told me about what happened to your fiancé and his daughter. And I remember reading about the case in the newspapers at the time.'

'It's OK, truly. I guess you and Josh must be close, huh?'

'Pretty much. Though you'd never think it if you'd seen us as teenagers, almost killing each other over who was next to use the shower. He's a good guy, Josh. Takes his work seriously and always did. I guess he's a man's man, if you know what I mean. Solid and dependable, even if he has his wild side now and then.'

I tried not to sound amazed. 'Josh has a wild side?'

'He never told you about his rock years? He's Springsteen's biggest fan. He also plays a mean electric guitar. He used to play lead in a rock band in college started by a girlfriend of one of his buddies. They called the band – wait for it – Joanie Salt and the Shakers.' Marcie covered her mouth as she laughed. 'Some name, huh? Don't ever tell him I told you about that. Me, I'm an R 'n' B chick. Rock just wrecks my ears.'

'I know what you mean.'

Marcie poured us each some more coffee. I was fast warming to her. 'Josh told me a little about his marriage,' I said quietly, trying not to make it sound like I was probing, which really I was.

For the first time since I'd met her the good humour left Marcie's face. 'He took it pretty hard, you know. Men often do. Statistically they find divorce and separation harder to get through than women. You believe that?'

I did, knowing how they'd taken their toll on David and Paul. 'How'd he cope?'

'For almost a year after the divorce Josh just retreated into himself, never spoke about it. When he finally came out of the tunnel, he was fine. But if you ask me he and Carla were never really suited. They met at a rock concert a couple of years after he'd finished college.'

'What was she like?' As soon as I asked the question I guessed Marcie had figured out I had feelings for Josh, but she didn't show it.

'Carla was an unusual kind of girl, mixed race, half Puerto Rican – exotic and sultry is how you might describe her, I guess. Josh was putty to her charm, but she was also a moody, selfish tigress and she had a short fuse. Carla wasn't really suited to motherhood or married life. Then suddenly she met this handsome, wealthy guy, fell head over heels, and that was it. She went out to San Francisco with him and left Josh a "Dear John" letter. Not so much as a goodbye to her son. Go figure that out.'

'It must have been so hard on Neal.'

Marcie sipped her coffee and put down her cup. 'The poor kid missed his mom so much, even if she wasn't much of a mother. He was confused for a long time, used to cry a lot at night. But Josh has been both mother and father to him, even though it hasn't been easy at times.'

'Didn't Carla ever call or want to see her son?'

'She phoned a couple of times for the first few weeks she was away, but then the calls stopped. To tell the truth, I think Carla was so far up her own perfect butt it was beyond her to miss *anyone* all that much.'

Marcie made me smile. She talked honestly and I liked her. 'And now? Doesn't she ever call? Even at Christmas or Neal's birthday?' I asked.

'Nothing. Maybe someday guilt will get to her, but it sure hasn't hit her yet.'

Marcie finished her coffee. 'I better go back up to Neal. Help yourself to more coffee, if you like, and I'll fetch that brother of mine. I'd take a guess that you two have some private talking to do.'

I sat in the kitchen listening to Marcie climb the stairs. I knew I had fooled myself into thinking that I had my plan to get out of this mess all worked out, but really I didn't. *It's a risky and dangerous plan and I need Josh's help. But will he think that what I intend to do is crazy?*

As I poured myself more coffee Josh came downstairs to the kitchen. 'How's Neal?' I asked.

'He's fine, gone to sleep. I guess the day took a lot out of him.' Josh looked tense as he noticed the coffee pot and cups. 'Did Marcie offer you something to eat?'

'We were talking so much I guess she forgot to, but I'm fine, honestly I am. What about you?'

'I could do with some cold water. I feel all wound up.'

'Let me get you some. Is tap OK?'

'Sure.'

I poured him a glass and he sat opposite me, placed the cold glass against his forehead to cool himself down, and said with concern, 'So how are you doing?'

'I really don't know. I thought I was fine until now but I'm having doubts,' I confessed.

'About what?'

I wanted to say: *'About the plan I've come up with that might prove my innocence. And I desperately need your help but I'm afraid to ask in case you think I'm crazy.'* For that reason, at that precise moment I felt as if a dark cloud were hovering right over my head, crushing me. 'About everything. I didn't do any wrong, Josh, I really didn't. I so much want you to believe that. I just don't know what the hell has been going on these last few days. It's got me scared and totally confused.'

He gripped my hand and I felt his strength. 'The best place to start is at the beginning. So just tell me what happened, Kate. That's the only way I can hope to understand this mess. Start at the very beginning and tell me every damned thing that's happened.'

125

I told Josh, and when I had finished I felt better for having unburdened myself. But the feeling of relief wasn't about to last. Josh shook his head and let out a worrisome breath. 'I agree that all that's happened in the last four days is pretty weird. But you're still in serious trouble with the Bureau, Kate.'

'You don't have to hammer it home.'

'Maybe I do. Maybe giving yourself up is the best course? *Think* about it.'

I shook my head fiercely. 'Josh, I've thought about it. If I give myself up I'll never get to the bottom of this investigation. I'd wind up stuck in prison, or out on bail if I'm lucky, but with a restraining order preventing me from moving more than a block outside my home. And there's something else you have to know.' I still hadn't told him about Lou Raines, but the time had come to be brutally honest. I looked Josh straight in the eyes. 'Lou's dead.'

Josh looked dumbstruck. He just sat there staring at me, wide eyed, while I told him every detail I could remember. I touched his arm. 'I'm sorry, Josh. I know how close he was to you and your family.'

Josh put a palm to his brow. '*Jesus.*'

'You believe what I've told you, don't you?' I said.

He shook his head and stared at me. 'Right this second I'm finding it hard to believe Lou's gone.'

'The killer shot him in the head, without a shred of mercy. There's no way he survived. It was Gamal who did it, I'm certain.'

Josh didn't answer.

I said, 'You think I'm fit to be certified, don't you?'

'I didn't say that.' But Josh's eyebrows knitted and all of a sudden he regarded me warily. 'What happened to Stone?'

I told him I'd seen Stone being attacked. 'He still managed to shoot at me so I figure he'll recover. He was so dazed after the crash maybe he thought it was *me* who beat him over the head.'

Josh sighed deeply, and I could sense his doubts. 'You must have got a good look at Lou's shooter?'

'Not so that I had a clear view of his face. I didn't have the time. But he sure looked about the same height and build as Gamal, and he uses disguises. That's why I didn't spot him straight away on the plane. What exactly he's up to I can't fully figure.'

Josh was still ashen as he shook his head. 'Come on, Kate. There's no way it could have been Gamal.'

'I told you, Yeta said that it's possible her brother survived. And I'm convinced I saw someone who could have been him.'

'I hear what you're saying, but heck, I just can't buy it that the killer you saw was Gamal.' Josh stood, moved towards the window and looked out at the garden, his knuckles resting on the worktop. He looked miles away.

I wondered whether subconsciously he was already trying to distance himself from me. I said, 'What are you thinking? That you're sorry you helped me? That you're sorry about what happened between us in Paris because it complicates things?'

He looked back and slowly shook his head. 'No, I'm not thinking that at all.'

'Then what *are* you thinking?'

'Two things. What in damnation's going on and how the hell are we going to get you out of this mountain of a mess? We've got to give this some thought, Kate. Look at it realistically. If not Gamal, then who might be behind this? Is there anyone you can think of who has a grudge against you right now?'

'Stone does. But I saw him get clobbered.'

Josh shrugged. 'That doesn't mean he couldn't have set it up to cover himself, or that he's not involved in *some* way. Anyone else?'

'I know this may sound weird, but Paul, my ex-husband, has

been behaving really strangely towards me these last months. He's become aggressive, and threatening. He's suddenly become very bitter that our marriage ended, even though he wanted the divorce. I have the feeling he's cracking up.'

'You think he's capable of being involved in something like this?'

I thought hard before I answered the question. 'There was a time when I would have said no, but now I can't be sure. It's like I don't know Paul any more. He's a completely different person. Something else about him you ought to know. He worked on one of Gamal's double homicides in the District six years ago, so he knows about Gamal's MO and classified details of his crimes. Paul's also on leave right now, and no one knows where he is. The last thing I heard was he'd been seen at Dulles airport.'

Josh arched his eyebrows. 'That's a very interesting coincidence.'

I stood up. 'I have an idea that may help answer some of our questions.'

He raised an eyebrow. 'I'm listening.'

'We open Gamal's grave.'

'You've *got* to be kidding me?'

'We have to verify that he was buried. There's no other way.'

Josh stared at me in amazement. 'Doing that could get us both in even deeper trouble.'

'Will you help me? And before you answer, I want you to know that I'll completely understand if you say no.'

Josh put up a hand to decline. 'It's asking too much, Kate. I've got Neal to think of. He needs a father who's employed, not one who's been discharged from the Bureau. He's proud of me. My dismissal would really upset him, never mind about me.' He held up a thumb and forefinger, a tiny gap between them. 'And I'm this close to being seriously reprimanded as it is, maybe even dismissed.'

I understood Josh's refusal but it hit me like a kick in the teeth, though I didn't let him know this. I couldn't expect him to risk his career for me. He could even go to prison, and he'd already done enough. 'I understand. There are no hard feelings.'

'Now what are you going to do?'

'Attempt it alone. I'll get some rest first, if you don't mind Then once it's dark I'll get out of your hair.' Exhaustion had begun to kick in after all the stress and travel, and I was feeling drained.

Josh shook his head. 'You're feisty, you know that?'

'Inherited from my mother. She raised three kids mostly on her own.'

'Be realistic, Kate. Call it off. You can't do it on your lonesome.'

'Maybe not, but I can try.'

126

Josh led me to the spare bedroom. Neal was still asleep and Marcie had gone, promising to return later that evening. 'The bad news is you've got the worst room in the house. The teenage kids next door like to play heavy metal.'

'Don't worry, right this minute I'd sleep on a rope.'

Josh had a pensive look, as if he was troubled by something. He said, 'Am I allowed to change my mind?'

'About what?' I asked.

'Going with you to the graveyard.'

'No, I really don't want you to get in any more trouble, Josh.'

'Seeing as I'm already in hot water up to my eyes I don't think it matters if I drown. Besides, I've decided that I can't let you do this alone. I'm adamant about that.'

I was puzzled. 'What made you suddenly change your mind?'

Josh sighed and looked into my eyes. 'Maybe part of me wanted to talk you out of going to the cemetery and getting in more trouble, but it didn't work. I guess if I'm honest with myself, and for what it's worth, I believe you're telling me the truth. That's really the bottom line.'

'Hearing you just say that is worth a lot.' It was just what I needed to hear and I got to my feet and hugged him.

He brushed my cheek with a kiss, and then he moved down to my neck and kissed me there. I didn't resist. His kisses were gentle and full of caring, and then suddenly his lips moved up to meet mine. For a long time we stood there kissing as I rocked back and forth in his arms, and it felt so good to be held and protected again, to feel secure in a man's embrace. Finally we moved apart. 'Are you OK?' Josh asked.

'I didn't mean for that to happen again,' I answered.

He grinned. 'Neither did I but it sure felt good. So good I'd like to do it again. Under different circumstances, I'd even ask you to sleep with me.'

'Under different circumstances, I'd accept.' I touched Josh's face.

His hand came up to hold mine. 'I've got to stay by Neal for now and give Marcie a break until she comes back later. I want to make sure he's OK.'

'I understand. You're a good friend, Josh Cooper.'

He winked at me. 'And you're a great kisser. How about I wake you around nine? That gives you six hours.'

'What about Neal? What will happen when we have to leave?'

'Marcie will stay with him.' Josh turned to look at me before he left the room, and I saw worry etched in his face. 'I hope to God we don't get caught at the cemetery or else we're both going to hell in a basket over this one.'

'There's still time to change your mind.'

He shook his head. 'It's made up. Try and get some sleep.' He winked at me, then crept out of the room and quietly shut the door.

I felt so exhausted I immediately lay down on the bed. Then I realised that on home soil Stone could track me down by triangulating my cell phone signal – my phone transmitted an identifying signal even when it wasn't being used. I flicked it off and slipped out the SIM card and battery. That would stop any signal being transmitted. In future, if I made any calls I'd have to keep them short and remove the SIM card and battery immediately afterwards. My mind was preoccupied with what I'd said to Josh about Stone and Paul. Could either of them be involved in this? *But why?* I tried to push away my troubled thoughts and get some rest. I lay down on the bed again and closed my eyes. In a little under a minute I fell fast asleep, thinking about our meeting of mouths, the feel of Josh's breath on my neck, and wondering what the hell I'd done to deserve a starring role in this fix I was in.

PART SIX

127

The mall looked like a movie set minus the cameras. Stone counted six local sheriff's cars, two ambulances and a couple of choppers hovering high in the air. The rotor-blade noise didn't help his headache: one of the medics had bandaged his cut and then insisted on taking him to the hospital, but Stone refused. The medic said, 'Don't be so stubborn, you may have cranial damage, sir. You'll need an X-ray.'

'Later. I've got work to do,' Stone insisted.

'Man, you're thick headed in more ways than one,' the medic replied.

Stone strode over to a vacant area of the parking lot, leaving the bemused medic staring after him. Now there was a third chopper in the air, a Bell coming in to land, and Stone watched it circle before it set its struts down on the black asphalt. As the rotor blades died, a tall man with stooped shoulders stepped out of the cabin. He was followed by Gus Norton. They ran forward, their heads bent low until they cleared the blades.

Stone offered his hand to Bob Fisk, the Senior Agent in Charge of the Washington field office. The two men had known each other a long time. 'Thanks for getting here so quickly, sir.'

Fisk was a Harvard man with a handsome, craggy face. He was also a moody bastard who had to be treated very carefully. 'What in the name of God happened here? It looks like a war zone.'

Fisk observed Stone's bandaged head, the ambulances and paramedics, the two crashed automobiles and the sheet-covered bodies of the cab driver and Lou Raines. Legions of locals and shoppers had had to be cordoned off from the scene by cops and mall security.

Stone ushered Fisk towards the crash scene. 'Let me show you, sir.'

He lifted the sheet from Lou Raines' head. It was tilted to one side, the mouth open. Fisk studied the corpse. His voice hoarse with emotion, he said, 'Lou and I joined the Bureau the same day, even graduated together. He was a true friend, a damned good man. Do we know what *animal* was responsible for this carnage and why?'

Stone replaced the sheet. 'We suspect it may have been one of our own agents.'

Fisk was astounded. '*What did you just say?*'

'Her name's Katherine Moran.'

'I know of Moran. You actually *saw* her shoot Raines?'

'No, sir. I was knocked unconscious for a time. But I know she fled the scene and now she's on the run. I figure she also stole my firearm and that maybe she used it to shoot Raines. I believe we'll have footage of her escape through the shopping mall – their security people are going through their videotapes as we speak. They say they've got cameras almost everywhere.'

'Why kill Raines, for God's sakes?'

'We don't know yet, sir,' Stone replied.

'What about video footage of his murder?' Fisk asked.

'Apparently the cameras don't reach this far. They cover only the immediate vicinity of the mall, inside and out, and a few of the parking areas.'

Fisk sighed and regarded the vast shopping precinct. 'Then what about witnesses?'

'The parking lot was pretty much empty at the time and nobody's come forward claiming to have seen anything.' Stone touched his bandaged head. 'I was out cold when the shooting occurred, so we'll have to wait until we've got ballistic results on the slugs in Lou's skull to be certain.'

Fisk was incredulous. 'I can't believe this. One of our *own* agents. It defies belief.'

'It had to be her, sir. Why else would she flee? I challenged her and fired but she disregarded my order and took flight.'

'You better tell me everything. What *exactly* did you see when you reached the mall?'

'I saw Moran get into the passenger side of a blue Landcruiser that sped away. I was too far away to tell whether she had help or took the driver hostage. We're having the roads scoured by chopper but so far we haven't been able to find her or the Landcruiser.'

Fisk looked stunned. 'I don't know what's harder to believe – Lou's cold-blooded murder, or the fact that Moran's our chief suspect. Has she any psychiatric history?'

'I know she's been under a therapist's care in the past,' Stone offered.

'Big deal, so's half the damned country. I'm aware her fiancé and his child were murdered by Gamal. Has she been psychologically unsettled or unhinged in any way recently? Did she show any symptoms of unbalance?'

'Maybe you heard about Gamal's claim that he didn't do the Bryce murders?'

Fisk nodded. 'I heard from Lou, but what's that got to do with all of this?'

'Well, you asked me if Moran had any psychiatric history. This morning she told Lou and me that she believed Gamal had survived his execution and that she suspected he might be behind the recent copycat killings.'

'*What?* You've got to be kidding me?'

'She's crazy, sir. But you've been out of the loop, so let me try to fill you in.' Stone explained the details and ended with Kate Moran's arrest at Baltimore and the shootings at the mall. 'I don't know if Lou told you, but I had my own theory that Moran killed her fiancé and his daughter. We arrested her on suspicion of the Fleists' double homicide, and I think it may have finally sent her over the edge.'

Fisk shook his head, aghast. 'Lou didn't mention a thing.'

'I guess the truth of it is that he and Moran were buddies and he found it hard to accept that one of our team could have committed murder. But I found evidence linking Moran to the crime, including a witness.'

'Go on.'

Stone elaborated and Fisk was horrified. 'This is all news to me. Why wasn't I kept up to speed on this?'

'I think Lou was having difficulty believing it for himself.' Stone looked down at Raines' body. 'Unfortunately, else he'd probably still be alive. If you want my opinion, Moran's completely flipped her lid now that she knows we're on to her. This episode only proves it.'

Fisk jabbed a finger at the dead cab driver. 'What part did he play in all of this?'

'The paramedics think he may have had a heart attack and lost control of his vehicle. It looks like Moran took advantage of the crash to make her escape.'

Fisk's jaw tightened and he slapped a fist into his open palm. 'I want a file on this entire case on my desk by late this afternoon. I want to personally review the evidence, you understand?'

'I'll see to it, sir.'

Fisk turned towards the chopper. 'I'm putting you in charge of this investigation, Stone. I want Moran apprehended. Do whatever it takes.'

'Yes, sir.'

As Fisk strode back to the chopper, Stone put a hand on his bandaged head and said to Norton, 'Moran's going to need help. Where would she run to?'

'Hey, you know her better than I do.'

Stone snapped his fingers. 'That brother of hers. Stake out his house, a twenty-four-hour watch, do it right away. She may try and contact him. Where's Cooper? We're going to need every agent we can get.'

'Lou suspended him, remember?'

'Where's he live?' Stone asked.

'Somewhere over in Gretchen Woods.'

Stone frowned when he heard the address. 'That's less than a ten-minute drive away.'

'So?'

'He and Moran seemed to get on pretty well, wouldn't you say? What does Cooper drive?'

'An old BMW.'

'You sure about that?'

'Yeah, why?'

Stone rubbed his jaw thoughtfully and gritted his teeth. ''Cause I've got another hunch, that's why. Find out his exact address.'

'Any particular reason?'

'Yeah, numb nuts. 'Cause we're going to pay him a visit.'

128

Lucius Clay was busy pruning the rose bushes on the front lawn of his house north of Richmond. He wore a woollen sweater with leather elbow patches and a pair of scuffed work boots, and as he clipped the bushes he heard the German shepherds barking in their kennel run at the side of the lot.

A blue Camarro halted at the end of the driveway and a man stepped out. Clay regarded him with suspicion as he approached the house. The dogs barked frantically. He had security cameras on each corner of the property and kept several handguns scattered throughout the house in case any of his former or current inmates decided they had a grudge against him. The visitor had a ponytail and pitted skin and looked like he might be a former prisoner. 'Stop right there, mister,' Clay called out.

The man smiled. 'Nice garden. Those roses look exceptional.'

Clay studied his visitor warily. 'If you're selling anything, my wife's already bought it. And if she hasn't I'm pretty sure we don't need it.'

'Warden Clay? I'm not a salesman, sir. My name is Dr Frank Moran, formerly with the FBI.'

Clay had the vague feeling he'd seen the man's face before, or else he reminded him of an actor. Was it Tommy Lee Jones? But with a scraggy ponytail. 'Do I know you?'

'No, but I believe you know my sister, Agent Kate Moran. I wonder if we could talk, sir?'

Clay whistled and the dogs fell silent. 'Have you got ID, Dr Moran?'

The man found his driving licence and held it open for the warden to see his photo. Clay studied it but was still cautious. 'What do you want to talk about?'

Moran replaced the licence in his hip pocket. 'I'd really appreciate if I could ask you a few questions, Warden. I think you may be able to help me.'

'Captain Tate told you all that?'

'Yes, Warden, he did.'

Clay let out a sigh. 'Then Tate's got a better imagination than I'd give him credit for. There's no way a condemned prisoner could survive the execution process, Dr Moran. There are too many safeguards in place. This academic paper you say you're writing, what's it for?'

'A respected medical journal,' Moran said vaguely. 'I happened to mention it to Kate and she suggested I might like to seek your opinion.'

Clay led the way towards the kennel run and the dogs whimpered as he approached. 'You said Miss Moran's abroad?'

'That's right.'

'When's she due back?'

Moran said, 'I can't be sure. Why do you ask?'

Clay shook his head. 'No reason. But to get back to our discussion, a condemned prisoner's survival during execution is not feasible. He couldn't feign death. That just couldn't happen.'

Moran said, 'Even with the help of someone senior inside the prison? What I was thinking was, if someone used their authority illicitly. For example, someone in your position, Warden. You could pretty much do as you wanted.'

Clay halted at the kennel run and regarded his visitor sharply. 'What exactly are you trying to imply, Doctor?'

Moran met the warden's stare. 'I'm being hypothetical. Tate seemed to think it might work with inside help. I wanted to know your opinion.'

'You've already had it,' Clay said sharply.

'Are you telling me you don't believe that anyone in a high-ranking prison position would use their authority unwisely, Warden?'

Clay avoided Moran's gaze, and when he looked back his eyebrows were knitted with suspicion. 'Tate's entitled to think what he likes. But do you mind if I say something?'

'Not at all.'

'Maybe you could tell me why I have the feeling that this interview has nothing to do with some academic study.'

Moran said simply, 'What gave you that idea, Warden?'

Clay was blunt. 'Because I've got a built-in shit detector. How about you just cut the crap and spit out exactly what it is you're trying to get at. I assume you are trying to get to a point, aren't you, Doctor?'

Moran looked down at the two German shepherds sitting obediently in the run, watching him with interest, then he kicked some gravel with his shoe before he looked back up at Clay. 'I thought I could be circumspect but I can see that's going to be difficult. Rumour has it you got yourself in trouble with the Department of Corrections because of your doubts about the efficacy of capital punishment. That you had ethical problems with carrying out the death penalty on the prisoners in your charge.'

'I'm not sure I follow the logic of this conversation.'

'I'm simply telling you about a rumour I heard,' Moran said. 'Have I heard right?'

Clay flushed. 'Are you in any way suggesting I might be inclined to interfere in the execution of a condemned prisoner because of my personal beliefs?'

'You tell me, Warden.'

Clay's temper flared. 'Tell you what? If it's your intimation, it's preposterous.'

Moran persisted. 'What about the execution of Constantine Gamal? How'd you feel about that?'

'Who in the hell are you writing for, Moran, and what's this really got to do with? Are you working for another one of those newspapers that tries to twist my words? I'll bet you are.'

'You've got the wrong end of the stick on that one, Warden—'

Clay cut in sharply. 'I don't have anything more to say. And I haven't the foggiest idea what you're attempting to imply, apart from trying to stick words in my mouth. You're trespassing, Moran, or whoever the hell you really are. I'll ask you to leave my property right now before I let my dogs loose and they run you back to your car.'

'I'm not a journalist, Warden Clay, honest. If I could just have another couple of minutes of your time I'll try and explain—'

'I've asked you to leave.' Clay gripped the bolt on the kennel and made to open the wire-mesh gate.

Moran saw the steely determination in Clay's face and then he sighed and touched his forehead with a finger in mock salute. 'Whatever you say, Warden. Don't worry, I think I can find my own way back.'

129

Gretchen Woods, Virginia

I tried to sleep, but after an hour of tossing and turning I woke from a light doze with a start. Brutal images from Paris and Istanbul flashed in my mind: I remembered shooting Jupe and seeing the brutalised bodies of Yeta and the guard.

I saw their faces float before my eyes. I was bathed in perspiration. Then I thought about Josh. He'd done a brave thing by offering to help me and had even put his career on the line, but I had the guilty feeling that I hadn't given him much choice.

I suddenly heard the sound of a car pulling up in the driveway, followed by doors slamming and footsteps coming up the path. My heartbeat increased. Some instinct made me get up out of bed and attempt to peek out of the window, but just then I heard Josh rush up the stairs. He burst open my door, looking ashen, and I heard the worry in his voice. 'It's Stone and Norton, they're outside the house.'

A second later we both heard the doorbell chime. My heart leaped. 'What are they doing here?'

Sweat beaded Josh's brow and he wiped it away with the back of his hand. 'I don't know, Kate. But don't move from the bedroom or make a damned sound.'

I was racked by fear as Josh went downstairs. I heard him open the front door and then I heard a mumble of conversation filtering up from the hallway, but nothing distinct, no raised voices, no complete sentences that I could make sense of. *What's going on?*

Despite Josh's advice I crept over to the door, but then suddenly I saw Neal appear from his room across the landing. He was still dressed in his pyjamas and he seemed startled to see me as he said aloud, 'Where's my daddy?'

I froze, fearful that he'd be heard downstairs. For a moment I panicked, not knowing what to do, and then suddenly my survival instinct kicked in. 'Neal, don't move, sweetheart. Your daddy's going to come upstairs very soon . . .'

'I want him now. My tummy's still sore.'

Jesus. What if Neal walked downstairs and started talking about me? '*Why is Kate still upstairs, Daddy?*'

I didn't even want to think about it. He started to move towards the stairs but I gripped his hand. 'Neal, sweetheart, *please* do as I say.'

But he wasn't listening. He struggled to free himself from my grip and then he started to cry. 'Neal, stay right there,' I whispered firmly.

'No, I'm going to see my daddy . . .'

I couldn't let him go downstairs or I was dead. I took his hand, but this time when he struggled to get away I whispered, 'You know what I liked getting done when I was a little girl and I felt ill?'

Neal stopped struggling, distracted, but he was still crying. He shook his head. 'I just want to see my daddy.'

His plea became a whine. I tried to keep my voice low. 'Neal, your dad's having a really important talk downstairs with some people he works with, and he can't be disturbed, but he asked me to look after you, and you know what I can do to make your tummy better? I can rub it for you. Did your mom ever do that?'

Neal stared at me, unsure.

I reached out and started to rub his tummy very gently. 'Did she ever promise you a surprise afterwards for being such a good boy?'

That got his attention. Neal was wide eyed. 'What kind of a surprise?'

'A big one.' I continued to rub his stomach in a gentle, circling motion. 'Is that nice, sweetheart?'

He nodded and sleepily rubbed his left eye. 'Yes, but I want my dad.'

'I know you do, but we have to be very quiet, Neal.'

'My tummy still hurts.'

'Let me rub it some more and make it better. And if you're very quiet I might promise you a *really* nice surprise. How's that sweetheart?'

Neal nodded, the deal done. Suddenly I heard more voices in the downstairs front room. *Has Stone heard us? What if he comes upstairs?* I tried to think of an escape plan. I looked around, saw a side window and pointed to it. 'What's outside that window Neal?'

'The garden.'

I saw that there was barely enough space for me to squeeze through. And I wasn't so sure that Neal was right. I tried remembering the external layout of Josh's house as I'd seen it when we drove in and I had a terrible feeling that the window dropped down to a siding of solid concrete. *But if it comes to it, I'll have to jump.* I started to pray that Stone wouldn't come up the stairs.

130

Stone hit the doorbell again, Norton beside him, and a form appeared behind the frosted glass. Cooper opened the door, wearing jogging sweats.

Stone offered a rare smile. 'Hey, Coop, sorry to bother you. But we were in the neighbourhood and I needed to have a word.'

'A word about what?' Cooper frowned. 'Look, my son's ill. Can this wait?'

'I guess not. We've got us an urgent problem,' Stone replied without offering an explanation, and fixed Cooper with a stare. 'You going to ask us in, Coop?'

Cooper sighed with frustration. 'Like I said, my son's ill. It's got me pretty tied up . . .'

Norton butted in. 'You're not listening, Coop. Vance means it when he says it's urgent. It's about Moran.'

'What about her?'

Stone studied Cooper's reaction. 'If you don't mind, I'd rather we discussed this *inside*.'

Cooper reluctantly led the way into the living room and gestured to the couch.

'So what's this about Kate?'

'You seen her recently?' Stone enquired.

'Paris, but I thought you knew that.' Cooper frowned. 'Look, don't I get an explanation?'

'How's your kid?' asked Norton.

'I already told you. Neal's ill. The doctor left him less than an hour ago.'

'You reckon he's going to be OK?' Norton asked.

'The doctor thinks so but he's got to be watched and I'm taking turns with my sister. So what is it with you guys? Is this a work-related problem or something?'

Stone grimaced. 'It's a problem all right, Coop. A major-league problem.' He went on to explain, and when he had finished he again studied Cooper's face for a reaction.

'Lou Raines is *dead*?' Cooper sounded shocked.

Stone moved over to the window, peeled back the curtain and peered out. 'That's what I said. And it may well have been your friend Moran. Right now, she's the only suspect we've got.'

'That's *crazy*. I can't believe Kate would murder Lou. *No way*.'

'Why?'

'She's not a killer. Come on, Stone, get real.'

Norton raised his eyes. 'Not a killer? What about the evidence we've got linking her to the Fleist murders?'

Cooper said, 'Maybe you've got something, but it sounds hard to believe. Me, I'd wait and see how the evidence pans out. But as for Kate Moran killing Lou? I mean, that's just way off the clock, guys. Too incredible.'

Stone started to wander around the room, idly studying the bookshelves and Cooper's selection of CDs. 'When you've been in this business as long as I have you get a nose for judging character. She did it, Coop, and make no mistake, I'm going to nail her.' Stone plucked down a photo of Cooper and his son standing beside a BMW. 'You still drive that Beamer?'

Cooper frowned. 'Sure . . . Why?'

'Nice coach. You don't own a Landcruiser?'

'No.' Cooper tried to look puzzled. 'Hey, where are you guys going with this? If you've got something to say, spit it out.'

Stone shook his head, replaced the photo. 'Just curious. It's going in circles, Coop. That's why we need all available help on this investigation. We'll be working round the clock and we're going to need you back on board. I'm in charge now and I'm removing your suspension. I appreciate that this is a difficult time for you but it's all hands on deck until Moran's apprehended. Is there any way your sister could look after your boy?'

442

Cooper shrugged. 'I guess later, when she finishes work, about eleven.'

Stone moved towards the door. 'Then I'll expect you at the office at eleven-thirty. I appreciate your cooperation, Coop. It means a lot.'

As Stone went down the path with Norton they looked back. They both saw Cooper's figure disappear behind the frosted glass when he closed the front door. Stone pursed his lips in a thoughtful expression. 'You get the same feeling I do, Gus?'

'I feel like eating. I missed lunch. What feeling have you got?'

'That there's something not right with our Mr Cooper. He was shocked to hear about Lou, sure, but by my reckoning not half enough. The guy was acting. And he was good, I'll give him that.'

They both climbed into the car and Norton shrugged. 'Can't say I noticed. But what did you expect him to do, roll around the carpet in floods of tears?'

'My instinct says Cooper's holding back about something, I'd bet my ass on it.'

'You reckon?'

'I reckon. I know the guy, Gus. I also got the feeling he doesn't trust me for some reason.'

Norton gestured at Stone's bandaged head. 'You're sure that bang on the skull ain't making you imagine things, Vance?'

'Funny. Just wait, I'll prove I'm right. We watch the house twenty-four-seven. But do it ultra-discreetly, use the best people. Cooper's a pro and he'd smell a tail a mile off. So have our guys be extra careful. And one more thing.'

Norton started the engine. 'Yeah?'

'Find out fast if any of Cooper's known family or friends own a blue Landcruiser.'

131

I heard muted voices in the hallway and then the front door being closed. Josh came bounding up the stairs looking worried and saw Neal and me on the landing. 'Hey, are you both all right?'

'Kate rubbed my tummy,' Neal said, going to his father's arms.

Josh lifted him up in one swoop and kissed his cheek. 'Hey, some guys have all the luck. You OK, Kate?'

'I guess Neal had me a little worried.' I explained what had happened.

Josh felt his son's stomach. 'Is that true? Is it still hurting?'

'Maybe just a little. But Kate promised she's going to buy me a surprise.'

Josh smiled. 'Well, there's a guy who's got it made. You got your tummy rubbed and you get a gift. You think you're going to be OK now, soldier?'

'I *think* so. I sorta feel better.'

'Good for you. How about I cool you down with a damp cloth, that ought to help too, don't you think?' Josh kissed Neal again and winked over at me. 'I'll be back once I get this little man settled.'

He carried Neal into his bedroom and I went back into my room. I was nervous as hell and didn't want Josh to leave me, but I was tempted to peek beyond the curtain and see whether Stone and Norton had gone.

I waited until I heard a car start up then peered through the crack between the curtains and saw their car drive away. I sat down on the bed and remembered the worried look on Josh's face when he'd bounded up the stairs. I figured *something* was wrong. Ten minutes later Josh returned carrying a basin of cold water and a moist face towel. He placed them on the corner desk.

'How is he?' I asked.

'A little anxious, but he'll sleep now.' Josh came to sit on the end of the bed.

'*Jesus*, that was close downstairs. I didn't know if I could keep my cool.'

'So what happened?' I was desperate to know.

Josh's face tightened. 'Stone's like a terrier hunting a rat, he's desperate to find you. I figure if he ever discovers what I've done, I'm finished with the Feds. I'll be walking the plank, big time.'

'Josh, I'm so sorry . . .'

'Hey, no grief here, it was my decision.'

'But I prompted you to make it.'

'No, you didn't. Bottom line is, I made up my own mind.' He smiled valiantly. 'If I get the electric chair will you hold my hand?'

'I promise. Besides, I could do with the change of hairstyle.' I attempted to make light of the situation, like Josh, but I was so tense I could barely smile.

He put a hand on mine. 'Hey, I know it's not funny, but sometimes you've got to try to laugh.'

'So what did Stone tell you?'

'Pretty much everything, except that the way he spun it you're their prime suspect. There's no denying he wants your head on a plate and he's put every available agent on the case. It's hard to tell whether he might have a hand in trying to frame you, but I wouldn't entirely trust the guy. It's just a feeling I've got.'

I felt caught between anger and despair and was close to tears. Josh must have sensed it because he squeezed my hand. 'I know you're not guilty. On that I'm sold. But I'm worried about a couple of things.'

'What?'

'Intuition tells me that maybe Stone suspects me of helping you in some way. But he's not exactly sure how.'

'Oh, *no* . . .'

'He even asked me if I drove a blue Landcruiser.'

I felt my heart sink farther. 'What did you say?'

'I told him no, but I've got a notion that after our little talk downstairs he just may be tempted to have the house watched. His excuse for calling by was that he wants me back at work tonight. The irony's pretty rich, don't you think? Me helping in the hunt for you while all the time you're hiding in my place.'

I got up off the bed. 'I'm not staying, Josh. Once we open Gamal's grave I'm out of your hair, no matter what we find.'

'You don't have to,' he said with conviction.

'Yes, I do. I'm not going to put you and Neal in any more danger.'

'And where will you go?'

'I'll think of somewhere,' I answered.

Josh picked up the towel and the water basin. 'We'll talk about it later. I'll go fetch some old clothes of Carla's that ought to fit you. Then I'll ask Marcie to come by about eight. We can go do our business at the cemetery and I can get over to the office by eleven-thirty.'

He made to leave, and suddenly I felt anxious again. 'Where are you going?'

Josh said, 'Down to the garage. If we're going to dig up Gamal's grave we're going to need shovels.'

132

God, how I hate the shitty taste of defeat. Hate losing. But Kate Moran wasn't going to get away with what she'd done to him.

'You get out here, mister.'

The Disciple shifted his gaze to the shuttle bus driver who had brought him out of his daydream. 'Thanks.'

The driver pointed ahead. 'Cab rank's just over there, or there's a bus service into the District, 'ever you wish, mister.'

'You're very kind.' A little politeness sometimes paid dividends. Made you avoid being considered suspicious.

'My pleasure.' The driver flicked a touch to his baseball cap.

The Disciple climbed down off the mall shuttle bus that hooked up with the local public transport. *So close.* He'd almost captured Moran until disaster struck and the other Fed showed up, sending the whole thing tits up.

He had tailed Moran towards the mall exit and seen her dart outside. Just as he was about to follow her he'd spotted the Fed climbing out of an ancient blue Cadillac driven by an old lady. *I thought I'd whacked the bastard hard enough to kill him.* Then he saw him raise a revolver and fire at Moran, but she kept running, right across the mall lot, and climbed into a blue Landcruiser which drove off.

Who was driving the Landcruiser and why had they helped Moran to escape? That puzzled him.

He'd decided there and then to get out of the mall – he figured the place would soon be crawling with Feds and cops. He didn't intend putting his plans in jeopardy because of his thirst to settle old scores. So he'd exited through one of the mall doors, seen the shuttle bus and hopped aboard. Now it had pulled up across the street from a cab rank, and he stepped off.

Next he needed someplace safe to hang out while he prepared himself for the final blitz, and he knew *exactly* where that someplace was going to be.

But what about Moran? Where would *she* hide? He knew as much about her habits as he did about his own. She wouldn't go to the cottage, not with the Feds and the cops on her tail. There were not many options. He reckoned one was her brother, Frank. The Feds would probably have his place staked out but her brother might still be able to help her find a safe hiding place.

Anyway, he figured he had a foolproof way of finding Kate Moran no matter where she hid. He felt for the bulges in his pockets where he still had the Glock pistol, the syringe and the spare vials. He was ready to rock and roll again. He walked over to the waiting cabs. The driver at the head of the queue was a Pakistani, a handsome man with a gold tooth. The Disciple climbed into the cab and the driver asked, 'Sir, where you want to go?'

'Just drive towards DC. I'll decide on the way.'

133

T he park was a short walk from the FBI field office on
Judiciary Square. Frank Moran sat down on the bench,
took his hands from the pockets of his dark blue windcheater
and blew on his fingers to keep out the cold. He looked left and
right and adjusted his pair of five-dollar sunglasses. Not that there
was much need for the glasses, the sun struggling behind bubbling
black clouds in the distance that told him a storm was on the
way.

He saw Diaz skating towards him from the right side of the
street. He wore black Speedos and a thick black sweater, his
athletic figure like a ballet dancer's as he expertly negotiated the
pavement walkers. He came to a halt beside Moran and grinned.
'Hey, Frank, how you doing, buddy?'

'Getting by, Armando. Trying to keep the demons from kicking
down my door.'

Diaz wore a slim pair of Ray-Bans. He eased himself on to
the bench and slapped Moran's palm in greeting. 'That mean
you're staying off firewater?'

'Trying to. I was watching you move. You keep skating like
that and you're going to saw your balls off, you know that?'

Diaz grinned. 'You reckon?'

'For sure, man.'

'I couldn't speak on the phone when you rang. I thought it
better we talk in private.'

Moran blew on his hands again. 'No prob.'

'You said you were looking for Kate,' Diaz offered.

Moran nodded. 'She left a message or two on my phone and I've been trying to get in touch with her but she isn't answering her calls. I thought you might know where she is. And I need a favour, Armando. I know I'm playing on the fact that we've worked a lot of investigations together and been friends a long time, but I was wondering what the latest is on the copycat case.'

Diaz frowned. 'Why? You're out of the game.'

'Let's just say I've got a professional interest. So what about Kate? I've been trying hard to find her.'

Diaz's face tightened. 'So's half the Bureau.'

Frank frowned. 'What do you mean?'

'They're looking for her.'

'I don't get it,' Moran answered.

Diaz removed his shades. His eyes looked serious. 'You know I like Kate, Frank. She's up there with the best in this business. But the way I heard it your sister's stepped into some grade-A shit.'

Moran said, 'What exactly are you talking about, man?'

Diaz sighed and slipped his shades back on. 'She didn't tell you? Then maybe I better bring you up to speed.'

134

Gretchen Woods, Virginia

I showered and dressed in the clothes belonging to Josh's ex: black Levis and a dark blue wool roll-neck sweater. Carla and I were the same size. As I finished tying back my hair Josh rapped on the door, poked his head round and offered me a wry smile.

'Am I allowed to ask what you're thinking?' I said.

'Am I allowed to say that those clothes look better on you than they ever did on Carla?'

'Thanks for the compliment, but you're probably lying.'

Josh's smile broadened as he came into the room. 'It's the truth. Dark colours for a graveyard visit. I thought we'd keep it respectful.'

'You always this smart-assed?'

'I try.'

I saw that he'd changed into a black roll-neck sweater, dark blue jeans and scuffed leather work boots. He looked pretty good in dark clothes – they emphasised his figure.

'How are we doing?' Josh asked.

'I feel nervous.'

'I guess the thought of exhuming Gamal's corpse is enough to jangle anyone's nerves.'

'You want to take a bet as to whether it's there or not?' I asked.

Josh raised an eyebrow. 'I'm not usually the gambling kind, but one thing I'd put money on is that Stone's got his watchers out by now.' He crossed to the curtain and looked tempted to crack it open to peer out, but he didn't.

I suddenly felt guilty again for putting him in harm's way. 'Josh, I don't like the idea of you taking more risks to help me.'

'Neither do I.' He smiled, his expression resolute. 'But I told you, the deal's done, so relax.'

I got the impression that arguing with him would be pointless. 'How's Neal?'

'I'm just going to check. You can come with me, if you like.'

We crossed to the bedroom where Neal lay sleeping. He wore his pyjamas and clutched a green stuffed monkey. His hair was damp and tousled, and one leg lay half out of the bed. Josh moved it under the covers and kissed his son's cheek. 'Before this little guy was born I remember people were always giving me that line – you know the one, about how you give your children the gift of life? But what they never said was that it works the other way around, too. They give *you* life, if you get my meaning.'

I heard the emotion in his voice and I felt another powerful wave of guilt. 'I can't let you do this, Josh. I can't let you risk everything that's important in your life. Neal's security, your career . . .'

'Are you still looking for that argument?'

'No, I'm not, but please listen to me—'

Josh sighed. 'Kate, it boils down to simple belief. I *believe* you're innocent and couldn't have harmed the Fleists or David and Megan, no matter what Stone says. I want to help you prove it.'

I felt so touched that I leaned over to kiss his cheek. 'Thanks for the vote of confidence. It means such a lot.'

Josh put up a hand to his face where I'd kissed him. 'Hey, thanks. But it's going to cost you more than just a kiss when this is all over and if we come out the other side in one piece.'

'Like what?'

'A weekend away together, some serious bedroom antics, and that's just for starters.'

'Are you always this tough a negotiator?'

He winked. 'Only with those I care about.'

'It's a deal,' I promised.

Josh headed towards the door. 'I better let you finish dressing, then we'll head downstairs. Marcie's going to be here any minute and if we want to get out of this house in one piece we better have our escape plan ready.'

Minutes later I followed Josh down to the kitchen, where he'd left two hefty garden shovels and a pickaxe by the back door. He handed me a couple of pairs of old gardening gloves which he plucked from the table, along with a powerful torch and a battery-operated power drill. 'Hang on to these and I'll take care of the digging tools. I think I've got everything we'll want.'

I touched the power drill, then the pickaxe. 'What did you ever need such a lethal-looking axe for?'

Josh said, straight faced, 'To tell the truth, there was a time during my divorce proceedings when murdering Carla seriously crossed my mind. So I bought the axe.'

I looked at him in mock disbelief. 'No kidding?'

He grinned as he dragged on a worn navy duffel coat he retrieved from the back of a kitchen chair. 'It was on special at Wal-Mart. One of those things you buy on green-fingered impulse and you never get to use. But hey, it's turned out I finally found a use for it.' Josh's face clouded. 'By the way, while you were finishing dressing I went into my bedroom in the dark and took a peek out through the curtains.'

My heart quickened. 'Did you see anything?'

'There's a cable TV repair van parked down the street that I never saw around here before. Seems pretty dumb if Stone has used *that* old ploy, but I wouldn't put it past him if he's desperate. And there are two private cars that I didn't recognise parked about fifty yards away. Might be one of my neighbours having visitors over, but then again it might not. But don't fret, I've got a strategy for getting us out of Dodge City.'

Before I could ask what it was the front doorbell rang and my heart jumped.

Josh said, 'That'll be Marcie.' He took a dark windcheater and scarf from a hook on the back of the kitchen door and handed them to me.

'Better put these on, it's going to be cold out there. Let me just go talk with Marcie before we make our exit.'

'What'll you tell her we're up to?'

'Nothing. The less she knows the better.'

I examined the power drill. 'By the way, what's this for?'

'Unscrewing the coffin lid.'

135

I waited in the kitchen while Josh left to answer the front door. I heard him talking with Marcie as he led her into the living room, and a little later I could hear their voices raised a touch, but not enough to suggest they were having an argument. A few minutes later Josh came into the kitchen with his sister.

'You look good in those jeans,' Marcie said to me. 'Wish I could squeeze myself into a smaller size. But maybe after all this worry's over and I've lost some weight, I will.' She turned to her brother and said with a puzzled frown, 'Why won't you tell me what you two are planning?'

'Marcie, no disrespect, but you're better off not knowing,' Josh told her.

Marcie sounded disappointed. 'OK, if that's the way you want it.'

'It's for the best. How's the family?'

'I called Dean and the kids at their grandmother's and they're all fine. I think Dean's glad to have a few days away from me bitching at him for getting under my feet.' Marcie took a look at the tools her brother had assembled and the leather work gloves in my hand. 'Looks to me like you two are about to do some gardening. Maybe when you're done you can tidy my back yard?'

What could I tell her? *No, we're going to exhume a body.* 'I'm sorry we can't tell you, Marcie. But Josh is right, the less you know the better.'

She shrugged. 'That's OK.'

'It's nothing dangerous,' Josh lied with a smile. 'Just a little gardening work, like you say.'

There was an accusing tone in Marcie's voice as she addressed her brother. 'Then how come all the subterfuge? You just better be careful tonight, that's all I'm saying. I want you back here in one piece for Neal's sake. You're all that boy's got.'

Marcie's statement rekindled my guilt but Josh suddenly took hold of my arm. 'OK, let's take the back way. Marcie, you better make yourself scarce and head upstairs. You know what to do – any problems, you call me on my cell.'

'Be good, and be careful.' She went out and seconds later I heard her climb the stairs.

Josh looked at me. 'Ready?'

'Josh, Marcie was right—'

Before I could speak another word he led me determinedly towards the back door. 'Here's how it's going to pan out. You follow me and don't speak unless you absolutely have to, OK?' He flicked off the lights and the kitchen was plunged into darkness. Then he opened the back door and ushered me out into the pitch black.

136

I followed Josh along a path to the end of the garden. The gusting wind made it feel like there was a storm brewing, the face of the moon appearing erratically behind masses of black rain clouds. We came to the tree house and I saw Josh's neighbour's property beyond the wall: two-storey, a light on behind closed curtains in an upstairs bedroom. Josh whispered, 'That's the Calvins' place, they live alone. Marcie's house is right across the street from there. All we've got to do is get over this wall, get out the side gate and over to Marcie's car.'

'You're sure there's not a catch?'

'Did I mention that the Calvins' have got a German shepherd with terrific hearing?'

'*Jesus Christ*, Josh . . .'

Josh grinned as he climbed up on the wall and pulled me up to join him. 'Don't worry, Rufus is almost one of the family. Besides, I've got this to keep him busy.' He took a clump of newspaper from his jacket pocket and I smelled fresh meat. 'Tomorrow night's prime rib dinner. See the things I do for you? Even starve myself.'

'I'm honoured.' I guessed the German shepherd smelled the meat too because I heard a single bark and then the sound of paws bounding across the lawn. A huge black-and-tan dog appeared out of the darkness.

'Hey there, Rufus, here you go, boy.' Josh tossed a slab of meat on the lawn and the dog began to devour it ferociously. 'Follow me over.'

'You're sure we're safe?'

'That dog doesn't know it but he's really a pussycat.'

As if to prove it, Josh jumped down into the garden. The dog paid him no attention and Josh held out his hand for me. I took it, jumped and landed beside the dog, who suddenly looked up and growled, as if uncertain about the stranger next to him. Josh took out another chunk of meat. 'Here, boy.' He threw the meat across the lawn and the dog raced after it, then Josh took my arm and guided me towards the side gate. He slipped open the catch, we passed through and he slid the catch shut again. I saw a road ahead, neat suburban houses either side, street lamps on.

'Wait here,' Josh said, and left me with my back to the gable wall as he went to peer out into the street. He came back a few moments later. 'Looks all clear. We'll take Marcie's husband's car this time.'

I followed him for a hundred yards to a bay-windowed house with a blue Volvo station wagon parked outside. The wind slashed at our faces as Josh took out a set of keys, unlocked the doors, slipped into the driver's seat and opened the front passenger door. I jumped in as he slipped the key into the ignition. At that precise second Josh's phone rang. He checked the number on the screen. 'It's Stone. Wonder what he wants?'

'You going to answer it?'

Josh hit the mute key. 'Like hell. Let him sweat.'

It was freezing cold and overhead tar-black clouds looked heavily pregnant with rain. The wind was getting worse, strong gusts buffeting the car. 'Looks as if we're in for a lousy night.'

Right on cue, the heavens opened and a sleety downpour hammered on the Volvo's roof. 'Perfect weather for a graveyard visit,' I said.

'You're telling me.' Josh started the car, flicked on the wipers and pulled out from the kerb.

The two FBI agents were enjoying a thermos of hot coffee. Each nursed a mug as they sat in the dark green Ford Taurus. They saw the woman enter Cooper's house down the street. One of the agents said, 'It looks like his sister's arrived. What you want to do?'

His colleague checked his watch. 'Give it a little while. See if Cooper leaves for work.'

Fifteen minutes later the rain was drumming on the Ford's roof but no one had appeared from the house. The agent pulled out his cell phone and punched a number. It answered on the second ring. 'Stone here.'

'It's Jackson. Cooper's sister came back a quarter of an hour ago, but Cooper still hasn't shown his mug or made a move to leave.'

Stone considered. 'Let me try him first on his phone. See if he's coming in.'

After a few minutes' silence Stone said, 'I just got his voice-mail. He's not answering.'

'What you think, Vance?'

'Is his car still parked in the garage?'

'Must be. No one drove out of there since we arrived.'

'Did his sister walk or drive?'

'Walk. And I wouldn't mind, but the sleet is coming down in buckets here, man. I can't put my finger on it but I've got a feeling about the situation. You want us to knock on the door and talk with the sister?'

A moment passed, and then Stone said, 'No, wait for me. I'm on my way.'

137

I kept checking the side mirror but it didn't look like we were being followed. Now that we were about to dig up Gamal's coffin I was jittery as hell, but Josh looked in control. 'You mind me asking how you manage to stay so calm and collected?' I said.

Josh patted his fist against his chest. 'Hey, you're easily fooled. It might look that way but inside I'm a bundle of nerves.'

'Don't go ruining it on me. I was counting on some premium leadership here.' I studied Josh as he drove and hoped my next question didn't sound too intrusive. 'Tell me about Carla.'

'What about her?' Josh flicked a look at me as he asked the question, then quickly diverted his attention back to the rain-slicked road.

'Did you really love her a lot?'

'Let's just say that you get to learn the hard way what love really is.'

'And what is it?' I asked.

Josh flicked the wipers on to double speed. 'Apart from what it should be about – joy, mutual support, companionship – it's about endless forgiveness. Being prepared to start each day together afresh, free of all the old hurts and arguments. But Carla wasn't that type. She'd hang on to an argument like a terrier hanging on to a dead rat. Me, I wanted any disagreements we had ironed out and settled the same day, but Carla was happy to let them run for months. It's Neal I feel sorry for because at times he misses her like hell. I guess sometimes I feel sorry for Carla that she's missed out on raising Neal. But that was her choice.'

Josh's cell phone buzzed. He checked the screen but didn't answer the call. 'It's Stone. What's the bet he'll leave a message?'

Sure enough, about a minute later the phone beeped and Josh called to check the message.

'What did Stone say?' I asked.

He smiled. 'Verbatim? "Where the fuck are you, Cooper? Call me immediately. It's urgent." How'd you like that? Cuss words from your superior.'

I felt suspicious. 'I'd take a guess from his tone that he's already on to us.'

'Relax, I would have heard from Marcie,' Josh answered.

'Would she talk if Stone called again to your home and questioned her?'

Josh laughed. 'It'd take a lot more than Stone to frighten Marcie. She's got a hide as tough as a jockey's ass. So where the hell's the graveyard?'

Gamal had been buried at Sunset Memorial Park in Chesterfield County, Virginia, a private non-denominational cemetery off Interstate 95. I checked my map. 'Take the next right and keep going straight. We should see it.'

Josh hung a right and we came to a small town with a few sparse stores, a Cracker Barrel restaurant and a couple of chain motels. By now the rain was coming down heavily and thunder rumbled, lightning flashes crackling in the icy black clouds overhead. 'The graveyard should be on the left,' I said.

'See it,' Josh replied as we drove up a wide street.

I saw it too. The cemetery was ahead on the left. *Oh hell.* I saw that right across the street was the local sheriff's office – a flat wooden beige-painted building – and the lights were on and blazing. Whatever shred of confidence I had disappeared.

Josh said, 'We're not exactly in luck. Looks like the dearly departed are well protected. A cop shop right across the road makes things even more risky.'

I studied the cemetery. A granite block wall surrounded the graveyard, topped by a wrought-iron fence. Behind the walls I glimpsed the dark outlines of jagged headstones and simple stone

461

crosses rearing up against the thunder-flash night sky. I was still determined to open Gamal's grave.

What will we find here? Are we about to come face to face with the rotting corpse of Constantine Gamal, or an empty coffin?

I felt apprehensive because either prospect freaked me out. And to make matters worse I saw shadows moving behind the wooden blinds in the sheriff's office. *What if we're caught in the act?*

'You seem nervous,' Josh observed.

'I am. Damned nervous,' I answered.

'And a little tetchy, maybe?'

My fear was so livid I had to stop myself from digging my nails into Josh's arm. 'I'm sorry, I'm just on edge wondering what we might find.'

'We'll soon see, so long as the local cops keep their heads indoors.' Josh cruised on past the cemetery until we saw a desolate track shaded by some trees. He turned on to the track, drove for thirty yards, pulled in and jerked on the handbrake. The sleety rain was slapping against the car. 'This is about as close as we can get. Just as well we brought the rain gear. We'll have to walk back and climb over the cemetery wall.'

I figured we were going to get completely drenched the moment we stepped out, but that was the least of my worries.

Josh opened his door and said, 'Don't use the torch unless you really have to, or the cops might see it from across the street. I'll fetch the things from the trunk and then let's go clear up this mystery.'

138

Icy sleet fell on us as we jumped out of the car and threw on our rain slicks. I grabbed the electric torch, power drill, gloves and one of the shovels, while Josh got the rest of the things and hefted them over his back in the canvas bag.

We moved towards the cemetery. Josh climbed up on to the railing and held out his hand to me. He pulled me up and we both climbed over and stepped down on to a gravel path. The freezing sleet slashed our faces. Josh said, 'Remember those really scary movies you saw as a kid?'

'What about them?'

'I've got a feeling that this is going to be worse than all of them put together.'

'You sure know how to cheer a girl up.'

'Force of habit.' Josh wiped his wet face as I followed him along the path and deeper in among the graves. 'I don't know about you, but I've never opened a grave in my life.'

'Me neither,' I said.

'So where's the grave site?'

We had moved towards the rear of the cemetery, the distant wash from street lighting just enough to see by, and I figured we were almost there. 'It's in the north-east corner of the cemetery, with just a wooden marker that ought to have some numbers. The location hasn't been made public but Lou was informed by the Department of Corrections.'

I kept the torch in front of me and flicked it on every now and then when I needed to. I kept my back to the cemetery wall, a hundred yards away. I was hoping the police wouldn't see the torchlight. I led the way past a clutch of fresh gravestones and finally saw a wooden marker plaque with the simple inscription: No. 1134562.

It was Constantine Gamal's prison number, denoting his grave. Right next to it was another, freshly dug, ready to receive another coffin. Earth was piled in a mound next to Gamal's marker and the open grave was covered by a green tarpaulin that sagged in the middle with a pool of icy sleet water. My stomach turned at the thought of what we were about to do.

Josh slipped on a pair of leather gloves and kicked the soil with his heel. 'It looks like the ground's soft enough so maybe we won't need the pick. But we better get started or we'll be here all night. And seeing as this is your idea, you want to do the honours and turn the first sod?'

'Kind of you, partner.'

Josh smiled with false bravado. 'Never say I don't know how to treat a lady.'

I stabbed the spade into the soggy ground, kicked my foot down and tilted the blade. The earth was soft and lifted easily and I tossed the first sod on to the grass. Then Josh joined in with his spade and we got to work eagerly, digging as fast as we could.

139

The two agents saw the black Chrysler pull up in front of their car. The headlights were extinguished, and Stone got out and ran towards them through the teeming rain, followed by Norton. The two men climbed into the back of the Ford and shook water from their coats, drenched after the short dash. 'What the fuck's been happening?' Stone demanded.

One of the agents said, 'Nothing's changed. The sister's still in there but Cooper hasn't come out, least not as far as we can see. Did you try him again on his cell?'

Stone gritted his teeth. 'Yeah, I even left him a text message, but the asshole never replied.'

'What else has been happening your end?'

Stone wiped rain from his face. 'We've got Frank Moran's place covered, but his sister hasn't showed up. Something else occurred to me – she suggested to Lou that Gamal's grave ought to be exhumed. You credit that? I figure she's lost her marbles. But I'm going to have the cemetery staked out in case there's a remote chance Moran shows up.'

'Are we just going to sit here and get pissed on?' the second agent finally asked.

Stone stared up at the house. 'No, I reckon it's about time we heard what the sister's got to say for herself.'

He climbed out into the downpour and darted up the path, followed by Gus Norton and the two agents. He rang the front doorbell and a few seconds later the porch light came on. Stone guessed Cooper's sister was studying her visitors through the security peephole, and he punched the bell again.

'Yes, who's there?' a woman's voice finally demanded.

Stone held his ID up to the peephole. 'I'm Special Agent Stone, ma'am, a colleague of your brother's. You mind me asking who I'm talking to?'

A pause. 'I'm Marcie, Josh's sister.'

'I'd like to speak with him, ma'am. It's really important.'

'Josh isn't here. He went to work about half an hour ago.'

Stone raised his eyes at the two agents and said to the woman, 'Is that so? Then I need to talk to you about that, ma'am.'

'I'm sorry but Josh's son is ill in bed and I can't leave him. You'll have to phone Josh—'

Stone said brusquely, 'Ma'am, I've already tried that. Now either you open this frigging door or we kick the damned thing down. You've got exactly five seconds to make the choice, so what'll it be?'

A blunt silence greeted Stone, except for the noise of the rain hitting the porch roof. Finally the front door was opened just enough for an auburn-haired woman to show her face, her expression angry as she blocked the way. 'Agent Stone, I don't know what this is about, but I do know my rights. You'll need a search warrant to come in here. So unless you've got one, I'd suggest you folks leave before I call the police.'

'I told you, I need to speak with your brother.' Stone was steadfast.

'And I told you, Josh left for work—'

Stone pushed the door in. 'Wherever the hell he left for, it wasn't work, lady. I think you and me need to do some talking.'

140

y bones ached from digging so I rested on my shovel. It was back-breaking work but we had excavated about four feet of earth and piled the clay on to the mound beside the open grave next to Gamal's. 'Who the hell in their right mind would want to be a gravedigger?' I remarked.

Josh stopped to catch his breath and wipe his brow with his free hand. 'These days they don't break their backs, they use those mini-diggers.'

I used my sweater sleeve to wipe rain from my face. 'Remind me to hire a mini-digger next time.'

'You mean there's going to be a next time?' Josh smiled but it didn't relieve the grim mood, and to make things worse the freezing sleet showed no sign of easing. Lightning sizzled in the black rumbling clouds and icy water was starting to fill the grave. We went back to digging and five minutes later we were down about five feet. The soil was mushy and the mound of earth we'd dug was beginning to tumble into the open grave next to us.

The sleet bit into our faces and I had to stop every now and then to wipe my eyes but Josh kept going until his shovel scraped against something hard. 'I think we've hit the coffin lid,' he announced.

We moved away some more earth, then I directed the torch and saw the pale varnished lid of a cheap wooden casket. *What will we find inside?*

Josh scraped the soil off the lid but the water level was rising fast and the open hole was turning into a muddy swamp. 'Instead of trying to lift out the coffin we can just remove the lid. There're usually some wing nuts holding it in place but I brought the power drill in case they used extra screws.'

'This was my idea, Josh. I'll do it.'

'You ever use a power drill before?'

'Once, when I had to fix some bathroom shelves,' I said.

'I'm impressed, but seeing as I'm down here I may as well do the honours.'

I aimed the torch as Josh started to unscrew the brass wing nuts on the coffin lid. After a while he stood up. 'I think I've got them all, so there's no need for the drill. The lid ought to come off easily enough. You ready for this?'

My heart fluttered so much my chest hurt. 'Are you kidding? I'll *never* be ready for this.'

'Here goes.' Josh kicked two footholds in the sides of the grave, about half a metre above the coffin. He dug his feet into the holds and firmed his balance, then he leaned down and tried to prise the lid with the edge of his spade. The wood didn't budge at first but after a couple more tries the lid creaked open.

'Got it.' Josh lifted the open lid with his gloved hand and a vile stench rose up.

'*Hell . . .* that's pretty bad.'

The stink of rotting flesh hit my nostrils. It smelled like noxious gas. I felt shocked. All I could think was: *Gamal's body is in the coffin, after all.*

I covered my mouth and flashed the torch just as Josh yanked the lid fully off, but I was so apprehensive I couldn't look inside.

Josh said, '*Jeez!* Kate, point the torch in the coffin.'

I forced myself to aim the torch and saw a rotting corpse that didn't look human. It was some kind of animal with hoofs, its flesh covered in filthy wool. The creature's head sported a pair of curled horns. I recoiled in shock.

'*What . . . what in God's name is that?*'

'A ram,' Josh answered. 'It's throat has been cut.'

I saw that the animal's neck had been slashed, and congealed blood had stained its wool a dirty crimson. I felt so confused that

I couldn't even speak, and then Josh gripped my arm. Suddenly we both heard a car engine and saw a pair of headlights sweep up the road towards the graveyard.

141

'So where the hell's your brother?' Stone paced the kitchen and then halted and fixed Cooper's sister with a piercing stare. 'I'm asking you a question, lady, and I'd advise you to answer. Cooper told me his son was ill and you were coming to look after the boy. After that, he was supposed to go on duty tonight. But so far he hasn't turned up.'

Marcie regarded Stone with contempt. 'You have no damned right to barge into Josh's home like this . . .'

'I've got every right. I'm in charge of an important murder case. Your brother's supposed to be working on it too, except now it turns out that he's gone AWOL in suspicious circumstances.'

'*What* suspicious circumstances?'

'My men were watching this house. Cooper never left. Or if he did, he didn't go out the front door, which means he must have sneaked out the back way. Now why would he do that? And he's not upstairs with his son, because we've already checked. He's not anywhere in the damned house. So where the frig is he?'

Marcie was unyielding. 'Agent Stone, has anyone ever told you that you've got a dirty mouth?'

Stone stared aggressively into the woman's face. 'Listen, lady, as far as I'm concerned Cooper's guilty of dereliction of duty. And that's a serious charge, one he could be dismissed for. So just answer the frigging question.'

'Or else what? You're going to slap me around?' Marcie said defiantly.

'No, but I'll have you arrested for obstruction,' Stone answered.

Gus Norton came into the room. 'I found these lying on a chair in one of the bedrooms.' He held up a pair of women's slacks and a grey top.

Stone studied the clothes and cracked a smile. 'Well, well, Marcie. What have we got here? You know who these belong to?'

'Josh's ex-wife.'

'Try telling the truth this time.'

'I don't know what you're—'

Gus Norton said, 'I recognise these clothes. They belong to Kate Moran. You know her, don't you?'

Marcie blushed. 'No, I—'

Stone said aggressively, 'Don't bullshit us, lady. These clothes tell me you're aiding and abetting a wanted felon, namely Kate Moran. So you better tell me what the hell you know or I'll arrest you right this minute on a bunch of charges. Then who's going to look after your brother's kid?'

Marcie bit her lower lip. A second later the door into the garage opened and one of the two agents from the car came in, his face beaming. 'You'll never guess what we just found.'

'Surprise me,' said Stone flatly.

'A blue Landcruiser.'

142

Sunset Memorial Park

I saw the car's headlights halt outside the cemetery gates.

'Stash the tools,' I told Josh as he climbed up to join me and we hunkered down. We dumped all the tools in the open grave next to us, all except for the torch. I kept it switched off as Josh and I crawled through filthy mud and squatted behind a pair of gravestones.

We saw the figure of a man step out of a dark-coloured SUV and enter through the cemetery gates. His parka hood was up and he shone a powerful torch around the head-stones. 'He could be a security guard doing his rounds,' Josh whispered.

I wasn't convinced. 'On a night like this?'

'Maybe he saw our torchlight and decided to investigate.'

'*Shit.*'

The man moved cautiously between the stones, flashing his own torch as he headed in our direction. Another few minutes and he'd be on top of us.

Josh whispered, 'I'm going to climb back down into Gamal's grave. Better come with me. If we pull the tarp over us we'll have cover.'

'Forget it, I'm not getting back down. Digging it was bad enough.' I shivered, remembering the rotting animal carcass. 'I've got the creeps.'

'It's the only place we've got to hide, Kate, for Christ sakes.'

I looked at Gamal's grave, water dripping down the open sides. I didn't have time to protest as Josh suddenly grabbed my hand, pulled me over to the grave's edge and ripped back the tarpaulin from the second grave site.

'Get in after me,' he urged, and slid himself into the muddy tomb. He planted his feet on the sides of the coffin, his chest above the grave's mouth as he held out his hand to me. I saw the intruder's torchlight moving closer with every second. But I still couldn't move. My body felt nailed to the spot.

I knew what we'd be lying on top of: the ram's maggot-riddled remains. I don't know what frightened me more at that minute, the torment of crawling into the grave or the final realisation that Gamal was still alive.

'*For Christ's sake, Kate, get in . . .*' Josh pleaded.

I forced myself to crawl over to the grave's edge, and Josh hauled me down into the hole. The rotting stench was nauseating. Josh yanked the tarpaulin over our heads and we were smothered in darkness. I could barely make out Josh's face as I lay on top of him. I felt his body grind against mine as he tried to find a comfortable position. My weight was probably crushing him. 'Am I hurting you?' I asked.

'Don't speak,' he whispered. The rain dripped down from a gap in the tarpaulin and coursed down our faces. My face nuzzled against Josh's neck and I could smell the musky scent of his soap, and was grateful – at least it partly masked the stench of the rotting animal beneath us. 'Not even a sound, Kate,' he whispered.

I felt something scamper over my left leg. *Was that a bug or a rat?* I recoiled just as I heard heavy footsteps sloshing through the wet mud. It sounded as if our visitor was moving right above us. Through a tiny gap in the tarpaulin I saw a flash of silver torchlight. It knifed into our hiding place and I instinctively looked away, and that's when I saw the ram's worm-infested head near Josh's shoulder. I felt like gagging but Josh clasped his hand over my mouth.

Seconds later the torchlight disappeared and we heard the man move away. We still didn't budge. It was another five minutes before we heard his car start up and drive off, then Josh said, 'Get up slowly.'

I clung to the sides of the grave and pushed myself up, then he clambered to his feet and yanked off the tarpaulin. 'You can't say it hasn't been a night to remember. Wait here while I go and make sure our friend's gone.'

'I'll go with you.'

'No, one is enough, I don't want us to be spotted.' Josh climbed out of the grave and disappeared between the tombstones, leaving me alone in the stench-filled hole. I could barely control my panic and wanted to clamber out. I was relieved when moments later Josh returned. 'It's OK, the coast's clear. Whoever it was, they've driven away.'

He offered me his hand and pulled me up out of the grave, and I saw a pair of red tail-lights disappear down the road. When I stared into what should have been Gamal's tomb, all the pent-up horror and disgust hit me again and I recoiled. Josh put his hand on my back. 'Take it easy, it's over now. You feeling any better?'

I looked at the grave. 'No. To be honest, now that I know Gamal is still alive it scares the living hell out of me. It's likely he's our killer.'

Josh knelt to gather the tools. 'Hey, we don't know that for certain. Something's sure odd, but don't go jumping the gun, Kate. You can call me a doubting Thomas but I still find it hard to believe he duped the executioner.'

'But it all makes sense.'

'Kate, be reasonable, you're too upset for anything to make sense right now.'

Maybe Josh is right. I looked down at the dead ram. 'We ought to cover up the grave before anyone else shows up.'

'You don't want to fill it in?'

'What's the point? I'll want our people to see what we found. Maybe then they'll believe me. Let's just use the tarpaulin, and you can get back into work, Josh, or else Stone's going to wonder where you've disappeared to. He's probably suspicious as it is.'

'What about you?'

'I'm going to see Frank and tell him what we found.'

'OK, but let's not lose our heads. We stick to our plans for now and see where things lead.' Josh climbed down into the grave and replaced the coffin lid before we laid the tarpaulin over the hole. 'You can take the car after I drive to the office.'

'Josh, you've done enough already . . .' I protested.

He shook his head. 'You want to take a bus, go ahead, but the car's yours. After tonight you've convinced me that something very weird's going down.'

I knew that we were still facing an uphill battle despite the evidence we'd found. 'How do we persuade Stone?'

Josh grabbed a shovel and shook his head. 'Hey, if this doesn't give him second thoughts, I don't know what the hell will.'

143

Washington, DC

Fifty minutes later we pulled up outside our field office on Judiciary Square and Josh said to me as he opened his door, 'Sure you won't consider trying to convince Stone in person?'

I shook my head. 'I wouldn't count on him capitulating so easily, but I wish you luck.'

Josh leaned across and kissed my cheek before he stepped out into the rain. 'I'll do my best. You keep in touch, you hear?'

'Promise.' I waited until he had reached the front entrance and then I started the car and drove. I was a hundred yards along the road when I remembered to check my cell phone for messages. I pulled in at the kerb, slipped in the SIM card and battery again and switched on. After a couple of minutes the phone beeped a bunch of times. I counted eight voicemail messages and I punched in the retrieval number.

Three of the calls were from Paul's cell phone but he hadn't left any messages, just hung up. The other five calls were from Frank, made over the last four hours, telling me to call him urgently, and with each couple of messages his voice seemed to become more anxious. He'd left the last message twenty minutes ago.

I flicked off the phone, slipped out the SIM card and battery, then I started the car and drove south for a dozen blocks and pulled in next to a gas station overlooking the Potomac. I stepped out, ran under the rain canopy of a payphone and called Frank's cell phone. He answered on the second ring. 'Moran.'

'Frank, it's me.'

His voice sounded urgent. '*Kate?* I've been trying to call your cell phone for hours. Where the goddamned hell are you?'

'I just got the messages. Listen to me, Frank . . .'

'No, you listen to me. I spoke to Diaz. He tells me Lou Raines was shot to death. He also says that Stone thinks you did it and he's gunning for you and he's even got evidence.'

'Lou's death wasn't my doing . . .'

Frank said reassuringly, 'Sis, I wouldn't ever think otherwise. But how about you tell me what in the name of sweet loving Jesus is happening here?'

'There's been a pretty sensational development. I can't talk over the phone and we'll need to meet somewhere safe. I think Stone might figure I'll try to contact you and have you watched or your phone tapped.'

Frank fell silent for a moment. 'Where were you figuring we'd meet?'

'Remember the place you liked to go for lunch?' I guessed he knew where I meant: a Cajun restaurant called Falgo's, off Constitution Avenue.

Frank said, 'Fine. Say about an hour.'

That gave me time to make an important phone call to Brogan Lacy. 'Frank, it's important that if you think you're being tailed you abort and leave me a message on my cell. I'll contact you again.'

'Whatever you say. By the way, you're not the only one with sensational news.'

I could hear excitement in Frank's voice. 'What do you mean?'

'That's why I've been calling. I've got something, Kate. Something so fucking weird that it's probably going to blow your mind.'

144

I drove to Falgo's, parked the Volvo in a lot across the street and walked over to the restaurant. With its yellow table lamps and tables full of diners it looked cosy and warm beyond the window. The sleet had stopped but it was still bitterly cold on the street.

For a moment I was tempted to step inside and order some fresh coffee to keep me warm, but I walked back and sat in the Volvo for another fifteen minutes. By then the rendezvous time had come and gone by five minutes, and my heart was sinking lower by the second. I was dreading the possibility that Frank had been followed and he'd decided to abort our meeting.

Ten minutes later and there was still no sign of him. I felt hopeless as I pulled out my cell phone and reinserted the SIM card and battery. Sure enough, a couple of seconds later a message envelope flashed on screen. I checked: it was voicemail from Frank.

'Kate, I hope you get this. I'm pretty sure I'm being tailed so we'll have to change our meet time. Call me.'

The call had been sent nine minutes ago. My heart raced as I called Frank's number. He answered on the first ring and sounded panicked. 'Are you near our rendezvous?' he asked.

'I'm sitting right across the street in a car,' I told him.

'Stay where you are. I may be a little while but don't move. Cut your phone off immediately, Kate. I don't want them getting a trace. Check for another message in ten minutes.'

Damn, nothing's going right. I removed the SIM card and battery. After ten more nail-biting minutes I was getting desperate enough to slip the card in again, ready to check for any messages, when suddenly I heard tyres screech and Frank's blue Camarro came speeding round the corner to my left. His exhaust left a plume of smoke in the freezing air as he drove past Falgo's. At the last second he swung a sharp right into the car park and turned off his headlights as he headed straight towards me.

I was convinced he was going to crash into the Volvo and I jumped out, but suddenly Frank nudged the Camarro into a shadowed parking spot between two cars. He climbed out, locked the door and ran towards me. 'I'm being followed,' he shouted as he threw himself into the Volvo. 'Get back in the car and keep your head down.'

I jumped in and ducked low just as a dark blue sedan with its headlights blazing screeched round the corner. The driver righted the vehicle then sped on for fifty yards before slowing. I noticed there were two men inside. They scanned the street before the sedan picked up speed and accelerated away. I turned to Frank and saw that his face was prickled with sweat. 'The bastards have been following me since I left the house. Stone must be pretty desperate to get a bead on your ass.'

'It looks like it.'

'Give me a few secs. I left some things in my car.'

I waited as Frank hopped out of the passenger side and dashed back to the Camarro. He removed what looked like a gym bag and a thick manila folder, then he locked the car and raced back to join me. 'You were right about the execution being videoed. It was authorised by the Richmond Medical Examiner's office for research purposes. Tate didn't know by whom. But it had to be the Chief Medical Examiner or one of his senior medical assistants.'

I frowned. 'Are you suggesting it might have been Brogan Lacy?'

'I'm suggesting nothing, but maybe you should ask her.'

'Why would she do that?'

'There you've got me. You intend seeing her?'

I nodded. 'Tonight at eight. I called her an hour ago and told her I wanted to meet to discuss Gamal's autopsy, and that it was urgent. She said she was working late at the examiner's office and agreed to see me. We better head there.'

'OK, but I've been working on a few ideas of my own,' Frank said.

'What do you mean?'

'All in good time. You first,' Frank said, stuffing the folder inside his jacket and dumping the holdall on the back seat.

'You're not going to believe me, Frank.' I started the Volvo and swung left to exit the parking lot.

Frank said grimly, 'Nor you me, but give it a shot.'

The sleet had stopped as the rented green Nissan sedan rounded the corner. The driver pulled into the kerb and left the engine running as he peered out beyond the rain-streaked windscreen. He had followed the Camarro all the way from Frank Moran's house, keeping a safe distance behind, but now the Camarro had disappeared. He'd been too damned careful, keeping well back, and now he swore bitterly to himself as he scanned the street.

Not even a pair of red tail-lights in sight. *The damned thing's vanished.*

He noticed the restaurant with its neon FALGO'S sign flashing in the darkness, and the parking lot across the street. He scanned the dozen vehicles in the lot but caught no sign of the Camarro.

Hey, wait a minute . . .

From behind the passenger seat of a silver Volvo a man's head popped up, and then a woman's rose to join him. It was too dark to see who the couple were, but next thing he saw the man step out of the Volvo and cross over to another car – what looked like a dark-coloured Camarro parked in the shadows. The Disciple at once recognised Moran's brother and grinned in triumph as he saw him take something from the Camarro then race back to the Volvo, before it started up and drove out of the lot, turning right towards the Potomac.

The Disciple gently revved the Nissan's engine, flicked off his headlamps and followed the Volvo.

145

For the next couple of miles I spilled my heart out – told Frank everything from the moment I landed in Paris to the murders in Istanbul and the graveyard discovery with Josh.

It seemed an effort for Frank to take it all in. 'You're *certain* you two opened the right grave?'

'As certain as I can be.'

'*Jesus*, that's fucking mind-bending.'

'I'd stake my life Gamal's still alive.' I'd hardly slept in the last two days, exhaustion was creeping in, and I felt a blinding band of tension around my skull. I massaged my forehead as I drove.

'Hey, you seem like you've been through the wars,' Frank said as I headed south on the Eisenhower Freeway.

'That about sums it up. What did you find out that's so important?'

Frank shook his head as if he were still in shock. 'To tell the truth, I *thought* I had pretty sensational news but I think I've been trumped.'

'Tell me.'

Frank said, 'Two things. First Clay. I called to see him at his home. I got a definite feeling he's hiding something. He got overly touchy after I asked him if a prisoner could escape execution with inside help. The next thing I knew he'd convinced himself I was another journalist trying to drop him in the shit. Or maybe it was all just an act to get rid of me. Then he told me to leave his property or he'd set his dogs on me. You credit that?'

'It doesn't sound like the Lucius Clay I met. What's he trying to hide?'

Frank pursed his lips. 'That's the big question. Second, I

headed over to Bellevue. I thought it might be worth having a look at Gamal's work records if I could get my hands on them. You know, maybe some notes in the files that might give us some pointers. I figured, what if there was a psycho at Bellevue that Gamal knew or treated who decided to emulate his killings?'

'The Bureau had to subpoena the hospital just to get file copies,' I told him.

'I know, but I went one better and got the originals, along with a whole bunch of his patient files and records that the Bureau wouldn't have got their hands on because of patient confidentiality.'

'How'd you manage *that*?'

'Charm and cunning.'

I glanced at the thick folder on Frank's lap. 'Are those the files?'

He nodded. 'I didn't get a chance to search through them all but I *did* find something incredible. And Kate, this is the part that's going to blow your mind.'

'What?'

'Brogan Lacy was once a patient of Constantine Gamal's.'

I was stunned by Frank's disclosure and pulled the car in off the highway. 'When?'

'Almost six years ago she suffered a breakdown right after her divorce. She spent a couple of months as a Bellevue patient and one of the psychiatrists who treated her was Gamal. It may mean nothing but it's sure kind of ironic, don't you think? Didn't David ever tell you about her treatment?'

'Not a word. But he probably wanted to respect her privacy.' I was startled by Frank's discovery and glanced at the holdall he'd thrown on to the back seat. 'What's in there?'

'The change of clothes you asked me to bring.'

I grabbed the bag from the back seat, unzipped it and took out a blue sweater, green Lycra pants and calf-length brown boots. All the clothes looked at least a size too big. 'Anyone ever tell you that you need to learn how to coordinate better?'

Frank grinned. 'Hey, you know I'm colour blind, it's the best I could do. They belonged to my buddy's ex.'

I pulled out on to the highway again. By a quarter before eight we had arrived at the Medical Examiner's office. I drove into a public parking lot across the street. It was almost empty, with only four other cars. 'You want me to go in with you?' Frank asked.

I began to change into the clothes. 'No, I'll do this alone. Company might complicate things. What's wrong? You look worried.'

Frank frowned. 'I'm thinking that the fact Brogan Lacy was once Gamal's patient somehow kind of muddies things. Do you think she might be mixed up in all of this?'

'I don't know what to think except that I can't imagine her having a motive for helping the man she believed murdered her daughter.'

'But Gamal claimed he didn't,' Frank reminded me.

Right at that moment I didn't feel sure about *anything*. Except that Brogan Lacy might help me answer some important questions. I pulled on the sweater Frank had brought. 'I need to talk with her. And I need more significant evidence before I can go see whoever I have to in the Bureau in order to get Stone off my back.'

'Gamal isn't in his grave, for Christ sakes, isn't that significant enough?'

Frank went on to explain Captain Tate's opinion as to how a condemned prisoner might survive execution. 'It seems to me we've got enough seeds of doubt to put a big question mark over Gamal's death.'

'I agree.' I told him what Yeta had said. 'But I want us to be certain. I want everything nailed down tight so that I've got overwhelming evidence.'

Frank looked towards the ME's building. 'OK, but if you have any doubts about Lacy just get the hell out of the ME's office immediately. And if you're not out in half an hour I'll call you, so you better keep your phone on. Don't fret about me, I've got enough reading material to keep me busy.' He grabbed the satchel from the back seat and flicked on the overhead light. 'There's still half the document folders to go through. I figure it's going to take me at least a few more hours, and you never know what else might turn up.'

I finished checking my clothes. 'Wish me luck.'

Frank put a hand firmly on my arm. 'Just go easy, OK? And watch out.'

'That's my intention.' I stepped out of the Volvo.

146

I walked up to the lobby of the Medical Examiner's office. I had expected to see a guard on duty inside but I saw no one. I slipped the battery and SIM card into my cell phone, powered up and punched in the number. It was answered on the first ring. 'Brogan Lacy.'

'It's Kate Moran, I'm outside,' I told her.

'I'll be right there,' Lacy answered.

I'd been on the line less than ten seconds and I figured there wouldn't have been enough time for Stone to track my location. Moments later I saw Lacy appear at the end of a hall. She wore a dark, two-piece business suit and carried a bunch of keys. She walked towards me and entered some numbers on a wall keypad before she opened the door.

'Come in, Miss Moran.' She led me inside, her manner distinctly cold.

'Isn't there a security guard on duty?' I asked.

'Yes, but Mac is probably on his rounds,' Lacy said as she led me to her office and indicated that I take a seat. 'You wanted to see me about the autopsy carried out on Gamal's body.'

'Did you carry it out personally, Dr Lacy?'

She almost looked offended. 'No, I did not. It was a young examiner, a fellow named John Murphy.'

'So there was *definitely* a body?'

She frowned at me. 'Of course there was a body. What's that supposed to mean?'

'I'll explain later. And what did the autopsy prove?'

'What it was supposed to. That cause of death was consisten
with execution by lethal injection.'

'Do you have autopsy photos?'

'Yes, of course. Look, where are all these questions leading?'

'I'll discuss that later. First, may I see the photos?'

Lacy sounded reluctant. 'I'm not sure I have the time, Mis
Moran. I'm going to be late for a dinner appointment with
colleague.'

'Please,' I persisted. 'It would save me a lot of trouble and
don't want to have to go over your head. Neither of us woul
like any kind of friction between the ME's office and the Bureau
but I really need to see those photos, Dr Lacy.'

'For what reason?'

'I can't divulge that just now.'

Brogan Lacy sighed and checked her watch. 'Wait here.'

She left the room and came back within minutes with a larg
manila envelope. She opened it and laid over a dozen colou
photos on the table. 'Shots of the body before, during and afte
the autopsy.'

I examined the pile then reached out and picked up one o
the colour photos – a head-and-shoulders shot of a man lyin
on a stainless-steel table, his eyes closed in death. The pictur
was sharp and face-on. I picked up another two shots of th
man's profile.

I took a deep breath and let it out. It was unmistakable. Unles
these photos were staged, I figured that the corpse I was lookin
at was definitely that of Constantine Gamal.

147

I sat there for several minutes, puzzled. It looked certain that Gamal was dead. I was stumped. I had half expected to see a different corpse on the slab. Had the photos been doctored or staged to make it look like Gamal was deceased?

'What's wrong?' Lacy asked.

I tried to hide my reaction as I finished scrutinising the photos, then gathered them up and replaced them in the envelope. 'Nothing. I believe the ME's office has a videotape of the execution. Apparently made for research purposes.'

Lacy reacted with surprise. 'How . . . how did you know about that?'

'When the warden led me into the viewing room I saw a guy setting up video equipment to shoot through the two-way glass. Executions aren't usually videotaped, so it didn't take much effort to find out that the Medical Examiner's office made the request. I need to know who authorised it.'

Lacy said calmly, 'I believe the Chief ME made the request personally to Warden Clay, but you'll have to verify that.'

'Not you?'

'No, of course not.'

'Have you seen the tape?'

Lacy shook her head. 'No, I haven't. I couldn't bring myself to watch the execution again.'

'May I see it?'

Lacy appeared reluctant. 'I really don't think that would be possible.'

'Why not?'

Lacy consulted her watch. 'As I said, I have an appointment.

This isn't the time and there are protocols involved. You'd hav
to make a formal application.'

'Are you trying to hide something from me, Dr Lacy?'

Lacy sounded defensive. '*Hide* something? What do you mean?

'Look, I was a witness to the execution. I saw everything tha
happened that night. What's the big deal if I see it again? It woul
save us both a lot of hassle if I didn't go the official route. Thi
way, no one's the wiser except us.'

Lacy thought for a moment. She still seemed reluctant bu
finally she relented. 'Very well. You better come with me.'

'Where?'

'There's a viewing room down the hall where the tape's kept

She led me to a room at the end of a hall. It wasn't mucl
bigger than a large closet, with a table and chairs, electroni
recording equipment and a secure metal safe. She opened th
safe with a key code. Inside were shelves of neatly stacked video
Their spines were covered with white identity stickers. She too
down one of the videos inscribed with the words: JANUARY 14TH
LIST NO. 2315B.

Lacy jabbed a finger at a button on the tape machine and th
green power light came on. She slid in the cassette but pause
before starting the tape.

'Ready?'

I braced myself. 'Whenever you are.'

148

I saw the screen turn blue and flicker. It took a few seconds before the execution room appeared in the frame, empty except for the metal gurney. The image was slightly out of focus. I heard a door open into the chamber and a grey-haired man poked his head round and said towards the video camera, 'You ready, Tod?'

'Ready whenever you are,' came the off-camera reply.

Lacy commented, 'We're seeing Tod Simpson and Fred Banks setting up the camera. They work for the ME's office.'

I saw an occasional flash of blurred fingers as one of the men adjusted the lens. Finally the picture came into focus, then faded, as if the camera had been switched off for a wait period. When it started to roll again a few minutes passed before the door opened inwards again and a struggling Gamal was marched into the execution chamber by the six guards before being strapped down on the gurney.

His hands, arms and legs were bound with leather straps and the blue plastic curtain was closed for several minutes. When it opened again the IV catheters had been inserted into his veins, three tubes attached to each arm. He arched his back violently against the straps, his eyes bulging as they searched the room. I remembered the chill I felt as Gamal fixed me with his hateful stare.

'Enjoy the show, Kate. Because you'll pay for this. You don't believe me? Just wait. I will defeat death and come back and take you to hell with me. You'll see. I promise you that.'

The memory jolted through me like a stab of electricity as the scene was repeated before my eyes. Soon the cocktail of lethal drugs began to work. Gamal's eyes flickered and his head slumped back against the gurney as the sodium thiopental was injected, sending him to sleep.

Then he went into a fit of coughing as the pancuronium bromide began paralysing his lungs. He gasped as he fought for breath, his body jolting violently. Then his lips quivered and he gave a final gasp and went still as the final shot of potassium chloride stopped his heart.

A hushed silence descended as one of the guards stepped behind the curtain, then reappeared and crossed the room to whisper to Warden Clay, who studied his wristwatch and spoke into the red telephone receiver to the Director of the Department of Corrections. '*Mr Director, inmate Constantine Gamal is pronounced dead at twenty-one hundred hours and nineteen minutes.*'

The warden left the room, and then a guard closed the viewing curtains. I watched for any sign of breathing but Gamal's chest remained deflated. Not a flicker of life, not even the tiniest twitch. Gamal *looked* dead. *But is the bastard dead? Has he duped everyone?*

Beside me, Brogan Lacy said, 'What's the matter?'

'Nothing – I'm fine.' But I could feel my body trembling.

Lacy leaned over and flicked off the video. 'Well, that's it.'

'Isn't there more footage?'

'What do you mean?'

'I mean after the execution.'

'I presume there may be some video of the orderlies removing the body,' Lacy answered.

'That's on the tape?'

Lacy shrugged. 'I'm assuming, but I don't know.'

'I'd like to see the tape to the very end.'

Lacy frowned. 'You realise that you still haven't given me a reason as to *why* you want to view it. What are you not telling me, Miss Moran?'

'I promise I'll tell you later. Could you go from the very start again?'

'What *exactly* are you looking for?'

'If I discover that, you'll be the first to know.' I knew there had to be *something* we'd missed. I was convinced that Gamal had somehow tricked us all. *But how?*

Lacy hit the rewind button.

149

Gretchen Woods, Virginia

'You *lost* him? How the *fuck* could you lose him? Are the guys you sent to do the job fucking blind?' Stone yelled into his cell phone. He was so enraged he kicked a chair halfway across Josh Cooper's kitchen. It clattered on the floor.

It was after 10 p.m., and his interrogation of Cooper's sister had produced zilch: the woman had claimed she knew absolutely nothing and had just sat there, brazen as hell, ignoring his threat to arrest her.

Marcie Cooper had gone upstairs to check on her nephew, and Gus Norton had gone with her to make sure she didn't step out of line. A minute after they'd gone upstairs Stone's cell phone vibrated, and the conversation that ensued made him bitterly angry.

'Frank Moran just disappeared, Vance,' the agent on the phone went on timidly. 'And we're still watching his sister's place but she hasn't shown up.'

'Tell me about her brother,' Stone snapped.

'We had two teams covering his home. He drove off forty minutes ago and our guys followed his car but lost him.'

Stone fumed. '*Two* teams? I'll tell you this for nothing – someone's gonna get their fucking teeth knocked out through their ass when this thing's over. We're up shit creek without a paddle. Do we even have the slightest idea *which* direction he might be headed?'

The agent said, 'We think towards the Eisenhower Freeway.'

'Terrific. That means he could have gone fucking anywhere. I'll take a bet that the asshole's gone to meet his sister. He's one of the few lifelines she's got and we have to go and fucking lose him.'

'We'll keep trying. Kate Moran's got to appear on the radar soon. And when she does, we'll get her, mark my words.' The agent sounded confident.

'Except you haven't made much of a fucking job of it so far,' Stone said bitterly. 'Where are you now?'

'Just arrived back at the office.'

Stone heard a disturbance on the end of the line. It sounded like voices raised in the background, and then the agent said uncertainly, 'Can . . . can you hold on, Vance?'

'Why, what's up?'

'Just hold for a sec, please . . .'

After ten seconds Stone had endured enough of the muffled voices on the line and shouted down the phone: 'Hey, what in the name of fuck is going on?'

A few more seconds passed until the agent came back on the line. 'Vance? You're not going to believe who's here. It's Cooper. He says he wants to talk with you right away.'

Richmond, Virginia

Frank Moran sat in the Volvo with the map light on, searching through the document folders. He'd gone through almost half of them and had still found nothing more of interest.

He heard a noise outside the Volvo and thought he saw a shadow moving. He frowned and scanned the darkened parking lot through the windscreen but saw damn all, so he rolled down the passenger window to get a better look.

Was it his imagination? *No, there it is again, a shadow moving across the car.* As he twisted to look towards the rear of the Volvo he suddenly felt the barrel of a gun prod his neck and heard the hammer being cocked. A voice said, 'Don't turn round unless you want a bullet in the head. You got that?'

Frank Moran nodded. 'Yes.'

'You follow my instructions and you stay alive, Moran. You fuck up and I'll rip your heart out.'

493

150

Washington, DC

'OK, Cooper, talk to me, my man.'

'I asked for Stone to be present, so where is he?' Cooper protested as he sat in the third-floor room at the Bureau's field office. He faced two agents, a flabby-faced senior named Jeb Walsh and another named Branson, both of whom he'd been introduced to the day he took up his posting.

Walsh said, 'Stone's on his way. But he said to save time you're to tell me what you've got to say.'

Cooper fell silent. Walsh said, 'We ain't got all night, Cooper. Either you talk or so help me you won't just have the book thrown at you, no sir, you'll have the fucking shelves as well. *Talk*, Coop.'

Cooper told his story and covered everything that had happened at the graveyard. The two agents looked at each other in disbelief and then Walsh said seriously, 'Are you on any medication, Cooper? You ever take drugs, recreationally or otherwise?'

'*No.*'

'You've got to be shitting us, man.'

'Everything I've told you is the absolute truth,' Cooper responded.

Walsh sighed and ran a hand over his flabby face. 'Look, this whole graveyard thing sounds weird, so why don't we just cut through all the bullshit and you tell us where Moran is. It's the only way you're going to help her, and it's the only way we can confirm your version of events. Tell you what, I'll even meet her personally and bring her in, before Stone gets his paws on her.'

'How can I trust you?' Cooper asked.

494

Walsh said, 'You've got no one else you *can* trust. This is the last-chance saloon, Coop. It's talk or walk. You really want to be turfed out of the Bureau?'

'If it's peopled by guys like Stone, maybe that wouldn't be such a bad thing.'

'You don't like the guy, do you?'

'I can't say I trust him. He's changed since I knew him in New York. He's bitter with grudges.'

Walsh leaned forward, his fingertips spread on the desk. 'Hey, Stone ain't all that bad. You do this right he'll go easy on you, I promise.'

'You meant it when you said you'll bring her in yourself, and not Stone?'

'That's what I said. So where's Moran?'

Cooper gave it some thought, then he said, 'Kate was heading over to the Richmond Medical Examiner's office.'

'Why?'

'She needed to talk with Dr Brogan Lacy about the autopsy that was carried out on Gamal.'

'When was Moran due to get there?' Walsh asked.

'She headed for Richmond over an hour ago. She should be there now.'

'You better be telling me the truth, Coop. Or Stone's liable to use your balls the next time he plays a round of golf.'

'It's the truth. Just do as you say and call her and go meet her yourself.'

Walsh smiled and picked up the phone. He began to punch in a number and Cooper said, 'Who are you calling?'

'Stone.'

'You lying bastard, Walsh!'

Walsh shrugged. 'Hey, I've been called worse. But Stone's in charge of this case, sonny. I'm just following his orders.'

151

Richmond, Virginia

The video started again and I said to Brogan Lacy on impulse, 'How about forwarding the tape to where Gamal is first administered the drugs.'

She hesitated, then fast-forwarded to where the guard was preparing to hook Gamal up to the catheter.

'Go from right there,' I said.

She hit another button and the tape slowed to normal speed.

I kept my eyes fixed on exactly what was happening as Gamal was strapped down on the gurney, his hands, arms and legs tightly bound. Then the blue plastic curtain closed for several minutes and when it opened again the IV catheters were inserted into his veins. I said to Lacy, 'Does that procedure look all right to you? I mean, the way the drug is being administered.'

She nodded. 'Yes. Why?'

'Explanations later,' I said, and watched as the tape progressed to where the sodium thiopental was injected. 'That looks OK too?'

'It all seems normal.'

I watched the screen intently, searching for a sign of even the slightest irregularity. 'I guess no one could tell from the footage exactly *which* drugs are being administered. That would be impossible, right? So for all we know there could be anything in the vials being injected into Gamal?'

Lacy shook her head. 'That's highly unlikely. I believe that very strict protocols are followed in the administration of the drugs. There couldn't be a mix-up, if that's what you're inferring.'

'Come on, Doctor, I think we've all heard of incorrect drugs being administered. What about in hospitals?' I suggested.

Lacy frowned. 'Yes, but as far as the prison and the administration of the execution are concerned there are only three drugs being used consistently, so a mix-up is highly unlikely. I've certainly never heard of it happening before. What are you getting at?'

'I was thinking out loud. Let's carry on.' I kept my eyes on the screen and eventually the third drug, potassium chloride, was injected into Gamal's arm. A few seconds later his body stiffened. *Had he started to hold his breath at that point?*

I didn't think so. Gamal's face turned a pale shade of purple, and then his eyelids flickered. I was convinced that by now he was dying, and that I'd seen nothing unusual. Absolutely nothing. But at the back of my mind was a niggling thought. *What have I missed? There must have been something.*

152

To all appearances Gamal was now dead as he lay on the gurney. Off to the right I again saw the warden start to give his spiel on the phone to the director. Then the warden left the room and the guard closed the viewing curtains.

I heard shuffling feet as the audience left and then the door into the execution room opened again and two white-coated male orderlies came in. One of them wore glasses and had a dark moustache, but the face of the second orderly seemed constantly masked by his colleague, and he had his back to the camera, so I couldn't see him. The drips were removed from Gamal's arm and the white sheet pulled over his face before the orderlies manoeuvred Gamal into a white body bag and wheeled the gurney towards the door.

'Do you know either of these two men?' I asked Lacy.

She frowned. 'I know this one . . .' She pointed to the dark-haired man on the screen. 'I believe his name's Buck Ryan. He's one of the prison guards. But I don't recognise the second man. How could I? I can't see his face.'

I stared at the second man: his head was turned away, his features not even in profile. *Was he deliberately making sure his face wasn't caught on camera?* It almost seemed that way to me. It was proving difficult to catch a proper glimpse. As he moved towards the door and exited the room he had to turn slightly to the right to manoeuvre the gurney out the doorway, but I still couldn't get a good look at him. *Am I on to something or just totally off track?* I was confused, had no answers.

I changed the subject and said frankly, 'Why didn't you tell me you were once a patient at Bellevue under Gamal's care?'

Lacy turned ashen. 'How . . . how did you know that?'

'Are you going to answer the question?'

Her tone suddenly became defensive. 'You had no right to pry into my private affairs. No right at all.'

'I'd like an explanation. Unless there's something you're trying to hide?'

Lacy said with consternation, 'What would I have to hide?'

'You tell me,' I said.

Lacy gave me a steely look. 'I don't have to tell you anything. But if you must know, I was depressed after David and I divorced. My decision to leave my marriage didn't come easily.'

'I'm not sure if I can believe that. David told me that the decision to divorce was his.'

Lacy said fiercely, 'You can believe whatever you want to. But my stay at Bellevue is none of your business.'

'It might have been my business if the FBI had known about a link between you and Gamal when we were investigating David and Megan's deaths. How did we miss that? I guess the fact that Gamal was the chief suspect right from the start and we didn't need to probe your private life.'

Lacy frowned at me. 'What are you trying to suggest?'

'I'm suggesting nothing. Just thinking aloud.'

'Then how about you just keep your nose out of my life, *Miss* Moran. It has nothing to do with you.'

For the first time I was witnessing another side to Brogan Lacy. She was like a different woman. *Is she really just angry that her privacy has been invaded or is there more to it?* 'I have only one last question. Why Bellevue?'

'I thought you would have known why,' Lacy said moodily.

I was confused. 'What do you mean?'

She hit a button on the video player and the tape ejected. 'Bellevue was glad to help in whatever way it could because David's father was once a hospital trustee and a very generous benefactor. The same way they helped David's brother Patrick try to cope with his severe mental disorders.'

'What?'

499

Lacy looked at me as if I were stupid. 'Among other things Patrick suffered from multiple personality disorder – or didn' David tell you that?'

I was astonished. 'No. He only told me Patrick suffered from depression.'

'It went much deeper than that. Patrick was diagnosed with so many comorbid mental dysfunctions that he was in and out of Bellevue for most of his adult life. The worst of it was his psychopathic tendency. But to tell the truth, Patrick didn't know who he was. When his condition worsened, he'd speak in different voices and mimic diverse characters, anyone but himself. To witness it was like watching an actor perform. Multiple personality disorder isn't uncommon in people who have suffered great trauma in their lives when they're young, such as sexual abuse or beatings. I imagine his death was probably a relief.'

'Are you saying something happened to Patrick in his childhood?'

'That's not for me to discuss.' Lacy was suddenly tight lipped.

'Was he ever under Gamal's care?'

'I'm sure he must have been, considering Gamal was one of the leading psychiatrists at Bellevue who dealt with the more serious cases.' Lacy stood, her patience obviously at an end and a bitter tone still in her voice. 'Now, if you'd please leave, I have to finish up here.'

I knew almost nothing about David's brother but I was desperate to learn. 'Did Patrick have a profession?'

Lacy slid the tape into its sleeve. 'His father insisted that he went to medical college but his bouts of mental ill health worsened when he was a student so he never graduated.'

I was about to ask her more but Brogan Lacy studied her watch and said coldly, 'And now I have work to finish. You'll have to leave.'

As she replaced the video cassette in the cabinet my cell phone rang and I answered the call. There was a brief silence, and then I heard Frank say, 'Kate, I need you out here, fast. I've turned up something in the file.'

'What?'

Another silence, and then Frank said, 'You better see for yourself. Kate. Listen, don't—'

The line clicked dead.

He had sounded urgent. I picked up my bag. 'I've got to go,' I told Lacy.

'What about my explanation?' she demanded.

'I'll call you later, Doctor.' I headed towards the door as fast as I could.

153

The security guard let me out through the front lobby and I crossed the street towards the parking lot. I was frustrated that I had got nowhere with the tape. And I was upset that David had kept the truth from me. It was so unlike him. *But maybe he found his brother's mental illness too difficult to discuss?*

I thought back to six months after David and Megan had been murdered: how I'd got a phone call from one of the doctors at Bellevue telling me that Patrick had been so overcome by the despair of losing his brother that he had left Bellevue, walked down to the Potomac and drowned himself. His clothes had been found abandoned at Headland Point. A suicide note had been left in his room, saying he couldn't take the grief any more. But his body had never been recovered and was assumed to have been washed out to sea by powerful currents.

And then a welter of thoughts assaulted my mind and made my legs go weak. I remembered some of the profile Frank had drawn up for our unsub: male, twenty-five to forty and physically fit, a diagnosed paranoid schizophrenic with psychopathic tendencies, above-average intelligence with a college degree. That part of the profile fitted Patrick closely. Except Patrick was dead.

But my imagination raced. Patrick had studied medicine so he'd have known about lethal poisons. And he was a Bellevue patient who most likely knew Gamal. The police had said his body had been washed out to sea by powerful currents but there was no solid proof of that. *What if Patrick is still alive and mixed up in this? What if he is our copycat killer? Or helped Gamal escape?*

But if Patrick was alive and implicated why would he conspire to help Constantine Gamal cheat the executioner? And why would he fool everyone into thinking he was dead? My brain was so addled that I couldn't figure out a single reason that made any kind of sense.

I saw the Volvo up ahead as I crossed to the car park. *If I tell Frank, will he think I'm crazy?* As I got closer I noticed that the internal map-reading light was on, but I couldn't see anyone in the vehicle. I peered inside. *Empty.*

I noticed that the keys were still in the ignition. For a second or two I froze with fear, but then I figured that Frank had probably gone to relieve himself so I looked around the darkened lot. That was when I noticed something weird. Earlier I had spotted four cars in the lot but now I counted five – among them a green Nissan sedan that was half in shadow. I was convinced I saw the dark outline of a figure seated behind the steering wheel.

A split second later a Taurus screeched into the lot, its headlights blazing. I panicked and ran towards the Volvo as the Taurus roared to a halt and Stone jumped out, followed by two other agents. Stone had his firearm out. 'You're under arrest, Moran! Get face down on the ground and place your hands behind your back *now!*'

I was five yards from the Volvo. If I made a run for it, I was certain Stone would shoot me dead – the look on his face told me that he wasn't in the mood for argument. There would be no reasoning with him. But I knew I *had* to escape. *Where's Frank when I need him?*

'OK, I'll do what you say,' I shouted back, trying to buy time.

Stone kept his gun aimed at me as I put my hands in the air and made like I was going to lie down. But I was closing the gap between myself and the Volvo, and when I was close enough I snatched the door open and flung myself in. A gunshot exploded as Stone fired off a round. I heard it smash into the windscreen as I scrambled to turn the ignition and the engine erupted into life. I saw Stone charge towards me like a bull and I slammed my foot hard on the accelerator just as another shot rang out, drilled a hole through the roof and zinged past my head. Then another round cracked past my right shoulder and shattered the rear window. I couldn't tell whether it was Stone or one of his men who had fired but I heard him scream, 'Stop or you'r fucking dead, Moran!'

I floored the accelerator, the Volvo's engine growled like a wild animal and I sped out of the parking lot with a screech of burning rubber.

154

Three more shots hit the Volvo – one more cracked through the windscreen and another two punched through the roof. I kept the accelerator floored and tried to see through the half-shattered windscreen.

I'd left the headlights extinguished and could barely make out what I was doing as I swung left, exiting the parking lot at high speed and bouncing off the kerbstone. I broke every set of traffic lights in my way and heard no more rounds strike the car, but two hundred yards farther on, as I approached a turning, I saw blazing headlights in my rear-view mirror. I knew that it had to be Stone and his men.

But by now I had a head start. I focused on the route ahead, easing off a touch on the gas until I'd cleared the next bend in the road, then I slammed my foot hard on the pedal. The Volvo's engine growled again as it picked up speed and I lost sight of the Ford Taurus.

Stone was in the Ford's passenger seat and Norton was driving, the engine snarling as he tried to narrow the hundred-yard gap between the cars. Stone was enraged: the Volvo was too far away to get a good shot. Suddenly Norton glanced in his rear-view mirror as a pair of powerful headlights approached them at high speed from behind. '*What the fuck . . . ?*'

'What's up?' Stone demanded.

'Some asshole's right behind us. Looks to me like he's gonna ram us!'

Stone leaned out of the passenger window to get a better look, just as a green Nissan sedan raced up beside them, its headlights ablaze. He couldn't make out the driver's face – it was in shadow – but whoever it was they deliberately swung left and rammed the Ford. There was a grating crash of metal and the car shuddered as Norton tried to control the steering wheel. '*Jesus*, that fucker's crazy . . .'

Stone noticed a bend up ahead and shouted in panic, 'Keep your eyes on the road, Gus . . . !'

But the car rammed them again with even greater force and the Ford started to skew across the road towards a crash barrier. Stone screamed, '*Jesus Christ* . . .'

Norton frantically tried to straighten the steering wheel but he lost control. There was a violent screech of rubber and the Ford smashed through the metal barrier.

155

I had driven another hundred yards before I looked in the mirror again. It appeared as if two cars were rounding the bend at the same time, but then suddenly one of the cars slewed across the road and vanished. I blinked, wondering whether I was seeing things. It appeared than one of the cars had ploughed through a crash barrier.

A single pair of powerful headlights was now speeding after me. My cell phone suddenly vibrated. I steered one-handed as I fumbled in my bag, thinking it might be Frank, but when I answered the phone it was silent. 'Frank? Is that you?'

After a pause a man's hoarse voice said, 'Kate, we speak at last.'

It wasn't Frank's voice, or anyone else's that I knew, and I felt a rising panic. 'Who . . . who is this?'

'I thought maybe you'd figured that out by now, Kate. Or do I really have to spell it out?'

The voice became familiar: *it almost sounded like David.* And then the penny dropped and my heart jumped. '*Patrick?*'

'Who's the clever girl?'

'W-where are you?' I was so perplexed it was all I could think of asking.

'In the car behind, but I wouldn't suggest you look back. We don't want you getting totalled, now, do we?'

I glanced in the rear-view mirror and saw that the headlights had caught up behind me. 'Where's Frank? What have you done to him?'

Patrick said firmly, 'Just shut up, pull in and keep your phone line open.'

'*Where's Frank?*' I persisted.

'Tied up on my back seat. But whether he stays alive or not depends on your cooperation, Moran. You give me a second's grief and I'll shoot him in the head. Understand?'

'Y . . . yes, I understand.'

'Then do what I say. Pull in, switch off your engine and step out of the car. Shut the door, keep your hands out by your side and turn to face my car. Do it right now! Pull in.'

I pulled into the kerb and did as I was told – stepped out, shut the Volvo's door and turned round. I saw a dark green Nissan sedan ease on its brakes and come to a halt right behind me just as a light flurry of snow began to fall.

The driver stepped out and I recognised the man from the plane. I knew that it had to be Patrick, but he'd changed – his hair was lighter and his face thinner than in the images I'd seen in his photographs – but the longer I looked at him the more I was sure it was David's brother.

He had an automatic pistol in his hand, and he moved to the Nissan's passenger side, yanked open the door and indicated for me to take the driver's seat. 'Get in behind the wheel.'

I climbed in and he slid in beside me. I glanced over my shoulder and saw Frank's body lying across the back seat. His hands were tied behind his back with thick blue nylon rope. I couldn't tell whether he was alive or dead.

Patrick said, 'Drive.'

'Where to?'

He stared into my face and I saw a madness in his eyes as he stuck the pistol in my ribs. His grin spread. 'Somewhere deep and dark where you're going to feel right at home, Moran.'

156

The snow started to fall more heavily and cover the Nissan's windscreen. I managed to find the wipers and flick them on but I found it impossible to concentrate on the wet road. Patrick was still pointing his pistol at me, and my hands shook as I gripped the steering wheel.

He said, 'Stay on the interstate, going south. And get this – you even think of fucking with me and you and your brother are going to get whacked.'

'I believed you were dead.'

Patrick smiled. 'So did a lot of people. Terrific, wasn't it? The pathetic suicide note about how much I missed David. What a fucking joke. I *hated* him.'

I was shocked. '*Why?*'

'Don't fret, maybe you'll get to hear the reasons before you die. I'm kind of looking forward to seeing your reaction. Keep driving.'

On the back seat, Frank suddenly moaned and fell still again. 'What did you do to him?' I asked.

Patrick's fingers mimed the plunger on a hypodermic. 'Gave him something a little stronger than a tequila slammer. Don't you worry, he'll soon come round.'

'What happened to Gamal? Is he dead or alive?'

Patrick was enjoying my curiosity. 'Hey, wouldn't you like to know. But I guess I can tell you that your old friend Constantine's waiting to meet you.'

A bolt of fear shot through me. 'Where is he? Did you keep him alive with an antidote? Is that how he escaped the execution?'

Patrick wielded the pistol. 'You'll find out soon enough when you meet him. And in case you're wondering what we've got planned, you'll find that out too. For now, just keep fucking driving.'

My stomach churned. *Gamal's alive.* I knew that Frank and I were about to be murdered, and if Gamal had anything to do with it he'd make it agonisingly painful. My heart was thumping like a piston as a car whooshed past in the rain, its red tail-lights reflecting on the slick road. 'What harm did I ever do to you? I can understand Gamal's hatred for me, but not yours.'

A look of pure venom erupted on Patrick's face, so intense that it almost overpowered him. 'Don't you see anything, you stupid bitch? Or are you that fucking dumb?'

'What are you talking about?'

Patrick's mouth twisted with malice. 'Don't play the fucking innocent with me. My parents didn't leave me a cent. They gave it all to my kid brother. *Everything.* Money that should have gone to me went to David, and then he goes and leaves it all to *you.*'

I said, stunned, 'So *that's* what this is really about – money?'

Patrick's malice turned to rage. 'You took every fucking thing that should have been mine! And then you wonder *why* I hate you?'

I saw everything then, the pieces fitting into place as I felt my anger growing. 'How could you kill your own brother and niece in cold blood? *How?*'

The venom spread on Patrick's face. 'David and his bitch daughter deserved to die. It was always David this, and David that. David the blue-eyed boy, David the guy who excelled at everything – sports, career, relationships. He got it all and I had to live in his shadow. And what did I get from my folks? I got a fucked-up mind that had to be locked up in a fucking psychiatric hospital.' Patrick grinned maniacally. 'Hey, but don't worry, David suffered for what he did to me. Megan did too, which I guess almost evened the score. I just thought you'd like to know that.'

I was overcome by a powerful feeling of hatred towards Patrick as I listened to his brutal words. I wanted to weep, wanted to kill

Patrick for what he'd done. I felt a searing pain in my chest just thinking about how he'd made David and Megan suffer. *How could anyone have a capacity for such brutality? How could anyone but someone truly evil enjoy seeing a fourteen-year-old die in agony?* 'David only ever tried to help you. And you killed him for *that*?'

'Hey, maybe I did kill him, maybe I didn't.'

'What are you saying?'

'You'll find out. Right now I don't give two fucks about David. What did he ever do to really help me? A few weekend visits? A few pathetic attempts at brotherly fraternity that never worked out? But Gamal, now there's a man who made me see what a dark and dangerous mind can achieve.'

'What do you mean?'

Patrick scoffed. 'Figure it out for yourself. Hang a left at the turnpike.'

We were already out into the Virginian countryside, and as we approached the turnpike I knew it was pointless trying to make Patrick see reason. Twenty years in and out of a psychiatric hospital hadn't worked, so I didn't have a hope. 'Gamal is waiting for us where we're going, isn't he?' I asked.

Patrick gave me a look that was pure evil. 'You're damned right he is. Hell, it's going to be fun seeing you two meet up again. So how about you just keep your eyes on the fucking road.'

157

Josh Cooper heard a key rattle in the door of the office he'd been locked into. The door was pushed in and Agent Walsh stood in the door frame, chewing gum. 'You comfortable in here, sweetheart?'

Cooper shrugged. 'A bed would be nice. Some magazines, cable TV, an assortment of snacks maybe.'

Walsh's grin vanished as he stepped into the room. 'Funny, but you won't need any of those comforts, Cooper. You're out of here on account of some bad news.'

Cooper glared at him. 'What are you talking about?'

'Stone was in an accident outside of Richmond. His car's a write-off, but he and Norton survived, apart from cuts and bruises. I guess God protects the righteous.'

Cooper jumped to his feet. 'What happened?'

Walsh took the gum from his mouth, rolled it into a ball between his palms and managed to flick it into a wastepaper basket. 'The bit I heard, it seems your buddy Moran has vanished again. She's like the fucking Scarlet Pimpernel – we seek her here, we seek her there, we seek her every fucking where. We've been busting our nuts trying to find her. You got any more ideas on that score, Cooper?'

'How the hell should I know? I've told you all I can.'

Walsh rubbed his palms and jerked his thumb towards the door. 'Stone wants to see you, he's gonna meet us off Interstate 95. Hey, you want some advice, Coop? You better have some right answers when you two meet. Because the mood Stone's in he's liable to rip your tongue out through your ass.'

Forty minutes later, Cooper found himself being escorted by Walsh into a Comfort Inn five miles north of Richmond. Norton opened the door to them as Stone talked on his cell phone by the bed. He wore a surgical neck brace and a couple of Band Aids decorated his face. A gauze bandage was wrapped around his left wrist and his right eye was bruised and badly blood-shot.

Stone finished his call and glared at his visitor. 'A word of warning, Cooper. You pull my fucking chain and so help me I'll clock you.' He jerked a chair round and sat facing Cooper.

Norton munched on a Dime bar and said, 'You need anything? Coffee? Coke? Some doughnuts?'

Cooper said, 'Coffee would be nice. Semi-skimmed latte, maybe. With a sprinkling of cinnamon on top. Sweetener, no sugar. Could do with a doughnut, too. Maybe one of those rasp-berry ones with the little sprinkly things on top.'

'I'm talking to Stone, you moron,' Norton answered.

Stone growled and slammed his fist on the table. 'Forget the fucking coffee, forget the doughnuts, Gus. Sit down, Cooper.'

'I thought he asked me what I'd like. I told him.'

Stone was red faced. 'Don't fucking try me. Just tell me again what happened at the graveyard.'

Cooper stared at him. 'I already told Walsh.'

'*Tell me*, Cooper. And move it along, because I ain't got the time or the patience.'

'I don't trust you, Stone. I get the feeling that you're up to something.'

Stone said impatiently, 'Cooper, you can have all the feelings you want but I'm in charge of this investigation from now and I promise you this, unless you want to be thrown into a cell and not get out until that kid of yours is a grown man, you better start singing, fast. That clear enough?'

Cooper looked at Norton and Walsh. 'Whatever the case with Stone, I'm hoping you guys are on the level.'

'What do you mean by that?' Norton asked.

'It means I don't trust Stone.'

'*Talk*, Cooper, before my patience snaps,' Stone advised. 'Tell me everything.'

Cooper spoke for a couple of minutes and when he had finished Stone got up with a sigh and put a hand to his injured face. He appeared to be deep in thought and seemed to be having trouble making up his mind.

Cooper said, 'Do you guys believe me now?'

Stone turned on him. 'Are you fucking kidding me? I'll believe nothing until we completely check out the cemetery. I've got more guys on their way there now. For all I know you two could have opened the wrong burial site. And the priority right now is finding Moran. My bet is her brother Frank's helping her – he's disappeared too. We're going to check out any calls to her desk phone and home phone in the last few days, and her e-mails, in case we get us a lead. So, Cooper, have you got any ideas where she is this time?'

Cooper rose angrily to his feet. 'No, I don't. You're telling me you *still* can't accept that she's innocent?'

Stone stared into his face. 'After what happened to Lou? After all that she's been implicated in? Never mind that she deliberately almost had me killed in an auto accident. I'm taking bets it was that bastard Frank driving the car behind Gus and me when we were run off the road.'

'I doubt that, Stone. And there's no way Kate harmed Lou. You're reading this all the wrong way. Kate or Frank wouldn't try to kill anyone.'

'That's fucking rich.' Stone pointed to his neck brace. 'You think I'm wearing this as a fucking fashion accessory? Listen to me, Cooper. It could be a bullshit story you're feeding me. As far as I'm concerned, that bitch is still as guilty as sin. This is the *second* time she's tried to kill me today. What's more, the next time I find her and she puts up a fight I think I can guarantee that she's as good as dead.'

Cooper said, 'What's this really about between you and her,

Stone? OK, so she makes you look a fool and you almost get killed. But what is it you want, an eye for an eye?'

Stone met Cooper's stare. 'I'm more the kind of guy who goes for both eyes.'

Cooper sighed. 'You know what your problem is? You're so clammed up with hate that you can't even accept the truth any more. You're just being dumb, Stone. *Seriously* dumb. Or maybe you're fooling us all and being really clever.'

'What's that supposed to mean?'

'You hate Kate so much maybe you'd go to any lengths to see her destroyed. Maybe you've even got something to do with what's been happening?'

Stone's face convulsed with anger and he grabbed Cooper by the throat and pushed him hard up against the wall. 'You think so? Then let me tell you what I think. You're the moron, Cooper. Because after this you can kiss goodbye to the Bureau, that I can guarantee.' He let go of Cooper and said to Norton, 'Have this loser thrown back in a secure room and let's go find Moran and finish this job.'

158

Virginia

My hands shook as I drove out into the Virginian country-side. The snow had stopped but it was so cold I figured we were soon going to be in for a heavy fall. Vehicles flashed by – even a cop car – but there was nothing I could do to attract attention without the risk of getting shot by Patrick. 'Are you going to tell me why you helped Gamal escape?' I was unable to control the fear in my voice.

He kept the gun aimed at me. 'You'll understand when we get where we're going. Keep fucking driving.'

I could see it wasn't worth trying to pursue a conversation because Patrick wanted to keep me in suspense. Like Gamal, he was someone who got their kicks from wielding power. But I still had questions that begged answers. 'Why did you lead me on a wild-goose chase? It was you, wasn't it? You and Gamal.'

Patrick's grin broadened. 'Didn't you enjoy our little game of cat and mouse, Moran?'

'Hardly, but I'd like to know why you played the game.'

'Easy. To make you see what it was like being hunted down like an animal, the way you hunted Gamal down. And we kind of liked the idea of pitting your mind against ours to see who'd win. You know what was terrific? That I could have killed you any time I chose, Moran. *Any time.* I could decide exactly *when* you were going to die. That's what made it so much fun.'

'Is that why Yeta was killed? Just for fun?'

Patrick's face again contorted with malice. 'That bitch betrayed her own brother so she deserved what she got.'

'Who killed her, you or Gamal?'

Patrick sneered. 'You still don't get it, do you? You still don't get what this is *really* about and what's ahead of you.'

'Get what?'

He didn't answer. I approached a turn-off and suddenly realised that we were somewhere near Angel Bay – we had approached it along a route I was unfamiliar with. We came to some woods, barely touched by snow. A strip of dirt track the colour of ground pepper led through the trees. 'Go that way,' Patrick ordered, pointing to the track, and when I hesitated he got angry. 'Didn't you just fucking hear me?'

My hands shook so much I found it hard to keep from veering off the track. 'I . . . I heard you. All this killing makes no sense, Patrick. Why do it? *Why?*' I was terrified, imagining what might lie ahead for Frank and me, at the mercy of two psychotic killers.

Without warning Patrick flew into a rage. He pointed the gun towards the back seat and squeezed the trigger. The silenced pistol coughed. I heard a dull *smack* as the round hit something soft, but not a sound came from Frank. *Has Patrick killed him?* I looked back with dread and saw that the shot had drilled through the leather upholstery above Frank's head. A stench of cordite filled the car.

'Next time it'll be his skull,' said Patrick angrily. 'Keep on the fucking track!'

I tried to keep my hands from shaking as I gripped the steering wheel, but I could see that Patrick was getting a kick out of my fear. 'I don't understand why you wanted me to get the blame for David and Megan's deaths.'

'To make the game all the more enjoyable, you idiot. We kind of figured if you were suspected of their murder it would be a terrific irony. All part of leading you a tortured chase before Constantine and I finally made you pay the price with your life. Ease off on the gas, Moran.'

I slowed as we approached a stone bridge over a narrow river. Beyond the bridge was a pair of open wire-mesh gates with wire fencing running off on either side. I realised we were at the rear

517

of Manor Brook. It was an old unused entrance road that I'd once strolled along with David.

'Drive on in,' Patrick ordered. 'Keep going until I tell you to stop.'

The car bumped as I went over the bridge and Frank moaned on the rear seat, then fell silent. A hundred yards farther on we came to the rear of the manor. The headlights washed over the granite. The house looked dark and gloomy. 'Get out of the car,' Patrick ordered.

My blood turned to ice, and I felt as if I were welded to the seat, fearing what was about to come.

'Get fucking out!' Patrick screamed, aiming the gun at me.

I climbed out, my legs buckling under me.

Patrick joined me and gestured to a stone stairway leading down to the basement. 'That's where we're going. You try to make a run for it and I shoot your brother in the head and you get one in the back.'

He slipped an electric Maglite torch into his pocket. 'Pull your brother out of the car.'

That was going to be impossible on my own. 'He's too heavy . . .'

Patrick cocked his pistol and pointed it at Frank, lying across the back seat. 'Too bad. Either you drag him down the basement stairs or I'll kill him right here and now. You decide. What's it to be, live or die?'

I tried to drag Frank from the seat, using both my hands and pulling him with all my might, but I barely shifted him. Suddenly Patrick brandished the pistol and said in a fit of frustration, 'Get back.'

'Please don't kill him,' I begged.

'I said get back!' He pointed the gun at my face and forced me to step away, then reached in and pulled Frank out of the car by the collar. He was stronger than I had thought, managing to manhandle Frank towards the basement steps. 'Get his legs,' he ordered.

The snow started to come down again as I grabbed hold of

Frank's legs and we dragged him to the bottom of the stairwell and halted in front of a rotting wooden door, hanging off its hinges. Frank was still out of it, his eyes shut, his mouth open, his body limp. The effort of carrying him was breaking my back but I daren't complain.

'Let him go,' Patrick commanded, and I released my hold on Frank's legs. Then Patrick kicked in the door and it crashed open. I stared into another stairwell, illuminated by Patrick's torchlight. I had never felt more scared in my life.

Patrick said, 'It's going to be cool doing the two of you. Killing in pairs, just the way Constantine always liked it. Only this time brother and sister.'

Without warning Patrick pushed Frank's limp body. It rolled into the black stairwell and moments later there came a dull thud that sounded as if Frank had hit hard ground. I felt a sickening sensation in the pit of my stomach. *What if he's cracked his skull?*

'You cruel bastard!' I shouted.

Patrick grabbed me savagely by the hair, enjoying my terror as he pulled my face up to meet his. 'Hey, the fun hasn't even started, Moran. I bet you're wondering what's waiting for you down those steps. But you know something? You're in for the biggest surprise of your fucking life.'

159

Patrick pushed me roughly and I stumbled down the stairs. He flicked a switch and a light sprang on, flooding the basement chamber. Frank was lying near the bottom of the stairwell. He was still unconscious and blood trickled from a gash on his forehead. I knelt and took his pulse. He was still alive and I felt a wave of relief.

'Keep it moving,' Patrick ordered, and jabbed his pistol in my back. 'Don't worry about Frank. Go straight on.'

I noticed a smell of burning incense. I was certain there was another smell underlying the incense but what it was I couldn't figure out. I moved forward reluctantly as Patrick grabbed Frank by the collar of his jacket and began dragging him along the ground. 'Face forward, Moran. And hurry up or your brother's going to get a bullet.'

I forced myself to look ahead and saw an arched tunnel, lined with dusty racks of wine bottles, which led to another part of the basement. On the floor were a rusting kitchen bucket and the remains of a shattered porcelain basin. My mind was plagued by one question: *Where's Gamal?*

My heart slammed into my ribcage as memories flashed before my eyes: of every crime scene where I'd witnessed Gamal's bloody handiwork. I tried to put aside any thought of my impending torture but it was impossible. *Death is waiting for me in this basement.* We reached the end of the arched tunnel and entered a large chamber. Patrick let go of Frank's collar. He was still unconscious as his head hit the ground. I saw a glow of candlelight up ahead but my attention was diverted as suddenly Frank moaned and came awake. That was as far as it got because Patrick slammed his pistol butt into Frank's skull. Rivulets of blood dripped down his cheek. His eyes closed and he made a gurgling noise. My stomach churned as I saw his head roll to one side. I made a desperate attempt to tend to him but Patrick grabbed me by the hair again and propelled me forward. 'Forget about playing nursemaid, Moran, I'll come back for him. Move it. I've got a surprise waiting for you up ahead. I can't wait to see your face.'

I stumbled forward through another archway. Patrick stretched out to touch a switch on the wall, then a second later I heard the hum of an electric generator starting up. Suddenly the entire basement was lit up by powerful halogen lights. Near a wall in a corner of the room I saw what looked like a metal operating table. Next to it was a wooden stand and laid out on top of it was a collection of surgeon's tools and butcher's knives: a drill, electric saws, hammers, brutal-looking serrated blades and meat cleavers. Alongside the deadly implements was a tan-coloured butcher's leather belt.

'We're here,' Patrick announced.

I shook with fear and realised that Patrick wasn't addressing me. I followed his gaze across the chamber to the far wall, where a circle of thick wax candles had been lit. What I saw next chilled me to the bone.

Standing in the middle of the circle, his face illuminated by the shimmering candlelight and his hands outstretched like those of a high priest, was Constantine Gamal.

160

Sunset Memorial Park, Chesterfield County, Virginia

The two special agents sat in their car in the pouring rain watching the cemetery. The snowy sleet had eased off and one of the men was dozing while the other sipped coffee. He spotted dipped headlights pulling up in front of the cemetery. A figure climbed out, wielding a flashlight as it entered through the front gates. The agent took one last sip of his coffee and stuck it in the cup holder, then made a grab for his rain cape on the back seat as he nudged his colleague awake. 'Hey, Sullivan, heads up, I think we're in business, man.'

They drew their guns as they entered the cemetery through the open gates. They saw the torchlight raking the back of the grave-yard, and when they got close enough they spotted a figure wearing a rain hood standing over one of the graves and flashing his torch.

He must have heard them approach because he spun round, raising his torch. Both agents aimed their weapons as one of them yelled, 'FBI! Get that frigging light out of my face and put your hands where we can see 'em!'

The figure obeyed instantly and the two agents approached their target. One of them pulled off the rain hood and they saw a frightened middle-aged man wearing a badged peaked cap that said ATLAS SECURITY.

'What the hell are you doing here, fella?' one of the agents asked.

'Just . . . doing my job. The company I work for handles grave-yard security.'

'You got any ID?'

'Hey, I could ask you guys the same question.'

The Fed showed his creds. 'Happy now?'

'I guess.' The guard displayed his ID, on a chain around his neck. 'You mind me asking what you Feds are doing out here on a night like this?'

'I believe I asked you first,' the agent replied.

The guard shrugged. 'I got a report that someone saw lights in the cemetery earlier and I've come by a couple of times to take a look.'

'Lights? What do you mean *lights*?' the agent asked.

'Like a flashlight. But I ain't seen nothing unusual, except over by that grave right behind you.'

The agents turned as the guard shone his flashlight at a green tarpaulin that had been disturbed; the tarp had sunk in the middle and was half covered with slushy rain. A cross with some numbers marked an obvious grave site. The guard said, 'That's what I was looking at when you people scared the living shit out of me. A graveyard ain't the place to give a guy the frights, fellas.'

'What do you mean, unusual?'

'An executed killer named Gamal was buried here maybe a couple of weeks back. Someone went and covered up the grave with a tarpaulin. I took a look under the tarp and discovered that the guy's grave has been dug up.'

'What?'

'Yeah, and you'll never guess what's in there, fellas.'

161

Josh Cooper paced the cell in frustration. He could hear Walsh moving about in the annexe, making himself some coffee. Beyond the cell bars he saw a medical first-aid kit mounted on the hallway wall and he called out, 'Walsh! I need you in here.'

Walsh appeared in the open doorway, munching a sandwich. 'What is it, Cooper?'

'You the only one doing guard duty?'

Walsh spoke with his mouth half full. 'Seems like it. Why?'

'I'm thirsty. I need some water.'

Walsh finished his sandwich and rubbed his hands with a paper napkin. 'Next thing you know you'll be wanting a take-out dinner.'

'Just water's fine.'

Walsh disappeared, and came back with a plastic cup filled with cold water.

'Never say I don't care.'

'Thanks, pal.'

'I ain't your pal, Cooper.'

'I guess that's obvious.' As Walsh turned to leave, Cooper gestured towards the wall. 'But how about you do your good deed for the day and find me a bandage in that first-aid kit over there.'

Walsh glanced at the wall kit. 'Why should I?'

'I think Stone sprained my arm when he pushed me against the wall. It's beginning to hurt pretty bad.'

Walsh grinned and his eyes narrowed with suspicion. 'Listen, Cooper, I wasn't born yesterday. I don't want no funny stuff on

524

ny watch, OK? Stone said not to let you out under any circumstances, and I ain't, so if this cell goes on fire, you're toasted, man.'

'I'm not asking to be let out. Look, just get me a bandage so I can bind my arm. When Stone gets back we can see about proper medical treatment. Hurry it up, will you? It's beginning to hurt like hell.'

Walsh frowned. 'I dunno . . .'

'You really think I'd be dumb enough to attempt an escape? I've got enough black marks on my copybook as it is.'

'Yeah, well, you shouldn't have been dumb enough to help Moran,' Walsh replied.

'Hindsight's always twenty-twenty. I made a big mistake. C'mon, Walsh, I'm locked inside a damned cell and going nowhere. Gimme the roll of gauze, for Chrissakes. What am I going to do with it, hang myself?'

Walsh studied Cooper's face, as if searching for the lie, then he stepped over and took down the first-aid kit. He opened the box and found a thick roll of gauze. 'That'll have to do.'

'Thanks. The pain's getting worse.'

Walsh handed in the gauze and Cooper wrapped it round his hand. 'There's got to be scissors in that kit, Walsh. Do me a favour and cut the gauze. I can't tear it with one hand.'

Walsh was wary. 'Scissors – you think I've lost my marbles?'

Cooper said in frustration, 'Then forget about it and just tear the damned gauze.'

As Walsh tore the gauze, Cooper's hands suddenly came out through the bars, grabbed him by the throat and manoeuvred him into a painful neck lock. 'You're fucking choking me!' Walsh croaked.

Cooper wrestled Walsh's gun from its hip holster, then fumbled in Walsh's pockets and found the cell keys. Walsh fought to release himself but it was useless, and his voice was a strangled whisper. 'You're fucking crazy, Cooper. When Stone finds out about this, your ass is barbecued . . .'

'Your kids ever tell you that you do a great Kermit the Frog impression, Walsh?'

At that precise moment the door burst open and Stone stoo[d] there, Norton behind him. Stone quickly took in the scene, slippe[d] out his Glock, pointed it at Cooper and said grimly, 'What t[he] fuck do you think you're doing, Cooper? Drop the gun and l[et] go of Walsh.'

Cooper didn't budge. 'I'm already in this up to my neck. A[ny] reason why I should, Stone?'

'Yeah. Because it seems like I owe you an apology.'

162

I stared at Gamal. He was an eerie sight, dressed in a black flowing robe with his arms outstretched. I broke out in a cold sweat.

Patrick's face radiated pleasure. 'Hey, you look scared, Moran.'

I was petrified. *Gamal's going to take his revenge on me.* The thought of what Frank and I would have to endure made me sick to my stomach. An instant death would have been welcome if it meant escaping Gamal's torture.

Patrick turned to Gamal and his voice boomed around the basement room. 'You want me to tell the bitch what we'll do to her, Constantine? What do you think? It's your call, partner.'

But before Gamal could answer, Patrick laughed. 'Hey, Moran, maybe we'll go the whole hog and go for a big, bad orgy of sex and violence. Screw you until you beg for mercy. Then butcher you alive for the finale. What do you think? Could you go for that, Katie, baby?'

I staggered back against a wall, terrified to be in the same room with both of these men. In the wash of the blue arc lights I saw that I had nowhere to run.

Patrick leaned in closer, his face so near that I could smell his acid breath. 'You know, it turns me on when a woman begs. So you better learn to beg for your fucking life. 'Cause if you don't, it's going to get a lot worse. Right, Constantine?'

Perspiration trickled down my face as I stared up at Gamal. He still didn't reply, his eyes staring straight ahead as if he was pondering what he would do next.

Patrick said aloud, 'You going to tell her how bad it's going to get, Constantine? Or will I?'

And that's when it hit me and I recognised the disgusting stench underlying the aromatic candles. It was the odour of rotting flesh. I scanned the ground around Gamal's feet but it looked bare except for the candles.

I continued to stare at Gamal's unflinching face. In the shadowy candlelight his skin looked the colour of faded parchment. And that's when the truth struck me and I suddenly understood where the stench was coming from. *No wonder Gamal hasn't replied to any questions.* I gaped at Patrick and stammered, 'He . . . he's dead . . .'

Patrick's grin widened as he flicked on a wall switch and another arc light snapped on and illuminated Gamal's lifeless body. Then Patrick reached over to the table and plucked up a frightening-looking butcher's knife. 'Hey, so you finally got it Kate. I guess the game's over and this is where the fun really begins.'

163

'What the hell's going on, Stone?' Josh stared frantically out through the windscreen as the Taurus sped out into the Virginian countryside. 'Tell me!'

He had been bundled into an elevator and rushed down to the car pool, and now the siren was on and Stone was driving like a madman, Norton in the back with Walsh. Six other cars had erupted out of the car park, split up into pairs and headed in different directions.

'My guys were at the cemetery and saw the grave,' Stone admitted as he turned off the Eisenhower Freeway.

Josh said angrily, 'I *told* you, Stone. Why wouldn't you listen to me?'

Stone sighed, ran a finger uncomfortably around the inside of his neck brace and admitted, 'Because I'm a dumb asshole, that's why. There's something else you need to know. It's about our trailer victim, Otis Fleist. He used to work for the Bryce family.'

'You're kidding me?'

'Five years ago, right after his parents died, David Bryce hired Fleist to help him with some yard work and gardening at the manor. Everything was dandy until months later when Fleist started making some unpleasant allegations.'

'About what?'

Stone kept his foot hard on the accelerator and the engine roared. 'Before I tell you that you need to know something. David Bryce had an older brother named Patrick.'

Josh frowned. 'What's significant about that?'

'Plenty. Patrick had a long history of psychiatric problems and was a patient at Bellevue. I met him once, when Lou and I had

to go break the news about his brother and niece being murdered.
I remember I even questioned the guy about Kate Moran, to try
to find out what he knew about the relationship she had with his
brother. But Patrick appeared to be at rock bottom with grief
and drugged up to his eyeballs.' Stone flashed his lights at the
car in front of them. '*Get the hell out of my way, pal.*'

'I'm listening, Stone.'

'But I wonder about that now, if it was all an act. Anyway, the
story you need to hear goes back to Fleist's allegations. Patrick
had been on new medication and showed promising signs of
improvement, so David Bryce had signed release papers for his
brother and legally became his guardian, hoping the progress was
going to be permanent.'

Josh nodded. 'Go on.'

'It wasn't. About a month later Fleist complained to the local
cops that Patrick Bryce had attempted to sexually assault his then
nine-year-old daughter. Apparently the kid was pretty traumatised and needed psychiatric care. Under court order, David
Bryce had to have Patrick recommitted to Bellevue until his case
came up. Then Fleist threatened a civil action, claiming his
daughter was mentally scarred by the assault. His lawyer wheedled a generous settlement from David, as Patrick's custodian,
and a week later Fleist decided to drop the charges so the case
never went to court. I guess now we know why Kimberly Fleist
never left the trailer much.'

'How come you know all this, Stone?'

'Moran had put out a bulletin looking for information on Otis
Fleist. A call came in a few days back from one of the local cops
from Angel Bay who was involved with the Fleist sex-assault case
five years back. We only got round to checking Moran's office
calls this afternoon and the cop who called gave us the lowdown
on what had happened back then.'

'Anything else you want to tell me?'

'Here's the really weird thing. The cop told us that a couple
of weeks back he was on night patrol when he questioned a guy
who was parked near Moran's cottage. He claimed he was stopped

to make a call from his cell phone and that he'd been visiting Moran. The cop said it was the next day that he realised that the guy bore a strong resemblance to Patrick Bryce. In fact, he's convinced himself that it *was* Patrick he spoke with.'

'You're serious?'

'I know, it's pretty fucking weird when you consider the same guy was supposed to have died by drowning, except his body was never found.'

Josh frowned. 'What does it all mean?'

Stone looked confused. 'If I knew that I'd have made director by now. The final nail is that I reckon Patrick was at the mall, trying to hunt down Moran. He even found time to kill Lou and beat me over the frigging head and steal my gun. We've got him on camera. One of the mall security guys gave us the tape and told us about this guy chasing Moran who claimed to be a federal agent. Show him the still shots, Gus.'

Norton took an envelope from his inside pocket and handed a bunch of still computer-printed photographs to Cooper, who examined them. He studied the man in the shots: he looked about forty, wore jeans and sneakers and a dark blue windcheater. 'How do you know for certain it's him?' Cooper asked.

'I don't,' Stone answered. 'I'm relying on instinct.'

'Your instinct has been wrong before.'

'You're right, Cooper. Except this time I'd bet my fucking pension on it.'

Josh handed back the pics and looked at the Virginian countryside flashing past. 'You mind telling me where exactly we're going in such a hurry? And what's with the other cars that left the lot the same time as us?'

Stone flicked a meaningful look at Norton in the rear-view mirror. 'Tell him the rest, Gus.'

164

Angel Bay, Virginia

I gazed at Gamal's corpse, lit by the powerful halogen lamp, the stench overpowering. His skin was eaten by maggots. A grin appeared on Patrick's face and I knew he was enjoying my distress. I wanted to ask the only question I could think of, but he was about to answer it for me.

'You're asking yourself *why*, aren't you, Kate? You want to know why I dug up Gamal's body, why do all this?'

'Y . . . yes.'

'Because it was all part of the plan, Katie, baby.'

'*What* plan?'

Patrick ignored my question. 'Move closer to him. I want to see you two come face to face.'

I wanted to say: *You're totally sick.* I didn't budge, and suddenly the back of Patrick's hand slashed across my mouth and he aimed the gun barrel at my head. 'You hear what I fucking said? Move closer, get right up to his face. I want you two to become acquainted again, just like old times.'

I tasted blood on my lips and forced myself to step closer to Gamal's corpse. Even the aroma of incense didn't mask the overpowering rotten stench, and I wanted to throw up.

Patrick laughed. 'Reach out and touch him. I want to see you shake hands with the Devil's Disciple.'

I couldn't bring myself to move a finger and I recoiled, but Patrick's hand came up, brandishing his pistol. 'You want me to put a bullet in that pretty face of yours? Make up your mind, sweetheart.'

I knew his threats were simply about power: killers like Patrick enjoyed exercising control and got off on seeing others suffer.

'Do what I fucking tell you. Shake his hand, *bitch*.'

Patrick pushed his pistol against my temple until it hurt. I closed my eyes and steeled myself as I reached out to touch Gamal's right hand. The moment had a surreal quality: it was *horrible* – Gamal's dead flesh eaten by decomposition.

Patrick laughed again. 'Shake his fucking hand! Maybe you'd like to tell him you're sorry for what you did to him.'

What was happening was so bizarre that I kept my eyes closed as I shook the rotting limb. It didn't move. I opened my eyes. That was when I noticed that a bulky nail had been driven into Gamal's palm. I looked at the other hand and understood the grisly truth. *Both* Gamal's hands were nailed to a black wooden cross that supported him, the nails concealed behind his sleeved garb. Patrick saw my reaction and snickered. 'You like that, Moran? I thought the black cross was a nice touch.'

I recoiled as Patrick struck me a blow across the face with his pistol. I was blinded by a cutting pain, and then I felt him snap something on my left wrist. *I'm being handcuffed.* It took a few moments to regain my senses, but even as I struggled Patrick forced the second cuff on my other wrist, binding my hands in front of me.

My jaw was on fire from the blow as Patrick savagely took hold of my hair and stared into my face. 'You wanted to know *why*, Katie? Hey, maybe it's time I told you the whole story.'

165

Patrick stood over me and tucked the gun into his trouse belt. 'I didn't kill them. Constantine did.'

'What?'

'It was him all along. He abducted David and Megan from the cottage on Thanksgiving morning. He entered the cottag while David and his kid were preparing dinner. He used th needle on them both and took them away in David's car an killed them at the mine. His last-minute confession was a lie, par of our set-up. What's the matter, Moran?'

I was stunned again. 'There were differences at the crime scen I never understood. In the way the crucifix was placed at Megan feet. And David had been shot . . .'

Patrick smiled. 'All I know is what Constantine told me, Morar When he dragged David into the mine he came awake and starte to fight back, so Constantine shot him twice in the head. Wh cares about the crucifix? Maybe some animal disturbed it, o Constantine was in a hurry and just tossed it there. Either wa you still got the message.'

'Then what about the murders at the Chinatown metro Gam admitted to?'

Patrick said, 'He did those too. Constantine told me he was o a high after doing David and Megan, knowing how much it woul get to you, and he wanted to kill some more. He did the black gu and his kid later that afternoon, and neatly rounded off the day.

I heard the cold brutality in Patrick's voice and felt a surge o revulsion. 'How could you be so heartless?'

I saw him pick something up from the table and slip it behin his back. He'd moved too fast for me to see what it was but m anxiety increased. *Has he selected one of the knives?* I felt my legs go weak. Patrick stared down at me. 'You think I care what you feel? See, the thing is, I reckon it was all fate. David and Megan were going to die anyway.'

'What do you mean?'

'Before Constantine did them, I'd been planning to kill them myself. When my parents made David the beneficiary of their will I thought that if I killed him and Megan I'd get everything I always wanted. Money, women, a nice life. I even had my escape route from Bellevue all planned, using a storm drain that led out of the grounds. I could have murdered them and been back in Bellevue without anyone being the wiser. Even made it look like Constantine's work. When your buddies Stone and Raines came to visit me at Bellevue, to tell me about the murder of David and Megan, I bet they never suspected me for a minute. But you want to know something? I remember that day pretty good. Your friend Stone, he asked me a lot of questions about you, he even gave me the feeling that he wasn't entirely convinced Gamal had done the job. I just played dumb, pretended I was hurt as hell and disturbed by the news. But the fact is, I'd thought about killing my brother for years, even before you came along. Sweet, money-grabbing Kate.'

I saw the look of pure venom in Patrick's face and responded, 'I never wanted David's money. That's not why I intended to marry him.'

Patrick picked up an oily rag from the table. 'No? But you still took the money, Kate.'

'I haven't spent a penny of it,' I answered.

Patrick produced a jagged knife from behind his back and began to polish the blade. 'Bet you would if you'd had time. You know my big mistake? I should have done my homework. After Constantine killed David and his brat the family lawyer came to see me, and what did I discover? That *you* got it all, David left you everything. And me? I'm a mental patient so I likely can't contest the will. Neat move, Kate. *Really* neat move. But that wasn't Constantine's fault. It was yours.'

I almost passed out as I watched the jagged steel in Patrick's hands. 'David drew up his own will, it had nothing to do with me. I swear . . .'

Patrick landed another stinging blow on my face and I staggered back against the wall. 'Don't lie to me. Want to know something else? If I can't have the legacy, no one's going to have it. I deserved that money after all the shit I had to take from my old man.'

I was handcuffed, couldn't escape, but I tried to stave off the moment when he'd start to use those butcher's knives. I changed the subject. 'W . . . where did you meet Gamal?'

'He treated me at Bellevue. I felt Constantine understood me, understood exactly what I'd been through with a shitty family who didn't give a fuck about me. But I didn't know all we had in common until after you caught him. Then I read all that stuff about him in the newspapers. That was mind-blowing, a fucking revelation. When I was a kid and misbehaved my old man used to beat the crap out of me and lock me in the basement too. No wonder I felt that Constantine and I shared a kinship. Crappy fathers and siblings who didn't care a shit.'

'David cared . . .' I said.

Patrick said with fury, 'Like fuck he did. But Gamal, now he was a different story. You killed a brilliant man, Kate. He'd had the balls to do what I always wanted to do – destroy the family who fucked up his life. It's your fault that the man I idolised was put on death row. That's why I promised Constantine I'd avenge his death.'

I saw Patrick stare up at Gamal with a look of awe, and I knew that he was totally deranged. 'How . . . how could you? You were locked up in Bellevue.'

Patrick started to polish the knife again. 'Warden Clay at Greensville happens to be an old family friend. After I got sent back to Bellevue he wrote me a letter offering to get me on a programme for sex offenders run by the prison shrink. He said it got good results, but I didn't even bother to reply. That all changed when I heard Constantine had been transferred to Greensville. I wanted to meet him again, so I wrote to Clay telling im that if his offer still stood I'd love to take him up on it. Hey presto, it worked. But I just wanted to meet Constantine.'

My pulse rate was soaring as I watched Patrick polish the blade. 'Clay helped you?'

Patrick nodded. 'The dumb prick pulled all the right strings and got me a temporary transfer to the same psychiatric unit in Greensville where Constantine was held. The prisoners are kept apart during exercise, locked up in special outdoor cages, but I could slip him written messages through the steel mesh. I told him I wanted to help him. That got him interested.'

'Help in what way?'

Patrick grinned. 'By trying to spring him from prison. That was my big plan, only it didn't work out. If you studied those drawings of Greensville you'd see it's impossible to escape without inside help. So we came up with another plan, this time to get back at you after the execution. My suicide and the copycat killings were all part of that.'

Patrick laughed and I said, 'What's so funny?'

'Clay. Don't you get it? He helps get me on a fucking rehab course and then I kill myself. I bet the idiot still blames himself for that.'

I wondered whether guilt had anything to do with Clay's reluctance to talk. And I worried that Frank was in pain and bleeding to death, but I had to force my concerns from my mind before they drove me insane. 'Where did you get the money to survive afterwards?'

'Constantine had a stash put by in a disused mine outside Fredericksburg. A couple of hundred grand in case he needed to get away in a hurry. I was to help myself to whatever I needed, including the name of a guy in DC who does a line in fake passports and cloned credit cards. So I laid low, created a new identity for myself and rented an apartment in Alexandria while I did my planning. Constantine and I figured the copycat killings would fuck up your mind, make you think he was still alive and was coming back to get you. Payback time. Hey, and it worked. Half scared you to death, didn't it?'

'Whose idea was it to dig up the body?'

Patrick gave another grin. 'Constantine and me figured it wou totally wreck your head. Especially when you found the remai of a dead ram instead of him. It was meant to be another min fuck for you. It worked, too, didn't it?'

'How could you know where Gamal was buried?'

Patrick replaced the polished knife on the table. 'After t execution I followed the mortuary van all the way from the pris to the Richmond Medical Examiner's office, just to make su that's where they took it. The next morning I called the offic pretended that I was from the funeral home and asked to confir the time they wanted the body picked up for burial. Smart, hu Then all I had to do was follow the hearse to Sunset Memori Park. That night I broke into the cemetery and dug u Constantine. Neat, huh?'

I still needed answers. 'There were no footprints at the mi shaft. How did you manage that? Did you brush them out, burn them away?'

'Sure, I used a blowlamp and lightly burned 'em off on n way out. Don't tell me you're only figuring that out now, *dumm* And you call yourself a criminal investigator?'

Patrick picked up an object from the table. I couldn't see wh it was as he held it behind his back. Had he selected anoth knife?

He said, 'I bet you didn't figure out Fleist either. Five yea ago he worked for David, until he claimed I assaulted his daughte I did, that's why I chose them as part of the plan, another enem to pay back. Clever, huh?'

'It was you who planted the misleading evidence. The stuff the trailer home, the drawings of Greensville prison and the blac cape, you put them there.'

Patrick inclined his head. 'It was all part of fucking with you head, Moran. And to send your investigation off on differe tangents.'

'You even pretended to be me arguing with Fleist,' I said.

'Hey, you're finally getting there. I reckoned it would dum

you deeper in the shit by making your colleagues think you were the killer. Wasn't I clever?'

'And the midnight phone calls? Did you make them from the cottage?'

Patrick gave me a baffled look. 'What the fuck are you talking about?' He stared impatiently at his watch. 'Time's up. Let's get this show on the road and do some cutting, Katie, baby. You first, then I'll finish off Frank.'

His answer had thrown me but I had no time to think about it as Patrick lunged. I staggered back but he held me in an arm lock and stuck a hypodermic in my arm. I felt the needle pinch and then moments later a strange sensation began to ripple through my body. The basement swam, the powerful halogen lights dimmed, and everything faded to black.

When I woke I was strapped down on the wooden table near the wall. I felt drowsy, and didn't know how long I'd been out cold. I tried to move but my arms and my legs were bound with straps. 'Welcome back, Kate. Looks like we're ready to begin the show.'

I turned my head and saw Patrick arranging the medical instruments on the table. I flinched. *This is not a bad dream. I'm going to die.*

He now wore the butcher's belt, complete with a collection of frightening-looking knives. I felt weak as Patrick plucked another one of the stainless-steel blades and ran a fingertip along the jagged edge. 'Don't you think it's kinda neat the way it all came together? The way I'm paying you back from both Constantine and me? At first, I thought I'd use the blades, but you know what? I think I'll try something just a little more interesting.'

Patrick slipped the knife back in the belt and picked up a miniature electric saw with a circular blade. He pressed the button and the saw whirred to life with a frightening high-pitched whine. 'This one's even got a diamond-edge blade for cutting through bone. You ready for the ultimate experience of being cut up, Kate?'

166

'We're going *where*?' Josh asked.

Norton said, 'Angel Bay. We figure Patrick may head to the old manor.'

'Why do you figure *that*?'

This time Stone answered. 'It's home territory for him. Killers like Patrick prefer to be on home territory when they're under pressure. It gives them a sense of security. And right now I reckon that he's under pressure. He'll know he's only got a limited amount of time once we're on his tail.'

'What if you've got it wrong?' Cooper asked worriedly. 'What if he's not at the house?'

Stone replied, 'You're right, he may not be. So we've hedged our bets and sent a half-dozen cars to the three nearest under-ground sites that Gamal used in this region in the past, just in case Patrick tries to head there to have his fun with Moran before he kills her. We reckon that's his endgame. The way it's panning out, he wants to kill her, but he'll want to play games with her first. Only God knows what his reasons are. Me, I haven't a clue.'

Cooper said angrily, 'This whole thing has been one big game but it took you a while to figure that out. You should have listened to Kate.'

'Yeah, well, I'm man enough to admit my mistakes,' Stone confessed.

'Except your mistakes could have already got her killed.'

Stone said grimly, 'I'm aware of that so don't rub salt in the wound. And don't be fooled, I'm just as worried as you look, Cooper.'

The communications radio was on and Cooper heard a metallic voice say, *'Charlie Three to Alpha One. You there, over?'*

Stone picked up the handset and said, 'Alpha One to Charlie Three. What have you got?'

'We're at the second site and it's all clear, no sign of Bryce, over.'

'Just stay with it, Charlie Three, and keep in touch, over and out.'

Stone put down the handset and Cooper said, 'Did you alert the local cops?'

Stone nodded. 'In every case. They've been given orders to observe the locations in unmarked cars in advance of our arrival, but they're only to take action on our instructions, unless it's an emergency.'

'What about Gamal? There's definitely no possibility that he's still alive?'

Norton said, 'There's no way, Cooper. Whatever's happened to his body it didn't climb out of that grave. He died the night of his execution, that's for sure. I spoke to the junior at the ME's office who did the autopsy and he told me Gamal was a stiff, no two ways about it. I even saw the autopsy photos and it was definitely Gamal on the slab. So we figure it had to be Patrick doing those killings, but as to why, like Vance says, we're clueless. Patrick was once a patient of Gamal's but that's the only connection we can figure.'

The Taurus slowed as Stone gently eased his foot down on the brake. Cooper saw the cottage fifty yards ahead, lights on inside. An unmarked car was parked along the road, its headlights extinguished. Cooper saw no one inside until they got closer and he spotted a couple in the car, who looked as if they were courting. The couple stepped out as the Feds halted. Stone handed Cooper back his weapon. 'Take it, Cooper, it's loaded. You may get to use it before the night's out.'

Cooper took his gun and checked the magazine as Stone climbed out of the car. The air was cold, the bay silent. The couple from the car came forward and Stone introduced himself. 'Well, you see anything?'

'I was just about to call your folks,' the male plainclothes cop answered. 'We saw nothing until I decided to take a walk around the back of the manor. There's a car parked there.'

'What kind?' Stone asked.

'A dark green Nissan sedan. It looks like it's been in an accident, has some damage to the passenger side and the front side panel's been dented. I had the plates checked out before I went to call you. The vehicle was rented from Hertz in DC over a week ago, to a customer named Patrick Swan.'

Stone raised an eyebrow. 'Well, at least he kept his first name. I'm betting it wasn't the only vehicle he hired or stole. You see signs of anyone?'

The cop shook his head. 'No, and we didn't hear anything, either. Except I saw what looked like a basement door that was open round the back. But I thought it best to head back here and make my report instead of going barging in alone.'

Stone removed his pistol. 'You and your partner better stay here and cover the exit.'

'Whatever you say,' the plainclothes answered.

'So what's the plan?' Cooper asked anxiously, as an icy wind from Angel Bay licked at their faces.

'The bad news is we don't really have one,' Stone admitted, handing round Maglite flashlights he took from the car. 'It's a case of suck it and see.'

'We're going to split up and take the front and back of the manor?' Cooper asked, taking a torch.

Stone nodded. 'Cooper, you go with Gus and check the basement door round the back, and Walsh can come with me. Only use the radios if you really have to, and for Christ sakes everyone go easy and don't make a fucking sound. If Patrick Bryce is in there, I don't want the bastard to know we're coming or he's liable to kill Kate straight away – that is if he hasn't already.'

167

I felt a stinging slap across my face as I came to again to the sound of Patrick's laughter. 'Wake up, you hear me? *Wake fucking up!'*

My jaw exploded with pain as he struck me again, this time with his fist. The frightening scream of the electric saw echoed around the basement and Patrick had a manic look on his face. There was no escape, no way to turn. *If I'm going to die then please God let it be over soon. Let me lose consciousness so that I don't feel anything.*

And then something happened: I became so resigned to dying that my fear ebbed away. Moments later I saw Patrick's sneer vanish and he flicked off the saw and the noise of the blade died.

I realised what was happening. *He gets off on seeing the fear in my face.* He must have sensed that I was reconciled to dying – for his pleasure to continue he needed to induce fear in me again. As if to prove it he replaced the electric saw on the table, and then made a show of carefully selecting a heavy meat cleaver with a sharp edge.

Patrick searched my eyes again for the one thing that gave him a kick of adrenaline – my terror. I felt the fear rise in me once more as he pressed the cleaver tip against the soft flesh of my arm and drew a line of blood. I winced with pain. He laughed. 'Hey, that hurt?'

I couldn't speak as the blood started to trickle down my hand. Patrick looked as if he was enjoying every second, then his gaze swept around the basement. 'You like it here? This place is a rabbit warren of tunnels. When I was a kid and misbehaved my old man used to lock me down here, just like Gamal's father.

Eventually I even got to like it because I got to do what I wanted. I used to catch wild animals in the woods and take them here and cut them up. Just like I cut up the others. Just like I'm going to cut you up.' His free hand started to tear at the buttons on my blouse.

'No . . . !'

'Scream as much as you want but no one's going to hear you.' Patrick ripped open my blouse, slid the cleaver under the middle of my bra and cut it with the blade, exposing my breasts. Then he leaned over and licked my left nipple. 'Like it, Katie? You getting off on it? Tell me, sweetie.'

I couldn't speak for fear as his fingers slowly moved down to my pants. *Let this be over with, fast.* Patrick roughly yanked down my pants, revealing my underwear.

'It's fun time.' He grinned, flicking his tongue like a snake. 'Let the party begin.'

168

Cooper advanced towards the rear of the manor, moving as fast as he could. He kept his gun drawn and ready, Norton keeping up the pace behind him, holding his weapon in both hands. Cooper flashed his torch when they came to stone steps that led down to a basement, a rotting wooden door hanging off its hinges. 'Let's try down here,' Cooper said. 'I'll go in first.'

'Won't argue with that,' Norton whispered back.

Cooper stepped quietly down the steps, flashing the torch as he went. When he came to the bottom he peered round the rotten door, brandishing the torch, and saw another stairwell. He listened but didn't hear a sound, then he looked back up at Norton, who was covering him from the top of the stairs. When Cooper beckoned, Norton gingerly followed him down the steps and wrinkled his nose. '*Jeez.* You get that? Smells like scented candles. But there's some kind of other smell, too.'

Cooper sniffed the air. 'I get it. Cover me.' He moved through the door and down the second set of steps. At the bottom of the stairwell he flashed his Maglite and saw several tunnels leading off in different directions.

Norton was right behind him, moving his torchlight over the walls as he whispered, 'If the manor house is anything to go by I figure this basement is fucking huge. *Hey*, you hear that, Coop?'

'Hear what?' Cooper said intently.

'*Listen.* Sounds to me like someone talking,' Norton answered.

Cooper listened, heard what sounded like whispered voices, and he tensed. 'There's someone down here,' he said.

Norton answered, 'Let me get closer, try hear what they're saying.'

As Norton moved past Cooper he kicked against something metallic and the noise boomed around the tunnels.

'*Holy fuck!*' Norton hissed angrily. He flashed his torch on the ground and saw that he'd struck a rusting bucket, and that the floor was covered with the remains of a shattered porcelain basin.

'*Jesus,* Norton,' Cooper whispered in alarm. 'You've done it now!'

At that precise moment they both heard a shriek, the cry echoing round the basement like the wail of a banshee.

'*Fuck,*' Norton said through clenched teeth. 'It's got to be Moran!'

Cooper didn't even reply. He was already darting forward through one of the archways, his gun at the ready, his heart drumming like a piston.

169

I couldn't speak as Patrick's fingers moved over my pants. I *hated* him, hated him for degrading me. *Let this end soon.*

'You enjoying this, Kate?'

I felt his fingers start to probe between my legs and I almost threw up. I wanted to say: *'Please don't do this.'*

Except I knew that once he heard me beg it would only spur him on. I saw Patrick's face spark with pleasure. He was enjoying humiliating me. Was this how Gamal had behaved when he had tortured David and Megan? Had he defiled Megan before he murdered her? Or worse, defiled her in front of her father? It was torment to even think about what might have happened to them. I struggled with rage against the leather restraints but it was useless, they were tied tightly.

Patrick leaned over, brandishing the cleaver. 'Hey, now you know what Gamal must have felt like when he was strapped down on the gurney. Puts a different perspective on things, don't you think, Moran?'

I couldn't take his taunting any more. *'Go to hell!'*

Patrick's eyes flashed with amusement. 'Hey, it's you who's going to hell, honey. And I'm the man who's going to send you there, but not before I've fucked you to within an inch of your life.'

Suddenly a noise rang around the basement, a metallic clatter that sounded like a small explosion. My body was as taut as a spring but I tensed even more and my imagination ran wild. What had caused the noise? Had Frank become conscious?

Patrick stiffened and looked behind him as an angry voice cried out from somewhere in the basement, *'Holy fuck!'*

The voice came from one of the tunnels. And it wasn't Frank's. I couldn't believe it. *Someone's out there.*

I did the only thing I could think of. I screamed.

Patrick exploded with rage and struck me a savage blow across the jaw that sent my ears ringing. 'Shut the fuck up, Moran!'

I reeled from the blow as Patrick crossed the room to listen at one of the tunnel entrances. A second later came the distinct sound of racing footsteps. Patrick lost it then, furious that his enjoyment had been interrupted, and he lunged at me with the blade. 'You're fucking dead!'

As he came towards me my survival instincts kicked in: *Think! Do something!* My body reacted almost by instinct: I twisted my torso, wrenched and flailed against the restraints so violently that the wooden trestle table keeled over and I collapsed on the floor, landing on my side, still strapped to the wood. The next thing I knew Patrick had kicked out at the table and I was flipped on my back. He stood looking down at me, his face contorted with hatred, the cleaver still in his hand. *I'm dead. There's no escape.*

Patrick raised the cleaver and slashed it through the air. I twisted again but the cleaver struck me a glancing blow, and I felt a searing hot pain in my arm as the blade cut flesh. Patrick laughed with triumph but as he raised his hand to slash at me again a voice said, 'Drop it, Bryce, *this instant,* or I drop you!'

Josh stood in the mouth of one of the tunnels, the Glock held in both his hands. 'Do it, Bryce, or so help me I'll send you to hell!'

Patrick didn't move and a grin spread slowly across his face. '*Last chance, Bryce!*' Josh roared.

Patrick smirked. 'Hey, whatever you say. Guess you've got me.' He knelt to lay down the cleaver but as his arm dropped his other hand came up and hit the wall light switch and the cellar was plunged into darkness.

There was an explosion as Josh's gun went off, a split-second flash of muzzle light that strobed the black and turned everything a silver white, and then the cellar was plunged into darkness again.

170

For a second or two nothing happened. My heart pounded like a power hammer in the darkness. And then Josh flicked on a torch and I glimpsed Patrick disappear through one of the tunnel arches.

'Don't let him get away!' I shouted.

Josh raced over towards the tunnel, flashed his torch into the dark and turned back. '*Damn*, he's gone.'

'We *have* to catch him, Josh.' I was frenzied. 'Frank's hurt, he's back there in one of the tunnels . . .'

Josh knelt and started to undo the leather straps that bound me. 'I know, he was coming round when we stumbled over him. Norton's with him and trying to call for medical help, and Stone and Walsh are outside with some local cops so Patrick isn't going anywhere.' He finished untying the straps binding my hands and then he noticed my unbuttoned clothes and gashed arm. 'Are you OK? Did he hurt you?'

I frantically helped him remove the remaining straps from my legs and I adjusted my torn clothes and buttoned my jeans. 'Just my arm, but he scared the hell out of me. Josh, this place is a warren of tunnels and Patrick will know every inch of the house. He'll find a way out.'

'Calm down, Kate. We've got it covered.' Josh studied the cut on my arm and helped me up. 'It doesn't look too bad.'

'Give me your gun.' I steadied myself on my feet.

'*What?*'

'He's mine. I want that bastard,' I answered.

Josh plucked a radio from his pocket. 'Kate, don't be so damned stupid. We'll search the basement and between us and the others

549

we'll find him.' He put the radio to his mouth. 'Stone, are yo
there . . . ?'

'*Yeah, I'm here,*' came the immediate reply.

As Josh was distracted on the radio I grabbed at his gun. '*Who
Kate, don't be so dumb!*' He looked stunned by my ferocity.

I felt like a woman possessed as I twisted Josh's arm into
lock. 'I said give it to me . . . !'

As he tried to wrestle with me he dropped his torch and radi
We could both barely see as Stone's voice crackled in the bac
ground. '*You there, Coop? What the hell's going on?*'

I kept pressure applied to the arm lock as Josh protested, 'Kat
goddammit, will you listen to reason . . . if you're not careful t
gun's going to go off!'

But I was past reasoning with. I wanted so badly to kill Patric
for all the evil he'd done. 'Let go of the weapon!' I screamed.

'Kate, are you crazy? Do you want to get yourself *killed* . . .

'I don't care, just give me the gun!' At that point *nothi*
mattered but apprehending Patrick. At last I managed to wrenc
the Glock from Josh's grasp, but I got the feeling that he let
go rather than have the weapon go off accidentally and kill on
of us.

'Kate!' he protested. '*Listen to me, for pity's sake . . .*'

But his protest fell on deaf ears and I grabbed the torch an
plunged into the tunnel after Patrick.

171

My claustrophobia was gone. My mind was crystal clear and I had only one purpose. *Find Patrick.* It was as if Gamal were alive again, and he and Patrick were two sides of the same coin. I advanced rapidly through the tunnel, clutching the Glock and shining the torch into every recess. Ten yards farther on I heard Josh race up behind me. '*Kate . . . will you listen? You just can't do this . . .*'

'I told you, he's mine.'

Josh was persistent. 'He can still be yours but you don't have to get yourself killed. Now how about you be sensible and give me my gun back? This is the time to be cool and measured, not lose your head. Don't let your anger overrule reason.'

I slowed down. I desperately wanted to kill Patrick, wanted it more than anything, and I didn't care if it cost me my own life. He hadn't killed David and Megan but he was part of an evil pact that had destroyed so many lives, and I wanted him to pay. But I knew Josh was right. I was allowing my anger to take control of me and I needed to calm down. My heart was still racing as I tried to breathe more slowly.

'You feel any better?' Josh asked.

'A little.' *But do I really?*

And then we both heard it. A *click* of shoe leather and the sound of footsteps receding. I aimed the torch towards where the noise had come from. It was a narrow recess, ten yards away. An open black-painted metal door appeared to lead into another part of the basement. The footsteps raced away, slapping

on stone, and then there was silence. 'It's him, Josh!'
  'Kate, will you hold on or you'll get us both shot . . . !'
But I was already running towards the doorway.

172

I halted outside the door and kept the Glock at the ready. I flashed the torch on the walls and saw a huge room with ancient wooden boxes stacked in the corners. Most of them were rotting. The place looked like a storage room. I could see no other exit. I wiped away the perspiration running down my face.

'Kate,' Josh whispered as he followed behind me, 'just wait for back-up, Stone's going to be here any minute . . .'

I put a finger to my lips for him to be silent. I could almost *sense* Patrick's presence. Then I heard a noise that sounded like heavy breathing. I flashed the light around the room and noticed a trail of fresh blood. Crimson spots, some as big as a dime, were spattered on the ground. 'Your shot must have hit him, he's in here somewhere,' I whispered back to Josh.

Before Josh could reply we both heard whimpering. I flashed the torch towards the noise and saw more blood on the ground. I followed the trail with my light and that's when I saw Patrick huddled in a corner. The blood trail ended in a pool at his feet. He'd been shot in the left side of his chest.

I still felt enraged, wanted to make Patrick pay for his evil, but then I saw that his face was beaded with sweat and his blood-shot eyes had a tortured, distant look. He didn't seem to recognise us. He looked at me like a frightened ten-year-old. '*Please* . . . please don't hit me. Don't hurt me, Daddy. I'll be a good boy in future, I promise I will,' he begged. 'I . . . I'll do what you tell me but don't beat me with the stick.'

What the hell's going on? Is this some kind of childhood regression he's experiencing under duress? Is this the storeroom where his fathe locked him and beat him up?

'Please, Daddy . . .' Patrick pleaded, and put his hands up t cover his face. 'Please don't hit me any more.'

He was weeping like a child now, tears streaming down hi cheeks, and he looked pathetic, but my natural caution kicked in *Is he acting, or for real?*

'He looks delirious,' Josh commented. 'As if he's in some kin of trance.'

'Josh, I'm not so sure,' I whispered.

Josh said cautiously, 'Neither am I. So let's just be careful her and take it nice and easy. Patrick, do you hear me? We're goin to get you medical help.'

Patrick didn't react but continued whimpering. He gave n sign that he recognised us. His hands still covered his face an like a frightened child he'd stuck a thumb in his mouth. He looke to be experiencing some kind of private terror. I noticed that th bleeding from his wound was getting worse. Josh said, 'He look like he's in severe shock, he's lost so much blood. But I bette pat him down.'

He addressed Patrick again. 'Put your hands against the wa where I can see them and kick those legs apart,' he ordered, the said over his shoulder to me, 'Keep him covered.'

But Josh had moved too hastily – he hadn't given me time t shield him with the Glock and I shouted, 'Josh, get out of m line of fire . . . !'

He must have realised his mistake but it was too late. In a instant Patrick had lunged forward, a blade flashing in his hand He caught Josh by the hair, and his other hand came up to hol the blade against his throat.

Patrick grinned. 'You dumb fucking bastard. Don't you kno never to trust the enemy?' He pressed the blade into Josh's neck 'Back off and get rid of the pistol *pronto* if you want your frien here to live, Moran. Or you're going to see blood.'

I took two steps back. Patrick's face and body were too clos to Josh for me to get a clear shot. I'd be taking a risk firing, an if I missed Patrick would cut Josh's throat before I could fire a second shot. Patrick patted Josh down with his free hand, searching for a weapon, but found only an ID and a wallet. He flicked open the wallet and showed me a picture of Neal inside the flap before he tossed the wallet away.

'Your friend's kid? He isn't going to have a father if you don't throw away that gun right now. Understand me, Moran? Or maybe you'd like me to cut your friend up the way Constantine did David and Megan?'

I felt a cold fury the moment I heard Patrick's taunt. I noticed Josh's eyes burning into mine and he flicked a look to the right, and then I saw him make a gesture in the same direction with his right hand. *What's he trying to tell me?* He repeated his actions twice and I thought: *This is just like Laval in the Paris catacombs. Josh is telling me he's going to attempt to move.*

If he could shift right he might expose enough of Patrick for me to get off a shot, but he still risked getting his throat cut. He stared into my eyes as if to ask: *You understand me?*

I nodded very briefly and Patrick screamed, 'Are you fucking listening to me, Moran?'

'Yes, I'm listening.'

'Then drop the fucking gun *now* or I'll kill him!'

I started to slowly lay the gun down. At that exact moment Josh twisted his body violently to the right. It happened so fast that Patrick was caught unawares. He slashed out with the knife and tried to manoeuvre himself behind Josh's body but for a second or two the right side of his skull was exposed.

I aimed and squeezed the trigger, praying: *Please God don't let me miss.* The Glock exploded. The round struck Patrick in the side of the head, shearing off part of his ear, and he screamed as his hand went up to clasp his wound. Josh wrenched himself free and grabbed Patrick's other hand and twisted it behind his back.

'You fucking bitch!' Patrick shrieked, his palm pressed to the side of his head, blood streaming from his pulped ear. '*I'll fucking kill you, Moran.*'

But Josh grabbed him in an arm lock and then Stone and

Walsh rushed in brandishing their weapons and the basement came alive with screams and torchlight. Walsh helped Josh handcuff Patrick, who was snarling like a wild animal. 'I'm not finished with you, Moran! You'll see! *You'll fucking pay.*'

I didn't see much point in replying but my anger got the better of me and I struck Patrick across the face. His head jerked, his lip cut and bloodied, and I met his stare. 'The down payment on a debt I owe you. You're the one who's going to pay. I hope you enjoy spending the rest of your days locked in a cell, you evil bastard.'

Then Stone and Walsh got a firm grip of his arms and dragged a screaming Patrick away.

173

My arm had been dressed at Mary Washington hospital and it was past eleven that evening when I got home. Frank wasn't so lucky. His head needed stitching and he was admitted with suspected cerebral bruising, but the doctors were optimistic. We had talked about what had happened as I'd lingered by his bed, holding his hand. I was so grateful he was alive that I'd told him over and over how much I loved him.

Frank slumped back on his pillow and offered me a twisted smile. 'Hey, it's not like I'm dying, sis. You better stop before you have me in tears. Later, we'll talk some more, but first you get some sleep. You want some free advice?'

'What?'

He said with concern, 'Stay at Josh's place tonight. Or book into a hotel. But don't go back to the cottage alone. You don't need those kinds of memories right now.'

'I'll think about it,' I said solemnly.

'That means you've thought about it. Don't do it, Kate. You'll only torture yourself.'

'I'll be fine. You just do what the doctors tell you, OK?' I knew that I had to go back. I had my reasons. I squeezed my brother's hand and we hugged goodbye and a little later Josh drove me home. The shore wind was icy cold and it had started to snow again as Josh helped me out of the car. I was exhausted, and by the time we stepped inside the cottage I felt fit to collapse. Josh followed me into the front room, and after he had flicked on the lights I saw him stare thoughtfully out at the bay before he closed the curtains for me. I said, 'You look like you've got something on your mind, Josh.'

'It's Lou,' he admitted, and he looked anguished as he met my stare. 'It's hard to believe the feisty old devil's gone. I'll miss him.

I felt a pang of emotion that brought me close to tears. 'We both will. I know the unit's never going to be the same without him. Will you come by tomorrow and accompany me when I go visit his wife?'

Josh nodded. 'Sure. But right now I think it might be better if I keep you company until you settle down and get some sleep. What do you think?'

'I'll be fine. You ought to be with Neal.' Part of me wanted Josh to remain, and I didn't want to give him the impression that I didn't appreciate his concern, but I had so many conflicting emotions battling inside me that I knew I needed to clear my head. 'I just need some time out alone. I hope you understand? But it would be good to see you tomorrow.'

Josh's gaze fixed on mine as he lifted his hand to touch my face. 'You could still come back to my place and sleep there.'

You've no idea how much I want to do that. I was tempted, but I knew what I had to do. 'I'd like that, but I *have* to stay here, Josh.'

'Have to?'

'It's like when a racing driver crashes. You know what he does if he recovers?'

'What?' Josh asked.

'He gets right back in a racing car again and drives. It's like that with Manor Brook. I have to prove to myself that I can beat the fear. I won't let Patrick or Gamal destroy all the good times I had here with David and Megan.'

'So long as you're sure.' Josh took my hand and kissed my palm. We held each other tightly and he whispered, 'If you need me, I'm only a call away. I'll drive by about noon. See how you are and we can talk some more, OK?'

Much as I wanted him to stay, I knew that the turmoil inside my head would make me poor company and I didn't want it to spoil whatever we might have. 'That sounds good.'

He kissed me on the lips, nodded a farewell and then I led

him to the door. He climbed into his car and was gone, the red tail-lights fading down the gravel driveway into the cold night as I waved him goodbye.

I closed the front door, went to the refrigerator and poured myself a large glass of cold Chardonnay. I brought the bottle into the living room. As I watched flakes of snow brush against the window I felt my unease return – I remembered Patrick's puzzled reply when I mentioned the phone calls, and it rattled inside my mind like a ball bearing inside a can.

'What the fuck are you talking about?'

I stepped into the lounge and stared out at the bay. It had been the most insane two weeks of my life, and my thoughts raged: about Paris and Istanbul, and Patrick, and above all about David and Megan.

And a voice in the back of my mind repeated a single mantra, as if to lessen the grief. *It's all over now and the guilty have been punished.* I tried to reassure myself with those words but I knew that punishing the guilty wasn't enough, and it never will be because retribution doesn't take away the pain or diminish the bitter anguish of losing loved ones.

And then Patrick's words came back again to haunt me. *'What the fuck are you talking about?'*

Was Patrick lying about the phone calls? The tone of his reply suggested that he was telling the truth. But could I trust him? Instinct told me not. *But maybe I'm wrong?* My unease was still there. Another thing troubled me: I still hadn't got an apology from Stone.

And then a breeze lifted the curtains, and I heard a faint noise behind me. My heart flipped as I spun round. Standing in my bedroom doorway, a pistol in her hand, was Brogan Lacy.

174

She stepped into the room. Her face showed no emotion. 'Put down your glass,' she ordered.

I was shocked. Had Lacy made the phone calls. *But why?* And had she helped Patrick in some way? It seemed crazy. Why would she help the man who had killed her daughter and ex-husband?

Lacy gestured with the gun as her eyes watched me intently. 'Put down your glass and sit over by the window.'

Her voice sounded dull and lifeless, as if she was drugged. I hadn't got my gun to defend myself, Josh was probably halfway home by now, and my cell phone was in my bag on the couch. Not that I could have made a call with a weapon pointed at my face. I thought about the spare Glock under my pillow but the room was too far away. My hand shook as I put down my wine and sat in the easy chair. 'How did you get in?'

Lacy dangled a key fob. 'This used to be my home, remember?'

I heard the tremor in my own voice. 'How . . . how long have you been in the bedroom?'

'Long enough. But you're here now and we can finally end it.'

I stared back at her. '*End* it? What did I ever do that would make you want to kill me, Brogan?'

She said bleakly, 'I thought you'd have figured that out by now.'

'All I understand is that you've got a loaded gun pointed at me and by the sound of it you're probably going to use it.'

'Not probably. Definitely.'

My throat felt dry. 'Do I get to know why?'

'You killed my child. You killed the one human being who meant everything to me.'

'*I* killed Megan? *How?*'

Her mouth pursed with anger. 'You were so determined to hunt Gamal down that you put David and Megan in harm's way. *You* made them targets with your selfish persistence. You caused them to be victims.'

I studied her eyes. They were blank pools, as if she was already past the edge of reason, although I hoped not. 'Brogan, maybe part of what you say is right. Maybe my determination to capture Gamal did put them in harm's way. But that was never my intention. Do you really think I haven't suffered torment every day since their deaths? Do you really think I haven't agonised over what I might have done? But I've learned that I have to move on with my life. Brogan, there's something that happened today I need to explain. I know it's going to sound absurd but if you'll just listen to me . . . Patrick Bryce is still alive. He never committed suicide . . .'

Her face sparked with a look of pure hatred. 'I knew you'd try to confuse and distract me. Don't tell me such ridiculous lies. *You* killed Megan. Your intrusion into her life caused her murder. That's all that matters.'

'Brogan, I know you're traumatised and there's nothing I can say to lessen your hurt, but you really have to hear me out. Why do you think I asked to see the tape? There's been another series of killings, this time by Patrick—'

She cut across me, aiming her pistol at the centre of my forehead. 'I don't have to listen to anything. I know all I need to know. Your friends, Stone and Raines, they came to see me. It was clear to me they were dubious about your role in David and Megan's deaths. I knew with absolute certainly after their visit that I was right all along.'

'Right about what?'

'That you'd destroyed my daughter's precious life with your recklessness. And that nothing matters but finishing this. Be silent and kneel down.'

Reason was having no effect but despair made me try again. 'Brogan, *think* about what you're doing. What will killing me achieve?'

'*Kneel*, or I'll kill you this instant.'

My legs trembled as I knelt. *She means it – she's going to kill me*. She stepped closer, pressed the tip of the gun against my temple. I felt the cold steel and saw tears well up in her eyes. 'You have no idea what it's like to lose an only child, do you?' she said.

'I lost Megan too.'

Her mouth tightened with vehemence. 'Don't patronise me. You lost nothing but an acquaintance. Megan wasn't your daughter. How could you have *any* idea what I'm feeling?'

I closed my eyes and listened to the rattle of the wind outside, knew that I was totally alone, that no one was going to save me. I had to do *something* to try to remain alive. I tried to figure out how I could make it to my bedroom and the spare Glock. I opened my eyes and looked into Brogan Lacy's face and said honestly, 'I know it's no consolation but I tried to imagine what it must have been like for you. How terrible your hurt must have been. But believe me, it's true what I said about Patrick . . .'

'*Liar*. Your distractions won't work. I told you, don't try to dupe me, or patronise me. It sounds so pathetic.'

'You made the calls, didn't you? But I heard David's voice. How was that possible?'

I saw Lacy's finger tighten on the trigger. Her eyes filled with tears and she said, 'You know what I do every night before I go to sleep? I play a videotape I once made of David and Megan down by Angel Bay. It was such a wonderful time, a summer seven years ago, before David and I began to come apart. I play the tape to remind myself how happy we once were and to see and hear them again. It causes me such pain but I still have to do it. I have to feel that pain because it reminds me of how much I loved my daughter, and how much I once loved David, too.'

Lacy's vacant gaze suddenly turned to contempt. 'I wanted you to share that pain. That's why I came here to the studio and played the videotape over the phone, a part with David's voice. At first I didn't think I could go through with killing you. I just wanted you to suffer for what you'd done. Torment you. Twice I came and played Megan's music and I let you hear David's voice but I still couldn't get up the courage to destroy you. But now I realise I want you to die. It seems a more fitting punishment.'

'A life for a life?' I asked hoarsely.

Lacy nodded and took a deep breath, as if she'd finally reached the end of things. 'Don't you understand? It's the only way I can find release, by making the person who was ultimately responsible for Megan's death pay for her sin.'

I knew at that moment that Brogan Lacy had lost all reason, and a voice in the back of my head said: *Maybe you deserve this. Maybe you deserve to join David and Megan.* But suddenly I felt angry. I *hadn't* killed David and Megan. I had done nothing wrong. 'How is killing me going to bring Megan back? *How?*'

I heard the sound of a ragged wind and a second later a gust lifted the curtain. Brogan turned and glanced across the room and I saw my moment and seized it. I lunged at her but she turned and fired. I felt a searing hot flame sting my right arm as I crashed into Lacy's stomach. She gasped as I collapsed on top of her, knocking over the coffee table and the wine bottle. The pistol was knocked from her grip and slid across the floor. I knew I'd been wounded as I staggered to my feet. I tried to see Lacy's pistol but I couldn't so I lurched towards my bedroom. I barely made it through the door when I felt the full weight of her body hit me and we landed in a heap on the floor.

I was pinned down as her hand slipped around my throat. She was far stronger than I had imagined and her grip began to choke me. I was only feet from the bed and I flailed my arms, trying to reach the hidden Glock, but suddenly Lacy's left hand came out of nowhere, clutching the wine bottle. The next thing I knew it had swished through the air and struck the top of my skull. I felt a blinding pain, Lacy's face began to cloud over and the world went black.

A hand slapped my face and I came awake groggily. I was lying on the bedroom floor and Lacy was standing over me with her pistol in her hand. 'Why . . . why didn't you just kill me?' I asked.

Her eyes were wet as she aimed the gun at my head. 'Because I want you to feel pain, the way Megan must have felt pain. I want you to suffer the way she must have suffered. And you'r going to, I promise you that.'

I'd been winged by her shot: a thin scarlet furrow ran for few inches along my forearm where the bullet had scoured flesh My blood was dripping in a shallow crimson pool on to the carpe and I felt weak. The Glock was only a yard away beneath m pillow, but I knew that if I moved Lacy would shoot.

Another gust of wind raked the curtains and lifted them in th breeze. This time Lacy paid the noise no heed, but a split secon later we both heard a door rattle outside in the hall. She flicke a glance towards the bedroom doorway and I seized my chance I slid my left hand under the pillow and wrenched the Gloc from its holster. In an instant I had it cocked and aimed at Lacy face. She stared back at me as I lay on the floor, saw the gun i my hand, but she kept aiming her own weapon at me, resigna tion in her eyes.

'Put down the gun, Brogan. *Please.*'

'This changes nothing,' she said vacantly. 'Except perhaps tha now we'll die together.'

That was when I heard the voice from across the room. 'D what she said, Brogan, and put your weapon down.'

Lacy glanced up in surprise as I saw Stone appear in th doorway. He barely gave me a glance, his attention riveted o Lacy. 'Brogan, be sensible and put down the gun. There's n point in taking Kate's life, now, is there?'

I could hardly believe the irony of Stone's presence, but Lac didn't waver as she kept her weapon pointed at me. 'You're s wrong. And don't think you're going to stop me from killing her

Stone shook his head. 'Trust me, I'm a better shot. You try t do that, and I'll shoot you first. So where's the triumph in that Just put down the gun, Brogan. *Please.* I don't want to shoot you Put down the gun *now.*'

Brogan Lacy hesitated, then a look close to madness sparke in her eyes and her finger quickly closed on the trigger. 'It's fa too late. It's gone way past that . . .'

'*No!*' I screamed, and I heard the gunshot explode.

175

No night should be so dark, no winter so cold. A little before midnight I went outside to sit on the veranda. I wore my overcoat which I'd pulled from my closet and I stared out at Angel Bay, at the snow falling, at the blue lights of police cars strobing the darkness while the lights across the bay watched me like a million unfeeling eyes.

The last hour seemed like a blur and I was still in shock. I remembered Stone grabbing his cell phone and calling 911 as I tried to stem the blood from Lacy's chest, binding it with a bedroom sheet until the paramedics arrived. The next thing I knew a medic was dressing my arm as the ambulance sped Lacy to hospital. I was so dazed I didn't recall much of what happened after that.

I heard footsteps and saw Stone amble out of the house. He parked himself beside me with a stiff groan. 'These bones of mine ache. Are you holding up, Moran?'

'I've felt worse. You think she'll make it?'

Stone shrugged. 'Maybe. The real question is whether she's going to feel happy if she survives. I guess not. But you'd be the same if you'd lost an only kid.' He looked at me sympathetically. 'I didn't mean to suggest that Megan's death didn't affect you, but you weren't her mother . . .'

'I know what you meant. It's OK.'

Stone sighed and ran a hand tiredly over his face. 'I had no choice, I had to shoot her.'

'I know that too,' I answered.

Stone plucked a pack of cigarettes from his pocket, lit one, blew a funnel of smoke into the cold air. 'And you were right. I let my bitterness get in the way of common sense.'

'I forgive you. After saving my neck you deserve it.'

Stone actually smiled. 'Gee, thanks, Moran. You've made n night. But maybe you still think I'm an asshole?'

'Maybe I'll amend my opinion in future. But why did yc come out here? You couldn't have known Lacy meant to kill m

Stone shook his head. 'I had two errands to run tonight. On was to call by Lacy's apartment and break the news about Patric I figured she deserved to know the full story. The other was call on you to apologise because I thought it was about time. called on Lacy first, only she wasn't at home and I couldn't read her on her cell so I decided to leave her until tomorrow, and drove out here. That's when I heard the first gunshot and can running. But you know something? Now I think about it, suspected all along that something wasn't right with Lacy.'

'What do you mean?' I asked.

'When I spoke with her on the phone before I interviewe her with Lou, she seemed like a woman close to breaking poin Then I called her yesterday to ask if she was OK and she sa she was fine. But she didn't sound fine to me. She sounded lil a woman on the edge, like she had serious problems and w on some heavy medication. So I asked Norton to do son discreet checking with a buddy of his at the ME's office. It turn out Lacy's been in and out of psychiatric hospital for the la year. She's had one hell of a rough ride and I guess her mind been shot to pieces.'

I studied Stone. 'Is this a new, more caring Agent Stone I se before me? You know it's going to ruin your reputation?'

'Hey, give me a break, Moran. And don't be a smartass.'

'I'm still in shock. You promise never to hassle me again? Nev to doubt my word?'

Stone raised his eyes. 'Hey, that's asking a lot. But I *will* lister

'I guess there's hope for you yet.'

He touched his neck brace and grinned. 'Don't say that un' I talk with my lawyer. He may advise me to sue you. What abo making a detour to hospital to get some proper treatment fo that arm of yours?'

I shook my head. 'In a few hours. If it was that bad the para-medics would have taken me with them. Right now I need to sleep. I haven't really slept in two days and I reckon I'm due some.'

Stone got to his feet and touched my shoulder in a friendly gesture. 'I don't think you're going to get much, not for a little while.'

'Why's that?'

Stone brushed his trousers and offered me a steady look. 'Because I called Cooper and he's on his way. He'll probably want to take you to the hospital himself.'

'Why'd you do that?'

Stone winked. 'Hey, we all need friends to comfort us. See you, Moran.'

'Thank you, *Vance*.'

'Hey, careful, you'll be bringing me coffee next,' Stone responded.

'I think I owe you that. Two sugars?'

'Six, but don't stir.' And Stone touched a finger to his fore-head in a mock salute and walked away.

It was three days later before I felt well again. Three days of recovery and soul-searching, and visiting Frank, and asking myself when I'd get up the courage to visit Brogan Lacy. I'd heard that she was past critical and hanging in there, that she'd been in theatre for ten hours and barely made it, and she wasn't going to be leaving hospital for quite a time. Whatever the condition of her body, I wondered whether her soul would ever heal. Somehow I doubted it. How could anyone truly heal after losing an only child? All I could do was pray for her.

Frank was bitching about still being in hospital but he was on the mend, and I got a surprise when I came home from visiting him to find that Paul had phoned me again, except this time to apologise. He left a message on my answering machine. 'I heard what happened to you, Kate. I sure hope you're OK? Listen, I'm sorry for being such a hurtful jerk. I know I went over the top, and you were right when you said I needed counselling. That's what I've been doing the last few days. I checked myself into a clinic here in Phoenix. I guess I felt I made a wrong decision about us getting divorced and the regret kind of sent me over the edge. I'm doing my best to move on but I just hope we can someday be friends?'

That same afternoon a bouquet of flowers arrived from Paul, along with a card, saying simply, 'I'm not trying to woo you back. But just to say thanks for all the good times we had together.'

It brought tears to my eyes when I read the words. I was pretty sure that within days Paul would revert to his old self again and start giving me grief, but right then I felt touched.

That evening Josh took me to dinner at Starlights Bistro along the bay and then he drove me home to the cottage and we kissed and held each other in his old BMW. I felt like I was seventeen again. When I asked him in I poured us both some red wine and a little after midnight we went into my bedroom and made love.

It was different to how it had been with David. Different but good. No Norah Jones playing softly in the background, no wind on the bay that night, but a calm, moonlit darkness. Instead of Norah I heard Josh's voice whisper how much he wanted to know me, how much he cherished making love to me, and I told him the same. And our lovemaking was sensual, so very sensual, his fingertips ghost-like as they traced tender outlines on my skin, touched my back, my legs, my belly, my face.

I thought: *I like this guy. I like him a lot, even more than I can say*. And I thought: *He was so right*. We are all hurt beings, and haunted souls. And there are some wounds that never heal. And I knew something else he was right about: the trick to surviving is simply to carry on. That's really all we can do if we want to endure. Hope that the next day will be better than the last. *Hope and dreams are all that keep us alive.*

After we had made love, we fell asleep. When I woke, dawn was breaking. I watched Josh as he slept and traced the outline of his kind face, watched him in the platinum light that streamed through the curtains, and then I left the bedroom and pulled on my clothes and stepped out of the cottage on to the lawn.

It was cold as I stared out at the harbour. Then I did what I had been dreading: what I had promised to do. I slipped David's ring from my finger. My eyes were moist as I raised the ring in my hand. I could imagine the soft *plop* as it made circles in the moonlit water, could imagine the words I would speak. *It's done now, it's over.*

But something held me back. I wasn't ready. Wasn't ready to let go completely just yet. But that felt OK, too. As I slid the ring back on my finger I heard footsteps and I turned and saw Josh come up behind me. His arms slid around my waist and he stood against my back, holding me, sleepily kissing my neck. 'What brought you out here?'

'A promise.'

'A promise to do what?' he whispered in my ear.

I wanted to tell him but I knew that now wasn't the time. *When we get close enough. When my heart is healed and I can tell you. Tell you all my secrets, all my hopes. Just as I want you to tell me yours.*

'Will you tell me?' Josh asked.

I didn't answer, and when he began to say something I turned and put a finger to his lips and whispered back, 'Someday soon when I get to know you better.'

He didn't speak, didn't ask me again, and I liked that. I liked the fact that he was patient with me – it was a good sign. I wrapped my arms around his neck. He kissed me, and then he took my hand and led me back up to the cottage.

We fell asleep again listening to the sound of the water. The last thing I heard before I drifted into peaceful oblivion was a flight of wild winter geese out on the Potomac. Their eternal music carried far over the cold salt marshes on Angel Bay, until finally they were gone and then everywhere was stillness again.

I doubt that the orchestra of nature was David's doing, a ghostly sign of his approval.

But a part of me would like to think so.

GLENN MEADE

Web of Deceit

'Compulsive and timely' *City Life*

New York attorney Jennifer March is haunted by the mysterious and savage slaughter of her family on the same night that her father disappeared, never to be seen alive again.

Two years on, his corpse is discovered frozen into a remote glacier in the Swiss Alps, the victim of a bizarre murder, and Jennifer sets out for Europe to find answers. It's a journey that's meant to unravel the frightening mystery of why her family was butchered, and to help uncover a dark secret at the heart of her father's past.

But instead, Jennifer March finds herself running for her own life, as her investigation draws her into a terrifying web of deceit, murder and betrayal, and a deadly conspiracy to hide an explosive secret.

HODDER